# The
# Girl Who
# Fell from
# the Sky

# The
# Girl Who
# Fell from
# the Sky

## SIMON MAWER

Little, Brown

LITTLE, BROWN

First published in Great Britain in 2012 by Little, Brown

Copyright © Simon Mawer 2012

The moral right of the author has been asserted.

*All characters and events in this publication, other than those
clearly in the public domain, are fictitious and any resemblance
to real persons, living or dead, is purely coincidental.*

A CIP catalogue record for this book
is available from the British Library.

Hardback ISBN: 978-1-4087-0350-2
C-format ISBN: 978-1-4087-0351-9

Typeset in Sabon by M Rules
Printed and bound in Great Britain by
Clays Ltd, St Ives plc

Papers used by Little, Brown are from well-managed forests
and other responsible sources.

MIX
Paper from
responsible sources
FSC® C104740

Little, Brown
An imprint of
Little, Brown Book Group
100 Victoria Embankment
London EC4Y 0DY

An Hachette UK Company
www.hachette.co.uk

www.littlebrown.co.uk

To the memory of Colette, one of the women of SOE.

# Foreword

The French section of the Special Operations Executive sent thirty-nine women into the field between May 1941 and September 1944. Of these, twelve were murdered following their capture by the Germans, while one other died of meningitis during her mission. The remainder survived the war. Some of these women became well known to the public through films and books that were written about them. Others remained, and remain, obscure. They were all remarkable.

Pour vivre heureux, vivons cachés.
*Florian*

# Trapeze

She's sitting in the fuselage, trussed like a piece of baggage, battered by noise. Half an hour earlier they manhandled her up through the door because she was too encumbered with her parachute to climb the ladder unassisted; now she is just there, with the sound drumming on her ears, and the inadequate light and the hard metal and packages all around her.

If only she could sleep, like Benoît. He's sitting opposite, his eyes closed and his head rocking with the movement of the machine. Like a passenger on a train. It's one of the most infuriating things about him, his ability to sleep wherever and whenever he pleases.

The dispatcher – young, gauche, prominent Adam's apple and slicked hair – stumbles towards her through the racket. He seems a kind of Charon, accompanying the souls of the dead towards Hades. Her father would love that thought. His classical allusions. 'Illusions', she always called them. The airman grins ghoulishly at her and bends to open the hatch in the floor, releasing night and cold into the fuselage like water rushing in from a sprung leak. Looking down she can see the huddled buildings of a town sliding beneath, smudged with cloud and lit by the moon, a mysterious seabed over which their craft floats. Benoît opens one eye to see what's going on, gives her a quick smile and returns to his sleep.

'CAEN!' the dispatcher shouts above the noise. He begins to

1

bundle packets of paper out into the blackness, like a manic delivery boy throwing newspapers to his customers in the darkness of a winter morning. The bundles crack open as they drop into the void. He thrusts one of the leaflets towards her so that she can read the news.

*La Revue du Monde Libre*, it says, *apportée par la RAF.*

''COURSE, THE FRENCHIES JUST USE 'EM TO WIPE THEIR ARSES!' he shouts. 'BUT IT MAKES JERRY THINK THAT'S WHAT WE'RE HERE FOR. GIVES US AN ALIBI, SEE? WE DON'T WANT THEM TO THINK WE'RE DROPPING SOMEONE LIKE YOU.'

She smiles. *Someone like you*. But who, exactly?

Marian.

Alice.

Anne-Marie Laroche.

A package to be delivered, like a bundle of leaflets.

Without warning the machine begins to pitch, a boat struck by waves. 'FLAK!' the dispatcher shouts, seeing her look of surprise. He's grinning, as though flak is nothing, and indeed there is nothing to be heard above the racket of the engines, no sound of shells bursting, no intimation that people down below are trying to kill them, nothing more than this pitching and banking.

'WE'LL SOON BE OVER IT!'

And sure enough, they are soon over it and the aircraft roars on, the hatch closed, through calmer waters.

Later, the youth brings her and Benoît a thermos of tea and some sandwiches. Benoît scoffs his down hungrily – 'Eat, *mon p'tit chat*,' he tells her, but she cannot eat for the same reason that she couldn't eat at the safe house before they went to the airfield, that slow, knotted constriction of her stomach muscles that had tightened up inside her from the moment that Vera had said, 'TRAPEZE is scheduled for the next moon. Assuming the weather's kind, of course.' That was when the pain began, a dull ache like period pains, when it wasn't her period at all.

2

'Are you all right?' Vera asked her as they made their final preparations at the airfield. She had the manner of a nurse enquiring after a patient – concerned, but with a certain detachment, as though this were no more than a task to complete before moving on to the next bed.

'Of course I'm all right.'

'You look pale.'

'It's the damned English weather.'

And now it's the French weather outside, buffeting the aircraft as it hammers on through the night. When she has finished the tea she manages to sleep, a nodding, awkward sleep more like a patient slipping in and out of consciousness than someone getting rest. And then she is awake again, with the dispatcher shaking her shoulder and shouting in her ear: 'WE'RE NEARLY THERE, LOVE! GET YOURSELF READY!'

*Love.* She likes that. English comfort. The hatch in the floor is opened once more, and as she peers down she sees something new, pale fields and dark woods skidding past below the aircraft, almost close enough to touch. *The vasty fields of France,* her father used to say. Benoît is wide awake now and alert, patting his pockets to make sure all is ready, zipping things up, checking his kit.

The plane tilts, turning in a wide circle, engines roaring. She can imagine the pilot up in the cockpit, searching, searching, straining to see the tiny glimmers of torchlight which mean that they are expected down there in the dark. A lamp comes on in the roof of the fuselage, a single, unblinking red eye. The dispatcher gives the thumbs-up. 'HE'S FOUND IT!'

There's a note of admiration and triumph in his shout, as though this proves what wonders his crew are able to perform, to come all this way in the darkness, eight hundred miles from home, and find a pinprick of light in a blackened world. He attaches the static line from their parachutes to the rail in the roof of the fuselage and double-checks the buckles of their harnesses. The aircraft makes one pass over the dropping zone, and

3

she can hear the sound of the containers leaving the bomb bay and see them flash beneath, their canopies billowing open. Then the machine banks and turns and steadies for the second run.

'YOUR TURN NOW!' the dispatcher yells at the pair of them.

'*Merde alors!*' Benoît mouths to Marian, and grins. He looks infuriatingly unconcerned, as though this is all in the normal run of things, as though as a matter of course people throw themselves out of aircraft over unknown countryside in the middle of the night.

*Merde alors!*

She sits with her feet out through the hole, in the slipstream, like sitting on a rock with your feet in the water, the current pulling at them. Benoît is right behind her. She can feel him against the bulk of her parachute pack, as though the pack has become a sensitive extension of her own body. She says a prayer, a baby prayer pulled out of childhood memory, but nevertheless a prayer and therefore a sign of weakness: God, please look after me. Which means, perhaps, Father look after me, or *Maman* look after me, but whatever it means she doesn't want any sign of weakness now, not at this moment of deliverance with the slipstream rushing past her and the void beneath, while the dispatcher gives her a nod that's meant to inspire confidence but only brings with it the horror of superstition, that you must never congratulate yourself, never applaud, never even wish anyone good luck. *Merde alors!* That was all you ever said. *Merde alors!* she thinks, a prayer of a kind, as the red light blinks off and the green comes on and the dispatcher shouts, 'GO!' and there's his hand on her back and she lets go, plunging from the rough comfort of the fuselage into the raging darkness over France.

# London

I

His name was Potter, which seemed unlikely. He had a queru-
lous, fluting voice and a distant manner, as though perhaps she
was not really suitable for his requirements but he would see
her anyway, out of politeness. 'Thank you for coming all this
way,' he said. 'And for taking time off from your work. Do,
please, make yourself at home.'

The exhortation seemed impossible to fulfil: the room itself
was stripped almost bare. There was the space where a bed
might have been – a headboard was attached to the wall and
there were two little shelves that would have been bedside
tables, but apart from that the only furniture was a table and
two chairs. A bare light bulb hung from the ceiling.

She sat, neither forward on the edge of the chair, nor back
as though she were in the sitting room at home, neither one
thing nor the other but upright, relaxed and watchful while
Potter sat opposite her and smiled benignly. He was an
undistinguished-looking man, the kind that her father called
a bank-manager type. Except bank managers always had
moustaches and wore dark suits; but this man was clean-
shaven and wearing a tweed jacket, with a waistcoat. A
headmaster, she decided. A headmaster about to interview a
difficult pupil, the kind of head who asks questions rather

than delivers lectures. The kind that lets you tie yourself in knots. The Socratic method.

'Now, I expect you are wondering why I've invited you here ...?'

His letter had asked her not to come in uniform. She'd thought that strange at the time, even slightly peculiar. Why not in uniform, when the whole damn world was in uniform? So she'd chosen something plain and businesslike – a navy skirt and jacket with a white blouse, and the only decent pair of shoes she had managed to bring from Geneva. She'd tried to avoid using them too much in the last couple of years. They were too precious. And silk stockings, she wore silk stockings. Her last pair.

'You said something about French in your letter. You had use for my language ability.'

'Exactly. *Peut-être* ...' Potter paused and smiled deprecatingly. '*Peut-être nous devrions parler français?*'

There was an English accent and a certain woodenness about the phrasing, as though he was using the language consciously rather than naturally. But he did it well enough. She shrugged, and followed his lead, slipping from one language to the other with that strange facility that she had and her father could never manage. 'The thing is, *Papa*,' she had told him once, 'for you it's two languages. But it's not for me. For me there's only *one* language. I simply use the bits of it that are appropriate at the time.' And so the rest of this conversation, a very guarded, evasive conversation, was in French, Potter with his quaint formalities, Marian with her rapid flutter of colloquialisms.

'I must emphasise from the start,' he warned her, 'that the work would be of a most secret nature. Everything about it, even our meeting here today, must be held in absolute confidence. It all comes under the Official Secrets Act. You do understand that, don't you? I believe you have already signed the act because of your work in the WAAF. But we do like to be sure.'

So she signed the form once more, a solemn little ceremony like a registry-office marriage, for which Mr Potter lent his fountain pen and waited reverently for the ink to dry.

'So tell me a little about yourself, Miss Sutro. The name, for example. Not Jewish, is it?'

'Sutro? It may have been once, I don't really know. My father is C of E, and *his* father was even a vicar. Which led to a certain amount of difficulty when *Papa* married my mother because she is Roman Catholic. That's how we were brought up – RC.'

'That all sounds most regular. But one has to be sure.'

'That I'm not a Jew? You don't want Jews?'

'We have to be sure that people of the, er, Jewish persuasion are fully aware of the risks.'

'What risks?'

There was a small tremor of impatience in his voice. 'Perhaps I should be asking the questions, Miss Sutro. I wonder, how did you acquire your command of the language?'

She shrugged. 'I didn't *acquire* my command of the language. I simply learned to speak, as everyone does. It just happened to be French. My mother is French. We lived in Geneva.'

'But you also speak excellent English.'

'That was from my father, of course. And at school we also spoke English as well as French. It was an international school. And then I spent three years at boarding school in England.'

'What was your father doing in Geneva?'

'He worked for the League of Nations.' She paused and asked, with irony, 'Do you remember the League of Nations, Mr Potter?'

II

At the second meeting he put his cards on the table. The expression was his. They met as before: the same place – an anonymous building on Northumberland Avenue that had once

7

been a hotel – the same room, the same two chairs and bare table and bare light bulb, but this time she accepted his offer of a cigarette. She wasn't really a smoker, but working in the Filter Room at Bentley Priory, particularly on nights, turned you into one; and anyway, it made her look older to have a cigarette in her hand and somehow she wanted to appear older in the eyes of this man, despite the fact that he knew her real age and so couldn't be deceived.

'How do you feel about our first encounter?' he asked.

She shrugged. 'You didn't really tell me anything very specific. The Inter Services Research Bureau could be anything.'

He nodded. Indeed it could be anything. 'At that meeting you talked, quite eloquently I thought, of your love of France, of the fact that you wanted to do something more directly for her.'

'That's what it was all about, wasn't it? My language.'

'More or less.' He considered her, watching her with an expression that was almost one of sadness. 'Marian, would you be prepared to leave this country in order to pursue this work?'

'Go overseas? Certainly. Algeria or somewhere?'

'Actually, I mean France itself.'

There was a pause. It might have seemed as though she hadn't quite understood. 'Are you serious, Mr Potter?'

'Certainly, I'm serious. The organisation that I represent trains people to work in France.'

She waited, drawing in smoke from the cigarette, determined not to let him see any change in her manner. But there *was* a change, a fluttering of excitement directly behind her breast-bone.

'I want to be frank with you, Marian. I want to put my cards on the table. It would be dangerous work. You'd be in danger of your life. But it would be of enormous value to the war effort. I want you to consider the possibility of doing something like that.'

She seemed to think about the suggestion but her mind had been made up long ago, before even this second interview had begun, when she had guessed that something extraordinary might be about to happen. 'I would love to,' she said.

Potter smiled. It was an expression entirely without humour, the tired smile of a man who deals with overenthusiastic children. 'I don't actually want your answer now. I want you to go away and think about it. You've got a week's leave—'

'A week's *leave*?' Leave from the Filter Room was almost impossible to come by.

He nodded. 'You have a week's leave. Go home and think it over. Talk it over with your father. The only thing you may let him know is that you may be sent on some kind of secret mission overseas, and that you will be in some danger. If you accept, you will go to a unit that will assess your potential for this particular work in greater depth. It may be that they will decide that my own judgement of your talents was wrong and you are not suitable for the work we are doing. In that case, after a suitable debriefing, you will return to your normal duties and no one will be any the wiser. If the assessment unit decides to move you on to training, then you will begin the work in earnest. Training will take some months before you go into the field.'

'It sounds fascinating.'

'I'm not sure that's the word I would use. You must warn your parents that if you accept this work, you will, to all intents and purposes, disappear from their lives until it is all over. Although your family will be contacted on your behalf by the organisation from time to time and informed that you are well, you will have no direct contact with them and they will have no further information as to your whereabouts. You must tell friends or relatives that you are being posted abroad. Nothing more. Do you understand that?'

'I think so.' She paused, considering this man and his solemn, headmaster's face. 'What are the risks?'

He breathed in deeply, as though preparing to deliver judgement. 'We estimate – it is no more than an estimate – that the chances of survival are about fifty-fifty.'

'Fifty-fifty?' It seemed absurd. The toss of a coin. How could she not feel fear? But it was the fear that she had felt skiing, the fear of plummeting steepness, the fear she had had when her uncle had taken her climbing, the awe-inspiring fear of space beneath her feet, a fear that teetered on the very edge of joy. She wanted to make a grand gesture, to laugh with happiness and cry 'Yes!', even to leap out of her chair and throw her arms around this strange man with his shrill portents of doom. Instead she nodded thoughtfully. 'What about my unit?'

'There is no need to return to your unit. If you decide to continue, your things will be collected on your behalf and your colleagues informed of your posting to another job. I must emphasise that no one must be told anything. No cousins, no aunts and uncles, no boyfriends. Do you have a boyfriend?'

She glanced down at her hands, lying passively in her lap. Did Clément qualify? When does a childhood crush metamorphose into an adult relationship? 'There was someone in France. We used to write, but since the invasion ...'

'Well, that's a good thing. You must, I'm afraid, break all such connections. No explanation, no farewell. Your brother – I gather he is in a reserved occupation ...'

'Ned? He's a scientist. Physics.'

'He must know nothing, absolutely nothing. When the call comes, you will simply follow our instructions and make your way to the Student Assessment Board. You will be there for four days, during which you will undergo various tests to see how you measure up to the kind of person we are looking for.'

'It sounds like an execution. You will be taken from this court to a place of execution and there you will be hanged by the neck—'

'This is not a matter for jest, Marian,' he said. 'It is deadly serious.'

She smiled at him. She had a winning smile, she knew that.

10

Her father told her as much. 'I'm not sure that I am jesting, Mr Potter.'

She walked out of the building, past the sandbags and the sentries, into the bright light of Northumberland Avenue. Did anyone take notice of her? She wanted them to. She wanted to seem extraordinary in the eyes of the anonymous passers-by – brilliant, adventurous, brave. She was going to France. However they organised these matters – would she go ashore by boat? or walk over the border from Switzerland? or land in a light aircraft? – somehow she was going to France. She crossed the street to the embankment to look at the river. The tide was out and sea birds picked over the mud – gulls laughing and crying. She wanted to laugh and cry with them – with joy and a breathtaking kind of fear. Trains rattled across the bridge overhead. People emerged from the shadows of the Tube station, blinking in the sunlight as she was blinking in the sunlight of her new life. Perhaps the next river she would see would be the Seine. How remarkable! Marian Sutro, living under some assumed name – Colette, she fancied – might soon be standing on the bank of the Seine beside the Pont Neuf and looking across the water, past l'Île de la Cité to the Louvre on the far side. All around her the people of the city would be wondering when and if the British were coming to rescue them from their misery, when in fact they would already be there, in her own small presence.

III

'We appreciate very much your volunteering,' the tall man said. He was wearing the uniform of a lieutenant colonel, and apparently he was in charge. Through the window behind him she could see the trees in the centre of the square. The faint sound of traffic came through the glass. The place was called Orchard

11

Court, and it was unclear whether it was a flat or a suite of offices. Rather it seemed a strange hybrid between the two: through an open door you might glimpse a bedroom with a made-up bed, or a bathroom with black and white tiles and an onyx bidet, and yet other rooms were clearly offices, with dull ministry desks and chairs and gunmetal filing cabinets.

Buckmaster, the man called himself. It was obviously a *nom de guerre*. No one could really be called Buckmaster. It smacked of a John Buchan thriller. Mr Standfast. 'I've taken the liberty of writing to your father myself,' he said, 'your being so young, and so on. I tried to reassure him that we'll look after you as best we can but I doubt it'll pull the wool over his eyes. I mean, he must know this kind of work can be perilous.'

He nodded, gloomily. You could sense the word being repeated in his mind. Perilous. It had a quaint, Old English sound to it. Castle Perilous. His *nom de guerre* seemed more dynamic than the man himself: he was balding and had a receding chin and feminine lips. Somehow he didn't inspire confidence.

'May I know what this organisation is really called?' Marian asked.

He looked discomfited. 'Actually, we don't ask too many questions.'

'I'm sorry,' Marian said, 'but I thought I ought to know.'

'No, don't apologise. It's quite understandable. But we prefer it like that. The less we know of each other the better.' He smiled at her. 'Of course, we know rather a lot about you, but then we need to, don't we? Whereas you don't need to know much about us. The need-to-know principle, d'you see?'

Did she see? Not really. It seemed ridiculous to have a name and then keep it secret.

'Well, I won't keep you any longer. Now that we've met I think it's time to pass you on to Miss Atkins.'

Miss Atkins was an elegant woman with a faintly supercilious expression. She invited Marian to sit down and offered her tea and biscuits and examined her with an air of detached curiosity, as though considering her for the post of scullery maid or something. If the tall colonel was the king of this particular world, then this woman was clearly the queen. 'You are very young,' she observed. 'Quite one of the youngest recruits we have ever had.' There was something unnatural about her voice, something strained and false, as though the carefully enunciated syllables were not naturally hers but had been learned for the occasion. 'People on the Student Assessment Board were of the opinion that you are too immature for what we are proposing. However, Colonel Buckmaster and I have decided to override their judgement and recommend you for training. So we will watch your progress with close interest.'

'You make it sound like school.'

'It *is* like school. And you have a great deal to learn.'

'When does it begin?'

'Immediately. The first thing is your position as a WAAF. We like our people to have commissions. It gives them more status in France. We will have you gazetted immediately as acting Section Officer.'

'An officer!'

'Exactly. However, for various reasons that I won't go into, we like all our girls to join the FANY.'

'The Fanny? What on earth is the Fanny?'

'The First Aid Nursing Yeomanry. You'll have the rank of Ensign and of course the uniform—'

'But I'm in the WAAF. You just said I would be made an officer.'

Atkins tapped her finger on the desk as though to bring the meeting to order. 'That is merely an honorary rank. It brings with it a salary that will be paid to you as appropriate, and a certain status when you are in the field. But while you are with us, you will be a FANY. It is the way we do things. Do I make myself clear? You must get kitted out with the uniform immediately.' She

13

paused, considering the girl in front of her. 'It is my duty to remind you that everything that happens from now on, in fact everything that has already happened since your first meeting with Mr Potter, comes under the Official Secrets Act. You do understand this, don't you? Your training, for example. Where you go and what you see and what you do when you get there. Everything. I know you've been doing secret work in the WAAF, but this is not quite the same thing. The secrets of the Filter Room are clearly circumscribed, but none of our work is defined in that way. From now on it is not that your *work* is secret; your whole *life* is secret. This obliges you to make judgements all the time. You must learn to say enough to allay people's curiosity without ever saying anything that awakens it. Do you see what I mean? You have to appear to be dull and uninteresting. It is a particular skill.'

'I'm sure I'll manage.'

'I suggest you tell people that you are doing preliminary training for liaison duties, with the aim of being sent abroad. Algeria is the obvious place, given your command of French. You may hint at this, but you need not say it explicitly. We like our people to learn to talk pleasantly and say nothing. You may begin to practise it now. And I must warn you that people will be reporting back to me, telling me how good you are with that kind of thing. They will be watching you all the time to see how you comport yourself. Am I making myself clear? Not everyone possesses the qualities we seek, and many fail during training. You must understand that failure is not a personal discredit; it is merely a sign that you do not quite have the qualities that we are seeking. We are looking for very particular gifts, Marian, very *particular* gifts indeed.'

Particular gifts seemed like particular friendships, those relationships that hovered on the boundaries of sin and awoke fear in the nuns' minds. 'In fact,' Miss Atkins added, with an expression of faint disapproval, 'some of the qualities we are looking for may not be entirely admirable ones.'

14

The hotel they found for her was in a narrow cul-de-sac tucked away behind Regent Street. Many of the guests appeared to be regulars and the hall porter seemed to know most of them by name. 'Good evening, Miss,' he greeted her as she went through the revolving door. 'I do hope you have a pleasant stay here.' And his expression suggested that, despite all the warnings about secrecy, he was well aware of exactly what this young woman with her shabby suitcase and her plain grey suit was all about.

She went up to her room, hung her clothes in the wardrobe and threw her new uniform onto the bed. It was an ugly creation in khaki barathea. F.A.N.Y., it said on the shoulder flashes. A ridiculous name, enough to make you blush. The uniform lay there lifeless on the bed, a corpse dragged into her life, something she would have to explain away when she next went home. It seemed daft. She was already in the WAAF and, for goodness' sake, they also insisted that she be part of this peculiar corps with the embarrassing acronym. Whoever they were – the Inter Services Research Bureau, as they called themselves – they appeared to be able to do precisely what they pleased.

She looked round the room indecisively. What should she do? It was far too early to go to Ned's. She'd rung him and told him she was at a loose end in London and he'd invited her to dinner. She'd have to explain why she was in London, which might be a bit awkward. Explain nothing, they'd told her.

*They.* She had no other word for them, the strange Colonel Buckmaster and the impassive Miss Atkins and their various minions. Perhaps they were watching at this very moment to see how she behaved. The idea amused and frightened her. She contemplated the stuffy room with its ornate wardrobe and overstuffed armchair and expansive bed. Concealed microphones? Hidden cameras? She stood in front of the mirror on the wardrobe door and examined herself. What would they see? Marian Sutro or *Marianne Sutrô*? Where did the stress and the accent lie? And what was now going to happen to this curious, hybrid being?

Standing before the mirror she undressed, tossing her clothes onto the bed and transforming herself from the confident young adult whom others might see into the timid child whom she alone knew, jejune, pallid, with awkward limbs and hips and small, pointed but pointless breasts. What to do with this creature who had never known a man, never stayed in a hotel alone before, never even been into a bar by herself? And yet here she was, on her own in the grey, battered city, about to begin some kind of training to prepare her for France. Was anything more unlikely?

She opened the wardrobe door and swept the young Marian aside. Taking out her cocktail dress, she held it against her. It had an elegance that you could no longer find in London; or maybe could never have found in London even before the war because she had bought it in Geneva from a couturier who always got the latest things direct from Paris. She had carefully nurtured it through the family's precipitate escape from Switzerland through France, and then through the tiresome months of exile in England. Only once had she worn it, at a dance to which one of the officers at Stanmore had taken her. He'd told her how fond he was of her, and ended up attempting to take the dress off in the back seat of his car. The dress would be entirely wasted on Ned, of course; but at least there would be no repetition of *that* particular embarrassment.

She washed and dressed and put her hair up – Clément always told her that she looked older like that. Then she did her make-up – still unfamiliar, still quite daring – took her coat and made her way cautiously downstairs. The bar was a place of smoke and noise and the male shout of laughter, the loud braying sound of the Englishman in his element. One or two men glanced at her as she pushed past and found a corner seat, but

16

most ignored her. These days a woman alone in a bar was no longer a matter of note. She nursed a gin and tonic and watched. Men outnumbered the women by three or four to one. They were officers, all of them. But now, apparently, she was also an officer, and a FANY as well. Goodness knows what that meant in the complex world of British protocol.

'May I sit beside you?'

She looked round. Everyone else in the bar seemed to have beer or gin, but he had a glass of red wine in his right hand and a stool in the other, and the accent was unmistakably French. A lighted cigarette bobbed up and down between his lips. 'You are alone and you are the most beautiful lady here, I think ...'

She shrugged and looked away towards the door, as though she was expecting someone. The Frenchman sat. He was young, no older than she was, and good-looking enough, with a casual, nervy manner, the kind of boy she recognised from Grenoble when she and her cousin had gone out in the evening, giggling and whispering to each other in the cafés, pretending they were older than they really were.

'You wish to smoke?' He offered a cigarette from a battered pack. It wasn't a Senior Service, or anything like that. It was a *caporal*. She shook her head. He shrugged. 'My name is Benoît. May I know yours?'

She was uncertain how to answer. Anyway, if she were to give her name, what would it be? Was she Marian or *Marianne*? The question was a delicate one. People were pushing all round them, and somehow she seemed united with this unknown French boy. Where had he come from? Why was he here? What was his place in this loud, ruined, irrepressible city? Someone shoved against her, apologised, then blundered on into the crush. And she wondered whether this Frenchman had been sent to trap her into giving something away.

'I'm Anne-Marie,' she said, on a whim.

'Ah, Anne-Marie. It is a beautiful name.'

'It's a name. Just a name.'

17

He sipped his wine and made a face. '*Pourquoi toutes ces gonzesses anglaises sont glaciales?*' he asked himself.

'I'm sorry?'

'You understand French?'

She hesitated on the edge of confession. 'Glacial, I understood glacial. What exactly is glacial?'

He grimaced. 'The English summer is glacial. *L'été glacial*, that is what I say. My English is so-and-so. Look, you are here alone. I am here alone. We talk, maybe? Have a drink together? It is a good idea, isn't it? I tell my life story.'

Marian considered. She liked the idea of being glacial. It gave her some kind of reassurance against the possibility of being thought a tart. Or a fanny, for God's sake. She tried not to giggle. 'There isn't time for your whole life story. I have to meet someone for dinner. You can tell me what you are doing in London.'

He drew on his cigarette. 'I escape from France.'

'You escaped? How remarkable. Did you swim?'

He laughed. His laugh was appealing. His manner was arrogant, an insufferable arrogance, but his laugh was a young boy's. 'In January it is not so good for swimming. I am in Paris and so I go south – over *les Pyrénées* to Spain. With a friend. We climb through the snow, and then when we get over the border they put us in prison.' He made a disparaging face. 'This is not so good. But then they let us out because we make so much trouble. So we get to *Algérie*, and here we are.' He smiled, as though it was a brilliant trick pulled off in front of an audience, an escape worthy of the great Houdini. 'And now I return to fight the *Frisés*.'

'Where is your friend?'

'My friend?'

'You said you were with your friend.'

'Oh, him.' He waved a vague hand. 'He finds someone for dancing this evening and I leave him go. Do you wish to dance? We can go find him.'

'I'm afraid not. I have to meet my brother for dinner.'

'Your *brother*? You 'ave no boyfriend?'

'It's nothing to do with you whether I have a boyfriend or not.'

The boy nodded, his face wreathed in the pungent smoke from his *caporal*. 'You 'ave no boyfriend. If you like, I can be your boyfriend.'

'I don't think that would be appropriate.'

'Appropriate?'

'It would not be a good idea.'

He looked glum, like a disappointed child. Surely his story of escape from France was pure fantasy. And yet he was here, a French boy in the noisy heart of the city, among the uniforms of a dozen nations. He must have got here somehow.

'Look,' he said, putting his cigarette down on the edge of the table. 'I play you a game, right? If I win, you come with me dancing. If I lose, you go and see your brother.'

'I have to see my brother whether I win or lose.'

'It is a very simple game.' He reached into his pocket and pulled out a box of matches. 'I show you.'

'I really don't want—'

'I show you all the same.' He began to lay out the matches in rows on the table between them – a row of three, a row of four and a row of five. 'Now you take as many as you like from any row. Then it is my chance. I take from one row like you do. Then it is your turn again, and so on. The person who has the last piece to take is loser.'

She shrugged and tried to look indifferent. 'But I'm not playing for anything. I mean, if I lose that doesn't mean to say that you're taking me dancing.'

He looked at her with a faint and infuriating smile. 'We see. You go first.'

So they played among the spilled beer and the empty glasses, the youth with a strange concentration, as though his whole future depended on it, Marian with a distracted impatience that told him, she hoped, that she didn't care for either the game or his company. Of course he won. She knew he would. He grinned at her and said, 'We play again,' and the second time he won again, and the third time.

'It's stupid,' she said. 'It's one of those games that you can't lose.'

'But *you* have lost.'

'Because you have the trick.'

'The *trique*?' He spluttered with laughter.

She blushed, understanding the double entendre and angry that she couldn't disguise her embarrassment. 'The way of doing it.'

'Ah, the *truc*! That is always the way, isn't it? You win always if you know the *truc*.' He gathered up the matches and returned them to their box as though they were valuable trophies. 'And now we find somewhere to dance. In this city of *merde* you eat always badly, but at least you can find place to dance.'

'I'm not going dancing with you. I told you.'

He looked at her with pale and erratic eyes. There was something unsteady about him, as though he had been drinking all afternoon and would continue all evening. 'You know what *truc* I am making? I am returning to France, do you know that? I am going back to *la patrie* and cut German throats. And you will not even dance with me.'

'You're drunk,' she said. 'I don't go dancing with men who are drunk.'

'And you are *frigide*,' he retorted. 'And I do not dance with women who are *frigide*.'

She picked up her handbag and got up from her chair. 'I must go.'

'Why must you go?'

'Because otherwise I will be late.' He made a grab at her hand but she shook him off. '*Tu m'emmerdes!*' she told him as she walked away. She didn't look back, not even to see the shock in his expression. How to get away? If she went to her room he

20

would probably follow her, and she damn well wasn't going to hide away like a frightened little girl. Pulling on her coat, she walked quickly through the foyer and out through the revolving doors. A taxi was delivering a fare to the hotel. She climbed into the empty seat.

'Where to, Miss?' the cabbie asked.

She gave Ned's address. 'Bloomsbury,' she said. 'Russell Square, more or less.'

'More or less Russell Square it is, darling.'

V

The cab crept through the darkened streets. There were cinemas open in Piccadilly, their faint lights cast down on the pavement. Black shapes shifted in front of them like shades in Hades, queues of silhouettes lined up along the pavements and edging towards the box offices. But beyond the borderline of the Tottenham Court Road there was no one around, and Bloomsbury was a dark maze.

'You all right here, Miss?' the cabbie asked as he let her down.

'Quite all right,' she said, handing over the fare. She scrabbled in her respirator case for her torch. By its feeble light she made her way to the door where Ned lived. There was a panel of bell pushes, but as she was about to press the one labelled *Dr Edward Sutro* the door opened and someone came barging out.

'I'm so sorry,' he said. 'Bloody blackout.'

She dodged past him into the hallway and the door slammed shut behind her. She felt for the switch, turned on a pale, watery light in the stairwell and climbed the narrow stairs to the third floor. It was a relief when Ned answered her knock.

'My goodness, Squirrel,' he said as he saw her standing on the landing. 'You look dressed to kill.' He hugged her to him. A

21

hug from Ned was like being jumped at by a Great Dane, entrancing but at the same time awkward and uncomfortable. His own clothes gave the impression they had been picked up at a jumble sale. His hair was awry, and his smile was the distracted grin of someone who is delighted to see her but whose mind is really on different, abstract things. 'Come in, come in,' he said. 'Tell me all about it.'

'About what?'

'What on earth you are doing. I spoke to the parents on the phone the other day. They said you'd left the WAAF. Something about going abroad. Father thought Algiers ...'

She followed him through into the sitting room. The place was typical of Ned. Books were crammed into every available shelf and piled on the floor. His desk was littered with papers. A couple of decrepit armchairs stood opposite each other across a Persian carpet that was old and worn but gave the impression that it might once have been a valuable piece. On the wall behind the desk was a framed print of the Collège de France.

'Doesn't anyone come and clean for you?' she asked. 'At least you had a scout at Cambridge.'

'Bedder. Scouts are Oxford. Here there's a charlady who comes round occasionally, but she's always complaining she can't clean if I leave it in such a mess. Perhaps there ought to be cleaners who'll come and clean your place before the cleaner comes.' He laughed his own, absurd laugh.

She sat in one of the armchairs and he brought her a drink, another gin that she dared not refuse because refusal would have made her a girl again and now she was a grown-up woman. She'd never been that before with Ned.

'So tell me, what's it all about?'

'I can't,' she said.

'What do you mean, you can't?'

'It's secret. They made me sign the Official Secrets Act – and that was at the initial interview. Even the interview itself was secret.'

'Oh, stop being mysterious. I'll bet it's translation or something. Or spying. Maybe they want you to spy on General de Gaulle.'

She felt like laughing out loud. Ordinarily he was never interested in what she was doing. 'Silly schoolgirl things,' was what he used to say. And then when she said she wanted to read law at university, he was derisive about her choice. Law will teach us nothing except how to evade it, was his view of things. Science will teach us the future. 'You don't tell me what you do, so why should I say what I do?'

'Because you are dying to, that's why. And I *do* tell you what I do. I work on super-high-frequency electromagnetic radiation.'

'But what's it *for*? That's what's important. What do you do this for?'

'I'm making a ray gun to shoot the Luftwaffe out of the sky.'

'Don't be silly. I know you're not. That's just science fiction.' He really was a fool. He was always telling her things like that. A super-bomb that would blow a whole city to dust. A beam of deadly rays that would kill people with light. Rockets that would hurl high explosive from one continent to another through outer space. The kind of nonsense you read about in bad novels. 'All I can tell you,' she said, 'is that this is my last evening in London. Tomorrow I'm off to Scotland.'

'Scotland?'

'Training.'

'It sounds dreadful. Scotland's all heather and haggis and men in skirts. But I suppose that if you're off to the land of haggis we'd better find you a decent meal first.'

The restaurant Ned had found was in Southampton Row. Apparently people from the lab went there quite often. The place was crowded, people pushing and shoving and trying to get a table even though the waiters insisted that there was none available. But Ned had reserved one, in the innermost depths, where they couldn't be overheard and where she could finally do what she had intended all the time.

'You must promise not to say anything to the parents,' she warned him. 'Or anyone else. You mustn't say anything. Swear.'

It sounded like one of their childhood games. He smiled condescendingly. 'I swear.'

'I mean it, Ned. This is serious. I've been recruited by this organisation. They're sending me for training, and then …' She shouldn't be saying this, she knew she shouldn't. And yet it was too exciting not to share with someone, and Ned was the only possibility. Ned had always been her confidant. She slipped into French. Perhaps it was safer to say it in French: '*Ils veulent m'envoyer en France.*'

'*En France! Pourquoi? Pas possible! Mon Dieu*, Marian, *t'es folle!*'

'It's they who are mad, not me. At first I thought the job was something to do with language, as you did. Translation, or something. That's what they led me to expect. But I was wrong. I'm off tomorrow for Scotland. Commando training. This is serious, Ned, completely serious.' It seemed even more incredible now she was telling him. At least within the Organisation you felt caught up by its mad logic, but here, at a restaurant table with her brother sitting opposite her, the whole story seemed crazy.

'So who are "they"?'

She glanced round at the nearby tables. Perhaps they had followed her here. Perhaps they were listening to see what she said. But the other diners were engrossed in their own conversations, indifferent to the couple in the corner whispering to each other in French. 'I've no idea. "The Organisation", that's what they call it. They've got a place in Portman Square. But the real name's secret.' She laughed. 'I ask you, what's the point of having a name if it's secret?'

'Maybe it's like the naming of cats.'

'The name that no human research can discover—'

24

'—but that the cat himself knows and can never confess.' They laughed. He'd bought her the book for her Christmas present in the first year of the war: whimsical poems about cats by one of the most serious of poets. 'Where will they send you? Might you go to Paris?'

Would she? She had no idea. The future was all mysterious, an unknown world.

'Because if you were to go to Paris, you might look up Clément Pelletier.'

'Clément?' Her surprise was feigned, part of a defence mechanism left over from childhood. She had already thought of Clément, of course she had. How could she not? As far as she knew he was still in France, but she couldn't be certain. That was what happened these days; families and friends dispersed, contacts lost, relationships blighted. Perhaps he had forgotten her by now, as she, occasionally, managed not to think of him. But memories remained, small nuclei of longing and guilt lodged within her mind. 'I haven't seen him for years. He'll have forgotten who I am.'

Ned grinned. 'I very much doubt that.'

Marian felt herself blushing. She looked away in the hope Ned wouldn't notice, but if he did he said nothing. Once he would have remarked on it and made it worse – *Marian has gone all red*, he'd say so that everyone would stare.

'Didn't he used to write to you when you went away to school?'

'Occasionally.'

'More than occasionally. I think he was pretty soft on you.'

'I was only fifteen, Ned. Fifteen, sixteen. Just a girl. He was more than ten years older.'

'You didn't *seem* that young.'

'And anyway, he's probably married with children by now.' She picked at her bread, sipped some beer – beer was all they had; these days wine was as difficult to find as oranges or bananas. 'Have you heard anything about him?'

25

'Nothing but speculation. I believe he's still at the Collège de France. There's the cyclotron that Fred Joliot had installed immediately before the outbreak. Presumably it's working now, unless the Germans have carted it off to Heidelberg or somewhere.' He shrugged, fiddling with the cutlery. 'God knows what's going on there.' He appeared distracted, as though mention of Clément and Paris had upset him. Only after the waiter had brought their food did he continue. 'You know, I've never really understood why Clément stayed behind in France. He had the opportunity to get out of the country in 1940 but he stayed put.'

'What are you suggesting? That he should have run away?'

'Others from the Collège escaped – Lev Kowarski, von Halban – and brought out a whole lot of equipment. Why in God's name didn't Clément come with them? He was there in Bordeaux. There was a berth on the ship. He could have been in England the next day. What did he have to lose?'

'Maybe his honour. The others aren't French, are they?'

'Russian and Austrian.'

'Well, there you are. Clément is French through and through. For God's sake, abandoning your country when it's invaded isn't particularly admirable. If more people had stood and fought ...'

'But he wasn't fighting, was he? He was doing scientific research.'

'So perhaps he felt above it all. Pure science, that's what he used to say.'

Ned gave a bitter laugh. 'One thing I've discovered, Squirrel, is that there is no longer any such thing as pure science. What I do, or what Kowarski does ...' He seemed to cast around for what he wanted to say but couldn't find the right words. 'Anyway, if you did get to Paris, it'd be interesting to get some idea of what's going on at the Collège. That's all I'm saying.'

'Who knows if that's where they'll send me? I'm not going on holiday, you know.'

'Of course I realise that. Don't be stupid.' He looked at her and smiled. 'You're still the same old Squirrel, aren't you? Getting all hot and bothered.'

'Well, you speak about it as though I could simply get on a train and go and see.'

He laughed. The momentary anger died away. It was always that way between them – sudden flare-ups of anger quickly dying away. They moved the conversation to neutral ground – the days before the war mainly, that strange Arcadian world that seemed so distant now, a landscape distorted by the passage of time and the intense gravitational field of subsequent events: the house on the lake at Annecy, the chalet in Megève, the sailing and the skiing, the noise and the laughter when the two families, the Pelletiers and the Sutros, came together. Madeleine who befriended her despite being five years older; and Madeleine's older brother Clément, who seemed touched by something like the finger of God. A graduate of the École Normale Supérieur. A physicist for whom a brilliant future was predicted. A second Louis de Broglie, they said, heir apparent to the king and queen of French science, Fred Joliot and his wife Irène Curie. Ned and he used to talk physics while Marian hung on their words and tried to understand. But they spoke of incomprehensible mathematics and obscure ideas and absurd enthusiasms. Let's play Piggy-in-the-middle, they'd cry, only they'd call it 'collapsing the wave function' and collapse with laughter at the joke that she, a mere fifteen-year-old trying to catch the tennis ball, couldn't share. And Consequences, they'd play Consequences, which Clément called Cadavre Exquis, the exquisite corpse. The Expatiating Physicist Preconceives a Stupendous Tintinnabulation. That was one of them.

The waiter came and took their plates. 'Look, I must go,' she said, pushing back her chair. 'I've got a long day tomorrow.'

Ned was suddenly attentive, helping her into her coat and patting her shoulders, as though he understood that she really was going and was off to do something rather remarkable, and needed his brotherly comfort however awkwardly expressed. 'D'you know, I envy you?' he told her. 'At least you're involved in something active. I've simply got to get on with my work and do what I'm told.'

'These days that's what everyone does.'

They went looking for a cab. There was nothing near the restaurant, and so they went towards the West End. It had come on to rain, and the flagstones glistened in what little light there was. She turned up the collar of her coat. Someone barged into them and shouted at them for getting in the way, then staggered on, muttering to himself. There were more people about now, shadows moving through the dark, voices talking and laughing but detached from their shapes so that the sounds seemed disembodied, the expression of the city itself. There were rumours about what happened in the blackout. Sometimes, it was said, people had sex there in the street, while strangers walked past without noticing. There had been stories about this among the girls at Stanmore. One of them had even claimed to have done it herself. A knee-trembler, she called it; and the other girls had laughed.

'Father thinks I should give up what I'm doing,' Ned said. 'He thinks it's an easy way out, and that I should be in uniform like you.'

'I'm sure he doesn't.'

'He abandoned his job in the Foreign Office in the last war.'

'And ended up sitting in a gun emplacement behind the lines and losing half his hearing.'

'At least he tried.'

'Your work is more important than anything you could contribute as a soldier. Once you get that ray gun to work.'

He laughed. They had come to a cinema. There was a dimly illuminated sign. EXCELSIOR, it said. People were streaming out, laughing and shouting. Taxis were waiting at the kerb and a man called, 'Anyone for Kensington?' He was wearing uniform – she made out captain's pips on his shoulder – and had two women with him. The women were giggling together, leaning against each other for mutual support.

Marian ran forward. 'Can you drop me off on the way?'

'No trouble at all, my dear.'

To Ned she said, 'Wish me luck.'

'Come on, love,' the captain called. 'The meter's going.'

As she climbed into the cab Ned broke into French. 'Do you know when you'll leave for France?'

She looked back, holding the door. 'I've no idea.'

'Come on, Miss. We've got to go.'

She sat back in the cab. 'Keep in touch,' he called through the window. 'How do I contact you?'

'Through the parents,' she said, 'how else?'

'I'll send his address. Clément's, I mean. Just in case.'

The taxi drew away. She watched him standing in the road until he gave a little wave and turned away. 'It's awfully good of you to wait,' she said to the others in the cab. 'I'm sorry I kept you.'

'Where are you going?' the officer asked. The women looked at her and giggled. Why did they? Were they drunk, or was there something comic about her?

'Just off Regent Street. I don't think it's out of your way, is it?'

'Didn't I hear you speaking French?' one of the women asked. 'Are you French? Golly, you sound awfully English to be French.'

Marian turned away to look out of the window. It had started raining again. She thought of Ned walking back through the wet. 'I'm both,' she said. 'Or neither.'

# Scotland

|

The journey was one of those wartime odysseys in which time and rationality seemed suspended. Occasionally the train moved with decisive speed. Often, for reasons that were never explained and never apparent, it stopped. Mainly it crawled with caution across a countryside as grey and damp as army bedding – mere fields, shallow hills, small, mean woods.

The compartment she travelled in was reserved. *Inter Services Research Bureau* it said on the booking docket on the door. The conducting officer was a Scots woman called Janet. Her charges made a strange, heterogeneous group. There was a middle-aged, man who called himself Emile, and a young Canadian who claimed to speak French but actually spoke a broken and uncertain québécois. Maurice, he was called. Marian guessed that it was really pronounced 'Morris' but he had put a French slant on it: *Mo-reece*. The third member was a woman called Yvette. She seemed as small and drab and anxious as a mouse. When they'd met on the platform at Euston she had whispered to Marian that she was so glad there was another woman on the journey and maybe they could be friends and wasn't everything so *vachement bizarre*? Now she sat in the window seat opposite, reading a book or watching the monotonous countryside pass by. Once she said, '*Ce pays de merde*,' then looked round blushing with her hand to her mouth, as though she had not intended to speak out loud. Emile laughed. 'I know shit compared with which this would be a bed of roses,' he said.

The journey went on, the grey-green flats of the Midlands giving way to industrial townscapes and then a desolate landscape of moorland and mountain. An England she didn't know. Passengers climbed on and climbed off, mainly soldiers humping their kitbags on their shoulders and cursing each other with a mixture of good humour and venom. She dozed and read, the one state merging into the other so that she was uncertain whether she had read something or merely dreamed it. Even the enclosed world of their compartment, with its disparate little group of travellers, seemed the product of some distorted imagination. Where were they going, and what were they meant to do when they arrived there? Was it all serious, or was it a joke, a hoax played upon four dysfunctional people, each of whom harboured the pathetic belief that he or she might contribute to the war effort? Maybe, she thought, with a small bubble of laughter rising in her throat, maybe she had actually gone mad during one of the long night watches in the Filter Room and now she was being taken off to some lunatic asylum in the far north of the country, away from the war, away from any danger of falling bombs, where they could all, harmless lunatics that they were, act out their various fantasies.

On the outskirts of Carlisle the train waited for half an hour for something that never happened before lurching forward across the border into Scotland. Rain, which had held off since Crewe, began to fall again.

‖

In Glasgow they stayed overnight in a hotel near the station. Marian shared a room with Yvette. Lying in bed in the darkness they did what, presumably, they were not meant to do: they talked about their private lives, speaking in French, as though the language were a code through which they could tell each other the truth. 'I want to go home,' Yvette confessed. 'I don't care whether the Germans are there or not, I just want to go home.' She must have been older than Marian, but seemed younger, lost in this strange, distracted journey and ill at ease in a country where her uncertain grasp of English gave her away as someone to be pitied, one of the dispossessed of Europe. Along with her English husband, she had fled south a few days before Paris fell to the Germans. They'd reached the coast and managed to get to Spain by taking a small boat from somewhere near Montpellier. It had been a brave and almost foolhardy journey, but somehow they had made it. 'Where's your husband now?' Marian asked.

The girl lay on her back in the darkness, a shadow with a voice. 'He's dead.'

'Oh. I'm so sorry. How awful.'

'He joined up, you see, and was sent out to Egypt. The ship was torpedoed somewhere near Sicily. He was called Bill. Bill Coombes. I loved him.'

There was silence. Was she crying silently in the darkness? Perhaps not. There was something cold and calculating about her, as though some vital piece of the human machinery had broken deep inside. Later she revealed that she had left her small daughter behind at her parents-in-law's house.

'You've got a *daughter*?'

The little voice pattered on in the dark, without stress, without anguish, a strange, featureless landscape of words. 'She's called Violette. The English call her Violet. Or Vi. She's two years old. Lovely little thing, but d'you know, I don't miss her? Isn't that terrible? I don't miss her at all.' And then unexpectedly she did weep, not for her child but for the fact of not being able to miss her. 'I'm sorry,' she said quietly. 'I must sound heartless. That's the trouble, I suppose. I *am* heartless. My heart has been turned to stone.'

Next morning the train left Glasgow in surprising sunshine, passing along the shore beside waters where dour warships lay at anchor, then inland, trundling slowly as though feeling its way into the wilderness. How far north could you go? And how far away from France? The landscape grew wild, the names of the stations acquiring a foreign tone: Ardlui, Crianlarich, Bridge of Orchy. They crossed a desolate moorland and went onward through the hills, past occasional platforms where no one waited, through valleys where no road passed. Eventually there was a glimpse of a few houses and they drew to a halt at a nameless station that suddenly became the focus of military activity. Doors slammed open down the train and other passengers got off, a few anonymous civilians but more men in uniform, bearing a mixture of regimental badges. 'There'll be transport down to the loch,' Janet told them, 'but we'll wait in here a while. We don't want the squaddies seeing ladies in this part of the world.'

And then Marian caught sight of a familiar figure. She was looking out of the window at the motley collection of passengers leaving the train and he passed by immediately below her window. There wasn't any doubt about it. He was only a few inches away, just beyond the glass – the French boy called Benoît.

People called out. Army lorries revved their engines and drove off. Janet led her flock to the door of the carriage and down onto the platform. Marian shivered against the cold wind, wondering where the French boy had gone, who he was and what he was doing here. It must be – that was the only explanation – that his boast had been the truth: he really was going to return to France.

A solitary truck took them down to the lochside where a motor boat was waiting. They clambered aboard and settled onto narrow seats, clutching their suitcases. The engine roared, the crew cast off and the craft headed out into the water. There was nowhere to go – only out into the desolate loch between empty hills that lined the shore. She thought of the lake at Annecy, with its dramatic alpine scenery. Would it become like this in some distant future, when the Alps had been eroded down to resemble these low, weary hills, and humanity had been reduced to a few miserable survivors? The boat puttered along for what seemed like hours, the water slopping, gunmetal grey, alongside. There was desultory talk among the group, part French, part English. Yvette and Marian huddled together for warmth. 'This is hell,' Yvette whispered. 'Hell is not hot, it is cold. And bare and bleak. This is hell.'

Eventually the boat docked at a deserted jetty on the south shore of the loch. There were two or three huts and a large sign that announced, in red lettering, WAR OFFICE RESTRICTED AREA KEEP OUT and a narrow valley that cut back into the hills. They climbed up onto the jetty, peering round like a group of refugees from some unnamed disaster wondering whether they had really escaped. Clouds of midges descended on them. 'I'm afraid we've got a short walk,' Janet told them. 'But at least it's no' raining.'

They humped their suitcases along a track that ran beside a small river. Scattered along the valley were a few huts and cottages, the remnants of a crofting community that had long since died out. It was a place as far from France as it was possible to imagine.

'Where are they taking us?' Yvette asked.

'The back of beyond.'

Yvette looked blank. 'Where's that?'

'It's a saying. *En pleine cambrousse.*'

The track rounded a curve in the hillside and there it was, couched in fir trees and clad in ivy like a suburban villa. They stumbled to a halt. In front of the building lay a wide lawn that did nothing to tame the setting: behind the house a rough hillside rose steeply upwards into cloud. There was the sound of wind and water all around, and an air of desolation. Wilderness, Marian thought: a strange, wild word with echoes of bewilderment woven

34

into it. Who had once lived in this place, and what had they done with their lives? It was impossible to imagine.

'Welcome to Meoble Lodge,' a young officer greeted them as they stumbled through the main door into the hall. He had a Scottish accent that made it sound like 'Mabel' Lodge, the kind of place a maiden aunt might stay at for her holidays, a place of sagging, broken armchairs and sofas and out-of-date editions of *Tatler* and *The Lady*. 'I'm Lieutenant Redmond, and I'm in charge of your course. We do hope you enjoy your stay with us.'

III

The lodge was a curious mix of military camp and university reading group, a world of much huffing and puffing, of pipe smoke and whisky and the smell of damp tweed. Outside, it rained. Inside there was a blazing fire and, after dinner, an open bar where the staff watched, so the story went, to see how well you handled alcohol. Much of what the students knew was the product of rumour and speculation, imagination filling the vacuum of secrecy. What exactly was this organisation that had recruited them? The Special Operations Executive, Emile said, but how did he know? And what were its aims? And why on earth were they shut away like this in the wilds of Scotland, amid the damp and the midges? Thus united in ignorance, the students drew together in some kind of camaraderie, in the way that prisoners unite against the common enemies of deprivation and discomfort.

They were woken on the first and every subsequent morning for PT on the lawn in front of the house. After that they had breakfast, which always included bacon and eggs, the kind of luxury most people had forgotten; but there was no luxury about the course itself. Together they climbed hills and crawled through soaking heather, in pairs they struggled over the assault course, in teams they waded through swollen rivers and constructed rafts to navigate the choppy waters of the loch. The two women had to get by as best they could. Yvette staggered in exhaustion through the exercises. At night she wept silently in the darkness of their shared bedroom. Whenever they talked it was obliquely, in low voices. The rumour had spread within the group – started, it seemed, by Emile – that their rooms had hidden microphones planted in the skirting boards or in the light fittings so that the instructors could listen in on private conversations and find out which ones were weak and which were strong. On one occasion Yvette crept, mouse-like, into Marian's bed to lie there in her arms like a child, the hot, wet pulp of her lips against Marian's cheek, whispering so that she would not be overheard.

Marian felt motherly towards her. It was absurd, this feeling of protectiveness. Yvette was eight years older and a widow. She had borne a child. She had escaped from France in an open boat and spent days at sea before making landfall in Spain. She was a woman and Marian a mere girl, and yet the dynamic of their relationship was this, daughter and mother, protected and protector.

'They think I'm shit,' Yvette whispered. 'All I want is to go back to France, so why do they have to do this to me? What kind of training is this? I just want to go home. I may as well give up. They're going to fail me anyway.'

The next night Marian was woken to shouts from her roommate. '*Va-t'en!*' Yvette was yelling. '*Va-t'en!*' But whom she was telling to get out was never clear. When she awoke, mumbling in the darkness, she had no memory of her dream.

While the nights were fearful and empty, the days were full. They went on forced marches for endurance, and ran the assault course for fitness and agility. They swung on ropes over imaginary rivers and climbed walls and crawled, bellies against the ground, beneath barbed-wire fences while a fixed machine gun fired live rounds over them, the bullets cracking deafening inches above their backs. Lectures and activities led one into the other, theory becoming practice so intensely that after a while this

36

learning and doing seemed normal, and their previous lives of indolence and ease an incomplete memory. Only in the evenings, after dinner, were they left to their own devices, but even then there were members of the staff on hand to watch. 'Of course they're assessing us,' Emile confided. 'It's an old trick. Play the friend and you'll find out more than you ever would at a formal interview. I used to do it myself when hiring people. Take them out drinking, that was the best thing. Get a few whiskies in them and have a bit of a laugh. That's when you find out the truth about a man. In vino veritas, as the ancients used to say.'

'When did you ever hire people?' Marian asked, and instantly regretted her question for the elaborate explanation it would conjure up.

'When I was in the Congo. In mining. A tough life it was. Makes this look like the life of Riley.'

In the rare periods of relaxation some of the students read – there was a small collection of French novels: some Colette, a few detective stories by Gaston Leroux, a much-thumbed copy of *Madame Bovary*. Maurice and Emile played chess almost incessantly while others studied the pamphlets that they had been given, on field craft and unarmed combat and how to shoot the one-hand gun in the manner of W. E. Fairbairn and E. A. Sykes.

Marian wrote letters. She wrote to her mother and father, to a couple of the girls she had worked with in the WAAF, and to Ned. Occasionally she was engaged in conversation by one of the instructors, a man whose French, though tainted by English, was fluent. He did the rounds of the students, asking them about their pasts, their connections with France, their views on the politics of Vichy and the problems of resistance. 'Where do you think the French communists' loyalties lie?' he asked her. 'With the French people, or with Stalin?'

'Are the two things in conflict?'

'General de Gaulle thinks they are.'

'And what do you think?'

'I'm asking *you*.'

He questioned her about others on the course, about the French Canadian with the terrible accent and about Emile.

'I wish he didn't *know* everything.'

The instructor smiled sympathetically. 'And how do you think Yvette is progressing?'

'I think she's fine.'

'Do you think she'll make it through to the end? Has she got what it takes?'

'I think she's a lot tougher than she seems.'

'And if she told you that she didn't want to carry on, what would you say?'

'But she hasn't told me that, so I couldn't answer.'

'Hypothetically speaking.'

'I think she can pull through. She's got a lot of guts.'

'Do you consider her a friend?'

'What's it got to do with you?'

'Everything is to do with me. Everything that might have a bearing on your mission. Where do your loyalties lie, Miss Sutro? With your friends, or with the organisation?'

She laughed at that. 'I really don't know what organisation it is. I find it hard to be loyal to something so nebulous.'

'So what do you think you are doing here?'

'I'm afraid you are better equipped to answer that than I am.'

Occasionally, to escape the watchful eyes and the attentive ears, she went out alone for a walk, loving the empty solitude of the place in the elongated dusk and prepared even to brave the midges. At least, she reasoned, out here I'm on my own. At least I can think.

IV

Time passed, with that curious relativity that brought Ned's physics to mind: relative time, elastic time, the hours of discomfort stretching out like days but the whole passage of the course compressing from days into what seemed like mere hours. They did weapons training – pistols, rifles, sub-machine guns, a dozen different types of each. They learned to prove a weapon, to strip it and assemble it, to charge a magazine and load it, to fire from the hip and the shoulder and prone. The shooting range was a simulacrum of a town street, built among the outhouses, with targets that were the silhouettes of malignant men that appeared momentarily and at random, pulled up by an artifice of levers and pulleys. The students ducked and weaved, turning this way and that, firing from the centre line of the body, arms out straight.

'Don't aim,' the instructors told them. 'Instinct is what we want. Like pointing with your finger.' They talked of Fairbairn and Sykes, twin deities of this strange world of killing. The Fairbairn-Sykes position: 'Square on to the target, legs apart, knees flexed. Raise the weapon to face level, both eyes open, the weapon obscuring the target. Then two shots in quick succession. Double tap. Bang, bang! If you don't kill him with the first shot, you kill him with the second.'

Marian found she could do it, that was the strange thing. Gun in hand she could weave through the shooting range and hit the targets with unerring accuracy. 'That's right!' the instructor cried. 'Show the gentlemen how to do it.'

Emile explained that he had once been a superb shot – even competed at Bisley – until something mysterious had happened in Africa and he had lost his edge as a result. 'But you're not bad,' he conceded grudgingly. 'Not bad at all.'

After weapons training they were induced into the mysterious world of demolition by a man with the joyous expression of a child with fireworks. '*Plastique*,' he said, showing them a lump of oily putty. 'As stable as chewing gum, as explosive as TNT.' They handed it from one to the other. It smelled of almonds. 'Detonate it properly and it'll bring down bridges. The resister's best friend, *plastique*.' Quite why he used the French name was never clear. Did this strange stuff originate in France? As though to help answer that question, he took the lump back and kneaded it into a shape that made the men laugh and the two women blush. And then, to demonstrate its stability, he tossed it on the fire, where the stuff burned and fizzed with a festive flame. Then he took them outside to a bunker among the outhouses and showed them how to tamp the explosive, how to wire up the detonator and finally, with a joyous shout as he wound the induction coil, how a few ounces of plastic could blow a car axle to pieces.

'Then there are the time pencils.' He held them up like a child showing his collection of bangers. 'Five minutes, ten minutes, twenty, thirty. You make your selection, twist the stem to break the capsule and Bob's your uncle.'

Time pencil. Again she thought of Ned, something he might invent, a pencil that could mark out the passage of time, a pen that could recall the past and predict the future, a quill that might consign the present to oblivion.

*Dear Ned*, she wrote. *I hope you are quite well. Here they work our fingers to the bone but in a strange way I am enjoying myself. When we get leave at the end of this course maybe I can get to London to see you.*

But she had little time to think about him. Here there were people of far greater curiosity than her scientist brother, men who knew how to kill and destroy, like the instructor in close combat, a middle-aged man with a brush of short, ginger hair and the gloomy manner of an undertaker. He delivered a first-aid course in reverse – how to cut the brachial artery with a knife slash to the forearm, how to dislocate the knee with a single stab of the foot, how to snap a man's spine by dropping him across your knee, how to inflict the maximum damage in the minimum time. You could render a man helpless with a handclap to both ears, knock him unconscious with a matchbox, kill him with an umbrella.

'Remember this: you don't want to get into a fight, but if you have no choice then you want to get out of it as quick as possible. The quickest way is to kill your opponent. I'm sorry if that offends the ladies' sensibilities, but that's the fact of the matter.'

It did not offend Yvette's sensibilities: with all the devotion of an acolyte committing to a new religion, she loved silent killing. She loved the heft of a knife in her hands, the wicked gleaming tongue of steel with the initials of the designer at the base of the blade: THE F-S FIGHTING KNIFE, it said, the plain truth engraved there without any euphemism. Fairbairn and Sykes again. The hilt lay softly in her hand, balanced between thumb and forefinger like a conductor's baton. 'I could kill with this,' she murmured.

They practised on one another with dummy weapons, and what started as self-conscious play-acting grew close to the real thing, something tense and terrific, as though a life depended on it. And Yvette showed the way, approaching her victim from behind, as quiet as a cat. The rest of the course watched, breathlessly, something that was at once compelling and obscene: the small woman moving, the sudden pounce, the knife striking down into the shoulder, right behind the collarbone where the subclavian artery lay deep among muscle and connective tissue, where, if you got it right, the victim would die within four seconds.

V

Marian lay awake and thought about killing. Killing in the abstract was fine. Killing at one remove, killing in theory. She remembered the Filter Room, a dozen WAAFs crowding round the table in the early evening with the calls coming through from the radar stations. The girls in a scrum, reaching out over one another to put tokens down on the map like gamblers at the roulette table placing their last bets. The excitement as single plots became dozens, became hundreds, tracks identified and called, pointing out across the bulge of East Anglia and heading

41

towards the sea, each single plot being seven men and that meant seven lives. Seven times seven hundred. Five thousand lives, give or take. They'd march soundlessly across the board and disappear beyond the edge of the known world and the girls would wait, smoking, drinking tea, chatting in a desultory fashion while the killing went on, distant killing that you couldn't see and couldn't hear, the pulverising of the German cities. But what the ginger instructor was proposing was different: killing when you could feel the man's throat beneath your arm, his breath on your cheek, his blood on your hands. How do you do that?

'Oh, it would be no trouble for me,' Yvette assured her. 'I think I would enjoy it.'

If it wasn't death, it was destruction. How to blow a door, put a car out of action, destroy a train. She found herself paired with Emile. He always knew everything about it even before the lecture had begun. 'Used to work on the railways in the Congo,' he explained when they were being taught how to sabotage a railway line.

'Was that before or after the mines?'

'That's a complex question.'

'No, it's not. It's not even one I want an answer to.' But she got an answer nevertheless, the precise chronology of his career as mine engineer, railway engineer, construction engineer, any kind of engineer you might wish for. 'It was a tough life showing the blacks the way forward.'

'You and Mr Kurtz, you mean?'

That puzzled him. It was always a triumph to puzzle Emile. 'Kurtz? I never met anyone called Kurtz.'

She hated him. She didn't often hate people, but she hated Emile. *One of the people on our course is a pompous KA*, she wrote to her father the next day. *The kind you abhor.*

They practised wireless telegraphy and Morse code regularly, tapping on the key with nervy fingers and trying to take down the irritating buzzing into a coherent sequence of dots and dashes. *The boat will dock at Dover on the fifteenth. The Test Match will result in victory for Australia.* Daft messages like that.

'Each operator has his own fist. As individual as handwriting.'

Hands stammered on the Bakelite knobs. Arthritis, they called Morse keying: like arthritis it brought a painful tension in the wrist, aching carpals and metacarpals, stiff and inflexible fingers. 'Accuracy is everything. Accuracy and speed. Lives may depend on it. Perhaps even yours.' Flimsies passed back and forth from instructors to students, misreadings underscored in blue crayon.

She keyed, without a mistake:

• ▬▬ •• •▬▬•• • •• ••• •▬ ▬ •• •▬▬• • ••• ▬▬▬
▬▬ • ▬•▬• ▬•• ▬▬▬ •▬▬ ▬ •▬ •▬▬•• •▬▬••

*Emile   is   a   tiresome   know - all.*

Often Marian thought of Clément. She tried not to, but she did. It seemed ridiculous to revisit a childish infatuation but the memories were powerful and disturbing, the kind of thing that could undermine your whole personality, disturb the equilibrium that adulthood had brought. She remembered him in Paris on that visit with her father a few months before the outbreak of war. She remembered walking with him in the English Garden in Geneva. She remembered other times and other places. Skiing at Megève. Sailing at Annecy. Sometimes it was difficult to get the chronology right. What had happened when? He and Ned used to play a kind of chess together, blind chess where each player could only see his own board. *Kriegspiel* they'd called it. They needed an adjudicator, to say whether a proposed move was legal or not. Madeleine always refused, so Marian was recruited. And she was willing, of course; happy simply to be in Clément's presence. Her task was to watch the two boards, while each player saw only his own pieces and had

43

to makes guesses and estimates of what his opponent was doing. The play had been strangely disjointed, groping in the dark with incomplete information. Exactly like physics research, that's what Clément used to say. Superposition and uncertainty. A quantum world.

Above all, she remembered that day on the lake. Always that. A day of sun and wind and a strange, opalescent light. A day of dreamlike difference, where shock seemed normal.

Clément.

# VI

They were given a free day. It was a rare day of sunshine and breeze, so Marian and Yvette decided to climb the mountain that had been the bane of their lives when they first arrived. Meith Bheinn was its name, a raw hulk of a hill that rose behind the lodge, guarded by crags and the ubiquitous Scottish bogs. But now the climb held no fears. Even Yvette had grown stronger, transformed from the city creature of the first days into someone who could walk with fair ease across this desolate landscape. So they slogged up the slopes, clambered over boulders, splashed, laughing through the marshy patches. 'Look!' Marian cried, seeing something scurrying amid the heather.

Yvette looked. 'What? Where?' But the animal had gone. A grouse perhaps, safer keeping to the ground than rising and being shot, living a clandestine life.

The climb took two and a half hours, and from the top they could see across the isles – Rum, Eigg and Muck close to the land and Skye lying like a shield on the edge of the Atlantic. They were too high for the midges. The wind blew cool but they found shelter in the lee of a boulder where they lay in the fragile sunshine and ate the sandwiches they had brought and talked about what might happen.

'I think they'll fail me,' Yvette said. 'I think they'll tell me I'm not good for what they want.'

'Don't be silly. You're doing fine.'

'No, I'm not. They want people to run over mountains and ford streams and things like that. But what about the cities? What about the towns? That is where the people are. That is where the resistance must be.'

'Maybe we'll end up in the Massif Central.'

'More likely we'll be in Paris and we'll wonder why on earth we were ever made to do this training.'

It was curious how they used the collective pronoun. *Nous.* As though they might be together. But there would be no 'we', surely. They would be on their own.

'What will you do when it's all over?' Marian asked.

Yvette shrugged in that fatalistic, Gallic manner. 'Find another husband, I suppose. A father for my little girl.'

'In France?'

'Of course, in France. Where else? Perhaps I'll live in a big apartment, and you and your husband will come to stay—'

'My husband!'

'That Clément you were talking about.'

'Clément's too old for me.'

'Maybe he was once, but age differences vanish as you get older. Look at you now. You're not a girl any longer, are you? You're a woman. You're catching him up. And there's a big advantage of having an older man.'

'What's that?'

'When he dies, you're young enough for another one.' They laughed at the idea, at the thought of men being their victims, lusting after them and being bent to their will.

After a while the wind grew chill and they decided to go back, but as they were preparing to descend from the summit they heard voices below them on the hillside. Was it someone from the lodge? They crouched in the lee of their boulder and waited, whispering.

The voices came nearer. Male voices. A burst of laughter. They were coming up from the north, directly towards them.

'Let's go,' Marian whispered to Yvette, 'we'll outflank them.' She led the way eastwards off the summit, keeping low, moving from cover to cover as they had been taught. They crept over tussocks of grass and round scattered boulders. And then they saw the group approaching, half a dozen men in battledress and cap comforters climbing the hillside rapidly, their boots clumping against the rocks.

'Commandos,' she whispered to Yvette. They had heard about commandos. Emile had told them. 'They train round here as well,' he'd said, 'Lochailort.' But he wouldn't say how he knew, merely gave that smug, know-all's smile. So the two women crouched behind a boulder as the six men climbed past. They were moving fast, almost as though they were in a race of some kind, and carrying weapons, Sten guns slung against their chests, and heavy packs on their backs.

Abruptly Marian stood up. It was an unpremeditated move, nothing that she had discussed with Yvette. She just stood up there on the hillside in the wind and the sun. 'Bang! Bang!' she shouted. 'You're dead!'

The men stumbled to a halt and grabbed at their weapons, looking round to see her standing there on a boulder, her hair blown out by the wind, looking for all the world like a Valkyrie, or something. 'What the fuck?' one of them exclaimed, and then looked embarrassed.

'A woman,' another said. 'What the devil's a *woman* doing here?'

And the others laughed, one of them raising his hands above his head. '*Je me rends*,' he cried. '*Je suis votre prisonnier*. Do what you will with me.' There was more laughter, and more French spoken. The one who had raised his hands in mock surrender was the French boy called Benoît.

The leader of the group came across. Yvette had appeared at Marian's side and stood close as though for protection.

'*Two* of you?' the man shouted. He wore captain's pips on his shoulders and his face was dark with rage. 'Who the hell are you? What are you doing here? Don't you know this is a restricted area? Where the bloody hell have you come from?'

'We're from Edinburgh,' Marian said. 'We've come for the weekend.'

'For the weekend? *Here*? Do you have identification? Where are your papers?'

'We left them down in the car. We didn't expect to meet a policeman up here.'

'I'm not a bloody policeman!' The captain was struggling with the possibilities, trying to work out what to do. His face was red, from exertion perhaps, or anger, or the embarrassment of meeting women in a place like this. 'Where in God's name are you staying?'

'At a hotel.'

'A hotel? Round here?' He shook his head in bewilderment. 'This is most irregular. You shouldn't be here at all. We'll have to escort you down.'

'Does that mean we're under arrest?'

'It means I'm keeping an eye on you until I can be sure of your story. As far as I know you could be spies.'

'We're not spies. Honestly.'

'Of course you'll say that. Spies would say that, wouldn't they?'

'I suppose they would. But actually we're secretaries, at the Office for Inter Services Liaison in Edinburgh. You can check if you like.'

'Inter Services Liaison? Never heard of it.'

'It's very important. It does liaison. Between the services.'

'However important it is, you shouldn't be here. You'd better come with me.'

So they set off down the hill, the captain leading the way, the two women following, escorted by the men.

'Will we be in trouble?' Yvette asked in a whisper.

'Don't be ridiculous.'

Benoît walked beside them. He was looking at her with a curious, sideways glance, as though trying to remember. Then his eyes lit up. 'You are Anne-Marie! *La belle* Anne-Marie who would not go dancing with me. *Mais qu'est-ce que vous faites là?*'

'Is it any of your business?'

He laughed. He looked quite different from the half-drunk youth who had tried to take her dancing. Younger, certainly, but dark and thoughtful. 'She is very surprising, our Anne-Marie. I didn't expect to see her here. I only expect to see sheep in this shitty part of the world, not beautiful women. And not London girls who suddenly show they are, in fact, French. You fooled me, you know. I never guessed you were French until when you walked away. *Emmerdeur*, you called me.'

'You were.'

'It was my last evening before coming here.'

'And mine.'

'We should have spent it together.'

'You should have been sober.'

The captain looked over his shoulder, suddenly alerted to the language that was being spoken. 'Are these women *French*? *Est-ce que vous êtes françaises?*'

The group stumbled to a halt. There was a further interrogation. What were two French women doing here? The faint suspicion arose in the officer's mind that he was being made to look a fool. 'Are you people from Meoble?' he demanded.

Marian smiled, as though it was a moment of revelation. 'Meoble Hotel, that's the place. That's where we're staying. Not really a hotel, more a work camp.'

'Look, are you taking the mickey?'

'Well, I wasn't going to tell you straight away, was I? It's all secret. I wasn't going to go blabbing to any Tom, Dick or Harry we bump into on a mountainside.'

The officer regarded her with something approaching fury. 'I am *not* any Tom, Dick or Harry. I'm an experienced alpine climber. I've climbed on Everest with F. S. Smythe. I've trekked up to the foot of Kanchenjunga. And I don't expect lip from a young girl out on a hiking trip. So you two come with me and we'll see what's going on.'

He turned and stormed off down the hillside with the rest of his group following on the broken slope, slipping and sliding at the steeper bits, herding the two girls among them. Benoît was still beside her. He tried to keep his voice low so that the captain wouldn't hear. 'So you *are* in training.' He shook his head in amazement. And admiration. 'What a *casse-cou* you are! Where are you from?'

'Geneva.'

'Ah, *une Genevoise*. I can hear it in your accent.'

'My father was an official of the League of Nations.'

'Posh!'

'He's not posh. He's just an ordinary man. He's my father.'

'And is the posh girl enjoying the course?'

'I told you, we're not posh.' But she admitted that she was enjoying it, in a masochistic kind of way. It was like a glorified expedition with her Uncle Jacques, who used to take her climbing in the Alps.

'Except for the weather?'

'Except for the weather.' They laughed. You had to laugh at the weather. The only alternative was to cry, and there was no point in doing that as no one would notice the tears. 'We've canoed across the lake,' he told her, and then corrected himself with elaborate sarcasm: '*Loch*. They get very excited if you call it a lake. And now we've been racing up to the top. It's some kind of competition. They love competitions, these British. Apparently there's a league table, like the football. I think that's what they think of the war – it's a competition, and whoever wins gets the Ashes. You've heard of the Ashes?'

'Of course I've heard of the Ashes.'

'Who would fight for ashes? Only the English.'

He was based at a place called Swordland, on the other side of the loch. Swordland seemed magical and fantastic, like something to do with the Knights of the Round Table. 'How strange that we should meet like this,' she said. But was it strange? So much seemed strange nowadays that all concepts of strangeness were distorted. Only a couple of weeks ago she had been a bored WAAF working shifts in the Filter Room at Bentley Priory amid the smoke from cigarettes and the smell from armpits. And now she was here in this remote landscape, with the vague promise of France ahead of her and a whole collection of skills that she would never have imagined acquiring. She knew how to kill a man with a blow to the neck and how to derail a train with a few pounds of explosive; she could signal with Morse and fire a Thomson sub-machine gun. She could move silently at night and penetrate barbed-wire fencing noiselessly and cross a river by pulling herself along a single rope. How was anything strange beside that?

'Perhaps we can get together when we have leave?' he suggested.

'Perhaps.'

'Where do you live?'

'Oxford.'

He looked disappointed. It was his disappointment that encouraged her. 'Are you in London?'

'Of course. They put me up in a hotel.'

She was about to ask other questions – where was he from? where was his family? how did he make it to Britain? all that kind of thing – when the captain looked round from the front of the group. 'What's all this talk? Where the hell has security gone? Bérard, you come up here with me, please.'

She laughed. 'Do as you are told.'

Benoît made a face, and hurried ahead to join the captain. 'Oxford *trente-deux quatre-vingt-neuf*,' she called out to his back. He glanced round and smiled. His smile was appealing, the smile of the little boy playing at being a soldier.

*

Down at the lodge, Marian and Yvette were ordered into the lounge like recalcitrant children, while the captain and Lieutenant Redmond conferred on the lawn. Marian stood back from the window so that she could see without herself being seen. There was much gesticulating and frowning.

'They're treating us like infants,' Marian said. 'I'll walk out. They can't stop me. I'll simply go home, and they can stuff their plans.'

Yvette sniffed. 'They'll throw me out.'

'Don't be daft. It's me they're after.'

'They think I'm no good.'

'Stop saying that. They're idiots. They take themselves so bloody seriously. And they make as many mistakes as anyone else. I mean, they're not especially clever or anything, they just think they are.'

'They're the ones in charge, though.'

The two officers disappeared from view. Now there were only the students from Swordland sitting on the grass in front of the house, six anonymous, khaki-clad men, with a heap of rucksacks and a pile of ugly-looking weapons; and that boy called Benoît who had seemed amused and self-contained, and accepting of her in a strangely familiar way, as though they had known each other much more than that chance acquaintance in a bar.

'I want to go to France,' Yvette said. 'That's all I want to do.'

'You'll go to France. I'm sure you'll go to France.'

Now the Swordland group was gathering up its kit. They must have been given orders that they were about to depart. She could see Benoît bending to lift his pack and sling it over his shoulder. Perhaps she should stride carelessly out and bid them goodbye and show everyone that she thought the whole incident the most colossal joke. That would put the cat among the pigeons. And then the door to the sitting room opened and there was the earnest Lieutenant Redmond summoning them into his office, exactly like the Mother Superior summoning her to the study for one of those humiliating lectures.

51

'What the hell were you two playing at?' he demanded. He sat at his desk leaving the two women standing in front of him.

'Soldiers,' Marian replied.

The lieutenant frowned. 'It's not a joke, Sutro. It was an appalling breach of security, and bloody foolish to boot. Surprising them like that. Jumping up like a pair of schoolgirls and ... what was it you shouted?'

'Bang bang, you're dead.'

'Bang. Bang. You're dead.' He said the words slowly, savouring them. 'Whatever you may think, this is not Cowboys and Indians, Sutro. Haven't you any idea of what danger you were in? They might have shot you.'

'*Shot* us? You mean they run around the country shooting innocent civilians at random? We might actually have been what we said we were – a couple of secretaries up from Edinburgh for the weekend. And I thought we did pretty well with our cover story, considering.'

He humphed. Like an old colonel, she thought. *Humph*. Perhaps that was his name – Humphrey Redmond.

'You seem to treat this whole thing as a game, Sutro. This course, the organisation, everything.'

'No, I don't. That's simply not true.'

'You're always making fly comments. You're always criticising. You seem to think you know everything. I'm damned if I'm going to have security breached and reports made all because of a hoity-toity girl with an aggravating smile and an insolent manner.'

Her eyes smarted. 'That's unfair.'

'This is nothing to do with being fair. It's to do with trying to train people to fight. Whether you like it or not, this is a military establishment and in military establishments officers don't like being made to look fools. The captain was bloody furious, you realise that, don't you? You even called him a policeman!'

'I was only being consistent with my cover story. Dizzy

secretary. Look, this is a bit of a nonsense if all we're talking about is hurt feelings.'

'And then you referred to him as "any Tom, Dick or Harry".'

'Well, which one is he?'

The lieutenant's expression faltered. For a moment it wasn't clear whether he was about to rage or laugh. 'He's two of them, actually.'

'*Two* of them?'

'Captain Thomas Harry.'

Incipient tears had metamorphosed into incipient laughter. She nodded thoughtfully, and tried to avoid the man's eye. There was something there, she realised now, some little spark of anarchy in his look, and a small pulse of sexual sympathy that passed between them. 'He's a bit of the other one, too,' she said.

Two days later, Yvette was told that she was being posted away. She should pack her bags and be prepared to leave first thing the next morning.

'I've failed,' Yvette said. 'I told you so.' Her face was drawn in tragedy. She suddenly seemed old, small and wizened, like someone who had suffered a bereavement: the downturned mouth, the clenched muscles in her cheeks, the dry and staring eyes. 'That silly business on the mountain did it. It's your fault.'

'Of course it isn't. They'd have thrown me out as well if that had been anything to do with it. Anyway, Redmond saw the funny side. And you're not being thrown out. You're being posted to another training place. You said so yourself.'

'That's just their way of trying to soften the blow.'

'Where did they say?'

'Thame Park, or somewhere. Where the hell is that?'

'Thame? Near Oxford. Perhaps we can meet up when they give us leave.'

Yvette shrugged. 'Who knows? I think they will send me home. I think I'm no good. I bet Thame is – what do they call it? The cooler.'

53

Emile came over with a glass of whisky in his hand and a smug smile on his face. 'You can go away for a start,' Marian told him, but he stood there, immune to animosity.

'They say they are sending me to Thame Park,' Yvette said. 'What is Thame Park? Is it where they hide the people who are no good? You said there was somewhere for that. The cooler, you called it.'

He knew, of course. He had all sorts of gen about the Organisation. He knew names and acronyms and code names. 'Thame Park's not the cooler. Thame Park's STS 52.'

'STS 52. What the hell is that?'

'It's the wireless telegraphy school. They're going to make a pianist of you.'

'*Une pianiste?*'

'Wireless operator,' he said impatiently. 'Don't you know the lingo yet?'

Marian was on her own now. It was a strange feeling, being the only woman among eight men. It gave her power – she knew instinctively the power of women over men – but also vulnerability, as though with Yvette gone she was now exposed as the next victim in line. But she would not fail. That she knew. The course was at one and the same time a training and an examination, and she would not be found wanting.

*Dear Ned,*
*There is a rumour that we will have leave when this is all over. Perhaps I can come and see you? Maybe even stay with you, if that wouldn't be getting in the way. Have you been to see the parents? I know how busy you are but you must make an effort and find the time.*
*On one of our few free days I went hillwalking with a friend. It was a rare sunny day, with the view from the top of miles and miles of deserted hills. And the islands. The Hebrides, that always makes me think of wind and rain. Is*

*it in the name? It sounds breezy and cool, doesn't it? Hebrides. Say it over to yourself. I know you don't like words. Numbers have no hidden meanings, you say. But it is the hidden meanings in words that make them so wonderful. When it is sunny like it was that day the place is as beautiful as anywhere in the world, but too often it is raining. And it also has the dreaded midge. These ought to be bottled and dropped on German cities by the RAF. The war would be over in a few days, although the Allies would probably stand accused of violating the Geneva Convention.*

# England

|

'What's that uniform?' her father asked as she came in the front door.

She shrugged, dumping her suitcase on the floor and accepting his kisses. 'I've been transferred to the FANY.'

'What on earth is that?'

'First Aid Nursing Yeomanry. It's like an army corps for gay young things with nothing better to do with themselves. That's what people say. As many titles in the FANY as in Debrett's.'

'Are you going to be a nurse? I thought you said—'

'They don't only do nursing, they do all sorts of things.'

'All sorts of things? Really, I don't know what you're talking about.'

'It's best not to ask, Daddy.'

'So how was the course?'

'Lots of hard work.'

Her mother came out of the kitchen and gave a little cry of happiness and surprise. 'You're looking very thin, darling.'

'I'm not thin, *Maman*. I'm fit.'

'And that uniform really doesn't suit you.'

'She says she's transferred to a nursing outfit,' her father said.

'Nursing? That's useful, I suppose. How was Scotland? What happens next? Where are you off to now?'

She wanted to tell them. She wanted to shock them with the truth: Parachute School, she wanted to say. And then B School, whatever that meant, and then into the field. But instead she shrugged the question away. 'More training, somewhere else. I don't really know. They don't tell you much.'

'Quite right,' he said approvingly, as one who understood such things.

'Oh, and there's a letter for you from Ned,' her mother said. 'You're very privileged: he hardly ever writes to us.'

She didn't open the envelope until she was in the privacy of her room. The letter was written – Ned's familiar scrawl – on the back of some Ministry of Supply pro forma, as though he had grabbed the first piece of paper that had come to hand. He said very little, of course. There was the usual greeting and a hope that all went well with her course, and then *'here's what I told you about …'* and an address, a Paris address in the place de l'Estrapade in the fifth arrondissement. *Numéro 2, appartement* G. And the name, Clément.

'What does Ned say?' the parents asked when she came down for dinner.

She shrugged the question away. 'Not much. Typical Ned. Have you seen him recently?'

They hadn't. He didn't really keep in touch. She waited for the conversation to drift on to other things – family, friends, the trials of wartime – before she asked her question. 'The Pelletier family. What happened to them, do you know?' She said it carelessly, as though it wasn't important whether they knew or not. But her father did know, of course. Gustave Pelletier had been in the French foreign office, on secondment to some department of the League. Shortly before the outbreak of war he'd been posted back to Quai d'Orsay to work under Bonnet, but he hadn't got on with his boss and was sent abroad again. 'An ambassador in North Africa, or something. Then he resigned and joined the Free French, that's what I've heard. Threw his lot in with Darlan, which wasn't

57

such a good idea. I think he's in Algiers now. Maybe you'll meet him ... '

'Clément used to write to you, didn't he?' her mother asked. 'I think he was soft on you.'

Marian blushed and cursed herself for it. 'He wrote occasionally. It's strange how Ned and he got on so well. They seemed such different types.'

'The attraction of opposites,' her mother suggested. 'And then they had their studies in common, didn't they?'

'Their research, yes.'

'All that atomic stuff. I didn't understand a word.' And then the conversation moved away, to other matters, other people, that world they had inhabited in Geneva, an international world that seemed so remote now when everything was narrow and focused and British.

The remaining days of Marian's leave seemed to drag by, sluggards compared with the frenetic sprinters of those six weeks in Scotland. The tedious domestic life of rations and queues at the grocer's and reading the newspapers and worrying about matters that were beyond her ken and beyond her power to influence. She had no friends in Oxford. The university city – introverted, supercilious, enmeshed in its own concerns – was no more than a temporary refuge for the Sutro family.

One evening the phone rang when they were in the sitting room reading. Her mother was deep in some turgid French novel that she had borrowed from the Taylorian. Her father was doing *The Times* crossword, agonising over a single clue: *Forges prose*, 9. 'I'll get it,' she said, and went through to the hall before either of them could move from their chairs. She even closed the door before lifting the receiver.

'Anne-Marie?' a voice asked. '*C'est toi?*'

It was Benoît. Benoît Bérard. She even remembered his surname. 'I was just thinking about you,' she said, and immediately regretted it. 'What are you doing?'

'Nothing. I was so bored, so I gave you *un coup de bigo* to see if you were at home.'

'What's that? *Un coup de bigo?*'

'A telephone call. *Le bigophone*. You don't know *bigophone?*'

She could hear his laughter on the other end of the line. 'You make things up,' she accused him. 'It's a load of nonsense.'

'*Bigo* is not nonsense, it is real. Doesn't the cream of Geneva society say *bigo*? "I give you a tinkle," that's what the Anglo-Saxons say. So tell me what you are doing at home. Have they sacked you from the Organisation?'

'Not yet.' And she suddenly understood that this boy was the only person she could talk to openly about what she did, that this telephone conversation, subdued so that nothing could be overheard, was a kind of lifeline, almost a confessional. 'I'm going to Parachute School on Monday. Can you believe that? Jumping out of aircraft.'

'They were going to send me there a week ago. And then there was a change of plan. There's always a change of plan. They're probably trying to work out a change of plan to get themselves out of the war.' He broke into his accented English: 'Ay say old cheps, ay'm afraid there is a change of plen. We are not, ah, fightin' 'itler any more, we are, er, fightin' Stalin.'

She laughed. 'And what are you doing now?'

'I'm on another of their shitty courses. How to put explosives into dead rats or something. All I want to do is go home, and all they do is send me on courses.'

'Maybe ...' she said.

'Maybe what?'

'Maybe we can see each other.'

'But there is no time. Perhaps in London.'

'Perhaps.'

And then the call was over and the receiver was dead in her hand and she felt abandoned.

That night she dreamed. It was a repeat of a childhood

dream, the falling dream, now fast, now slow, like Alice down the rabbit hole. People watched her as she fell. She knew them all but she didn't recognise them, that was the strange thing. Except her parents. They were there among the audience. And the French boy, Benoît. He was laughing at her.

On Sunday she accompanied her mother to Mass at St Aloysius on the Woodstock Road. The church was full, as though Catholics had multiplied in the war years.

*The sun shall not burn thee by day*, the choir sang, *neither the moon by night.*

*Maman* prayed long and hard after the blessing, and when she finally stood up to leave there were tears in her eyes. 'I prayed that you will be safe,' she said as they left. 'Wherever you are going.'


||


Parachute School passed in a blur of sensation. They learned how to fall from a ten-foot wall, they shot down slides and swung in harnesses from a gantry inside a hangar, they crunched to the ground on mattresses and coconut matting, they ascended in a tethered balloon and dropped to earth from five hundred feet. There was the same exhilaration you found in skiing – the same thrill of surrender to gravity, the same heart-stopping breathlessness that gave, for a moment, a glimpse of dying. At the end of the week they climbed, bound up in parachute harnesses, into an aged Whitley bomber and flew over Tatton Park where they lined up inside the fuselage to plunge out into empty space. 'Go! Go! Go!' the dispatcher called, urging them on like a trainer urging athletes to run faster, jump higher, throw longer. And she plunged out into the air and the wind hit her face and snatched her breath away and the falling dream became reality, people on the ground looking up at her and a disembodied voice calling to her to keep her feet together and flex her knees, before the ground came up and threw her in a crumpled mass into the grass.

After three drops you gained your parachute wings, but women weren't allowed to wear them on their uniform jacket lest questions be asked. 'Why the hell should questions always be asked about *women*?' Marian complained, but no one paid her any attention. Immediately after the ceremony, transport took the members of her course to the railway station at Ringway to catch the train back down to London. The B School course started the next day near Beaulieu in Hampshire.

III

At Beaulieu, any pretence about what they might be doing was set aside: this was training for the clandestine life. A school for spies, someone said. They'd given her a field name, and that was how she was to be known. *Alice*. It seemed fitting. The school was based in a large country house tucked away in the middle of the New Forest; but everything was French, all casual conversation was French, even the reading material was French. It was as though she had stepped through the looking-glass and emerged at a house party in a remote and rather dilapidated château in the French countryside, inhabited by a motley collection of people who knew only that they should not be known, who understood that they should not necessarily understand.

'Remember,' a rather louche young man with brilliantined hair explained to them, 'the smallest detail you pick up here may one day save your life.' The Knave of Hearts, Marian thought. A recent arrival from France, he spoke about the intricacies of the rationing system and the problems of day-to-day life. 'France is no longer the place you knew before the war. You will arrive there and you will be strangers in what you think is home. Don't walk boldly into a café and ask for a *café au lait*.

61

There is probably no milk, and there certainly won't be any coffee. And when you've got whatever it is they give you – roasted acorns, probably, or chicory – don't ask for sugar to stir into it. There is no sugar. All you've got is saccharin. If you do ask for sugar, they may wonder where you've been for the last two years.'

There was advice on how to comport yourself in a country whose leadership you loathed and whose views you hated; how to blend in and how to fade away, how to see without ever being seen.

'*Pour vivre heureux, vivons cachés,*' the lecturer insisted, quoting someone. To live happily, live hidden.

There were lectures on the German armed forces and security forces, their uniform, their ranks and their manners – the Wehrmacht and the SS, the *Sicherheitsdienst* and the *Geheime Staatspolizei*, the whole taxonomy of occupation and terror. 'The Abwehr hate the SD, the SD despise the Abwehr. The battle between the two is almost as vicious as the battle between them and us.'

They explained how to recruit local agents and how to arrange a rendezvous, how to set up dead letter drops and arrange safe houses, how to think and out-think. There were practical lessons in how to tail someone and how to detect that you were being tailed. There was instruction in lock-picking and burglary given by a weasel-faced man who was the only one to speak English and who, so the story went, had done a dozen years in Wormwood Scrubs.

'If he was such a bloody awful thief that he got caught,' one of the students asked, 'why the hell is he teaching us?'

There was a course in encryption and wireless telegraphy. A young man with a prominent Adam's apple explained the intricacies of the B2 wireless set in terms no one could understand, and then they spent hours learning how to write a message and turn it into apparent gibberish using a double transposition cipher. You chose a poem that you knew by heart and used words from that to generate the cipher key. If the operator at the other end knew your poem, then she could reverse the process and turn the message back into clear. Marian chose a sonnet by Elizabeth Barrett Browning that she had learned at school.

> *How do I love thee? Let me count the ways.*
> *I love thee to the depth and breadth and height*
> *My soul can reach ...*

The words almost brought tears to her eyes, sentimental tears that were soon dispelled by lessons on what to do if you were captured, how to deal with interrogation, how to deflect the questioning, how to survive on your own, afraid and uncertain, convinced that your position is hopeless. They even came for you in the dead of night and dragged you out of bed and bundled you into a car and drove you to another house where there were bare cells, and anonymous men in the uniform of the SD who interrogated you for hours; shone bright lights in your face; shouted at you. You stood in your nightclothes while they threatened you with violence. Stories went round that they even stripped you naked, but Marian and the only other woman on the course tried to reassure each other by dismissing such rumours as nonsense. They'd never strip a woman. They might try and make it as realistic as possible, but they'd never do that. Still, the fear always lurked in the back of your mind.

The other woman was called Marguerite. She seemed a purely English kind of person, a bit of a busybody, the kind of woman who might be a housekeeper or a district nurse; but her French was perfect, spoken with a Belgian accent and figures of speech.

'Have you come across someone called Yvette?' Marian asked her. They were like convicts in prison, getting rumours from one another, trading snippets, hearing things on the grapevine.

'You mean that silly woman who married an Englishman?'

'Probably. Coombes was her married name.'

'She was in the course before me at Thame. We bumped into one another through some muck-up with the transport. Seems an empty-headed creature.'

'We were in Scotland together. I tried to help her.'

'Did you now? I doubt it was worth it.'

*Dear Ned,* Marian wrote. *Training goes on. More peculiar than you can imagine. At this rate I'm afraid I'll end up fully trained just when the war ends. Tried to ring you but couldn't get through. Maybe I'll get some free time ...*

## IV

The course finished with a four-day scheme. 'The Scheme,' they announced portentously, as they might have spoken of some kind of ordeal by fire, an initiation into the secret rites of the faith. For her scheme, Marian was to invent her own cover, travel to Bristol, find somewhere to stay and then carry out a series of assignments. First, she had to make contact with an agent operating in the city. Once this was done, her task was to set up cut-outs and dead letter drops and make a move towards recruiting likely people who might provide information about aircraft manufacture in the city. In this charade – that is what she called it – the British police were to be her enemy. They would have been informed that a suspected enemy agent was in the area, and it was her job to evade them as surely as she would try to evade the *Milice* and the Gestapo.

'And if they catch me?'

'Use your cover story for as long as you can. If things get silly—'

'It's been pretty silly all the time.'

'This isn't a joke, Sutro. This is as near to being real as we can

64

make it. In a few weeks it *will* be for real, and then you'll get no second chance. If things get really difficult with the police, insist that they make a call to this number and ask for Colonel Peters. He'll tell them that you are an agent in training and he'll come round and pick you up. That number is your Get Out of Jail card, so you'd better not forget it.'

And so she stepped through a further looking-glass, this time into the person of Alice Thurrock, graduate of the University of Edinburgh and teacher of French, a rather plain woman of twenty-eight who wore flat shoes and a shapeless tweed skirt, and had her brown hair gathered into a bun. She didn't wear make-up, but did have a pair of horn-rimmed spectacles that rested asymmetrically on her nose and gave the appearance of a squint. She had been in Paris until the summer of 1940 and returned to Britain a week before the Germans marched in. Since then she'd joined the WAAF, but last spring she had been discharged on medical grounds, and now she was trying to get things back on an even keel, to do something useful even if the military were no longer interested in her. There was no one else. Both parents were dead, her father in the flu epidemic of 1918 and her mother two years ago of cancer, so she was on her own, more or less. There was a brother in the army but he was out in the Middle East. Unfortunately all her stuff – her degree and teaching certificates, recommendations from former employers, all of that had been left behind in Paris. She had little more than what she could carry in her suitcase. A whole life.

The next few days were a kind of game, with the whole damaged city as the board and those few people she encountered, the pieces. But who was watching? She travelled on buses and tramped the pavements. She made a rendezvous with a threadbare man in a bookshop who gave her various messages to pass on to agents who didn't exist. She chose flats for wireless transmissions and anonymous sites for dead letter drops. At a girls' school in Filton, where she managed to get a job as a temporary

65

teacher, she selected the unwitting school secretary as a cut-out. A newsagent in Queens Road became another. She spent one afternoon identifying possible dead letter boxes – a loose stone in the steps of the Bethesda Chapel in Great George Street, and the space behind a fuse box beside a cinema in Whiteladies Road – and choosing other sites as suitable places to rendezvous with hypothetical agents. She had no idea what relation all this would have with reality but, her natural cynicism suspended for the moment, she played the game with gusto.

> *Dear Ned, this is the most tremendous fun, like an elaborate game of Hide and Seek but with the whole city to play in. Am I a spy or a mysterious criminal? Or am I just Alice who has stepped through the looking-glass? I remember your explaining that Tweedledum and Tweedledee stood for real matter and a new kind of material that is the exact opposite. Terrene and contraterrene, was that what you called it? Maybe I am like that. Everyone around me is real and I am unreal. Perhaps that is why they don't notice me ...*

Suppers were sorry affairs in a cheerless dining room with the other lodger, a girl called Maisie who worked for the Ministry of Supply. The landlady cooked them a thin stew with many potatoes and little else. An Oxo cube gave an approximation to the flavour of meat. 'Might as well be in prison,' Maisie muttered when the landlady was out of earshot. Apart from that little moment of controversy they talked of neutral things, films they had seen, books they had read, film stars they liked. And boyfriends. 'You got a man?' Maisie asked.

Marian thought of Clément, of what was and what might have been. 'Not really.'

'Don't blame you. It's not worth it nowadays. I had a boy but he was called up and now he's in the Middle East or somewhere. Hardly ever hear from him. I have to make do with my own comfort, if you get my meaning.' The girl laughed, blushing. 'Well, what else can you be sure of these days, eh?'

'Nothing, I suppose.'

'You just got to look out for yourself, haven't you?'

'I suppose you have.'

Marian lay in bed that night and considered Maisie's confession. Once upon a time she had thought such an act to be against the God who looked over her and admonished her for things done and things left undone. Although that particular belief had gone it had left behind a grimy residue of guilt, a feeling that this was a mean-spirited and dishonest act. But Alice Thurrock decided that she had no such inhibitions. She was a practical person. If you wanted a few moments of intense and careless ecstasy, then why not? It was your body, to do with as you wanted. You had to look out for yourself because no one else was going to. So she lay in bed quite without compunction, her legs open and her knees drawn up and her fingers involved in the soft intricacies of her vulva. She tried not to think of Clément. She tried not to think of anyone else but herself, this creature of flesh and blood and bone, of awkward limbs and sterile but sensitive breasts, this mortal coil stroking itself to a climax that ransacked her body and washed through her mind and left her placid and heavy with sleep. But still she thought of Clément.

'Alice Thurrock,' she said to her reflection in the cracked mirror the next morning, 'you are a shameless woman.'

V

On the last day of the exercise they arrested her. They came in the middle of the night when the household was asleep and courage was at its lowest ebb, half a dozen men banging on the front door and pushing past the landlady's feeble attempts to stop them. They burst into Marian's room as she struggled into

67

her overcoat and dragged her downstairs to a waiting car while Maisie and the landlady looked on. From there she was driven to some anonymous house in the Clifton area where she was handcuffed to a chair beneath bright lights and interrogated for hours about who she was and what she was doing in the city.

'Tell me your name.'

'Alice Thurrock.'

'Your middle name.'

'Eileen.'

'Your date of birth.'

'October the eighteenth, nineteen fifteen.'

They'd taken away her overcoat and she had nothing on beneath her nightdress. The light dazzled her so that she could see nothing of her interrogators but she felt violated under their gaze, as though their hands and not only their eyes were on her body.

'I want my clothes,' she said, but they ignored her.

'Where were you born?'

'Oxford, I was born in Oxford.'

'Tell us what you are doing in Bristol.'

'I want my clothes.'

'Never mind your clothes. What are you doing in Bristol?'

'I'm trying to find a job. I was in the WAAF but I was dis-charged on medical grounds—'

'You're lying!'

'No, I'm not. Believe me, I'm telling the truth. My parents are both dead and my brother—'

'I don't want to hear about your bloody brother. What were you doing yesterday? You were wandering around, checking places out, trying to talk to people, trying to wheedle informa-tion out of them. What were you doing in Filton?'

It was like diving, like holding your breath and diving deep down, swimming down against the lift of the water, your breath held, your lungs bursting, knowing that you could always come to the surface and break through into the air and ask them to stop.

'I went for a job at the Filton Ladies' Academy. They were looking for a French mistress.'

'Where did you learn your French?'

'I studied French at university.'

'But you've been to France?'

'Many times. As a child I went on exchanges with a French family during the holidays.'

'Tell me the name of the family.'

'Perrier.'

'Where did they live?'

'In Paris.'

'Where?'

'In the fifth, near the Panthéon.'

'What was their address?'

'Look, I want my clothes. I'm cold and I want my clothes. You can't keep me like this—'

'We can keep you how we please. We can strip you naked if we like. Now tell us their address.'

It was like a masquerade, where the pretence has worn thin and tempers are frayed. But she played the game, knowing that one day it might not be a game any longer and she wouldn't have a Get Out of Jail card and the men behind the lights would be members of the Gestapo.


VI


Miss Atkins turned a page. 'It seems you did well at Beaulieu. "Tolerated arrest and interrogation. Kept to her cover story throughout and made no slips", that's what it says.' She looked up, smiling bleakly. 'I'm putting you forward for immediate deployment in the field. You'll go in the next moon period. Your circuit will be WORDSMITH, in the South-west.'

Marian felt a small snatch of emotion, a blend of fear and excitement from which it was impossible to recover either. The

South-west. Toulouse, maybe. Or Biarritz, on the coast. Or perhaps Montpellier and the Mediterranean. She searched her memory in vain for anything more. Not Paris. Ned's idea of her seeing Clément evaporated in a cloud of relief and disappointment.

'The organiser is one of the most successful of our agents,' Atkins was saying. 'Field name Roland. Perhaps you have heard about him? I know how word gets round, despite our best efforts at security. He has been in the field for over a year.'

More than a year! It seemed impossible. A year of the clandestine life. Your cover story would become more real than your true story. The lies would become truths, and truths lies. Lies like beauty.

'The circuit is very dispersed. It covers a huge area – from Limoges down to Toulouse – and Roland has been struggling to keep the thing under control. He has a pianist who's been with him for months now, but he desperately needs a courier. One man can't get round that area on his own. You'll be dropping with César. He's going to the same circuit, as a weapons and sabotage instructor. You won't have much to do with each other in the field, but you ought to get acquainted. I've arranged for him to come and meet you. He should be here any moment.'

But César was late. They waited, making awkward conversation and glancing at the clock on the desk. Fifteen minutes after the appointed time there was a cursory knock, the door was flung open and there he was, with a faint smile on his face and profuse apologies on his lips and a kind of childish insolence about him that seemed to appease even Miss Atkins. Apparently there had been a mix-up over appointments, a meeting with someone in RF section. He was most very sorry because he knew how much you British value punctuality, but anyway, here he was, better late than never, isn't that what you say?

'This is César,' Atkins announced primly. 'As you may see, he has the gift of the gab.'

'We've already met,' said Marian.

'Already met?'

'We bumped into each other in a bar here in London.'

Atkins pursed her lips. 'In a *bar*?'

'And again in Scotland. On a mountainside.'

'On a mountainside? It sounds most irregular.'

'Just a vein,' he said.

'A vein?'

'Don't you say that?'

Marian giggled. '*Un coup de veine*. Chance, pure chance.'

Atkins glared at the two of them, as though she might be the butt of some private joke. 'I'm not sure that I approve of chance,' she said. 'As I told you, César is going as a weapons instructor. You won't have much to do with each other in the field …'

Marian tried to ignore Benoît. He was attempting to catch her eye, trying to snare her into laughing. 'When do we go? You said the next moon …'

'It depends on the weather. But we have a slot for you in the middle of next week. That'll give you time to sort matters out, get to know the geography, that kind of thing. César will have useful tips for you – he was in France not long ago and knows exactly what it's like. Perhaps …' she made a small gesture of dismissal, 'you can find somewhere to discuss things.'

They found a corner of what had once been the living room. 'My little Anne-Marie,' Benoît said. 'You see, it is fate that we should be together.'

'I'm *not* your little Anne-Marie,' she said, but the idea amused her. Despite seeming no older than she he still had that air of instant superiority, of Gallic arrogance. 'I think we should use field names anyway. I'm Alice.'

'But I *hate* César. You are lucky. Alice is lovely. But César! Not even a Frenchman. And an emperor to boot.'

'So was Napoleon.'

'That's even worse. I'm not a Bonapartist or a monarchist or

71

any of those things. I am a republican! Look, let's get out of this place. Let's go for a walk. We don't have to sit around in here just so they can keep an eye on us.'

So they escaped like children from school, amused by their suddenly being thrown together. Somewhere up in the sky the moon was waxing but you couldn't see that; all you could see were clouds and blue and the sun chasing itself in and out of shadow, and barrage balloons floating like great, airy maggots. The moon seemed a long way away. Talking together, they walked down to Marble Arch and into the Park. It was easy, this talking, despite their unfamiliarity with each other and the differences in their backgrounds. Benoît was a *colon* from Algeria with something of the hot Mediterranean littoral in his blood, and a sense of alienation. 'They call us "Black Feet", you know that? What does that mean? That we're part Arab? That we're not quite as good as the rest of them? Maybe it means that we've stepped in shit.'

He had been called up in the general mobilisation in 1939, and after the fall of Paris his whole unit had surrendered. On the night that they were to be taken off to a prisoner-of-war camp in Germany, he and a friend had jumped the train. He shrugged it off as something of no consequence. 'You seize the moment. You can't think about it for too long or the moment's gone. You've just got to act, and if it works ...' another shrug, 'good luck to you.' Much of the time he shrugged; or grinned, as though what he had done was no more than a boyish prank. With his friend he had made his way across the demarcation line into the unoccupied zone where they'd worked as farm labourers for a while before continuing southwards. Eventually they had crossed the Pyrenees into Spain, where they were flung into jail.

'We made such a fuss that they let us go after a week. Pamplona, that was the place. Do not go to Pamplona. Full of shits. From there I got back to Algeria and joined the Resistance. Then this fellow approached me and suggested that I could go back to France if I sold my soul to him.'

Her own experience, so dramatic at the time, appeared banal beside his. When she told him, almost apologetically, about Geneva before the war – the large house, the servants, the privileges that accrue to the family of an international civil diplomat – he shrugged it all off. 'You can't help that. I can't help being a *pied-noir*; you can't help being the daughter of a big shot. At least you've not become a spoiled brat. At least you can take what they throw at you.'

He grinned at her. 'Let's go and get a cup of tea. Isn't that what the English do? *A nice cup of tea*.' He said it in English, his French accent overlaid with a clumsy Cockney imitation: *Uh noice cuppa tey*. It made her laugh.

Over tea they talked about what they might do during these tiresome, anxious days of waiting. Benoît was staying in a hotel that the Organisation had found for him. They didn't want him living with other members of the Free French Forces. 'They guard me jealously because I should be working with the Gaullists but they want to keep me for themselves.'

She looked at him thoughtfully, her head on one side. 'Why don't you come to Oxford? I'm going back this evening. Why don't you come and stay next weekend?'

It was an idea plucked out of the air. Why not bring this French boy to see *Maman*? She would love him, wouldn't she? It was not the kind of thing Marian had ever done before, but then she was no longer the kind of person she had ever been. She wouldn't even ask. She would simply tell her mother: '*Maman*, I've invited this French guy for the weekend.' *C'mec*, she'd say. Her mother hated that kind of slang. 'He's at a loose end in London, and I thought it would be nice for him to see a bit of family life.' Family life. That is what would win her mother over.

That afternoon she discovered whom she was to be. 'Anne-Marie Laroche,' an earnest, bespectacled Frenchman informed her. 'Anne-Marie as you suggested. Laroche because it is common. So, a plain name, an ordinary name, a name that is as completely forgettable as you will try to be.' Like a bridge player laying out his hand to take all the remaining tricks, he displayed the identity cards and ration books of this fictitious woman.

'Anne-Marie Laroche. I like it.'

He shrugged, as though liking a name were an irrelevance entirely confined to women. 'As you see, I have made her twenty-six years old. The same colouring as yourself, of course. But I'm afraid you'll have to make her, er ... less *striking* than you are. Good looks are not considered an asset for an agent – you don't want to go turning men's heads.' He glanced up at her and blushed and fiddled with the papers in front of him. 'Now you need to get to know *mademoiselle* Laroche as well as you know yourself.'

Afterwards she had a briefing about the use of ciphers with a flirtatious young man called Marks. He introduced himself as 'More Groucho than Karl', and asked her if she remembered from her lectures at Beaulieu how to do a double-transposition cipher and laughed out loud when she told him which poem she had chosen for her key. 'You and half a dozen other women agents,' he said. She needed something original, something that no German cipher expert could possibly know. Did she write any poetry of her own?

'There's something.'

'Let me see.' She picked up a pencil and wrote out a poem that she'd written years ago:

> *I wonder whether*
> *Or ever*
> *You'll love me*
> *Forever*
> *Or always*
> *Our pathways*
> *Will keep us apart*

74

*Perhaps never*
*But never*
*We'll share love*
*Together*
*Yet always*
*Through all ways*
*You're close to my heart*

'Who was he?' Marks asked.

She smiled and blushed a bit. 'An old friend. I haven't heard from him for ages. I thought I was in love with him but maybe it was no more than a childish crush.'

He shrugged. 'Crush and love, the only difference is how long it lasts. Let's see if he brings you luck.' So he set her an exercise to see how many mistakes she made using her poem, and she gave a small smile of triumph when she made none.

'Close to my heart,' he said approvingly, and with apparent reluctance released her to her next appointment, which was with a Jewish tailor in Clifford Street who would make her a couple of suits and a coat in French cloth and in the best French manner. The stitching, the lining, the cut, everything was different, he explained, huffing and puffing around her and decrying English fashion. But it would take time. You cannot rush these things. These people always ask for everything by tomorrow.

## VII

In the evening she took the train back home. The ups and downs of her present existence bewildered her. One moment she was in the world of the Organisation with its tricks and puzzles, its truths and half-truths and downright lies: the next she was at home enveloped in the certainties of childhood. The only thing she carried over from one world to the other was the ability to lie.

75

'They've told me to prepare to go overseas,' she explained to her mother. 'Algiers, I expect, but it might be Morocco. They're terribly vague. I want some stuff that won't look out of place, clothes and things. Can I see what you've got? Oh, and Benoît is probably coming to stay for a couple of days.'

'Who is Benoît?'

'I told you. This *mec* I met during training. He's coming for the weekend.'

'What on earth do you mean, *mec*?'

'Boy, then. What do you want me to say? Chap?' She said it in English – *chep* – with mockery in her tone.

'Well, whatever you call him, we don't know him. How can we have someone to stay whom we don't know?'

'But if he doesn't come to stay you'll never know him.'

Her mother made that face, the little moue of anger that she always showed when either of her children bested her in an argument. 'Anyway, there's also a phone message for you. Something else to do with your work, I suppose. A colonel, he said.'

'A *colonel*?'

'That's right.'

She thought: Buckmaster. She thought: disaster, a change of plan, the whole carefully constructed artifice brought crashing down by an outside agency, some matter of chance or coincidence. Maybe in Bristol, or maybe some other hitch. The head of WORDSMITH didn't want a woman. Perhaps it was that. Or perhaps Buckmaster and Atkins had revised their opinion of her at the last minute and decided that no, she was not suitable material for going into the field. Instead it would be the limbo of the 'cooler', where she would kick her heels in frustration while doing nothing, because she knew what she knew, like some kind of radioactive substance that was too hot to handle and had to be kept in isolation.

But her mother had written the message down on the notepad beside the telephone and the name was not Buckmaster but Peters: would Marian meet Colonel Peters at Brasenose College at ten o'clock the next morning? It took a moment for her to recognise the man's name – her Get Out of Jail card during the scheme in Bristol, the number she never had to ring.

VIII

The college, like everything else, had been taken over by the military. Where you expected gowned figures stalking the quadrangles, instead there was a coming and going of men in uniform, and that sense of shabby impermanence that haunts military installations, as though the enemy is approaching and administration might be making a bonfire of the files at a moment's notice. In the shadows of the main gate a notice from the Commandant exhorted officers of the Directing Staff *to kindly address all problems of a domestic nature to the adjutant rather than the domestic bursar.* Someone had ringed the split infinitive in red ink.

She stood hesitantly in the gatehouse wondering why she was here. Alice, she thought, in some eccentric wonderland. But no white rabbit scuttled across the green velvet of the lawn; instead a figure in sports jacket and flannels stepped out of the shadows of the porter's lodge, held out his hand and gave a little half-bow. 'How good to see you again, Miss Sutro, and looking rather more *habillée* than at our previous encounter. My name is Peters.'

He had a stooped, donnish air about him and seemed rather too old to be on active service. She frowned. 'I'm sorry. Perhaps there's been some misunderstanding ...'

'Oh, no misunderstanding at all. But our previous encounter was a little one-sided, I'm afraid. I was witness to your interrogation in Bristol.'

The revelation was a shock. She remembered shadows behind the lights, men asking questions of her, shouting at her,

77

wheedling, threatening, men whose interest in her seemed almost lascivious. Why did she feel embarrassed by the knowledge that this man had been one of the watchers?

'I must say,' he added, 'you conducted yourself in exemplary fashion. To the manner born. I've always had my doubts about young women getting mixed up in this kind of thing – there's been quite a bit of opposition to it, d'you know that? – but girls like you show that my doubts were ill-founded.'

'Is that a compliment?'

'It's not an insult.' He took her elbow and guided her into the golden light of the quadrangle. 'I wrote a glowing report for Colonel Buckmaster. Told him I'd have been happy to have you working for me when I was in the game. Just the ticket.'

Men in uniform walked past them, young officers laughing and joking about something. Through a shadowy archway was another quadrangle with a military-looking tent pitched on one of the lawns. Under the eye of a corporal a soldier was carefully painting cobblestones white. She thought of Alice again, the gardeners painting white roses red. 'What is this all about?' she asked, and Peters nodded thoughtfully, as though she had posed a most penetrating and perceptive question. 'Of course you are curious,' he said. 'Of course you are. And we will satisfy your curiosity all in good time.'

He led the way into one of the staircases and up narrow stairs to a door that opened onto a room overlooking the small quadrangle and the end wall of the college chapel. There was a sofa and two armchairs and a low table between them. And rising from one of the armchairs was a second man, rather younger than Peters. He wore a dark blue pinstriped suit, and in his top pocket was a white silk handkerchief. His name, so Colonel Peters said, was Fawley. Major Fawley.

They shook hands. The man contrived a smile of sorts. He wore glasses, perfectly circular glasses that gave him an owlish look. Would she like tea? Or perhaps, what with her French background, she would prefer coffee?

'I don't want anything, thank you, Major Fawley. I just want to know what I am doing here.'

'Of course you do. And I will tell you shortly, but before I answer I must emphasise the extremely confidential nature of what we have to discuss. All of this conversation must be considered most secret. Nothing of what we say here must be repeated to anyone, either within your organisation or outside it.'

'What about Colonel Buckmaster?'

'Not Colonel Buckmaster, nor Miss Atkins. No one.'

'But they are my superiors.'

Fawley nodded. There was something measured about him, something of the stillness of a priest who would understand any point of confusion and have the doctrinal answer ready to hand. 'I comprehend your difficulty, Miss Sutro. Of course I do. If everything goes well, Colonel Buckmaster will be made aware of our conversation in due course; but for the moment let's say that this meeting is outside even his remit.'

Was this another test? Was it some stupid charade put on by the Organisation to see how good she was at keeping things secret? 'I really don't understand—'

'You see, I work for a different government department from the one that recruited you—'

'Different? What do you mean, different?'

'In my father's house are many mansions, Miss Sutro. I'm afraid I am unable to identify the department, save to say that it is most secret. More secret even than the one so ...' he hesitated, 'so *admirably* run by Colonel Buckmaster.'

'I don't follow—'

'I'm sure you don't. Let's say that we are all on the same side, all working towards the same ends, but in different ways.' He reached inside his jacket and took out a cigarette case. 'Do you smoke?'

Did she? It seemed a question as difficult as all the others seething in her mind. She thought of the girls in the Filter Room

79

during the night watch, the haze of smoke above their heads, the desultory conversations when there was nothing happening, the sudden action when the radar stations called through and plots began going down on the table. An explosive tension like a parachute jump, not this nagging anxiety, this confusion. She took the proffered cigarette and leaned forward to accept his light. As she sat back in her chair Fawley said, 'I understand that you are due to leave for France at the next moon.'

She tried not to betray her shock. At Beaulieu they'd warned her – they'll surprise you with unexpected knowledge. They'll find out things from other prisoners and they'll try and shock you with what they know. But you've got to seem indifferent, as though you've no idea what they're going on about. You know nothing, remember that. Nothing. So she tried not to show shock, she tried not to glance at Peters, she tried to appear indifferent. 'I don't know what you mean.'

'I think you do, Miss Sutro. For the moment, all I want to say is that when you get to Paris—'

'Major Fawley, I can't make any comment about this kind of thing.'

He nodded. 'Of course you can't. Let me put it this way: if the *chance* should arise of your going to Paris, we would like you to do something for us.'

'Something?'

'We'd like you to make contact with your friend Dr Clément Pelletier. Would you be happy to do that?'

The two men seemed to be held in a great stillness. She was aware of a sound from the quadrangle below, the clatter of army boots on paving stones, the sound of men laughing, someone calling in a loud voice across the open space.

'Clément Pelletier?'

'Exactly.'

Thought seemed difficult, as though demanding more strength than she possessed. Like trying to run when waist-deep in water. 'How do you know about Clément Pelletier?'

'Dr Pelletier has long been known to us.'

'But how do you know that *I* know him?'

'It has come to our attention in the course of events.'

'But *how*, Major Fawley? How exactly has it come to your attention?'

The man smiled benignly. 'You were put through the cards, Miss Sutro. Inquiries were made about your background, your contacts, whom you know and have known. The security people can be very thorough. You must understand these things by now.'

'Perhaps I'm just beginning to. So what exactly would be the purpose of my contacting Dr Pelletier? Assuming that I were to go to Paris?'

'We would like you to take a letter to him. Of course we can't expect you to carry an ordinary letter in an envelope. Instead, we have a rather special letter.' He reached into a pocket and took out a leather wallet. From inside this he took a key, an ordinary key that might have opened a front door lock. He handed it to her. 'I imagine you carry a key ring of some kind? When you go to France, ensure that this key is on it.'

She held the thing between thumb and forefinger. 'It's just a key.'

Fawley shook his head. 'Not *just* a key. You see the maker's name, Lapreche?'

'Of course I can see it.'

'Well, if you file the metal down at the letter "R" you'll find a small cavity. In the eye of the letter. You need to do it carefully but I'm sure that a person of Dr Pelletier's ingenuity is quite capable. Inside that cavity – it's less than two millimetres across – is what we call a microdot. Maybe you are already familiar with such things? A piece of photographic film little bigger than a full stop.'

She turned the key over in her hand. It shone in the light, a bright silver. LAPRECHE. However close she looked, there was no sign that it had been tampered with.

'Under a microscope the microdot will reveal itself as a letter from a certain Professor Chadwick. I can assure you that Professor Chadwick is a most important person in the world of science.'

She looked from one man to the other. 'I know perfectly well who Professor Chadwick is.'

'Of course you do.'

'So why me? If it's only a matter of sending a letter from Professor Chadwick, couldn't any agent of yours have done it? You must have people working for you in Paris.'

'Perhaps we do. However, the letter invites Dr Pelletier to come to England—'

'It does *what*?'

'—which is where you come in. We thought you might be more persuasive than a mere letter. I believe – forgive me if I'm wrong – that there is a degree of fondness between you and Dr Pelletier.'

She felt the colour rise in her cheeks. 'What do you mean by that?'

'Just what I say. Fondness.'

'Yes, he was fond of me. Like a brother.'

The man continued in his placid, inquisitorial manner. There was something of the barrister about him, carefully cross-questioning a witness, asking the questions in his own time, never being deflected from his purpose. 'Dr Pelletier wrote to you when you were away at school, didn't he?'

'How on earth do you know that?'

'In most affectionate terms.'

'I asked how you knew.' She felt a burst of rage. Ned, she thought. Her own brother betraying her confidences. And then another possibility dawned. 'The nuns. You've spoken to the nuns.'

Colonel Peters shifted uncomfortably in his chair. He looked like a reluctant witness to an unpleasant surgical intervention. Fawley leaned forward and stubbed out his cigarette. 'I believe

82

the good Sisters were under the impression that Dr Pelletier was your uncle. That, apparently, is what you told them. Although when they consulted your parents—'

'They did *what?*'

The man allowed a sympathetic smile to escape. 'It seems that we are not the only ones to have made enquiries about you, Miss Sutro.'

'The nuns checked with my parents? Is that what you are saying?'

'Dear old *Oncle* Clément offering kisses to his beloved niece seems a different thing from an unrelated man, only a few years her senior, doing the same. Doesn't it?'

*Je t'embrasse.* She recalled the thrill of reading his words, and the image that she clung to in the cloistered confines of the convent. 'His letters stopped. I thought he'd grown tired of writing—'

'So I imagine.'

Understanding dawned, like a revelation: 'The nuns kept them from me. They stole them.'

Fawley removed his spectacles and polished them with a large, white handkerchief. 'Miss Sutro, what the nuns did or didn't do with regard to one of their flock is no concern of mine. And believe me, it is no concern of mine what your relationship may or may not have been with Dr Pelletier three years ago, except as far as it might help us. But you do seem uniquely placed to assist us in our efforts to get Dr Pelletier to come to England, don't you?'

She didn't know whether to be angry or not. She didn't know what to say. She felt bewildered, almost violated, as though people had been discovered ransacking her room, going through her private possessions. Thieves in the night. 'What work is Clément doing? Why in God's name is this so important?'

Fawley looked sympathetic. 'If I knew the answer to that question, Miss Sutro, I couldn't possibly tell you.'

## IX

'The nuns, *Maman*.'

'Which nuns, my dear?' As though there were whole flocks of them out walking round the city.

'The nuns at school, of course.'

Crows. That's what they used to call them. 'Look out, a crow's coming,' they'd say, and hurry to hide whatever illicit thing they were doing, reading a forbidden book in all probability. Or writing a secret letter.

'What about them?'

'Did they contact you about Clément? About how he used to write to me?'

Her mother looked vague. Marian knew that look, the expression of someone wondering whether to remember or not. 'I believe they did. I got a rather concerned letter from Sister Mary Joseph. She asked … Oh, I don't recall. She asked, is he Marian's uncle? Or something like that. And I replied, no of course not, whatever gave you that idea? But he *is* a family friend, and how can there be any harm in a family friend writing to you? That's what I said.'

'That's what you said?'

'Of course, my darling. Why on earth are you asking about all this? It was ages ago, when you were a child. You're anything but a child now, it seems. These days people grow up so fast. It's the war, I suppose.'

'They stole his letters to me, do you know that? The damned nuns stole my letters!'

'Please don't use that kind of language, darling. All this military service has made you coarse. And whatever the Sisters did would have been in your own best interests.'

She didn't know whether to argue. A year ago she would have. A year ago she would have exploded in a great burst of anger. Now she merely shrugged. 'I'm going up to London tomorrow,' she said.

'But you've only just come home. Always rushing around. I don't know what's going on. Is it that French boy?'

'It's nothing to do with him. It's Ned. I'm going to see Ned.'

X

'Fawley.'

Ned kicked ineffectually at a stone. 'What about him?'

They'd abandoned his flat for the garden in the centre of the square. She didn't want to be inside. She didn't want to be cooped up, trapped. She wanted to be out in the open where she could breathe fresh air. She needed to breathe deeply, to let anger out and something resembling calm take its place.

'So you do know him?'

'I've met him.'

'How? When?'

'He was involved with Kowarski and von Halban, getting them out of France in 1940.'

'So who is he? And why is he so interested in Clément?'

'It's to do with the war effort.'

'Everything's to do with the war effort, Ned. You're to do with the war effort, I'm to do with the war effort. You've got to be a child or a geriatric not to be.' She looked round at the garden, stripped of railings, its lawns dug up and given over to growing vegetables. 'Even this bloody garden is to do with the war effort.'

'Squirrel, you've learned to swear. It's not very ladylike.'

'I'm not ladylike. They knocked the lady out of me in Scotland. They taught me how to kill, Ned. Do you realise that?' Her voice rose. 'Do you?'

'I suppose that's part of the training. Why should it only be men who are taught to kill?'

She looked at him. Once she would have entrusted him with her life; now matters weren't so clear-cut. She didn't know him

85

any more, that was the problem. The Ned of old was like a childhood memory – uncertain, distorted by time. 'This man Fawley paid me a visit and all he did was speak about Clément. What's so important about Clément, Ned? That's what I want to know. For God's sake, Fawley and his henchman came all the way to Oxford to proposition me. They've set themselves up as some alternative to the organisation that has recruited and trained me.' She felt herself hovering between tears and anger, wavering like something balanced on a fulcrum with only two ways to go, both of which involved falling. 'I've got no idea what the hell's going on, and no means of finding out. These people are asking me to do something for them and I want to know what it's all about. You know and you're not telling me. Christ alive, I'm your sister, Ned!'

He looked at her thoughtfully. 'I'm afraid I simply can't tell you. It'd put you in danger if you knew.'

'What a bloody pompous thing to say! I'm not a child any longer. I'm up to my neck in stuff that's just as secret as yours. And why should it be all right for you to know but not me? Typical bloody man. The dear little woman can't know, but I can.'

'It's not that. The fact is, you're going to France. You know what the risks are.' He shook his head. 'You mustn't know, Squirrel. Really.'

'But you should?'

'It's not my choice. I was part of the team that debriefed Kowarski and von Halban when they got out of France in 1940. I spent that year at the Collège before the war. I know all about their work.'

She looked at her brother with sudden clarity, an intense white light of revelation. 'You've been briefed to tell me all this, haven't you? You're working with them, aren't you?'

He barely hesitated. 'Of course I am.'

She looked round at the ruined garden. What did Ned's

answer mean? Were they no longer brother and sister? Did she now have to judge even her relationships with her own family through the distorting prism of secrecy and connivance? 'It was you who told them, wasn't it? About me and Clément.'

'Certainly, I told them.'

'But why? For God's sake, why?'

'They came a couple of weeks ago. Shortly after I saw you the last time. I thought it was security screening. You know what it's like. Lots of questions.'

'What questions?'

'About you. Family and friends, our life in Geneva before the war, that kind of thing. And then they asked, what about Clément Pelletier?'

'How did they know?'

'They know I worked with him. It's not a secret, for heaven's sake. And then they asked, how well does your sister know him?'

'And you *told* them?'

'Of course I did. Why shouldn't I?'

Anger was an organic thing, occupying parts of her body. The brain, of course, but also the chest and the stomach, a tumour of anger, a metastasis of rage. She spoke French. French was a weapon she could use, a rapid, caustic, light flutter of fury. 'Because it sounds to me rather like betrayal.'

'Oh, don't be melodramatic. All I said was that you were quite close.' He looked away, avoiding her eyes. 'This is ridiculous, Squirrel. Like brother and sister, I said; nothing more than that. You and me, Madeleine and Clément. I had no idea where it was leading.'

'That's the trouble, isn't it? I have no idea where it is leading either. And you don't help because you won't even tell me why they're so interested in Clément Pelletier. Christ, you're a coward, Ned. I always looked up to you, thought you were my big, clever, brave brother. But now I see you for what you really are.'

At last there was some reaction from him, some glimmer of shame and anger in his look. 'And what is that?'

'You're a cold fish, Ned. You don't understand the basic human decencies. You shun the parents, and now you're shunning me. Soon you'll have nothing left except your stupid bloody physics.'

There was silence. They stood there in the garden with the wreckage of their relationship between them, like two children looking down on a broken toy. Ned glanced over his shoulder, as though it were all his fault, as though he had smashed the thing in temper and the adults were coming to see what the fuss was all about. But there were no adults around, nobody at all, only the trees in the garden and the blank windows of the houses that surrounded the square.

'All right, I'll tell you,' he said. 'If that's the only way you'll see how important this all is. I'm putting you in danger, even more danger than you were in before, but I'll tell you. Clément was part of Fred Joliot's team at the Collège de France, you know that. Well, they were working on the idea of an atomic bomb.'

Time, that flexible dimension, stopped. She thought of Ned's jokes – death rays, devices that could see in the dark, bombs that could blow up whole cities. And the silly games they'd played – Pig-in-the-middle, *Kriegspiel*, Consequences. 'An *atomic bomb*? Are you serious?'

He laughed, that little snorting dismissive laugh that so annoyed her. 'Of course I'm serious.'

'Clément was working on an atomic bomb?'

'That's what I said, isn't it? He's still there, still in Paris, and as far as anyone knows, still working at the Collège de France.'

'And working on a *bomb*?'

'Who knows if that's what he's still doing? But he was.'

'You mean it could happen? Some sort of super-bomb?'

'It's easy. That's what makes it so frightening.'

'Easy?'

'Uranium. You must have heard me talking about it, that Christmas before the war. Everyone was talking about it at the time. If you fire a neutron at a uranium nucleus it splits apart into two new atoms – different elements. Barium and krypton.'

She remembered now. 'You and Clément came home for the holiday and we all went to the chalet in Megève. We wanted to ski but all you and Clément did was talk about science. I remember no one understanding a word you were saying. Daddy said it sounded like alchemy, turning base metal into gold. The philosopher's stone. "What will you physicists come up with next?" he kept asking. You got angry with him.'

'As always, he was missing the point. He thought it was a joke, some kind of esoteric conjuring trick. That's the trouble with diplomats. They're all classicists. Not a scientist among them. Any scientist would have realised how fundamental it was.' Fundamental was one of Ned's words. He could batter you into submission with it. 'It was totally unexpected, this splitting. I mean, really amazing. As startling as firing a pea-shooter at a diamond and – ping! – the diamond splits open ... and becomes two new jewels altogether. Ruby and sapphire, say. And at the same time energy is released, a massive amount of energy.'

'But wasn't all that done in Germany? What's it got to do with Clément?'

'Hahn and Strassmann were the first to publish, in December 1938. Yes, they were in Berlin. But Irène Curie and Pavel Savitch had got exactly the same experimental results a year before at the Radium Institute in Paris, only they hadn't interpreted them correctly. I must have told you about this at the time.'

'We were hardly listening, and when we were we didn't really understand.'

'It's not that difficult.' He looked impatient, almost angry. 'That's the trouble with people. They just don't *try* to understand. You see, atomic nuclei are held together by huge forces, and at the time everyone thought that they couldn't come apart

89

like that. But they can. If the nuclei are big enough, they can. And when they do the energy equivalent to those forces is released. Then Fred's lab showed something more: when this fission takes place – that's what they call it, fission – as well as the energy it also emits neutrons. These neutrons will then hit *other* uranium atoms and cause them to split as well. If each decaying atom releases at least *two* neutrons then those neutrons could hit two more uraniums, making them split up in turn. You understand the idea? Atomic billiards, but each single collision creating the possibility of *two* further collisions. You'd get a cascade of uranium atoms splitting up, one causing two others, two causing four, four causing eight, and so on. An exponential increase. They call it a chain reaction. Joliot and his team showed that it would happen. Not that it might happen – it *would* happen.'

She was used to conversations like this. Ned had tried to explain his world to her many times. It seemed a bizarre place, of nebulous ideas and cloudy realities. Remember, he'd told her, the atom is mainly nothing at all, a hard nucleus, where all the matter is concentrated, with acres of empty space all around it. If the nucleus were the size of your fist – he'd held up his own – then the outer limits of that one atom, the outer edge of its emptiness, would be about half a mile away. Reality is so much empty space.

'And this chain reaction makes a bomb?'

'Think of the energy,' he said. 'When a uranium nucleus splits, you've suddenly got two nuclei right next door to each other.' He made a ball of his hands, fingertips touching, and then collapsed the ball into his two fists. 'But nuclei shouldn't be close together like that. They should be—'

And suddenly she saw it. 'Half a mile apart! No, twice that. They should be a mile apart!' She almost laughed. She saw into his world for the first time: the pure outrage of having two nuclei so close together was something shocking, against nature.

He nodded, as though it was obvious. 'They should be a mile

90

apart and instead they are *touching*. So they fly apart at colossal speeds to take up their correct distances. We don't know exactly how fast they move. Maybe a tenth of the speed of light. The energy involved is vast. We talk of electron volts. Each uranium atom that splits apart like this releases two hundred million electron volts of energy. That's ...' He seemed to scratch around for a way of saying it. 'Oh, tiny, useless, enough to move a grain of sand. You can't do anything with it, not in practical terms. But each kilogram of uranium contains a vast number of atoms – imagine twenty-five with twenty-three zeros after it, that's the number. If all the atoms split one after another in this chain reaction, you have to multiply the amount of energy released from each nucleus by the total number of atoms. Suddenly you've got an immense amount of energy. Do you see what I mean? Potentially unlimited.'

She thought of Clément trying to explain his work to her. It's exactly like *Kriegspiel*, he had said: groping in the unseen with incomplete information and trying to find out what's possible. And what was possible was some kind of bomb. She remembered the very last time they'd been together, at Easter time in Paris with her father and Ned, shortly after her seventeenth birthday. They'd walked close together. Occasionally their hands had touched. You mustn't be frightened, he'd said to her.

'You're not listening, are you?' Ned was saying. 'You're not paying attention.'

'Yes, I am.'

'If you want to understand, you've got to listen.'

'I *am* listening.'

'The point is, you must have a sufficiently large mass of uranium. That's crucial. Remember what I've told you before: atoms are mainly nothing at all. The nuclei are like dust motes in an empty room, hard to hit and far apart. Neutrons can go a long way before encountering one, so if you haven't got enough mass the neutrons simply escape into the air before they actually hit other atoms. Francis Perrin, another man in Joliot's team, made an estimate of how much uranium you'd need to guarantee that the chain reaction happens. He called it *la masse critique*. He calculated forty-four tons. Or, with a casing that could reflect escaping neutrons back into the mass, a mere thirteen. He published that in the *Comptes Rendus* so it was completely open to the public. All that I've told you was published before the war for anyone to read and work it out for themselves. However, a short while later Joliot's group filed a secret patent with the Caisse Nationale de la Recherche Scientifique entitled *Perfectionnements des charges explosives*. It's a patent on how to make an atomic bomb.'

It was a beautiful day. It should have been cold and miserable, threatening a storm. But instead the sun was shining, and leaves were glistening in the light.

'And all this work was done in Paris?'

'All in Paris. At the Collège de France, and at their other lab at Ivry. You came to the Collège once with *Papa*, don't you remember?'

'Of course I do. We took you and Clément out for lunch.'

'It wasn't the happiest of meals.'

'You got angry over the slightest thing.'

'I got angry over the way Clément pandered to you.'

She hadn't understood at the time, but now she did: the intricate complex of Ned's jealousies. After lunch they'd walked along the *quai* where artists were selling paintings of the usual scenes: the cathedral directly across the river and the Eiffel Tower and nostalgic views of the alleyways of Montmartre. Clément had strolled along beside her, while Ned was condemned to walk ahead with their father. 'Hurry up,' he'd complained, looking back at them. 'We must get back to the lab.'

Clément had ignored him, leaning close to share his thoughts with her, laughing with her, teasing her. 'I want to pull your leg,' he said, using the English expression, which seemed to delight him but sounded outrageous to her, so outrageous that it had made her blush.

'And what part did Clément play in all this?'

'He worked on the critical mass problem. Natural uranium is made of two different kinds, different isotopes. Most of it, more than ninety-nine per cent, is uranium 238. A mere 0.3 per cent of natural uranium is the other kind. It's called uranium 235. Clément worked on the calculations Perrin had used. Mean free paths and cross-sections and probabilities, a whole lot of stuff. Thermal neutrons and slow neutrons. And then he made a crucial observation: if it was only the uranium 235 that was responsible for the fission and if you could obtain a relatively pure sample of 235 then the calculations would be different. A forty-ton, even a twelve-ton atomic bomb is a lot of bomb. An aircraft couldn't deliver it. But if you can increase the proportion of uranium 235 in your sample, then the value for the critical mass comes down dramatically.'

'How dramatically?'

'It depends on the degree of enrichment, and even then the maths is not certain. Clément's revised calculations were in the order of pounds, not tons. Say ten, maybe even less. No mass at all.' There was a rockery among the bushes at the centre of the garden. Ned went and picked up two large stones and brought them over. 'Imagine these are lumps of uranium metal, each one a fraction below the critical mass.' He handed them to her. 'Imagine it's uranium. It's greyish and shiny. Quite decorative, really. Now smash the two together.'

She did as she was told. A children's game. Crash! And there was a faint and sulphurous smell of sparks.

'There! That's all there is to it. You've just blown London off the map and out of history. Vaporised.'

'Merely by doing that everything *vanishes*?'

'Merely by doing that. If the two lumps are below the critical mass, as long as you keep them separate nothing happens. Smash them together and the chain reaction begins, fast, almost as fast as the speed of light. The atoms break up in a cascade, each one causing the next two to split in turn and release their energy. If one kilogram of uranium went like that it would release the equivalent energy of twenty thousand tons of TNT, all detonated in a flash.'

She knew TNT. She knew all the explosives: plastic, Nobel 808, ammonal, gun cotton. She knew how to shape a charge and how to fuse it and how to detonate it. She could break a railway line and put a train out of action, or a car. She might have a go at destroying a bridge, although you'd need to be an expert for that, like Benoît was. But not this, not a whole city, in an instant.

'This is all theoretical, isn't it?'

'It's as certain as existence itself.'

She tossed the stones back among the bushes and brushed the soil from her hands. 'I don't believe you.'

'That doesn't make any difference. Whether you believe it or not doesn't change the facts. It doesn't depend on belief.'

She looked around. There was the garden with the old plane trees, their camouflage trunks and shivering leaves; and beyond, the buildings of the square, one or two of them hollow shells, but still there; and the city itself, battered by the bombing but still incontrovertibly there. It was beyond imagining that it could all be blown away in an instant simply by banging two lumps of metal together.

'And now they know all about me and Clément.' It seemed unreal, circumstance and happenstance and pure coincidence coming together to create a small but terrifying explosion.

She looked at him with an expression that tried to mollify her previous anger. 'Do you remember playing Pig-in-the-middle, with me in the middle?'

'We called it "collapsing the wave function".'

'It used to make me furious.'

'But you kept playing, didn't you? Because of Clément.'

'That's what I feel like now. The pig in the middle.'

He smiled, a bitter little smile. 'You always were,' he said.

'And I've got to keep playing?'

'I'm afraid so.'


## XI


The Cambridge train was full. All trains were full these days. Soldiers, airmen, men in dark suits carrying significant brief-cases, academics in careless tweed jackets and ill-fitting grey flannels. IS YOUR JOURNEY REALLY NECESSARY? posters on every platform demanded, but half of England seemed to have reason enough.

'Whose idea was this?' she asked as the train trundled out through the London suburbs, 'yours or theirs?'

'Mine,' he said.

'Do they know about it?'

He nodded. 'They thought it a good idea. The personal touch. You'll be more persuasive if you've met him.'

'Who are they, Ned?'

He smiled and shook his head, looking out through the window at the passing buildings. 'You know I can't tell you that.'

Cambridge itself seemed smaller than Oxford, more delicate, more vulnerable, as though its only foundation, the fragile sub-soil of learning, had been eroded by war and put the whole place in danger of dissolution. They took a bus from the station into the centre and walked a few minutes to where Free School Lane threaded its way between close, medieval buildings. Halfway along the lane there was a gothic gateway that might have belonged to a fourteenth-century monastery but actually announced itself as the Cavendish Laboratory. The porter had the manner of a household butler, at once obsequious and knowing. 'You'll be looking for Dr Kowarski, won't you, sir? I think you'll find him in his office.'

'Thank you, Dawkins.'

'Good to see you back, sir, if only for a brief visit.'

'It's good to be back, Dawkins. How are things going?'

'Pretty strange, sir. Not many undergraduates these days, and an awful lot of hush-hush, if you get my meaning.'

'I do, Dawkins, I do.'

They climbed stairs and walked along corridors as cold and cheerless as a reform school. An open doorway gave a glimpse into a laboratory where a technician was fiddling with some elaborate piece of glassware. A poster explained the fire drill and where to assemble in the event of an evacuation. Windows were criss-crossed with adhesive tape. Finally Ned knocked at an anonymous door and a gruff voice called them in.

The office they entered was as cluttered as a bear's den. The window ledge was littered with the bones and sinews of electrical apparatus. On the desk was a scattering of files and open books. At the desk sat the bear himself. His hair was cut short, giving him the appearance of a Prussian army officer in one of Low's cartoons but his manner was more the bluff heartiness of a Russian than a German. Yet he spoke French, that was the surprise – fluent French with a strong Slav accent. '*Mon cher Edward! Je suis ravi de vous voir!* And this lovely young lady is …?'

'My sister Marian.'

'Of course, of course. How charming.' The bear took her hand and raised it to his lips. The gesture was curiously graceful, as though inside his great bulk there was a slender dandy trying to express himself.

'This,' Ned explained unnecessarily, 'is Dr Lev Kowarski.'

Kowarski cleared a chair for Marian to sit. 'Ned has told me much about you. He promised me you were pretty, and instead I find that you are beautiful. That is the Englishman in him, mixing one with the other. A true Frenchman would never make such a grave mistake.' He gave an expansive smile. 'And neither would a Russian.'

'I'm not sure how to answer that.'

'There's no need. Just accept the compliment. Ned tells me that you may soon meet up with a mutual friend of ours.'

'Possibly.' It seemed appalling. Her mission, her whole existence was meant to be secret yet here were people who knew all about it: the faceless Mr Fawley, the apologetic Colonel Peters, the Russian bear Kowarski, her own brother. How many others?

'Well, you must tell him that *I* need him here. Forget Professor Chadwick's invitation, forget the damned war effort – Lev Kowarski needs him!'

'Will that be enough to persuade him?'

The man grinned, looking at her sideways. 'He's a Frenchman. Put it to him this way: I need him because otherwise the whole project will be dominated by the Anglo-Saxons. Worse, by the Americans. France used to be in the lead in all this, and now she is being elbowed out of the way, so he is needed to help the French cause. Tell him …' His eyes narrowed. 'Tell him that they are running away with Fred's work. Tell him that von Halban and Perrin have gone to Canada and left me here on my own. Tell him that I am nearly at the critical point – can you remember that? The critical point. Tell him …' He glanced at Ned for a second. 'Tell him that I am on the trail of element ninety-four. Remember that. Element ninety-four.'

'That's easy enough. But what does it mean?'

Kowarski laughed again. It was a typical Russian laugh, humour on the surface but with a cold, dark current flowing underneath. 'It means,' he said, 'the end of the war. Maybe the end of the world.'

XII

She waited beneath the clock at Paddington station, thinking about Alice. A young girl adrift in a sea of dreams, surrounded by monsters. *It means the end of the war. Maybe the end of the world.* It was a relief to see Benoît coming through the crowd carrying a kitbag and wearing Free French uniform. That's what he had told her when they'd spoken on the phone: 'I'll wear my uniform. Maybe they'll even mistake me for a gentleman.' And she didn't care whether he was a gentleman or not as they walked along the platform to the Oxford train – he was French, a lifeline to France, a real Frenchman against her dubious, hybrid Anglo-Frenchness. And a straightforward man against the anguished complexities of what Clément may or may not have been to her, or what he may or may not have been doing in the laboratories of the Collège de France.

He flung open his arms and embraced her while the other passengers looked on with condescending smiles. Why was she up in London again? Was she seeing another man? Did she have lovers all over the country?

She laughed at his absurd ideas, and wondered whether she would tell him what had happened. 'I saw my brother. We went to Cambridge for the day. King's College chapel. Punting on the Backs. All the tourist things.'

He didn't know the Backs. He didn't know what a punt was. She tried to explain – *une barque à fond plat* – while people stared. Speaking the language in public made her feel different, as though a mere change of syntax and vocabulary could transform the reserved English girl into a vivacious Gallic: Marian into Marianne. They talked throughout the journey, volubly, carelessly, confident that the others in the compartment would never be able to follow their rapid flood of French. Did he have news of their departure?

'Any time from next Wednesday, that's what they said. Once the moon is into its first quarter. But the shitty English weather means that there's a queue of people built up. It's like the London rush hour in the rain, everyone waiting for taxis.'

They took the bus from the station and reached the house in the Banbury Road in time for dinner. Her mother fell for him.

He was tall and good-looking and, above all, French; and he seemed to understand exactly what manner of words would delight her. 'Now I understand where Anne-Marie gets her beauty from,' he told her when they were introduced.

There was a fleeting puzzlement behind her grateful smile. 'Anne-Marie?'

Benoît reddened.

'*Marianne*,' Marian said. 'He's always fooling about with names. Sometimes he calls me Alice as well.'

'From Wonderland,' Benoît added, and even that seemed to be a Gallic compliment. Her mother smiled and the faux pas was forgotten, but as soon as they were alone together, he protested: 'I am invited to stay at this girl's house and she hasn't even told me her name! You aren't Anne-Marie? You are *Marianne*? You make me look a fool.'

'I completely forgot to tell you. And I rather like Anne-Marie. It's my cover name, you know that. Anne-Marie Laroche.'

'So what are you really called?'

There was something thrilling about telling him a truth. 'Marian,' she said, 'Marian Sutro.'

'Sutro? What kind of name is that?'

'It's English. As you can see, my father's very English.'

'Seeming English doesn't mean a thing. Half the bloody English *seem* English but aren't. Look at Churchill. He's half American. And look at your king. He's mostly German, for God's sake!'

They went to the cinema that evening, sitting in the sweltering darkness of the back stalls with other couples all around them, heaving and grunting. The first feature was a Pathé News report that spoke of fleets of bombers thundering across the sky between Britain and northern Germany. *Hamburg Hammered*, it was called. Aircraft trailed long plumes of vapour across the sky, with American airmen aiming machine guns at unseen enemies. And then the city at night, a galaxy of flame. The RAF by night, the USAAF by day. Round the clock, the commentator said. He talked of seven square miles of the city laid waste, twelve thousand tons of bombs dropped, fifty-eight thousand dead, numbers impossible to comprehend. The audience stirred in their seats and emitted a sound, something atavistic, both horrified and gleeful at one and the same time.

The main feature came as a relief, some concoction of intrigue and romance starring Joseph Cotten. As three and a half years of war had taught, she pushed the horror aside and felt sixteen again, awkward in the presence of a half-known youth beside her, wary of his motives and intentions, and her own. When he put his arm around her something stirred inside, an emotion that seemed akin to fear – the same pulse, the same sweat of panic – but when he turned her head and kissed her on the neck and then on the mouth, she turned away. 'Please,' she whispered. 'Not now.'

She sat there in the darkness with Benoît's arm around her, wondering what she felt. And Clément, what she felt about Clément. She still had his letters, those that had been allowed to reach her. Scraps of paper that she held to herself and treasured and reread as though they were mysterious messages, with hidden meanings enciphered within the plain text. *Je t'embrasse*. The sense hovering between kiss and embrace and love. My uncle, she had told the nuns. Only my uncle. And as though they were written in some strange code, they never guessed what the words meant. But Fawley, the placid, thoughtful Fawley, had understood.

After the film they walked home, their shaded torch casting a feeble light on the pavement at their feet. The clouds had cleared to discover a curved, white nail paring of moon hanging low over the roofs. The moon ruled their lives. It kept them here and it told them when they might go. It held them in safety or plunged them into danger. The idea seemed impossibly romantic and at the same time rather sinister, as though, as astrologists claimed, the movement of the celestial spheres determined what happened in the sublunary world.

'Minions of the moon,' she said. 'That's what they've trained us to be.'

Benoît didn't understand, either the source of the quotation or its meaning; but she felt her new life as an unfolding drama in which she knew there would be betrayal and hatred without yet knowing the precise dynamics of the plot, the motives and the denouements. Would she tell him about Paris? Knowledge was a burden. Should she lighten the burden by explaining about Clément, and the man called Fawley and the Russian bear Kowarski?

'What are you afraid of, Marianne?' Benoît asked. 'Is it what we're doing, going to France, all of that? I tell you, there's no need to be frightened! You'll see when you get there. It's just … France. Occupied by people we hate. When you are there, what you feel more than fear is anger.'

She shook her head. 'It's not that.'

'What is it, then? I think,' he said, and hesitated. 'I think you have another man.'

'Another man?' She laughed. 'No, I don't.'

'I don't believe you.'

'There was—'

'Ah, you see,' he said as though with sudden understanding, 'my little Marianne is pining for a loved one—'

'Don't be silly. There was a flight lieutenant on the staff at Stanmore. We went out together a couple of times, to the theatre in London and then to a dance. Nothing more. He was posted away. And before the war there was someone in France. He was older than me. I suppose it was a schoolgirl crush, really … but he felt the same about me. I still think of him sometimes.' She looked at Benoît. 'That's it. The story of my love life.'

'And where is this older man now?'

She knew about confession, how you could pour out your guilt and see it washed away. Confession, contrition, absolution, things that the nuns had taught. 'Somewhere in France, I suppose. We lost touch when the war came.'

'So you are free to do as you choose ...'

'Of course I am. It's just that I don't really understand myself.'

'Why should you understand? That is typical of you English. You spend all your time trying to understand yourselves and not enough time getting on with life. That is why so many English girls are frigid.'

'How many have you tried?'

His laughter saved the moment. 'Absurd,' he said. 'You are absurd.'

At home, they let themselves in quietly so as not to disturb anyone. Outside her bedroom she allowed him to kiss her; but she put her hand on his chest when he made a move to come in. 'You must let me think,' she said.

'Not about yourself still?'

'No, about you.'

The next morning they went for a walk along the river. The introspection of the previous evening was dispelled by sun and wind. Willows blew lightly in the breeze beneath a sky of ragged cloud and fitful sun. They held hands, and as they walked sometimes they came close together so their bodies touched. She told him a story that sounded so English – about three young sisters and a couple of Oxford clerics who, one summer's day eighty years ago, had rowed up the river here telling stories. Perhaps her own field name brought it to mind. 'This is where it happened,' she said. 'On the river right here.'

'What happened?'

'*Alice in Wonderland*, of course. Charles Dodgson was his real name but he called himself Lewis Carroll for the books.'

'Even he had a field name.'

It was the kind of joke that she could share with no one else. There were so many things that she could share with no one else. Conversations round the table over breakfast had been a careful obstacle course, as difficult as any interrogation at

Beaulieu. 'But what are you going to *do* in Algiers?' *Maman* had asked. 'And what's all this about nursing? I really don't understand.'

'It's all very vague, *Maman*,' she had replied. 'I don't think they know themselves.'

'And you, Benoît. What are *you* going to do?'

'I expect they will put me behind a desk and make me sharpen pencils. French pencils, of course.'

Afterwards they laughed at their careful evasions of the truth, but still she couldn't tell him the one thing that mattered, the question of Paris and Clément.

By lunchtime they reached a pub beside a weir. She felt hot from the walk, sweat staining her underarms, her body strangely vulnerable in her thin cotton dress. They carried their beer and sandwiches to an empty table outside by the edge of the weir where the sunlight was smudged by spray. Nearby were a couple of RAF pilots and a girl with buck teeth and a loud, braying laugh. Weeping willows made a backdrop that was as iridescent as an Impressionist painting, and even the buck-toothed girl looked beautiful.

'Benoît,' she said, and then hesitated, knowing what she wanted to say but not finding the words, or the nerve.

'Tell me.'

In the water there were trout beneath the surface, hanging in the flow and swinging their tails against the current. That was what an agent had to be, one of the instructors at Beaulieu had said: a fish in water, entirely at home. But at Meoble Lodge they had learned how to catch trout by placing their hands in the icy stream beneath the animals and then flipping them, helpless, out onto the bank.

'I don't know quite how to say it ...'

'You have to decide,' he said.

She looked up at him. 'I'm a virgin,' she said. *Vierge*. The word seemed ridiculous. *La Vierge Marie*. A plaster statue in blue and white, with stars round its head and a crescent moon at its feet. If Benoît had so much as smiled she wouldn't have continued. If there had been a glimmer of amusement in his expression, she would have told him to go to hell. But he didn't. He just watched her as though she were telling him something of solemn importance, as though he were a priest listening to her confession. But this confession was taking place across a wooden table by the side of the weir, across two glasses of beer and a plate of corned-beef sandwiches.

'I don't want to go to France a virgin,' she said. 'That's all.'

## XIII

She waited until everything was still, her parents in bed and all the lights out. Then she got out of bed and opened the door to her room and crept down the corridor to the spare room. They'd even been taught this at Beaulieu – how to move through a building soundlessly, how to open doors without any noise, how to be unseen and unheard.

She opened the door and stepped inside into darkness. 'Are you there?' she whispered.

'Of course I'm here.'

She crossed the room by feel alone, her naked feet sensing the floorboards and the carpet before accepting any of her weight. At the side of the bed she lifted her nightdress over her head and dropped it on the floor, then felt down to find the edge of the bed and slip in beside him.

She lay quite still, on her back, feeling his presence beside her, a warmth within inches of her body. '*Ma p'tite Marianne,*' he said, but she put her finger on his lips and shushed him to silence.

'Not Marian,' she whispered. She didn't want any recognition of who either of them might be. She wanted this to happen not to her but to someone else. To Alice Thurrock with her spectacles and her blunt, practical manner. To Anne-Marie Laroche. To anyone except Marian Sutro.

'Alice,' he said. 'My Alice.' There was the hesitant touch of his hand on her breast. It moved down to her belly, paused at her navel and ran like an errant drop of warm water into the rough hair. The contact brought a shock, like a pulse of electricity coursing upwards through the basin of her body. She lay there while he stroked her, softly and methodically.

'*Ma belle*,' he whispered. '*Ma fleur*. Do you like that? Is it all right?'

'Yes, it's all right. Like that.' And it was, in its way. Pleasurable despite the shame, the small stroking of the quick of her, as though he had found a deep root of her nervous system and was bringing it to life. But there was no giving on her part. Wasn't that supposed to happen, a mutual exchange of delight, a giving and receiving at the same time? Yet she felt that she had nothing to give him, no wish to hold him, to have anything to do with the alien fact of him there in the darkness beside her. Maybe it could continue like this, anodyne and indifferent. But then he moved onto her, his invisible weight bearing her down into the mattress, his thighs pushing her legs apart, his belly against hers. Something dull and blind, like a nocturnal animal, nuzzled at her. She gave a cry that might have been pain, might have been rapture; and then she was full of him, fuller than she had ever imagined possible, gorged with him. He made a sound, a small note of surprise, pushing into her as though trying to discover her depths, the movement going on and on, insistent and intrusive; and then just as suddenly he slipped out of her and his penis lay between their two bellies, convulsing like a dying animal spreading its lifeblood.

He rolled off her and away. She felt the wetness under her hand, something glutinous that she had drawn out of him. There was a smell, of earth mould and mushrooms, quite distinctive. 'A handkerchief,' she whispered, groping in the dark at the bedside table.

'Shall I put the light on?'

'No!' She rolled out of bed and felt for her nightdress on the floor. Had she bled? That was part of it, wasn't it? Blood and pain. What the hell would her mother say, finding the sheets stained, with blood or sperm or both? 'I must go.'

'Wait. Wait, *ma p'tite*. Don't be in a rush. You were so beautiful.'

Was she? What did beauty have to do with it? She was Marian Sutro, no longer a virgin. She pulled the nightdress over her head. The shame, kept at bay until now, came flooding in. She left the room in the same manner as she found it, feeling her way in the darkness down the corridor, but this time going to the bathroom. With the door safely closed behind her she could turn on the lights and see herself as she was, the lean form of an adolescent girl, the pale curve of her abdomen dimpled with her belly button, and below it the flock of hair clotted with his sperm. There seemed to be no blood, but she felt sore. The taps shuddered as she drew water. Would the noise wake her parents? She washed and towelled herself dry, then returned to her room and the cool, clean sheets. Was she now a woman? But the difference was only physical: nothing had changed in her mind. The experiment, if that is what it had been, was a failure. She fell asleep, thinking not of Benoît but of Clément Pelletier, and two lumps of stone crashing together in her hands.

At breakfast the next morning she hardly looked at him. Perhaps her mother would think they had quarrelled; her father would not even notice. 'We must get back to London,' she told her parents.

'So soon?'

'I told you it was only for the weekend. We could be leaving any day now.'

'For Algiers?'

'Probably, Mother. I've told you, we can't be sure, and anyway it's all very hush-hush.'

On the train they sat apart, a clear two inches of space between them. Benoît looked hurt and puzzled. 'What have I done wrong, *mon chaton*?' he asked.

Nothing, she insisted, nothing at all. But she rejected his attempts to take her hand and re-establish even a faint image of their intimacy of the night before. And she didn't know why – that was the problem. She found his presence beside her on the train an intrusion greater than anything that may have happened between them. 'And please don't call me *mon chaton*,' she said. 'I don't like it.'

'*Minou*, then. I'll call you *Minou*.'

She turned away from him and looked out of the window, wondering at her own caprice that seemed something beyond her conscious control, a childish manner that had somehow survived her becoming a woman.

At Paddington they took a cab to Portman Square. The door to Orchard Court was opened to them and Parks the butler was inclining his head and ushering them into the world that they had, for a few days, escaped.

# First Moon

|

Colonel Buckmaster had a guest. Sir Charles, he was called. He was tall and elegant and polished to a shining smoothness. 'Sir Charles is CD,' the Colonel attempted by way of explanation.

'Seedy?'

The man in question smiled, confident that the description didn't remotely fit. 'It's not the most flattering acronym, is it? I'm actually the executive head of this organisation. Anyway, it's a delight to meet you, Miss Sutro. I might say that your name has been mentioned in the highest circles. The very highest.'

'Delight' confused her; 'the highest circles' confused her. She'd worked it all out in the train – she would resign. Her private life was being dragged into this whole mess. People had poked around in her past and read her letters and spoken to others about what there was or wasn't between her and Clément, and she wasn't having any more of it. They could send her to the cooler for however long they liked but she didn't care. She'd resign. And now she was being greeted with delight and talked of in circles that floated like haloes high above the head of a person even as exalted as Sir Charles.

'Someone has been trying to poach you,' Buckmaster said abruptly.

A look of pain passed across Sir Charles's features. 'Please,

Maurice.' He had the quiet, self-assured manner of a man who possesses all the privileges of life. She recognised it from people she had met in Geneva, British diplomats who had come to the house, men who believed that whatever might befall the world, their place high up the pyramid was guaranteed. 'A sister organisation would like our help in something,' he explained. 'Sometimes their way of going about things is a little high-handed.'

'It's damned inconsiderate of them,' Buckmaster said. His hands were behind his back, slotted together as though he were on parade but standing at ease. One hand flapped at the other as though beating time to some unknown and unexpressed tune. 'But exactly what we've come to expect.'

Sir Charles reached into his jacket and took out a cigarette case. 'D'you smoke?'

She took the proffered cigarette and leaned forward to accept a light from a gold lighter. 'I feel like the pig in the middle,' she told him, but actually it was worse than that – this was a new variant, one that had elements of *Kriegspiel* in it. The wretched victim, the one standing bemused between the two players, was blindfold.

'I'm sure you do. The trouble is, the secret world is a crowded place and occasionally we tread on each other's toes. They want things from us; we want things from them. Quid pro quo, so to speak. I couldn't possibly say more than that, except to make it clear that you remain responsible to this organisation.'

'So do we go ahead with whatever they have suggested?' *We* and *they*. Her choice of words was deliberate. She and the Colonel together, and Miss Atkins and all the other staff of F Section. All of us together, against *them*. With Sir Charles Whoever-he-was smiling benignly down on them from the highest circles.

'We have agreed that you should do whatever our friends have in mind. As long as it does not compromise your mission with us.'

Buckmaster said, 'A typical bureaucratic fudge, if I may be

allowed to voice an opinion. The plan is to drop you in the southwest of France in the next couple of days. It's far too late to divert you to another circuit, and WORDSMITH has been crying out for assistance for months. But you may have to make a trip to Paris to attend to this matter.'

'So I gather.'

'Paris is a dangerous city.'

'Of course it's dangerous. I know it's dangerous.'

'Above all, your loyalty must be to your colleagues in the field. That is how I see it. Nothing you have to do should put them at risk. In Paris you will be in the ambit of one of our most important circuits.' He looked at her with those cold eyes. 'Have you heard of PROSPER?'

She looked from one to the other. PROSPER was a name to conjure with, a thing of whispered rumour, the largest circuit in France, with subgroups spread all across the north from Lille to Brest. Francis Suttill was the organiser, the great hero, Buckmaster's golden boy. You weren't meant to know these things, but you did. The insidious penetration of rumour and gossip. 'I've heard something.'

'Well, you are to expect no assistance from any member of PROSPER, do you understand that? Once in Paris you will be on your own.'

'I'm sure Miss Sutro will be able to carry out her mission with the utmost facility.' Sir Charles drew on his cigarette and smiled encouragingly. 'I gather that the plan is to *exfiltrate* – I believe that is the term we use these days – a certain person. For that, of course, you will need assistance.'

'Gilbert is our movements man for the Paris area,' Buckmaster said. He attempted to pronounce the name in the French manner but it came out as *Jill Bear*. Sister of Rupert Bear, Marian thought. Cousin of Teddy. For a moment laughter, hysterical, forbidden, bubbled up inside her. Like giggling in chapel. She coughed and looked away and thought of Benoît, how he would have delighted in her discomfiture.

'Gilbert should be able to set something up,' Buckmaster was saying. 'And these Lysander chaps – quite brilliant. Regular as clockwork, never a hitch.' He made it sound like an airline service: Croydon to Le Bourget every weekday. 'This operation is of the utmost importance to us. Nothing you do should compromise their work, do you understand that?'

'Of course I do.'

Sir Charles smiled. 'That's settled then. I'm sure Colonel Buckmaster can fill you in on the operational details but I'm afraid I really have to dash.' He stood up. 'It has been most pleasurable talking with you, Miss Sutro. I would wish you the best of luck in your mission, but I gather that is not considered quite the form in F Section, is that right?'

'*Merde alors*,' she said. 'That's what we say.'

Sir Charles considered the matter. 'Best not translated, eh?' He held out his hand. '*Merde alors*, then. How about that?' He made it rhyme with turd, which seemed appropriate.

||

The holding centre was red brick, Georgian, rather elegant – like a country hotel, someone remarked. There were worn sofas and battered armchairs and a bar that always seemed to be open. Poor weather during the previous two moon periods had created a backlog of agents waiting to leave. Emile was one of them, propping up the bar and pontificating about meteorology and the cause of fog. 'Temperature inversion,' he was explaining to anyone who would listen. 'All to do with the adiabatic lapse rate.'

People avoided his eye lest they be drawn into the lecture but Marian couldn't escape. 'So you made it, did you?' he called when he caught sight of her across the room. 'You survived the rigours of Beaulieu.'

'Did you think I wouldn't?'

'Headstrong, that's what I thought.'

She poured herself a Dubonnet. There was ice in a bucket, but no lemon. 'Is headstrong bad?'

'Headstrong's got to be moderated with intelligence,' he said.

A record was playing, a bittersweet thing by Mireille and Jean Sablon. '*Puisque vous partez en voyage*', it was called. A couple on a railway platform discussing the pains of departure, which seemed fitting.

'What about Yvette?' she asked. 'Do you know what happened to her?'

'Ah, Mrs Coombes. The redoubtable Mrs Coombes who wanted to kill Germans. Well, don't tell anyone, but I've heard that she's already got her opportunity. They needed someone in a hurry and they've thrown her to the wolves.'

'She's already gone? Where?'

He sipped his whisky and glanced round as though people might be eavesdropping. 'I've heard it was Paris. They must have been out of their minds putting her in the field in the first place – but Paris!'

'She'll be all right,' Marian said. 'She's tougher than you think.'

'She's a little girl in a man's world, that's what she is.'

'And me? What am I?'

Before he had an opportunity to answer, Benoît appeared. He didn't want a drink. He was smoking and his expression was low and glum, which made him look like a spoiled child. He tried to draw Marian away. 'Can I talk?'

'That's all we do round here,' said Emile. 'Talk, talk, talk. What about some action, eh? I've no idea when the hell I'm going. What was it that von Clausewitz said about war? Fog and moonshine. We've got the one and they tell us the other.'

Marian and Benoît found refuge in another room, a lounge where people went if they wanted a bit of peace and quiet. 'Why are you looking so boot-faced?' she asked.

'What do you mean, "boot-faced"? Face like a boot? You

mean I am not beautiful enough for you? You want one of your smarmy English men who really prefer boys to girls?'

'Don't be silly. It's just an English expression.' She wished that he would not do this, that they could step back from one another and just be friends.

'An English expression. Hah!' He pretended to laugh. 'Is it an English expression to ask me to screw you?' He used the word *baiser* with its strange vagaries: to kiss or to screw. 'In fact, you practically *beg* me to screw you. And then you more or less tell me to piss off.' He said that in English – peece off! – which only made it worse because it made her laugh, and her laughter precipitated a row, an absurd and meaningless conflict, mere frustration boiling over into anger.

'You just play with me,' he shouted. 'You want this and then you don't want it. What am I meant to think?'

'I thought you understood.'

'Understood? I understand all right. You're nothing but a fucking cock-teaser!'

Someone put his head round the door, looking startled. It was one of the conducting officers. 'What the devil's going on?' he asked.

'Nothing,' Benoît said. *Rien.* So much more expressive than the English word, which seemed so elaborate, so full of import. *Rien!* A nasal expectoration, like clearing your throat. Marian took the opportunity to escape to her room, and when he knocked at the door a few minutes later she didn't even tell him to go away. She just ignored him.

|||

TRAPEZE was the code name for the operation. Everything had a code name, even the task of dropping them into a field somewhere in France; even they themselves had code names particular to this operation: she was FLORIST and Benoît was

113

MILKMAN. Like that childhood game she used to play: Happy Families. The next morning there was the name TRAPEZE on the noticeboard outside the office, scheduled above all the others despite the crowding of the last few weeks.

'What's so special about Florist and Milkman?' Emile complained, but she shrugged him aside. In the briefing room a pallid flight lieutenant pointed to a map of France and talked to them about the weather, and explained that if the fog lifted they would be going late that afternoon. 'Of course we can't be sure of conditions over the dropping zone.' The dropping zone seemed an abstract concept, a place in a different world so distant as to seem beyond belief.

Benoît took her arm as they were leaving the briefing.

'I'm sorry about yesterday,' he said. 'I was a pig.'

She shrugged. 'It doesn't matter. Forget all about it.'

'You don't mean that, do you?'

'Of course I do.'

Throughout the morning there was excitement, anticipation, the curious, heart-threatening flutter of anxiety that she could relate only to trivial things – the preparation for an exam or a school hockey match or going on stage. She went to the lavatory twice, her bowels as loose as blancmange. At midday they were given a large lunch that they couldn't eat, with real coffee afterwards.

'Like condemned men having their last meal,' Benoît said.

She snapped at him – 'don't be so negative' – and immediately regretted it because he had meant it as a joke. Gallows humour was allowed. It was good, even. *Génial*.

They spent the afternoon checking their kit, going over the maps of the dropping zone and rehearsing their cover stories. Then, after tea, mugs of hot, sweet tea, they were driven to the airfield in a limousine with white-walled tyres, the kind of thing King Farouk might have driven around in. They were privileged and they were pariahs, treated like nobility but kept away from ordinary human intercourse: on the far side of the airfield there

114

was even a special section made available for them, a cluster of farm buildings which was strictly off limits to ordinary personnel. It was bitterly cold and the remains of the fog skulked around the outhouses, but there was a blur of white light in the sky overhead and a faint wash of blue breaking through. 'It's going to be all right,' someone said as they went into the final briefing. The same flight lieutenant explained about the flight and the weather and probable conditions over the dropping zone. 'Of course we can't be certain how things will pan out, but the local fog is lifting. Over the DZ' – the officer shrugged – 'who knows?'

Benoît leaned across and whispered in her ear. 'You scared?'

'Of course I'm not.'

He grinned infuriatingly. 'You are, though.'

They were led across the farmyard into what looked like a wooden barn. A stove burned in one corner creating a thick fug of heat. Miss Atkins had come up from London and she greeted them with that oblique smile, as though she knew everything that was going to happen but wasn't allowed to let them know. She gave Marian a money belt stashed with francs – 'For Roland,' she said – and then went through her pockets and her handbag in a final search for those things that she might be taking over into the next world that could betray her recent presence in this one. For a moment she held the key ring in her hand, peering at the keys, on the lookout for the giveaway, a British maker's name, perhaps. They passed her scrutiny. 'Is everything all right, my dear?' she asked, and Marian replied that yes, things were OK, of course they were.

'You look pale.'

'It's the damned English weather.'

She smiled reassuringly. 'There's this for you,' she said, handing Marian a powder compact. It was gold, gleaming slyly in the light from the bare bulbs. 'Just a small token of our appreciation.'

Marian sprung the lid open to disclose the little bed of

scented powder, and a mirror from which Anne-Marie Laroche's eyes looked back at her with an expression of faint puzzlement. She thought of grave goods she had seen in the British Museum, the fragile and pointless trinkets that accompanied a pharaoh into the afterlife. 'It's lovely,' she said, not knowing how to react, as one never knew with presents. 'I don't really know what to say.'

'You don't have to say anything. Take it as thanks for what you are doing.'

How kind. That was what *Papa* always said when given a present. How kind. Even when he didn't want the thing.

'And there's this,' Atkins added as though it was an afterthought. She held out her hand. In the palm lay a small oval capsule covered in brown rubber. It looked like a dried bean. 'Just in case.'

The L pill.

'Of course.' Marian took the thing from her and slipped it into a pocket almost apologetically. Cyanide, they said. You crushed it between your teeth and swallowed. It would only take a few seconds. Swallow it whole and it would go through you and come out the other end. So they said.

Then the two of them climbed into parachute suits and zipped useful things into various pockets and checked their personal suitcases. There was nervous banter as last cigarettes were smoked. An airman bent down to strap up Marian's ankles. She was jumping in her town shoes and would need the support on landing. 'The last thing you'd want is a sprained ankle,' he said.

'The last thing I want is my parachute not to open,' she replied, and the airman laughed.

Benoît was ready, looking like the Michelin man in all his gear. She tucked her hair up into her helmet and they said their goodbyes. '*Merde!*' they said. '*Merde alors!*' as though invoking the worst would naturally bring with it the best. Like actors about to go on stage: break a leg!

Outside, out of the fug of the barn it was damp and cold. The car drove them around the airfield to where their aircraft stood waiting on the concrete apron, a dark silhouette in the fading light, like the giant Roc that carried Sinbad the Sailor. They hobbled towards it, weighed down by their parachutes as Sinbad was weighed down by the Old Man of the Sea who sat on his shoulders and wouldn't let go.

The aircrew were waiting in the dusk to shake hands and assure them that everything would be all right. 'Nothing more than a milk run, really,' the captain said. He looked no older than Benoît. An airman standing at the steps to the aircraft offered to help. 'Come on, sir, I'll give you a hand up.' And then: 'Oh blimey, I'm sorry, I didn't realise you was a lady, ma'am.' But he shoved her up just the same, with just the same lack of ceremony.

The inside of the fuselage was a narrow space of ribs and stretchers, like the hold of a boat. There was an unidentifiable smell that seemed to be a mingling of rubber and metal. Another airman was there already, organising packages. Benoît reached across and squeezed her hand, as though she might be frightened, as though the whole thing, the prospect of never seeing England again, never seeing her parents again, never being able to recapture this life of Marian Sutro again, might scare her. She grinned back at him and wondered why she felt no fear. What they were about to do defied all logic, all common sense, and yet she felt only a great rush of excitement.

Outside their metal cocoon there was a sequence of loud explosions and the engines began to roar. The noise was deafening, so loud that it was difficult to think. Perhaps it was better like that. With a jerk the machine moved forward.

117

# France

|

It's the dream. The falling dream, the flying dream, the dark hole down which she plunges or floats, watching the world go past her sometimes slowly, sometimes too fast to see clearly. This time it's cold and she gasps with the shock and cries out in her sleep. This time it's fast and the world cartwheels round her, giving a glimpse of trees and a slanting, sly shine of water. This time there's the dull black of the earth and the luminous black sky, and the moon swirling round her. Then the crack of her parachute overhead like the sound of a sail filling with sudden wind and the boat keeling over and somewhere someone laughing with the pure pleasure of it. A terrifying, exhilarating ride. She swings in the wind for a moment. Ahead of her the black bulk of the aircraft roars on, shedding another parachute, Benoît's, the canopy opening out and floating like a great white jellyfish in the flood of night. And then the ground, which for a moment has been something remote and theoretical, comes up to hit her and she is rolling in the earth and grass and being dragged by the billowing silk until she does what they were taught to do at Ringway, pull on the rigging lines to empty the air and collapse the canopy into something manageable, a great bundle of silk sheet.

*

Silence, the muttering silence of night-time, full of strange whisperings. The aircraft is a distant thing now, a crucifix turning against the moon and tilting in salute before the sound recedes and is gone for good. She is alone. Where has Benoît come down? It's like scattering seed, some falling on stony ground and some among thorns. Where is he?

Far away, a dog barks. After months in which she has been watched and pandered to, led and cajoled, bullied and pacified, treated like a lady and like a schoolgirl, she is alone with this muddy field, this slant of woodland on a hillside across the valley, this cold air and cold moon and fragments of cloud. There is the smell of crushed grass and ordure and a whisper of water nearby. France.

How will anything, ever again, be as exciting as this?

With her parachute in her arms she hurries to the edge of the field, to the illusion of safety provided by the shadow of a hedgerow, to search for somewhere to hide the chute. Where, she wonders still, is Benoît? Where, come to that, is the reception committee? She removes her helmet, shakes her hair out and sits to unbind her ankles. Her town shoes now seem ridiculous in the middle of this muddy field in the middle of the night.

Where is Benoît?

Somewhere from the darkness comes the sound of voices. In the pale, monochrome moonlight shadows seem transformed into objects and objects into mere shadows. But the sound of voices is something different, a patter of whispers on the night, a laugh, an exclamation.

Training takes over, the natural caution that has been drummed into her. She pulls her pistol from her jumpsuit and holds it at the ready. Stories did the rounds during training of people being dropped into the hands of waiting Germans and carted away to a prison cell before they even had time to speak a word of French. A cautious agent is a live agent, that's what they said, time and again. Watch, wait, listen. Think before

119

acting. Pause to consider. 'Wonder, don't blunder,' that was how one of the instructors put it.

Two shadows emerge from the backdrop of dark.

'*Par là*,' a voice says. '*Il est descendu par là.*'

It takes a finite time, a measurable moment of absurd uncertainty, for her to realise that they are speaking French. Still holding the pistol at the ready, she stands out from the shadows. '*Bonsoir, Messieurs*,' she says.

One of them exclaims, almost in fright: '*Ah!*' while the other flashes a torch in her face. '*Alice? Vous êtes Alice?*'

'*Bien sûr. Qui d'autre?*' She senses heavy figures behind the light and feels a tough hand grab hers. '*Bienvenue en France, Mam'selle*,' the man says. And then he kisses her – rough, unshaven cheeks – on both cheeks; and ridiculously – there is no preparation in the training for this – she finds herself in tears.

||

They walk through the night, along paths and over hills, it seems interminably. Like one of the night exercises at Meoble, even to the French being spoken by these shadows who walk with her. Except she knows now that the dream has become real.

'Here we are,' one of them says. The building is nothing more than a block of shadow against the hillside, with the smell of animals around it and a dog barking somewhere in the back. And then a slice of shadow opens and a yellow light streams out and a woman is silhouetted in the stream of light. 'Come in,' she says, 'come in, come in.'

They crowd into the front room of the farmhouse, five men in blue overalls suddenly discovered from the darkness.

'This is Alice.'

ALICE. From mere theory – a field name, a *nom de guerre*, almost a joke – it has become hers. 'Alice!' the farmer's wife exclaims, and clucks and fusses around her like a hen with a chick. Later Benoît appears, looking like a prisoner being brought in from hiding, glum and bad-tempered because they had found him hanging in a tree by his rigging lines and had to spend almost an hour getting him down. 'It seems such a farce,' he mutters to her. 'As though I was some kind of string puppet.'

'But it's not your fault,' she points out.

'It *seems* that it is. There's no *dignity* to it.'

'This is César,' one of the men says. Benoît scowls at the sound of his field name and in his scowl she sees what is so often obscured, that he is little more than a child, a boy who finds older people tiresome and younger people tedious. Someone claps him on the back and asks what the matter is, which only increases his displeasure at the whole thing. Outside the building there is the noise of men coming and going. 'The containers,' someone announces, coming breathless into the house. 'We got the lot.'

Apparently the *parachutage* has been an unqualified success. Twelve containers in all. Arms, explosives, even cigarettes and coffee. All kinds of stuff. Bounty from the sky, like one of those cargo cults in the Pacific islands, gifts descending from the heavens.

'Tomorrow you'll meet *le Patron*,' the head of the reception committee tells her. 'For the moment you're staying here.' He is a dark man with slicked-down hair and three days' growth of beard. A farmer, he says. Pigs. Well, those that the *Chleuhs* have left him, anyway. He has a narrow, suspicious face and, despite being called Gaillard, seems slow and thoughtful.

'What are *les Chleuhs*?' she asks.

He laughs at her ignorance. '*Les Boches.*'

She doesn't know *les Chleuhs*. She doesn't know anything. Benoît always knows, and now he smiles at her ignorance, that smile that so infuriates her.

'Did *you* know what *les Chleuhs* were?' she asks crossly.

'Of course I did. Moroccan tribe, actually. Ignorant morons, see?'

She feels like a victim of shipwreck cast up on a foreign shore and being humoured by the natives. The accents all around her are strange, their manner of speaking hard to follow. Yet they are French, incontrovertibly, absurdly French, with the gruff humour of the countryside and a hint of arrogance: impudent Gascons, watching breathlessly as she unzips her jumpsuit and peels it off, as though she might be naked underneath and about to expose herself entirely to their gaze. But beneath the overalls she is a city girl in plain skirt and sharp jacket and a white crêpe de Chine blouse, ordinary enough in the town but incongruous among these workmen and farmers in their blue overalls.

'My shoes are ruined.'

'They'll clean up well enough,' the farmer's wife assures her. 'But they're not much good for round here, anyway. City shoes.'

They are forced to eat. She isn't hungry and all she really wants is to sleep, but Benoît sits opposite her across the table and consumes the most gargantuan meal. Is this how they live, here in occupied France? Ham and pork and cheese and vegetables and a rough red wine that she refuses after the second glass because it makes her feel light-headed. And then a flan with apples and even – is this possible? – fresh cream.

'I need to sleep,' she insists, but perhaps she is speaking a different language and they don't understand her request. 'Eat,' she is told. 'Eat.' She feels like a goose being force-fed with corn, one of those geese that the farmer surely has out in one of the sheds. *Foie gras* in the middle of wartime.

'Tell us,' they ask, watching the two new arrivals carefully as though to be sure to take any morsel that they let fall. 'When is the invasion going to happen? How long do we have to wait?'

Benoît shrugs. Alice doesn't know the answer any more than he does but she wants to give them something. 'Soon,' she assures them. 'Just as soon as everything is in place.'

'We've waited so long. What's keeping them?'

Their insistence seems annoying. Can't they see that fighting a war is a difficult operation? It isn't simply a matter of

Churchill and Roosevelt giving an order and everything working out for the best. 'Where is *le Patron*?' she asks, to change the subject.

'He was meant to be here, but someone was arrested and he's in hiding.'

'Hiding?'

'At Montalban. At the Delacroix place.'

How can he be in hiding if they all know where he is? She thinks of Beaulieu, of the constant nagging about security. Tell no one who doesn't need to know. Don't talk to people. Don't strike up casual conversations unless it is suspicious not to do so. Don't draw attention to yourself. A cautious agent is a live one.

'I must lie down,' she insists, putting the food aside and no longer caring whether she offends them or not. 'Please.'

So the farmer's wife leads the way to a room upstairs while Benoît stays downstairs with the others. He'll sleep on the floor beside the fire. He's quite all right, he can sleep anywhere.

The room upstairs is a small attic under the eaves with white-washed walls, a single bed, a cupboard and a chest of drawers. Alice feels like a giant, bowing her head beneath the sloping ceiling. 'My son's room,' her hostess explains. 'Please, make yourself at home.'

'Where is he?'

The woman's face is suddenly weary, as though the whole thing has become too much for her, the life on the farm, the men crowding into her house, the lateness of the hour, the war and everything. 'He was sent to Germany. To work.' She shrugs. 'Now you get what sleep you can.' She leaves an oil lamp on the table beside the bed, gives a brief, fugitive smile and goes out, closing the door gently behind her.

Alice pushes her suitcase under the bed, then straightens up to look round the room. It smells of damp but she doesn't care. What she does care about is an escape route. Always look for a second way out of a room, a second exit from a bar or a

123

restaurant, a second way out of a railway station. That's what they taught her. But the window is jammed shut, the frame thickly crusted with paint. She crouches to peer through the narrow panes. The moon is almost down, visible through trees just above the horizon. That means that the sun will soon be up and whatever is to happen will happen.

There's a soft knock on the door. She opens it to find Benoît standing there with that wry, ironical look that was once so appealing. 'I came to say goodnight,' he says.

She accepts a chaste kiss on the cheek. He hesitates in the doorway. 'May I come in? All those people downstairs ...'

'No,' she tells him, 'no, you can't.'

'But *mon chat*—'

She puts her hand in his chest and pushes him back. 'No,' she repeats. 'Don't be an idiot. And for God's sake stop calling me that. I'm not your cat or your dog or anything.'

'*Ma puce*,' he says laughing.

'Go away.'

After closing the door she waits to hear his footsteps going down the stairs. There's no lock on the door, so she props a chair against the handle then turns to undress. Through the mottled silvering of the mirror on the wardrobe her reflection looks back at her, an indistinct image of an indistinct individual unbuttoning her shirt and stepping out of her skirt and standing there in her petticoat. She thinks of Benoît, recalling those days in England. The memory is vivid and yet it seems distant in something other than time and space, as though she has stepped through that looking-glass into another world, another dimension. ALICE. Alice with no surname and no story, no parents, no brothers and sisters. Just Alice, *à travers le miroir*.

Where, she wonders, is Marian Sutro?

She shrugs, dismissive of her old personality. She wants to be Anne-Marie Laroche, whose identity card, clothing coupons and ration book – the ration coupons carefully extracted until yesterday – she now carries in her handbag. Anne-Marie

Laroche, student, who left Paris in search of the peace and quiet and decent food of the countryside in order to recover from a bout of pneumonia. Paris is impossible. There are all manner of useless luxuries available but you can't get fresh eggs and meat. Except at an exorbitant price on the black market, of course. And how could she afford anything like that?

What was she studying in Paris?

Well, she was about to start a course in literature at the Sorbonne, but when the war came all that stopped. And now she doesn't know what on earth to do, really. She thought perhaps she'd find some work as a nanny. She loves working with children.

Where is her family?

She has no family, no immediate family at any rate.

Where was she born?

You can see it there on the identity card. Look. *Genève, Suisse*. Her father was in the hotel business.

Was?

Yes, he's dead. So's her mother.

She frowns at Anne-Marie Laroche's reflection in the mottled mirror. 'I'm on my own, really,' she says out loud. 'I've just got to muddle through.' Muddle through. It's so much better in French than English: *je dois me débrouiller*, with all its fogginess and confusion.

Outside, through the dirty panes of glass, the sky is already growing pale. Feeling that strange light-headedness that comes with lack of sleep, she lies down in her slip with her coat over her and a blanket over that and her pistol beneath the pillow. In thirty seconds she is asleep, dreaming of a rocking, roaring tube of darkness, and falling and swinging, the daring young girl on the flying trapeze with people below her applauding. There's Benoît there too, able to see – a moment of great embarrassment – right up her skirt; and then, in the way of dreams, Benoît becomes Clément, and she suddenly finds that she has no knickers on.

125

III

Morning is a new, bright world full of cold. There's been a light frost overnight, the first frost of autumn, and sunlight ricochets off ice crystals as though they are diamonds. You don't get days like this in England. You have fog and dank and a raw kind of cold that is like a caustic chemical escaped from a laboratory. Instead, this cold is champagne.

When she comes down, Benoît is still lying on the broken couch in the corner of the living room beneath a pile of blankets and overcoats. He grunts when Alice greets him. 'I did not close my eye all night,' he complains, in English. His tone is reproachful, as though Alice sleeping soundly has somehow denied him the possibility of doing the same. The farmer's wife fusses round them. There's bread and home-made plum jam. And real coffee that they brought with them.

'We must speak French,' Alice admonishes him as he joins her at the table.

'I want that they think I am English.'

'That's ridiculous. And bad security.'

'Look, I must instruct these people in arms and explosives. They think all Frenchmen are losers and they will not take instruction from another Frenchman like they will from an Englishman. It would be even better to be American.'

'But you don't *sound* American. You don't even sound English. When you speak English you sound like Maurice Chevalier.' She struggles not to show her amusement.

'I don't know what's so funny. And I do *not* sound like Maurice Chevalier. Anyway, they would not know if I did, would they?'

'Maybe you should put on an English accent when you speak French. That way they'll be sure you're English. Although they probably won't understand a word you're saying.' In vain she tries to contain her laughter. The conversation seems absurd: a

126

Frenchman pretending to be an Englishman pretending to be a Frenchman.

By the time they have finished breakfast Gaillard has come with the car. It's a black Citroën *traction avant* with a large cylinder like a water heater at the back. '*Un gazogène*,' he explains. 'You have *gazos* in England?'

Alice doesn't think so, but she doesn't even want to consider the question. England is not where she wants to be, even in the minimal way of a fleeting thought. She is Anne-Marie Laroche who has never been to England.

They pile their suitcases onto the back seat and Benoît sits among them as the car jolts along narrow country roads. They travel through an empty countryside, on byroads that are devoid of traffic, past isolated farms and the occasional hamlet. Where are all the people? The countryside seems deserted, the villages empty. The size of the landscape strikes her, the miles and miles of farmland and woodland, the distant villages and even further towns, the vasty fields of France. What is she and what is Benoît in all this space? How can they achieve anything?

Benoît is dropped at one of the villages on the way. People are expecting him, a group who have already gone into hiding, young men who have evaded the forced-labour laws and live a clandestine life, sleeping in barns and in remote farmhouses. He gets out of the car and leans in at Alice's window to give her a kiss. 'Cheerio, Mouse,' he says, in English. 'Take care of yourself and keep your knees together.'

She doesn't know whether to laugh or be angry with him. He has so often been like that, flippant and immature. It is something of a shock to see him go, and something of a relief. For the last few days he has been there to cajole her, laugh at her, show her how things are and how they might be, and now he is no more than a figure seen through the small rear window of the car, diminishing as they drive away, diminishing in importance as well as size.

'He shouldn't speak English,' Gaillard says. He smokes as he drives, a cigarette wedged into the side of his mouth.

She shrugs, trying to feel indifferent about Benoît and his little quirks. 'When do we get to Lussac?'

'Not far now. You mustn't worry,' he adds, almost as though he can sense her anxiety. 'There are no Germans there. The gendarmes …' He shrugs, as though gendarmes are of no consequence. He keeps his eyes only partly on the road. Otherwise they are on her, on her face or on her bosom or on her knees. She tugs at the hem of her skirt, but somehow she is sitting on it and her knees remain resolutely exposed to his view.

'Your stockings.'

'What about them?'

'Women don't wear them round here. That's Parisian.'

'Well, that's where I'm from, isn't it?' She stares out of the side window, not liking the man, uncomfortable under his gaze that is at the same time critical and lascivious.

'You'll need to think about these things. What to do and what not to do. When to order coffee and when not to order coffee, that kind of thing. However well you may think you know it, this is not the country it was, nor will it ever be again. Some things are permanent.'

'I know all that.'

He smiles disparagingly, as though no one can know who has been away even for a few weeks. 'At Lussac you'll go to an address I'll give you. Gabrielle Mercey is your contact. She doesn't know you've come from London, all right? She's a helper but she doesn't know much. I've just picked you up from the station, from the Paris train. It's better that way.'

'They'll think I'm French?' Benoît's ridiculous pose as an Englishman has infected her, and now the idea that she won't only have to deceive Germans but also French men and women seems a task beyond her abilities.

'Of course.' That sideways glance, to face, to bosom, to knees. 'Aren't you?'

'Yes,' she says, wondering if he is being sarcastic. 'Of course.'
*Bien sûr*.

## IV

Lussac is a small, dull market town with the memory of a castle
in the centre and the vague recollection of walls round the
periphery. Place de la République forms a triangle with a church
at the apex and the *mairie* at the base, Church and State in
uneasy juxtaposition as they have been for centuries. A *tricol-
ore* hangs limply from the flagpole in front of the *mairie*. A
couple of market stalls have been set up in the square where
women in headscarves argue over the price of potatoes.

Alice walks the pavements of France for the first time, alone,
like a child in a nightmare. The sun is bright on the *pavé* but
there is something dark about the people, as dark and shuttered
as some of the houses. They hurry past, heads down. One or
two glance at her indifferently, although somehow she expects
them to stare with wonder, as though it is written across her
forehead that she does not belong, that she is a performer, an
artiste who has swung down from the sky, the daring young girl
on the flying trapeze. There is nothing to support her, no safety
net beneath. She can ring no one, ask no one, rely for help on
no one. She has nowhere to go but along this line of frontages
towards an address that Gaillard has given her: *numéro* 23, rue
de la Bastille.

'Tell her that Gaillard sent you,' the man said as he dropped
her off near a bus stop.

'There's no password?'

Gaillard laughed. 'I can tell you've just come from London.'

Twenty-three, rue de la Bastille is on a side street off the
main square. When she knocks, an elderly woman opens the
door and stands there on the step looking down at her with
suspicion. 'Yes?'

'Gaillard sent me.' For a moment, looking at this pinch-faced woman with the scraped hair and the narrow mouth, she feels panic bubble up inside. 'Are you Madame Mercey? Gaillard said you'd put me up for a few days. My name is Alice. I've been in Paris.'

Is the woman going to react? Alice looks round to see if anyone is watching. Never approach a rendezvous directly, they taught her. Always look for signs that the place is being observed. Always make sure that you are not being followed, that you are not leading them to the next link in the chain. If it's a house, walk straight past the first time, as though you are going somewhere else. Watch for anything out of the ordinary. Watch for watchers. Watch for the man in the window of the house across the street, or the street sweeper leaning on a broom, or the couple talking and pretending to kiss. Only then, if everything seems OK, make another pass.

But she has done none of this. She has simply walked along the street and up to the door as though it were peacetime, as though the world weren't at war and the country occupied by the enemy.

Tell them Gaillard sent you.

'Please,' she says. 'Gabrielle Mercey?'

The woman shrugs, but stands aside and cocks her head to indicate that Alice should enter. At that moment there is a clatter of footsteps on the stairs and a younger woman appears from the floor above. 'Alice!' she exclaims. She is in her thirties, and bright and smiling in contrast to the older woman's dour expression. 'Are you Alice?' She comes down the stairs and scolds her mother for not being more welcoming and grabs Alice's hands to shake. 'Come, give me your suitcase. I'm Gabrielle. You must be confused, but you'll soon get used to us. *Maman* is a sour old puss. She's always grumbling about me and my ways, but she's good at heart. Come through to the back. Have you had breakfast? Did you sleep well? Goodness, you can't have had more than an hour or two, can you? Are you exhausted?'

She leads the way through to the kitchen. The old mother is already seated by the kitchen range knitting a tube of brown wool. 'Socks for the men in Germany,' Gabrielle explains. 'Isn't that right, *Maman*? Socks for the prisoners.' Her voice gets louder when she speaks to her mother, drops back to normal to speak to Alice. 'There's only the two of us, you see. Maybe Gaillard explained? Goodness, it's wonderful to have you here at last. All the way from London!'

'How did you know? Gaillard said—'

'Oh, Gaillard. He thinks I'm a fool. We heard the plane last night. It's obvious, isn't it? You can work out the connection. But don't worry. I'll be very discreet. What are you called? I mean, who are you here? Not your real name, of course not. For us you'll be Alice anyway, but just so I know.'

'Anne-Marie Laroche.'

'Anne-Marie. What a lovely name! I have a cousin called Anne-Marie.' Gabrielle chatters on aimlessly, as though there is no war and no worries. 'How long are you staying? It doesn't matter to me. You can stay as long as you like. We'll have fun together, won't we?'

Fun?

'I'll say you're my cousin, what do you think about that? No, I suppose that wouldn't fit in with your cover story, would it? An old friend, then. Where did we meet? In Paris? I was in Paris for a year, living with a family and looking after the children. Les Invalides. You should have seen the house. He was a surgeon and she was, well, terribly chic, which meant that she really didn't want to be bothered with kids. We could say we met in the Luxembourg Gardens, how about that? I used to go there with the children so it'd all fit in. Or the Champs de Mars. Wherever you like.'

'I'm not sure ...'

'Where did you stay in Paris?'

*Paris*. The name seems like a threat.

'What do you mean?'

'In your cover story, silly.'

'Oh.' She casts around for what to say, thinking of Clément. 'In the fifth, I suppose.'

'There you are, that's perfect. We met there in the gardens and got talking and became friends, how about that?'

She's being organised and she doesn't like it; this woman trying to embroider her cover story and stepping into areas that are off the map, where she shouldn't stray. 'I think I'd better wait until the boss arrives.'

'Just as you please. If that's what you want I'll leave you alone. Whatever you want. You're the one who matters here, not me. I'm only a pawn, but you're the queen.'

'Don't be silly.'

'I'm not being silly. It's true, isn't it? They've all been waiting for you for weeks, and now you've come.'

'How do you know all this?'

'I'm not stupid, am I? People think I'm stupid, but I'm not.'

V

*Le Patron* comes the next day. That is how everyone refers to him. *Le Patron*, the Boss. Never by his field name. He arrives by bicycle and Alice listens to his heavy footsteps climbing the stairs towards her room and tries to picture him before he appears. It's like trying to imagine an announcer on the wireless from the voice, and when the door opens he is nothing like she expected. He's a short, nervous, sour-looking man with a tooth-brush moustache, but a toothbrush that has been used for many months and become ragged and unkempt. She was expecting something better, but quite what she can't say. Younger-looking, of course. Tall, if only as tall as she is. Maybe even handsome in a raffish kind of way but she knew that that idea came from the films, which was hardly a mature way of thinking. Yet not quite this inconsequential, anxious man, the kind her father would refer to disparagingly as a travelling salesman type. Travelling in ladies' underwear. That was one of his more risqué jokes.

'Welcome to WORDSMITH,' *le Patron* says, looking her up and down. He laughs at something unsaid and fiddles open a packet of Gitanes. His hands are curiously effeminate, with narrow, tobacco-stained fingers and nails bitten to the quick. 'You don't smoke, do you?'

'Not really ...'

'Good. Keep it that way, at least in public. Women don't get a cigarette ration. You'd stick out like a sore thumb.'

His face is worn with tiredness and worry. She recognises the look from the days of the bombing in London, the expressions on the faces of the rescue workers, the men who tunnelled into the rubble to pull corpses out, the women who drove the ambulances through the wrecked streets, the people who were up all day and all night and lived constantly in the shadow of death.

'Was the drop OK? I hear it went well. At least you and César got here in one piece.'

'It went fine.'

'Couldn't do it myself. Jump, I mean.' He laughs, as though being scared of parachuting is a sign of strength rather than a weakness. 'Depending on the equipment like that. Depending on some bloody fool to pack the chute properly. Depending on the pilot not to drop you too low. Darn sight safer by boat. That's how I came, by boat from Gib. So long ago I've almost forgotten. We landed near Narbonne.'

He walks towards the window, smoking and staring sightlessly through the glass. Maybe he's remembering, or maybe he's checking for an escape route. Alice has already worked it out. You lift the window – she has established that the sash is working – and climb down onto the kitchen roof immediately below. From there you can jump down into the back garden. Then there would be an eight-foot wall to negotiate before reaching the alleyway that runs down the back of the gardens. She could manage the jump easily enough, and the eight-foot wall – the assault course at Meoble Lodge and the parachute school at Ringway saw to that. Physical confidence, that was what they tried to instil, and succeeded sometimes. It was the other kind of confidence that was more difficult.

'I've brought the money,' she tells him. 'I'd rather hand it over straight away if you don't mind. It makes me feel like a bank robber.'

'Of course.' She turns away from his gaze in order to pull up her shirt and undo the money belt. The notes are counted out in piles on the table, five hundred thousand francs in all. Two thousand five hundred pounds. More money than she has ever seen in her life. Some of it is stashed away in the pockets of his overcoat, and some in a suitcase he has brought. 'You'd better keep some. You'll need it to pay people.'

'Don't we have to keep accounts of some kind?'

He laughs derisively. 'You must be joking. Write nothing down, didn't they tell you that? No names, no addresses, nothing. Now, let's have a look at your papers. Let's see what London has given you.'

He flicks through the documents expertly, like a poker player assessing his hand, frowning slightly as though to mislead his opponent into thinking that he's not got good cards. She asks, anxiously, 'They're all right, aren't they?'

'The ration cards are OK but the identity card is no good. Oh, it looks all right, almost the real thing, but they've got you as having been in Paris yet there's no record of your having crossed the demarcation line. So you're living here illegally.' He laughs, and then his laughter breaks into a deep, raucous cough that shakes his body. She almost tells him. I'll have to go back to Paris some time soon. But she doesn't.

'I'll sort it out,' he says. 'You know the best source of documents? The bloody issuing office itself. I know someone in the *commune* who'll get the real thing for you. All you need to do is provide some photos. Have you got photos?'

She has. London provided them, just in case.

'We'll get you more than one identity. You can be different people in different parts of the circuit. The danger is if you travel with more than one set of cards at a time. You've got to be careful of that. One good ID card is all right. Two good cards is a ticket to the Gestapo. In the meantime you lie low.'

'And do nothing?'

'Much of our job is doing nothing. The rest of it is running around like a scalded bloody cat. It'll be a couple of days.'

'I could use the original for the moment, couldn't I?'

'Look, I'm alive, right? I've been out here eighteen months and I'm still going. It's a record. And you know why?' He laughs, that racking laugh. 'Because I'm bloody careful, that's why. Because I never trust anyone I don't know and only a third of those I do. Because I don't allow written messages and post boxes. Because I don't make meetings with people I don't know. Because people don't know where I live or where I go. Because I have genuine papers and a genuine reason to be wherever I am. Because, Mademoiselle Alice, I'm bloody careful. And making do with a second-rate ID card is not being bloody care-ful. And if *you* get caught they'll be on to *me* in a trice. See what I mean?' He's looking at her aggressively, his small eyes narrowed. He's challenging her to argue and preparing to shout if she does.

'What about your accent?'

'My accent?'

She shrugs. 'Well, you don't *sound* French, do you? I mean, I can tell you're not French by your accent. And you don't get the syntax right. Doesn't that rather give you away?'

He glares at her, his narrow eyes narrowing, and for a moment it is unclear whether he is going to explode with anger or turn the matter into a joke. Then he draws on his cigarette and laughs through the smoke. 'Because I'm *not* bloody French, am I? I'm Belgian. That's my cover. Belgian, Flemish, came here

135

from Ghent in 1940 and found myself a job working for the local council. Agricultural inspector, and a bit of black-market stuff on the side. That's how I get away with it. So don't you think you're so bloody clever that you can put me down with your *lycée* French and your airs and graces. You listen to someone who's been around a bit.'

She smarts beneath his invective. She thinks of Buckmaster and the man called Sir Charles and how they treated her like someone of importance, and here's this man speaking to her as though she's a skivvy. The temptation to tell him is there, in the forefront of her mind. The temptation to say that she may be a woman but she's been chosen for something special, something more important than he could ever imagine. 'I'm sorry. It's just—'

'I don't care what it's just. You're here to do a job of work and I'm here to tell you what to do, is that clear? I've managed to survive here for almost as many months as you have hours, just you remember that. Jesus Christ, how old are you? You look about eighteen and act sixteen. Who in God's name recruited you, and why?'

Tears start to her eyes unbidden. 'Maybe,' she says quietly, 'maybe they recruited me because I am French.'

That seems to shut him up, for a moment at least. Then he laughs and then he shakes his head and lights another cigarette. 'I'm tired. I'm sorry, but I'm tired. I asked them for a man, that's all. Someone who might be able to take some of the strain. And all they've done is send me a girl. It's not your fault.'

'I don't think of it as a fault. It's a benefit. Men are suspect, aren't they? Either they've evaded forced labour or they're in the black market, or something. Anyway, they're suspect. But a girl can get away with almost anything. And I passed the A School training all right – the assault course, the weapons training, the unarmed combat, all of that stuff. There were no concessions. I can do anything a man can do.'

He watches her through cigarette smoke. 'And a few other

136

things besides, I don't doubt. Do you really know what you've got yourself into, I wonder?'

'Of course I do. That's half the training. They warned me right from the start.'

He laughs. 'Who was it recruited you? A friend of a friend of Daddy's, was it?'

'It was nothing to do with my father. They sent me a letter out of the blue, asking me to an interview in London. I suppose it was my French. I was in the WAAF at the time, at Bentley Priory.'

'What the hell's Bentley Priory?'

'Fighter Command Headquarters.'

He laughs that racking, smoke-filled laugh. 'Bloody typical, isn't it? The Germans would put themselves in a castle and have done with it. But we find ourselves a priory. Full of old women, I imagine. Anyway, get your things together and I'll show you where you'll be staying. It's a farm out in the country. I hope you can ride a bike. You're bloody well going to need to.'

## VI

Plasonne. It's the name of the farm itself as well as the surrounding area, a small, secluded valley in the hills above the town of Lussac. The farmhouse is set into the side of the slope with the front door looking across the valley. There's a muddy yard between the house and a large and decrepit barn. Chickens pick their way through the yard in search of seeds, warbling gently to themselves. From the end of a long chain, a dog, named Xavier but always known as Clebs, barks at strangers.

'You'll be all right here,' *le Patron* assured her as he showed her the place. 'It's tucked out of the way and yet it's only a half-hour's bike ride to Lussac. And the people are good. They'll not let us down. Of course,' he added, 'I've told them you're from Paris. Even if they don't really believe it, you'll keep up the pretence.'

Of course. Her whole life is a pretence. Lies are the currency of what she does and is. Deceit is the capital she has stored up against discovery. Anne-Marie Laroche, student, born 18 September 1918 Geneva, daughter of Auguste Laroche and Émilie Grenier, both deceased.

Living on the farm and being lied to are the farmer and his wife, Albert and Sophie, and their son Ernest, who is simple. Simple, but not exactly stupid because he has a kind of cunning, the intelligence of an animal who has lived in these hills and woods for all his life and knows them as a fox knows his surroundings. His moral life is bereft of complexity: he knows what is good and what is bad and between those poles there is nothing of any importance. Fortunately Alice is good. He looks at her across the table in the narrow dining room of the farmhouse and grins, and says her name, 'Anne-Marie', as though it is a source of wonder.

Albert and Sophie's other son is in Germany working in some factory or other. Every two weeks they receive a letter from him – a few lines written on a standard form: *My dear parents, I am quite well, thank you. We work hard but are well treated. I hope all is well with you on the farm. Give my regards to Ernest. Your affectionate son, Hugues.* That kind of thing. Ernest shows Alice one of these missives, pointing to his own name which, despite his not being able to read, he can recognise well enough. 'Ernest,' he says emphatically, in case she has not understood. Ironically the very quality that seemed to make Ernest useless as a farmer's son – his mental deficiency – has actually ensured his usefulness: because of this deficiency he will never be called up under the *Service du Travail Obligatoire* and is therefore free to help his father on the farm.

Albert is a taciturn man with a dry sense of humour. At times he seems to regard the occupation as nothing more than an ironical manifestation of the absurdity of nature, like a random storm that has destroyed a standing crop in his fields, or a disease that swept through his small herd of dairy cattle and carried them away. His wife Sophie is different. Warm and placid, she quickly becomes a surrogate mother to Alice. In Alice's mind the name Sophie is associated with softness. Of course she knows that its origins lie in the Greek word for wisdom, and softness is merely an association of sounds that only works in English, not French, but Sophie embodies this assonance, being big-breasted and maternal. She has never been outside her *pays*, her region, but Albert has travelled. Like many men of his generation it was war that widened his horizons, showed him for the first time that he was a citizen of what until then had been little more than a vague idea: *La République Française*. Serving as a *poilu* on the Verdun front, surviving two years in the trenches, taught him that his country is France and his country's enemy is Germany. He refers to the Germans as *les Frisés* or Fritz, the terms he and his comrades used during the First War, or sometimes *les doryphores*. *Doryphores* are beetles, agricultural pests that have swept away crops as the occupying forces sweep away farm produce to feed themselves. On public buildings in the towns and villages there are posters warning farmers about *doryphores*. *Eliminate these pests!* is the exhortation. People still derive a certain amusement from it even though the joke is old.

Alice's room is upstairs under the eaves of the farmhouse. There is a low window from which she could get down onto the roof of the dairy at the back of the building. From there it would be possible to jump to the ground, go through a fence and climb the sloping meadow that lies behind the buildings. Within a few seconds she could reach the woods that cloak the hill. It seems impossible that this small world of farm and fields and forests might ever be invaded, but still she has prospected the escape route just as they taught her.

'You don't have to do anything,' Sophie tells her when she offers to help around the house. 'You have enough work.'

What do they imagine she is up to? They ask her no questions, yet she tells them lies: she is Anne-Marie Laroche, a student of literature recently come from Paris. Her only family is a brother in Algiers. She spent some of her childhood in Switzerland and some in the Haute-Savoie. She is twenty-five years old. This is what she tells them when she tells them anything. What they think is another matter.

Living this bucolic life, she becomes something of a country girl. She pins her hair up anyhow. She wears no make-up. She leaves her legs and her underarms unshaven. She wears no perfume. Some perverse part of her likes the smell that she acquires: the russet, autumnal scent of sweat. Most mornings she wakes as early as her hosts, snatches a quick breakfast and gets on her bike for the journey to Lussac. It's a half-hour ride through the dark countryside, with the cold wind bruising her face and the tyres threatening to skid on the bends. When she arrives in the town she leaves the bicycle with Gabrielle Mercey, then hurries to the main square to catch the bus. To get on and find an empty seat she has to battle – elbows and knees – with women carrying baskets and men carrying briefcases, and when finally she is seated she buries her head in her book and hopes that no one will talk to her. She still finds it hard to believe that she does not have the words *British agent* branded across her forehead. When a gendarme gets on and pushes through the crowd of standing passengers checking everyone's papers, she can't believe that he isn't stupid and the fact of her deception obvious.

'*Merci, Mam'selle,*' he says as he hands the identity card back. His eyes flick down to the topmost button of her dress and the small shadow of cleavage that lies couched there. Being a woman has this advantage, that officials look at things that are clearly not false while ignoring the possibilities for deception that may lie elsewhere. She smiles up at him. She has learned this smile. It is cool and distant, a demonstration of politeness that excludes the possibility of any further conversation. It is also false.

The bus takes her to one of the neighbouring towns where she has messages to deliver and information to receive and pass back to *le Patron*. Messages to *le Patron* will often go from him to the circuit's wireless operator, their pianist, another woman known only by her field name: Georgette. Alice hardly ever sees her. Georgette lives in a shadowy world, moving between safe houses in various villages, where, in attics and barns and back rooms, she crouches over her silks, enciphering and deciphering; or over her wireless set, tapping out messages for London in the strange insect language of Morse; or listening in her headphones for the staccato buzzing in the ether that comes – the idea seems almost beyond imagining – from the key of a FANY RT operator sitting in a room with twenty similar FANYs in yet another country house in southern England, this one in the village of Grendon Underwood, some twenty miles from Oxford. Even *le Patron* does not always know where Georgette carries out her task. The less you know the better, is his watchword. 'That's why we're still here,' he explained on his first meeting with Alice.

The reach of the *réseau* WORDSMITH is wide, covering much of the south-west of the country and overlapping in places with other circuits, other resistance groups. The limits of each circuit's territory is vague and often unknown, even to the organisers. If Alice is going further afield, south to Toulouse perhaps, or north to Limoges, the bus takes her to the nearest railway station where she can catch the train. Here there is a further hurdle to surmount, for the stations are picketed by the French *Milice* or the German military, and the scrutiny of papers is more thorough than any cursory examination on the buses.

'*S'il vous plaît, Madame,*' a German officer says, holding out his hand.

She gives him her papers and waits. How would she behave if she were entirely innocent? That is the trick you must discover. What would Anne-Marie Laroche do? She would stare over the officer's shoulder, breathing in sharply and then expelling air in a small explosion of impatience. 'The train is coming,' she points out. 'I don't want to miss it.'

The man is indifferent to her anxiety. He indicates the trestle table beside him. 'The suitcase, please.' Others are walking past unchallenged, black marketeers with suitcases full of illicit farm produce being allowed to go while she is opening her suitcase for this young man to go through her spare dress and nightclothes and underwear, her wash things and her few pieces of make-up. For a moment his hands linger over a pair of her knickers. He glances up at her thoughtfully, then folds them and puts them back. 'I am only doing my duty, Madame. Thank you for your cooperation.'

'I hope it made you happy,' she says, and immediately regrets the comment as one sentence too many, one step too far. But he takes no notice and merely turns to the next passenger in the line, leaving Anne-Marie Laroche to continue to the train where she might find a seat if she is lucky, or might be offered a seat if luckier, or, because of the hold-up at the *poste de contrôle*, will in all probability spend the next four hours in the corridor sitting uncomfortably on her suitcase.

Where is she going? To Limoges, where there are three Allied airmen who are being fed through the escape line towards the Pyrenees and the Spanish border; to Auch to pass on a message from *le Patron* to his lieutenant in the town; to Condom to see about a problem with one of the French resisters who has been arrested for black marketeering; to Montauban, to arrange for a *parachutage*, her first, which is planned for the next moon period. The possibilities are endless. All the detail of a complex, disjointed, secretive organisation, united in little more than the conviction that salvation will come in the form of an Allied invasion, after which the fragile unity of resistance can crumble

away and everyone can get on with being a republican or a roy-
alist or a communist or a socialist.

Benoît she sees occasionally, when she is in his sector. They
meet with that strange familiarity that is born of things she
cannot deny because they have happened, and what has happened is irrevocable and irredeemable. The fact is there, in the
past. And it throws its shadow forward even into the world of
Anne-Marie Laroche. '*Mon p'tit chat*,' he says, 'I miss you.' *Mon
petit chat*, my kitten. There are things about him that she misses
too, but not that. His laughter and his companionship she
craves; the feeling that with him she is somehow safe. What an
absurd thought. If anyone thinks he is safe in this obscure
world, that is the moment when he begins to run the greatest
risk.

Clément?

Clément is there, like a shadow following her in the dark,
always there, his footsteps matching her own, his figure indistinct and elusive. When it's light he's nowhere to be seen. But
she knows that sometime soon she will get the call to Paris.

# Second Moon

|

The men smoke *caporal* cigarettes and drink *piquette*, a thin, sour apology for wine. A paraffin lamp adds its unctuous smell to the dark scent of tobacco smoke. Alice knows the men by sight but not by name. They are Gaillard's men, blunt and cautious farmers who know the land and have worked it, and have the ingrained suspicion that what might seem promising will work out badly in the end.

Between them on the farmhouse table is a map, her map, the map that she has marked. Gaillard puts his finger down where there's a tiny cluster of houses and a track leading off into the fields. 'We meet Marcel's group at the Bonnard place. We'll have to use a cart to get the stuff to the nearest road. It's not ideal but it won't attract attention.'

'Why there?' one of them asks. 'It's bloody miles away.'

'It's safe. Alice says it's safe. The *Milice* has never been seen round there, let alone *les Chleuhs*. And there's the reservoir above Dompierre. That gives the pilot something to steer by.'

'Water is the best landmark,' she explains, wanting to convince them. 'A lake or a large river. Water shines in the moonlight. And the shape, the pilot knows the shape exactly, from maps and photographs.' This is her first *parachutage*, and it's impossible to underestimate the value of a successful drop.

A *parachutage* is the mark of recognition, the assurance of help, the manifestation of a deity that lives out of sight beyond the horizon but who may care for His children there in the benighted world of occupied France.

The men grunt, unconvinced; but still the plans are laid – who'll carry the lights, where they'll stand, how the wind is blowing and where containers are likely to come down, how they'll be disposed of once they have been emptied.

'Let's hope it goes well this time,' one of the men says. The others mutter agreement.

'Five days, we've got to allow five days,' she warns them. 'Things can go wrong.'

'Something always seems to.'

'Why can't they get it right?' another complains. 'Don't they know what it's like here?'

Alice watches these men with a mixture of incomprehension and admiration. It seems absurd that she should be telling them what to do. She wants to help them; sometimes she feels almost maternal about them. They need her comfort and her succour but there have been too many postponements and too many failures in the past. The month before she arrived an aircraft circled the carefully arranged dropping zone for half an hour while they flashed the code letter up into the sky. Maybe the pilot never saw it, or maybe he was off course, looking for a different reception committee with a different code. Whatever the reason, eventually it turned away and vanished into the night. Gaillard has given her the sorry history. On another occasion a thin ground mist appeared like a malevolent ghost to shield the dropping zone. And further south near Albi there was an incident when the pilot dropped too high and the containers drifted away on the wind (maybe the wind had kept him high, maybe he was nervous about descending to the approved five hundred feet) and only half had ever been recovered. Some of the missing equipment – Sten guns, pistols – had turned up in the hands of the *Milice* a few days later, so the story went. That put paid to that dropping zone, so that now they were on this new one, near the Dompierre reservoir, chosen by Alice, with Marcel and his men in attendance. Marcel is a communist, that's what Alice thinks. A communist who pretends he is a socialist. He has gathered a group of disaffected youth around him, kids who have evaded the *Service du Travail Obligatoire* and have taken to the hills. There are also a couple of Spaniards, veterans of the civil war, and a deserter or two from the French army. But such a motley collection of resisters is not unusual. Gaillard's group is a mixture of monarchists and republicans, liberals and socialists and self-styled Gaullists, an almost farcical embodiment of the political problems of the country.

'It'll happen,' she reassures them, remembering the crew that brought her and Benoît a month ago, their nonchalance, their casual confidence. 'This time it'll happen.'

'Let's hope so,' says Gaillard.

They go out into the gathering dusk and climb into Gaillard's Citroën van. It's another *gazogène*, the charcoal fire already humming with heat. Smoke rises, steam rises. Alice sits in the cab beside the driver while the others climb into the back. There are complaints about the dirt, about the cold, jokes about how Alice gets the best treatment as long as Gaillard is allowed to put his hand on her thigh. She sits against the door as far away from him as possible, precisely to avoid this possibility, while he looks at her sideways through cigarette smoke, smiling. Saturnine, she thinks, pulling her *canadienne* tight about her throat. Denied a view of the opening of her blouse, his eyes slide down to her knees. 'You'll be cold.'

'I've got thick stockings. And a blanket.'

'Still. A woman's legs.' He says the words thoughtfully, licking his lips – *les jambes*. 'I'll rub them for you if you like.'

Once she would have felt prim and vulnerable, unable to deal with his lechery. But not now. 'Oh, shut your face.'

He laughs. The truck climbs upwards through the darkness,

146

the engine straining against the slope and its faint headlights showing no more than a vague suggestion of the verge, the dry hedges, the rough tarmac of a road that soon surrenders to gravel. The moon is rising behind the trees, casting the cold light of reason on the landscape. 'At least there's no cloud,' she says. 'At least it's a clear night.'

Gaillard grunts.

Marcel's men are waiting for them at the cluster of three houses where the Bonnard family live. They've congregated in the farmyard like itinerant workers looking for a job, stamping their feet and coughing cigarette smoke. There is the sullen gleam of weapons. A pair of oxen sigh steam in the cold air. Overhead a display of stars has grown like crystals of frost, Orion tilted like a windmill, Cassiopeia like the letter W scrawled across the sky. By coincidence that is the very letter that she will flash up into the night sky to bring the aircraft in. Dot-dash-dash. An omen or a cosmic breach of security? Do the constellations care about what goes on in this cold, sublunary world? Ned would say no, of course. The universe is indifferent.

After a brief exchange of orders the men disperse into the half-light, knowing their places, knowing how to gather this improbable harvest. Alice walks with Gaillard, trying to avoid contact with him. Despite her efforts, at one point he grabs her by the elbow to help her over a fence and across a ditch; later he succeeds in putting his arm round her. '*Ma petite Alice*,' he says. 'You're a tough little kid, aren't you?' *Petite môme*, he says. It's hardly flattering.

'I'm a British officer. I'm not a kid.'

He laughs. 'Only a joke. Can't officers take a joke?'

They blunder through the dark for half an hour before they reach the place. There's a thinning-out of the trees, an open stretch of grassland cropped close by sheep. In the distance is the high ground of the massif, matt-black mountains against the luminous black of the sky. A faint breeze comes cold from the east but it is nothing to put the drop at risk. Everything should be all right. Gaillard goes off to tell the men where to stand with their torches, three of them in a line in the direction of the wind, with Mam'selle Alice standing at right angles, facing the aircraft as it comes towards them, if it comes towards them, if the whole enterprise comes to a happy conclusion. Others are detailed to stand guard. They are the ones with the weapons – a couple of Sten guns from the last *parachutage*, and four rifles dating from the last war and stolen from a French army barracks.

And then there is nothing more to do than wait. Alice sits against a hillock, wrapped in a blanket, harassed by cold. Gaillard is smoking. She can see the glow of his cigarette in the shadows. At Meoble they warned you not to do that, not to smoke out in the open. It's like a beacon. But when she mentions it to Gaillard, he merely laughs.

Time passes. The constellations wheel overhead, a vast and implacable chronometer with the moon climbing blindly towards its apex. Alice wonders. She wonders about Ned, she wonders about Clément and Benoît, she wonders about Anne-Marie Laroche and Marian Sutro, about the past and the future. Her pistol – a Browning automatic that she only takes on operations like this – is pressed into her side like an accusing finger. Can she be bothered to move to make herself more comfortable? To move is to feel cold. This must be how Antarctic explorers die, keeping still to conserve their heat. Maybe Scott himself, the quintessential British hero, sat still like this, willing his own little envelope of warm air not to dissolve away into the icy night. She looks up into the stars and for a moment, a fraction of a moment, she feels the depth of space, the void, that aching absence. What is the temperature of outer space, up there between the stars? Surely Ned knows things like that, Ned with his wayward and persistent mind, Ned with his brilliance and his anxieties.

She listens. There are night sounds all around her: the hush of the wind among the nearest trees, an owl's hoot and the brief scurry of some mammal through the undergrowth, the whisper of cold and decay. And then there is another sound on the air, something muttered and distant, a rumour of war. She stiffens, moves her legs, feels the shock of cold.

'There.'

Gaillard is another shadow, crouched against the hedge. 'What?'

'Listen.'

The noise waxes and wanes, nothing more than a murmur rising and falling on the night, like a sea lapping on some distant shore.

'There it is,' she says, struggling to her feet. 'Come on!'

Gaillard follows, calling to the men. There's a sudden urgent bustle, shadowy figures coming out of the shadows, shouting to each other and in their turn being ordered to be quiet.

'In line!' Gaillard calls. 'In a fucking line, fifty metres apart like I told you. Christ, it's worse than herding sheep. At least sheep have got brains.'

The sound is nearer now, the drumbeat of aero engines, somewhere out there to the north, somewhere in the dark, too small to be seen against the stars.

'Turn the fucking lights on!'

The men are holding bicycle lamps, mere pinpricks against the black of the earth. Alice stamps her feet and blows on her fingers, fiddling with the switch of her torch. She points the thing in the vague direction of the sound, in what she hopes is the direction, fishing for the thing, dangling the bait of •━ ━ and again •━ ━ until her fingers begin to hurt with the effort of turning the switch on and off.

•━ ━   •━ ━   •━ ━   •━ ━

A shout comes from someone in the shadows at the edge of the meadow: 'There it is!' But she can't see the machine, just hear the engines rising and falling as the plane circles, imagine the propellers clawing at the air, dragging the great beast round.

•━ ━   •━ ━   •━ ━   •━ ━

W for WORDSMITH, perhaps.

'There!'

And now she sees it, a shape running against the stars, a black cross tilting and turning, coming nearer like a great bird, overbearing and overweening, the engines sounding louder and louder, roaring at them down there on the ground. She finds herself waving ridiculously, in the hope that up there in the aircraft they can see this figure below them. There are tears in her eyes and a stinging in her nose, tears of joy that these unknown men, seven of them, have flown all across France to make this strange rendezvous, them up there and still attached somehow to England, and the reception committee down here, two distant worlds coming into brief and tenuous contact out here on a desolate hillside above Dompierre. The aircraft thunders over them at a thousand feet or so, and turns and circles towards the south, banking against the stars and momentarily blotting out the moon. And then it is back, confronting them, moonlight glinting on its cockpit canopy, the wings adjusting their grip on the air as it feels its way down to five hundred feet. She wants to embrace it, or have it embrace her. She wants to have its power inhabit her body. She wants it more intensely than she has ever wanted anything, from her father's approval to her mother's love, to the craving she once felt for Clément. It is an experience, sliding overhead as loud as a train, a thundering, magnificent call of defiance greater than any childish longing. And the parachutes appear, sudden celestial globes emerging from it like eggs from the belly of a great fish, eggs that float in a stream on the tide of night, settling towards the earth where they might hatch out their offspring.

'Over there!'

'Look out!'

One of the containers lands a few yards away, a cylinder about six feet long. Another thumps into the ground fifty yards further on, the parachute canopy settling over it like a ballerina's skirt in a *plié*. Men are running after the containers, lugging them to the edge of the field where the ox cart waits. All is motion in the cold moonlight: shadows flitting back and forth, the aircraft climbing away from the drop, engines bellowing as it climbs and turns back for a second run.

'Keep your eyes open!'

'They're coming back!'

And here it is again roaring overhead, dispensing its bounty to the worshippers down on the ground, the whole world vibrating with its power as it climbs away from them and, tilting its wings in salute, turns and recedes over the countryside, a presence that has for a few minutes occupied their minds and their bodies but is now suddenly detached, a remote thing leaving their collective consciousness for ever. And in the darkness, as the men run around collecting the containers and lugging them towards the waiting ox cart, Alice weeps for her moment of ecstasy and her apprehension of loss.

## ‖

There's a meeting with *le Patron*, at Gabrielle's house in Lussac. She doesn't like this way of meeting – she'd prefer cut-outs and dead letter drops and all that stuff that they taught her at Beaulieu, but this is *le Patron*'s manner. 'They don't know their bloody arses from their elbows,' he said when she objected right at the beginning. 'You need someone who's been in the field to teach you, not some pimp from Whitehall.'

They meet in the same back room that she has stayed in from time to time, the one with the view over the back roofs and the little alleyway, the room she occupied after her drop. It seems like part of her history now, part of the memory of Anne-Marie Laroche – that morning of excitement and anxiety, the sensation of being safe in one place only, this small, sequestered space with the floral quilt on the bed and the picture of *la Vierge Marie* on the wall. She's waiting at the window, looking out on the back garden when she hears his footsteps on the stairs, and the rasping of his breath as he flings open the door.

'Come in,' she says but he seems not to notice her sarcasm.

'The *parachutage* went well, then?'

'As well as could be hoped.'

'I hear they used Marcel's men?'

'That was Gaillard's decision.'

'Gaillard is a blithering idiot at times. We won't be able to trust them when the balloon goes up.'

'They're all right.'

'What the hell do you know about it? They're bloody commies.'

'Their hearts are in the right place.'

'You don't fight with your heart. You fight with your head. All they want is the chaos when the landings come and then they'll be shooting everyone in the back. Including us.'

'Is that what you came to see me about?'

'As a matter of fact it's not.' He lights a cigarette and looks her up and down speculatively, like a farmer trying to assess how much he might get for her at market. That's not the way Gaillard looks at her. Gaillard looks at her with the eager eye of a prospective purchaser. 'You'll have to go to Paris,' he says.

'Paris?'

'Yes, Paris. You heard.'

'What for?'

*Le Patron* coughs at some smoke, then clears his throat. The sound of sandpaper. 'It came through on Georgette's last sked. They've lost touch with one of the circuits. CINÉASTE. They think ...' his mouth turns down in disgust, as though he knows that thought is the one thing they are incapable of '... they *think* that it may be a simple thing. Broken crystals or a duff valve, or something. They want you to take some replacements. My guess is they don't know their arse from their elbow. My guess is that CINÉASTE has gone down with the general mess in Paris. You know about PROSPER, don't you?'

'I've heard of it.'

'Well, PROSPER's coming to pieces. That's what I gather, anyway. The whole damn circuit.'

'How do you know that?'

'The grapevine.'

'And I've got to go to Paris when all that is happening? What for, exactly?' But she knows. Fawley's there in her mind and he's talking about Clément. *We thought you might be more persuasive than a mere letter.*

*Le Patron* shrugs. 'Apparently you know the pianist, that's the point. So you can recognise her. Her name's Yvette. Yvette Coombes.'

'Yvette!'

'So the name means something to you? You know the damned woman?'

'Yes, I do. We were together at A School. They posted her away before she'd completed the course. Someone said she went to Thame.'

'That's it then. Apparently her field name's Marcelle. There's an address which she was meant to be using, but nothing else. You're to try and make contact and take her the spares. That's the idea. They included them in that last drop.' He takes a final drag on his cigarette and stubs the thing out, then takes a waxed paper packet from his pocket and hands it to her. 'Of course you can break it up. Two valves and two crystals. The crystals are the dangerous ones. You might pass the valves off but the crystals would give you away. So you'll just have to be careful.'

She opens the packet and there they are, part of the mystery of electronics: two valves like small light bulbs and two wireless crystals, squares of Bakelite the size of postage stamps with two metal contacts poking out of one end. She never really understood what they did. Ned would understand, of course, but for her there is nothing more than the memory of a lecture at Meoble, talk of diodes and triodes, of crystals and megacycles

153

and 'skip'. What is skip, that sounds so childlike and happy? Ned would know. She picks up one of the crystals and examines it.

'Quite easy to conceal against a spot check, I suppose.' *Le Patron* laughs. 'Tuck them down the front of your knickers, or something. But if they really search you, you're stuffed.' He hands her a scrap of paper, rice paper that can be swallowed in a moment. 'There's an address of a safe house you can use. A staff nurse at the Salpêtrière. She's called Béatrice. You were sent by Ricard. She'll know Ricard. And remember, Paris is not like here. Here things are safe enough if you know what you're doing. But in Paris ...' He shrugs and smokes, and looks at her with something like concern. 'It's the usual pile of shit, I'm afraid.'

|||

After *le Patron* has gone she stands looking out of the window at the small back garden, thinking of Clément. And the smooth man in the pinstripe suit called Fawley. Excitement is close to fear: there is the same pulsing heart, the same dry mouth, the same thin rime of sweat beneath the arms. So which of the two does she feel, knowing she must go to Paris? Excitement or fear? Or is it both?

And then she thinks of Yvette, that child in a woman's body, the little girl lost in widowhood and motherhood and the chaos of war, who wept on her cheek and whispered that she was no good, that they would never send her to France. What, she wonders, is Yvette's part in this little rigmarole?

She cycles to Plasonne to collect her things and warn Sophie that she will be away for a few days. Paris, she adds, and then regrets it when she sees Sophie's expression of fear. 'Don't worry. I'll be back in a few days. I've got to go and see a friend.'

Back in Lussac, Gabrielle Mercey thinks differently. 'You're going to Paris!' she exclaims, clapping her hands in delight. 'Let me come with you!' And then, when it is made clear that they cannot make the journey together, she says, 'Wait a second,' and disappears for a moment to come back with a slip of paper with an address written on it. 'These are my friends. If you need help you can always contact them. I'm sure they'd give you a place to stay if you need ...'

Alice packs a suitcase. She will be able to wear the suit that she arrived in and has never worn since because it is too *parisien* and the shoes that were bought in a little shop off the rue du Faubourg Saint-Honoré shortly before they left Paris for London, *Maman* and *Papa* and she, in the spring of 1940. Gabrielle watches her preparations devotedly, an acolyte at the altar. She is always doing things to help – sewing on buttons, darning stockings, turning the collar of Alice's blouses – that kind of thing. Her treadle-driven sewing machine is constantly whirring away in the back room of the little house, making and mending in the days of privation. 'You'll look so lovely dressed up for Paris,' she says. 'I can imagine you strolling in the Luxembourg, sitting at a café on the Champs-Élysées, attracting the men.'

'I don't imagine I'll have time for that.'

'Maybe after the war. Maybe we can go to Paris then.'

'Perhaps.' After the war seems like a fiction, in the way that paradise is a fiction, a time and place of unlimited plenty, of peace and harmony and eternal light. An antidote to the theology of terror.

Alice looks down at her packed suitcase and considers the two wireless valves that she has to carry. The trouble with attempting to hide things is that if they are found then you really *are* in the shit. That was how one of the Beaulieu instructors put it. If you can get away with it, better use wide-eyed innocence rather than a hiding place. So she wraps them in a face flannel and packs them among her clothes. If there is a *barrage* and they

155

are found, then she will have to bluff her way out. But she can't bluff with the crystals. There is no getting away with them. People listen to radios in all innocence, but no one transmits in innocence.

For the moment she leaves the crystals on the chest of drawers and follows Gabrielle down to the kitchen. They eat supper together, sitting opposite each other with Gabrielle's mother at the head of the table. The old woman's jaws work methodically although she doesn't seem to eat much. It looks as though she is chewing over the past. 'So how is Mathilde keeping?' she asks Alice.

'Don't be silly, *Maman*. This is Alice. You know it's Alice.' Gabrielle has already explained: Mathilde was her mother's younger sister. She died of TB during the Great War.

The old woman looks angry. 'Of course I know it is Alice. But she *seems* like Mathilde.'

They all go to bed early. 'Alice has to get up early tomorrow,' Gabrielle explains. 'She has to take the train at Toulouse.'

The old lady laughs. 'Toulouse!' she exclaims, but quite what amuses her is not clear.


IV


Alice sleeps fitfully, her waking haunted by fear, her sleep punctuated by dreams. In her dreams she is in Paris, with Ned, with Yvette, with Madeleine and Clément. Clément smiles at her, and reaches out his hand to touch her. Sometimes Paris is London. Once, Benoît is there and they are in bed together, but this seems to be a public thing, with Clément and her own mother watching; and then Benoît becomes Ned and then Clément, with that weird facility that dream figures have, to be different persons at the same time. And then she awakes, soiled with guilt, with the luminous hands of the clock on her bedside table pointing to five-thirty.

She creeps downstairs to boil some water. Back in the

bathroom, using the hard, unyielding bar of soap that is all she can find, she shaves her legs. For the first time in months, she applies make-up – a pale foundation, prominent red lips, eye shadow and mascara – and then she has to deal with her hair, combing it out and tying it up in a chignon. Finally she files her nails to even them up, then applies a blood-red nail polish. From being a country girl she is transformed into a city woman: sharp, *raffinée* and older.

Wrapped in her bath towel, clutching it to her with her elbows but holding her fingers out to let her nails dry, she tip-toes back to her bedroom where she hesitates for a moment, looking at the wireless crystals that have lain on the chest of drawers like an unspoken threat since the previous evening.

What were the words of Marguerite, the woman she trained with at Beaulieu? 'We girls have an advantage over the men.' That prim little smile. 'We can always carry items – messages and the like – where no gentleman will ever see them. You might call it inside information.'

Alice blows on her nails to hurry their drying, then carefully picks up the crystals, places them head to tail in cotton wool and wraps them tightly in a square of lint. From an inner pocket in her suitcase she takes out a condom. She puts the crystals in the condom, tosses her towel aside and sits on the bed with her knees up and her legs spread open. She looks down at herself. What did the nuns used to say? You should not be overfamiliar with your own body. It is the temple of the Holy Ghost, and it is not yours to do with as you please. Rather, you must honour God with it.

She moves her finger up and down until she is moist, then takes the package of crystals and eases it up into her vagina. When she stands the thing feels uncomfortable, something vio-lating her, an ugly presence thrusting against the neck of her womb. Perhaps it will make her sore, but it'll have to do.

After that, she dresses – a crêpe de Chine blouse and her smart, Parisian suit – and takes her L pill from the drawer where it has lain hidden ever since she came here. She glances at it for a moment before slipping it into the pocket of her jacket. Then she picks up her suitcase in one hand and her shoes in the other so as not to make any noise, and opens the door. But when she emerges from her room she finds Gabrielle waiting at the head of the stairs in her flannel nightdress.

'You were trying to sneak out!'

'I didn't want to disturb you.'

'I wasn't going to let you go without saying goodbye.' Gabrielle looks her up and down. 'You're beautiful.'

'I'm nervous. I hope it doesn't show.'

'Of course it doesn't show. You look like queen of all you survey.' She throws her arms round Alice and hugs her tight. 'Be careful,' she whispers against her cheek. 'Promise me that. I won't wish you good luck.'

'*Merde alors*,' says Alice, and Gabrielle giggles. '*Merde*,' she echoes as Alice goes downstairs carrying her suitcase and her shoes, pausing in the hall to stand awkwardly on each leg in turn to put the shoes on before opening the front door and stepping out into the cold, dark, morning street. '*Merde alors!*'

V

She is out of place among the passengers on the bus, but she doesn't care. She is travelling to Paris. A woman going to Auch for the market makes a bit of extra room for her to sit, as though mere contact with ordinary work clothes might sully Alice's outfit. The gendarme who checks documents nods appreciatively as he hands her documents back. The bus, as overcrowded as ever, lurches out of the town square, past the church and the *mairie*, down over the bridge and onto the main road. She is going to Paris, away from the drudgery of the countryside and the sheer labour that she has expended over the last weeks, away from farmers and their families, who are the salt of the earth but like salt have one flavour only. Paris has many flavours. It is a place of possibilities.

From Auch she takes the regional train to Toulouse, and from Toulouse the overnight train to the capital. There are no sleeping compartments these days, no couchettes, only bare wooden seats or the faded plush of first class. She travels first class. Money is no object. She is *raffinée* and wealthy: money descends on her like a gift from heaven. In her purse she carries thousands of francs. In her vagina she carries two wireless crystals.

VI

The journey is one of those wartime treks that she recognises from Britain, a voyage of fitful movement and inconsequential stops magnified by the size of the country, as though perceived through a distorting lens of space and time, something Ned and Clément might have talked about in one of their mad discourses about the dimensions of the universe. The space–time continuum or some such nonsense – didn't they try and explain that to her by talking about people on a train? Relative speeds and time dilation. Sharing this experiment in time with her are two middle-aged men who look like government officials of some kind, and an ancient woman who wears elaborate jewellery and views the world through rheumy and disapproving eyes. 'I can't think why they don't have *wagons-lits*,' she complains. 'What can they be using the things for these days? Carrying soldiers? Of course not. So it is pure inefficiency. Or jealousy. Perhaps it is jealousy, denying us our comforts.'

The men grunt and look out of the window, trying to ignore her. Being party to a conversation that criticises the system is dangerous. People listen and report and lever themselves up the tortuous ladder of preferment by denouncing others. But the woman doesn't seem to care. The train jolts and sways and she continues to complain: 'It's the fault of the Jews, this mess we're in. That fellow Blum. A Jew and a communist. What can you expect?'

Alice takes out her book and reads. More passengers get on at Montauban and Brive until the compartment is almost full. Time dilates and space contracts. She is squeezed against the window by a large man wearing a heavy overcoat and carrying a massive suitcase. With great effort he lifts the case onto the luggage rack overhead.

'Is it safe?' she asks.

'Of course it's safe. Why wouldn't it be safe?'

'Because it might fall.'

'It's safe.'


The train clatters on through the night, stopping and starting, going slowly when there seems no good reason, pausing for long, indeterminate periods in the middle of the countryside. With the blinds down the compartment is illuminated by a feeble blue light, barely sufficient to read by. When they halt they turn out the light and put the blinds up and wipe condensation from the windows. But there is nothing to see in the darkness outside.

Alice sleeps fitfully, her head lurching sideways with the sway of the carriage. Once she awakens to find that she is resting her cheek on her neighbour's shoulder. He has been too considerate to disturb her. 'I'm sorry,' she says, embarrassed. 'I'm awfully sorry.' Then she falls silent. That is what France is reduced to: silence between strangers because conversations would be compromised one way or the other. Better to keep quiet.

In the early morning the train rumbles across a bridge and grinds to a halt in a blacked-out station in a great sigh of steam. 'Vierzon,' someone says, peering through the glass. Doors slam. There is German spoken on the platform and the sound of movement in the corridor. Soldiers clump on board. Doors can be heard sliding open, and people shouting. In the compartment her fellow passengers look at one another more directly than throughout the whole journey, a look entirely without sympathy. Who is going to be caught doing what? Beside Alice the fat man sweats and fidgets, his fingers fluttering like sea creatures caught in some wayward ocean current. Alice feels the crystals inside her, accusing fingers pointing towards her womb.

And then there is a sudden cry, a shout, a scurrying of footsteps and a scream beyond the spectrum of human sound, something animal that nevertheless carries within it words that are recognisable: France! Shit! Bastards! Followed by a rapid running and a single rifle shot that is loud, flat and final.

'Communists,' the old lady decides.

Alice peers out of the window. In the light of lamps she can see figures move, dragging something. 'Someone's dead.' She looks at the old lady. 'Communist or not, he's dead.' Immediately she regrets the comment, which goes against everything she has been taught, that she should say nothing of any note, that she should enter into no argument or discussion, that dullness is the best camouflage. *Pour vivre heureux, vivons cachés.* That was the motto at the school in Beaulieu.

'But there you are,' the old lady continues with a patient smile, as though the young woman has missed the obvious. 'They believe in nothing, so what does it matter?'

Alice looks away. People push past along the corridor and a German officer peers into the compartment. He is wearing a silver breastplate that she knows to be the sign of the *Feldgendarmerie*, mere military police, to be treated with respect but not feared in the way that some of the other units are to be feared. He catches her eye and for a moment they look at one another like beings from two entirely different habitats, a fish in the depths of a pond examining a fisherman on the bank. Then the man nods and passes on. Moments later the door slides back and a young man enters the compartment, settling opposite her in the one empty place. When he catches her eye he gives a wry smile; she ignores him and buries her head in her book, anxious not to get drawn into conversation.

The soldiers are leaving the carriages. Doors slam shut and the train, ancient and arthritic, flexes its joints and moves forward. 'What happened?' someone asks.

The newcomer shrugs.

'Well, at least we didn't have to wait long,' one of the civil servants remarks.

'A small inconvenience,' the young man agrees. His smile is faint and supercilious, as though he knows more about inconveniences than anyone else.

Later the young man stands up, excuses himself and steps over legs and feet to gain the door. Perhaps he has gone to the lavatory, or to stretch his legs, or to smoke a cigarette; but she wonders. His empty seat seems as suspicious and threatening as his presence. When he returns he seems just the same: young, anonymous, indifferent. And yet she cannot rid her mind of the idea that he is watching her, smiling knowingly whenever their eyes meet, wondering who she is and what she is doing. When the ticket inspector passes there is a moment's confusion as tickets are handed over and then identity cards. There is an awkward juggling and Alice's card falls to the floor. She leans forward to retrieve it but the young man is quicker, picking it up from between the jumble of feet and straightening up so that his face is close to hers and she can smell some kind of soap on his skin. He is close-shaved but his chin is brushed with blue, like the blueing of tempered steel.

'Please,' he says, handing her the card. She takes it thankfully and returns it to her handbag. Outside the windows of their compartment a thin stain of dawn is smeared across the sky, like blood and lymph oozing from a wound. Acres of railway sidings are visible.

'Juvisy,' the young man says. 'We're almost there.'

# Paris

|

Gare d'Austerlitz, early morning. The *Feldgendarmerie* have set up a *barrage* at the head of the platform with trestle tables and soldiers going through people's luggage. Queues have formed. One or two people – officials, men in uniform, a mother with her children – are waved through but everyone else has to queue. Alice stands in line, with the crystals nudging her womb.

A story did the rounds at Beaulieu: one agent carrying his wireless set in a suitcase was faced with just such a search. Noticing a woman with a baby in her arms and two young toddlers trailing along behind her, he lifted the younger child into his arms. 'Let me help,' he said to the harassed mother, and, along with his newly acquired family, he was waved through the checkpoint without being searched.

No such brilliance here, only the slow plod forwards in the line until finally Alice reaches the front of the queue, puts her suitcase onto the table and opens it. She stands indifferently while the policeman sorts through her clothes, waiting for him to find the wireless valves. Her heart beats loudly – surely he can hear it – but somehow her mind seems calm, as though she is about to go on stage and she knows her lines and the tension is what she needs to play her part well.

'What's this?'

The racket of the mainline station is all around, enveloping her with its echoes from the roof, a stunning contrast to life in the countryside at Lussac. Even Toulouse seems a small town compared with this.

'Those? Oh, they're for a friend.' She shrugs. 'His wireless has broken and he wants to listen to *Großdeutscher Rundfunk* and he can't find spares for love nor money. I managed to find something in Toulouse. I hope to goodness they're the right ones.' She smiles at him. He is young, as young as she, and being male means that he looks even younger because those things that happen to men – the hardening of the features, the toughening of the jaw, the rough growth of stubble – have not yet happened to him. A mere boy.

The boy turns the valves in his hand, then glances up at her and returns her smile. '*Gut*,' he decides, then tries it in French: '*Ça va. Vous pouvoir aller.*'

'*Pardon?*'

'*Allez*,' he repeats, '*allez!*'

She feels a small stir of triumph deep inside her where the crystals lie. Of course she may go. Why on earth would he wish to detain her? She smiles at him, takes up her suitcase and makes her way to the ladies' cloakroom. In the cubicle she drops her knickers and hitches up her skirt and squats, feeling with her finger, probing inside and levering out the package of crystals. Then she opens her case and wraps them in a towel, adjusts her clothing and goes out. Benoît would have laughed.

The deserted station forecourt is slick under a grey sky, the sky of Paris that she has dreamed about, imagined, feared, almost forgotten, and is lain now like a blanket over her childhood memories of the city. Walk purposefully but without hurrying. That's what they said at Beaulieu. Always know where you are going and why. Always have a story to explain yourself. But she has no story to explain what she is doing, nothing beyond the simple fact that she wants to look, wants to see the city for the first time in years. So she crosses the road to the embankment and stands looking at the view across the river, remembering that time in London, the day after that first interview when she walked onto the Embankment beside the Hungerford Bridge with the trains rattling overhead. Then she envisaged this moment, looking out across the slow slick of the Seine from the *quai*, imagined the drama of her presence here. But the reality is that she is small against this great sweep of river and sky, and insignificant. Anything she might be able to do is as nothing. And yet she feels again the weight of two stones in her hands and smells the acrid stink of sparks and hears Ned's voice: *That's all there is to it. You've just blown London off the map and out of history. Vaporised.*

A voice behind her says, 'Hello again.'

She turns. It's the young man from the train, her companion since Vierzon. He has followed her. He has managed a shave and a change of shirt – she notices that – and he looks appealing enough, except that he is *not* appealing, that no casual encounter appeals these days, that the whole vacant city lies around her and none of it is appealing because it is a threat of unknown proportions and unperceived dimensions, and everyone within it is a possible enemy. She turns back to the view. 'What do you want?'

'It's Anne-Marie, isn't it?'

She feels a sudden emptiness inside, as though, with the crystals no longer there within her, her bowels have dissolved into a loose and insidious fluid. 'How do you know that?'

'Laroche. Anne-Marie Laroche. When you dropped your identity card. I'd have spoken during the journey, but with all those others around ... and at the *barrage* I didn't want to distract your cheerful young soldier just as he was smiling into your eyes.'

'Are you trying to pick me up? Because if so, I'm not interested.'

He laughs. There is something familiar in his laughter – a lightness, an honesty, rather like Benoît's. 'I thought we might have a coffee together. Or breakfast. Have you had breakfast? We can get something near here. I happen to know the owner, and there's a chance that I can persuade him to give us some real coffee. How about that?' He talks fast, his words sliding easily over her request to be left alone. 'My name's Julius, by the way. Julius Miessen. Julius, Jules, whichever you like. I thought you looked a bit lost in the big city, and ...'

'I'm not at all lost.'

'That's fine then. But you can't go far lugging that suitcase. Let me give you a hand.' He moves to pick up her case but she pushes him aside.

'Leave me alone!'

He steps back, smiling, holding up his hands in mock sur-render. 'I'm sorry. Only wanted to help, that's all. Paris isn't an easy place to be these days. You need friends. Rationing's a nightmare and the black market has gone through the roof, but a young woman like you can have a very comfortable time.'

'What are you talking about? Look, leave me alone, will you?'

'Do you need a place to stay? Or I can find you work, if you like. Easy enough. You'll make a thousand francs a day.'

'What the devil do you mean?'

'You know the kind of thing. Nothing you wouldn't want to do. There are lots of men in this city who are crying out for a bit of companionship.'

'What the hell do you think I am?'

He laughs. 'An intelligent, respectable girl who needs a bit of cash. That's all. Where are you from? I can usually place people but not you. Educated, though.'

'Go away, will you? I don't need your work and I don't want it. Now leave me alone or I'll call the police. Do you hear me? I'll call the police.' She looks round, as though there might be policemen just ready for her cry of distress; but the *quai* is deserted, trees blowing in the breeze, one or two cars passing down the road, cyclists going past, cyclists everywhere. Even one of those *vélo-taxis*, a rickshaw contraption with a skinny man pedalling and two German soldiers sitting in the back laughing.

The man shrugs. 'Here's my card. Miessen sounds German, doesn't it? But don't worry, it's not. Dutch. Dutch father, French mother. If you're ever hard up don't hesitate to get in touch.'

She takes the card just to get rid of him; then picks up her suitcase and walks off along the embankment as though she had a purpose in going out of the station, as though she had somewhere to go here on the banks of the Seine between the Gare d'Austerlitz and the Gare de Lyon. At the bridge she turns and glances back. He's standing there, watching. What does that mean? Who is this man, with his rapid talk, his knowledge of her name, his offer of work? A pimp? An agent? A man who preys on young women coming to the capital, trying to recruit them for whatever business he has going? Entertaining Germans, probably. She shivers with revulsion. The word *prostitute* sounds in her mind, with its hissing sibilant. She can't go back now. He is there between her and the station, and she can only pretend that this walk across the river was what she intended all along. So she picks up her suitcase and crosses the bridge, walking on alone beneath the neutral sky and the sullen river, feeling exposed. Crows and pigeons wheel overhead like predators. The silver city lies all around her, tarnished and battered, a once beautiful artefact reduced by misuse to something you might find on a stall in the flea market, fingered by punters looking for a bargain. Downstream there is a familiar view, the hunched back and splayed legs of the cathedral squatting in the midst of the stream like a great arthropod, but even that seems tawdry, something remembered from a dream, the dream of childhood when fears could be laughed at in the light of day.

On the far embankment bicycles clatter past like an army of insects, locusts swarming having stripped the landscape bare. An army lorry overtakes them, hooting. There are German soldiers in the back. One of them catches her eye and gives a jaunty little wave. She shrugs and turns away, crossing the road in the wake of the lorry, dodging through the bicycles. Where should she go now? A train rattles past somewhere nearby. She can hear it but not see it: a *métro* line out of sight below the bridge. But where is the station? The train emerges from beneath the embankment and climbs onto the next bridge to cross back over the river. How to get on to it? She feels angry and incompetent, a refugee adrift in the big city frightened by the attentions of a strange man, forced against her will to make this detour.

'Just over there, dear,' a woman replies when asked. It's obvious now, the sign obvious, the occasional pedestrian going down to the platform obvious. Also obvious is a black Citroën parked near the entrance with two men standing beside it, smoking and watching people pass by. Belted raincoats and trilby hats, but you can't pretend it is anything other than a uniform. Don't panic. Keep calm. Breathe deeply and walk slowly but with purpose.

As she approaches they stop a man and demand to see his papers, then order him to open the bag he is carrying.

Walk confidently. Don't catch their collective eye. Ignore them as you would ignore anything that doesn't concern you. But they watch her. She can feel their eyes touching her legs and thighs, patting her backside. *Stuff you*, she thinks, and strides past looking the other way, sick with fear.

The *métro* station is a refuge, somewhere the anonymous congregate within the milieu of this strange city that is a simulacrum of the Paris that she knew. There is a poster showing a young man looking out from a dark doorway towards a bright and hopeful horizon. IF YOU WANT TO GET AHEAD, it says, COME TO WORK IN GERMANY. She waits, her suitcase beside her, for the next train going south to place d'Italie, back the way she has come, back on track, confusion conquered for the moment.

When the train arrives the carriages are packed. She edges in among the passengers and pushes down the car, stepping over legs and feet, apologising as she goes. Someone offers her his seat – '*Je vous en prie, Mam'selle*,' he says, smiling – and she turns to see that grey-green uniform, those black and silver badges of rank: a German officer, a *Hauptmann*. Should she refuse him or accept? Is the spirit of resistance to shun the occupiers? She knows how to behave in Lussac, or Agen or Toulouse, but here in Paris?

The train swings onto the bridge and rattles across the river. 'Thank you,' she says, and sits primly with her knees together and her eyes straight ahead, conscious all the time of his standing over her, watching. No one else looks at her, though. No one cares. Just a girl, *une gonzesse*, being eyed by a *Frisé*. She is safe; for the moment, beneath the appreciative gaze of a German officer and circumscribed by the indifference of the city, she is safe.

||

The house is in a run-down street near the place d'Italie, an area of narrow, sloping lanes and crowded cottages. The *pavé* glistens with rain. On the corner is a small café and next to it what was once a print shop but is now a shuttered shell, the owners departed, leaving behind nothing more than the ghost of their presence, their name on the shop sign: *Imprimerie Bertrand*. Paris is a city inhabited by ghosts. Ghosts of young men, ghosts of Jews, ghosts of communists and socialists. A poster advertises thousands of francs' reward for anyone giving information about a wanted 'terrorist', but a long strip has been torn out of it so that the face is no longer there. Is *she* a terrorist? Presumably she is. She places her suitcase down on the pavement outside number 45, rings the bell and waits, conscious that people might be watching, conscious that she is exposed there on the street without a decent cover story. What if there is no one at home? What will she do then? But after a while

169

there is the sound of someone shuffling around inside and a man's voice calling out, 'Who is it?'

Alice speaks softly and urgently, leaning towards the door. 'I'm looking for Béatrice. I'm a friend.'

An old man opens the door a few inches so that he can peer through the crack. He is wearing a blue boiler suit and a black beret. His lips are sunken, as though he has not yet put his teeth in, and wisps of white hair poke out from beneath the beret. In the shadows behind him hovers a woman of similar age. 'I've come from Ricard,' Alice says. 'Is Béatrice here?'

'No, she's not.'

'She's at work?'

The man glances over his shoulder at the woman as though for guidance. 'She's gone away.' He tries to close the door but Alice holds it open.

'Ricard sent me. Please let me come in.'

'I said she's gone away.'

'You can't leave me standing here on the pavement. I've nowhere else to go.'

As he relents and opens the door further, she seizes the opportunity to push past into the narrow hallway. There's a smell of drains, the claustrophobic stink of fear and deprivation. Unbidden she goes into the front room, thankful to be off the street and out of the view of strangers. Lace curtains blur the view of the houses opposite. There's heavy flock wallpaper and a large dresser occupying one entire wall. A holy picture – the sacred heart of Jesus – offers the narrow room its blessing. On the other wall is a framed photograph of Marshal Pétain.

'You've got to leave,' the man protests, coming after her.

Seeing the weakness of her husband, his wife takes over. 'You can't stay here. It's too dangerous. They came looking for her. We don't know what she was mixed up in but they are looking for her. They may have followed you. For all we know, they're watching the house …'

'No one followed me.'

170

'You've got to go.'

'Look, I've just come from Toulouse. On the overnight train. I'm exhausted and I need somewhere to rest. Can't you let me stay one night? Then I'll be gone and you won't hear any more from me.'

'It's not safe.'

'Is Béatrice your daughter?'

The woman nods. 'My daughter, yes.'

'She's gone,' says the man. 'And now you must leave too. Don't you understand?'

Alice looks at them, at the implacable faces of rejection. The nightmare has become real: she has nowhere to go. She puts her suitcase down on the floor. 'Can I sit for a moment?'

The woman sucks her lips and watches her, as though expecting her to pull some kind of trick. 'Let her sit,' the man says. 'Make her some coffee.'

There is a moment of unspoken argument between the couple, a shared look that encompasses a whole lifetime of marital conflict.

'Only a moment, and then she's out.'

Once she has gone the man stays watching, like a prison warder, while Alice sits on one of the uncomfortable, over-stuffed chairs. She's faint with tiredness, but she has to think what to do next. The prospect of finding a hotel or a *pension* looms ugly in her mind. Her name would go down in a register. She would have to surrender her papers to the scrutiny of hostile eyes. She would be exposed to the regard of the authorities, as vulnerable as a nocturnal animal caught outside in the daylight. But perhaps she can try and make contact with Yvette directly. Perhaps the solution lies there. Or the address Gabrielle gave her – could she trust that?

'I'm sorry to make things difficult for you,' she says to the man.

'You're a friend of Béatrice's, then?'

'A friend of a friend.'

He nods. Something in his eyes betrays sympathy. 'It's not that I don't want to help, but it's the wife, see? She gets frightened. It's the priests, they put all kinds of ideas into her head, about what you should do and what you shouldn't. Béatrice doesn't go along with any of that any more than I do. But the wife …'

'I quite understand.'

'If it was up to me …' He looks away, embarrassed, trying to justify his weakness. 'Used to work on the railways. A union man all my life …'

She thinks of the address that Gabrielle gave her. Could she throw herself on the mercy of strangers? And then she considers the other possibility, the one that stares her in the face. The former railwayman is talking on, about strikes before the war, about how they didn't stand for no nonsense, about demonstrations and sabotage. 'We dealt with *les jaunes* as they deserved,' he is saying. 'Oh yes, we didn't take no shit from them.' And part of her mind is wondering who 'the yellows' could be, while the other part recalls the address that she already knows, the reason she is here in Paris, whatever the business with Yvette. Place de l'Estrapade.

Clément.

The woman comes in with the coffee – a filthy concoction of acorns and chicory – and they drink in awkward silence before Alice gets to her feet to leave. Outside it has begun to drizzle, a thin, bitter drizzle as unpleasant as any ersatz coffee.

|||

From place d'Italie she takes the *métro* once more, gets off at place Monge and surfaces at the barracks of the Garde Républicaine. Over one of the gates an inscription exhorts the people to *Travail, Famille, Patrie* where once it was *Liberté, Egalité, Fraternité*. Against that institutional power she feels as nothing, just a girl with a suitcase of clothes and a couple of radio crystals. What use is that? She turns up the hill, going by the memory of the street map that she has in her pocket. Always know where you are going. Always move with purpose. Always have a reason for doing what you are doing. But what is her reason now?

In rue Lacépède she pauses, vague with tiredness, puts her suitcase down and looks in a shop window. Is anyone following? That dreadful man Julius Miessen, perhaps. But there is no one in the milky reflection, no figure floating in front of the dusty items behind the glass – pots and pans, a colander, a half-moon chopping knife, things that are used for preparing the food that has all but vanished from the shelves. She glances round for confirmation. The narrow street behind her is empty. Bicycles chained to lamp posts. No cars. No people. She stands for a moment, flexing her shoulders like an athlete, before picking up the suitcase once again and going on up the hill into the place de la Contrescarpe, a small, rain-swept square with two run-down cafés round the edge and in the middle a urinal and a single blighted tree. She chooses one of the cafés – a low-beamed, shadowy place – to sit and eat and think; above all she needs to think.

A waiter brings something that the menu calls onion soup, a brown swill in which a few onion scales float and a flaccid piece of bread lies drowned. She sips the soup and buries her head in a book, trying to ignore the fact that she is the only female customer in the place and that one of the other clients is eyeing her thoughtfully. Tiredness brings with it a dangerous wandering of the mind. She can't concentrate. She has to concentrate. She is out in the open, with the hawks hovering all around. She needs somewhere to sleep, somewhere to relax for a while, somewhere to summon up the courage that was instilled into her in Scotland and Beaulieu and Bristol; and the only place she can think of is Clément's.

'D'you want the *plat du jour*?'

173

She looks up, startled. The waiter is hovering over her, taking the soup bowl and wiping vaguely at the table. 'Yes,' she says hurriedly in case he should suddenly withdraw his offer, 'yes, please.'

He nods and goes away. She turns a page unread and recalls sailing on the lake at Annecy, remembers the Pelletiers' house fronting the lake, with a lawn and a landing stage where they kept the skiff moored. And they went sailing. She remembers that – the kick of the wind in the sails, the dash of spray, and laughter, an open, equal laughter. And a sensation somewhere inside her, an organic compulsion quite novel and disturbing, something whose focus was Clément, in shorts and an old torn shirt, with his hand on the tiller of the little dinghy, the boat beating into the wind and the spray flying and both of them laughing.

'Where shall we go?' he shouted. 'America?'

Clément, with whom she would have gone anywhere.

The *plat du jour* arrives. It's a slab of something rusk-like, swimming in a thin, brown sauce and entitled, with a fine irony, *gâteau de viande à la mode*. With it come thin strips of *rutabaga*. She knows *rutabaga*. A fearful alien in the French cuisine, she knows it from boarding school: *rutabaga* is swede. She eats with distaste, thinking of the food at Plasonne and how different life is here in the city. The occupation has reversed the norms – the city is reduced to penury, the countryside has become a place of riches. Where, in all this poverty, she wonders, do Clément and his sister stand?

Something makes her look up from her food. There's a disturbance in the square: a black Citroën *traction* has driven in and parked opposite the café. Through the window she can see the white chevrons on the radiator, and behind the windscreen the silhouettes of the occupants. What do they want? What are they watching? Panic seethes below the surface of her composure. What are they doing, watching this place? What if they suddenly come in and start a search? What if there are others

174

waiting in the side streets and she were to find herself in the midst of a *rafle*? What if ...?

'What are they after?' she asks the waiter, but the man gives nothing away. Just that Parisian shrug. 'Who knows?'

Meanwhile the watchers in the car do nothing, merely sit and watch while the desultory life of the café goes on. She forces herself to take a few more mouthfuls before picking up her suitcase and heading for the ladies' lavatory down in the basement, an odorous place with a single cubicle and a squatting plate in the floor. The door doesn't lock, but she has no choice and anyway there don't appear to be any other women among the customers. She places her case on the floor and opens it. In a pocket sewn in the lining are the two crystals, wrapped still in their little bed of cotton wool. Rapidly, with nervous fingers, she assembles her little packet, then drops her knickers and crouches, legs awkwardly spread, to push the thing inside her. There is no hint of that unexpected and delicious thrill she felt the first time: this is like some unpleasant medical procedure, a lumpy, intrusive insertion. Cautiously she straightens up and moves her hips and thighs to make certain that the thing is in place.

What would Benoît say if he knew? Make some ribald joke, probably. Or an offer of help. Suddenly, shut in this squalid cubicle, isolated in the midst of the city, she wishes she could see him again. All would be forgiven. His bewildered and bewildering attentions would be welcome. She'd let him go there if that was what he wanted; anything rather than this.

The momentary weakness is pushed aside. There's a box of cleaning things beneath the basin. She upends it and steps up to reach the lid on the top of the cistern. The valves will go in there. She can't hide them anywhere else, but she can tape them to the underside of the lid, exactly as they showed her at Beaulieu, and then return to reclaim them some time later. 'Unless they've called the plumber in the meantime,' the instructor said. He

175

meant it as a joke, but it doesn't seem so funny now. Nothing seems funny: fear chases away humour.

She slides the lid back, steps down and composes herself. She even touches up her make-up in the cracked and discoloured mirror before going out and finishing her meal. The Citroën is still there. 'They don't seem to be doing much,' she remarks as she pays her bill.

'You never know,' the waiter replies, guardedly.

Picking up her suitcase she heads towards the door and the dank outside, and the *traction* with its anonymous occupants. Her wooden heels clip on the *pavé* in a brisk percussion. She strides with confidence, her public façade belying the fear inside and the foreign presence pressing against her womb.

She draws level with the car.

Nothing will happen. She is merely unsettled by the strange environment, by Paris with its grim poverty, its cowed silences, its passivity. She has got the wind up for nothing whatever. They aren't looking for her, they aren't interested in her, they are only doing what they always do: instilling fear and uncertainty.

As she passes the car, the passenger door opens and a woman gets out, a small, almost dainty woman, dressed not in a uniform raincoat but in a leather jacket with a fur collar.

'Come here!'

Alice stops. A woman is worse than any man. A woman knows the intricacies of the female mind and body. A woman knows what women can do.

'Me?'

'You.'

The single word, peremptory. Expecting to be obeyed. She crosses to the car and stands like a schoolgirl summoned by one of the prefects, the prefect who is always ordering you around, the prefect who seems to be amused by you alone.

'Papers.'

Her papers are scrutinised. But papers mean nothing: they lie

176

as often as they tell the truth. That is the nature of the things. The woman's small, almost perfect, almost pretty face looks up at Alice. It is framed with golden curls but the features are hard, like porcelain. 'Lussac? Where's that?'

'The South-west.'

'So what are you doing here?' The woman's French is native, her accent Alsatian. She's a hybrid like Alice is a hybrid. An amalgam of things. German and French, English and French, it doesn't make much difference. A bastard.

'Visiting.'

'Visiting who?'

Never give away more than you are asked. Never volunteer information. Appear amiable and slightly slow-witted.

'Friends.'

'Why do you have friends in Paris?'

'I used to study here.'

The woman considers this, looking up into Alice's eyes. 'Where are you from?'

'The South-west. I just said—'

'Where were you *born*? Where were you brought up?'

'Oh, I'm sorry. Geneva. It says on my card. Geneva. But my parents were French.' And while Alice speaks, the woman lifts her head almost as though she is sniffing at the words that issue from Alice's mouth, searching for hints of accent, assonances and intonations that may prove, or disprove, her story.

'French from where?'

'Grenoble.'

A nod. Apparently she is satisfied that what Alice says is true, that there are hints of Switzerland and the French Alps in her victim's voice. 'Your case.'

'My case?'

'Yes, your case. Open it.'

'Oh, I see. Of course.' An ingénue: willing, confused, apologetic, slightly frightened because no one is entirely legal these days. She looks round for a place to put the case, and, deciding that there is nowhere more convenient, opens it on the ground. The woman crouches to rifle through her things, leaf through the underwear and the sweaters, the sanitary belt and towels, the skirt and jacket, her slender hands going down into the corners like small animals searching through undergrowth for things to eat and coming up with three brown paper packets. 'These?'

'Presents. Coffee.'

'Where did you get them?'

'Toulouse.'

'Black market?'

'No.'

The woman sniffs them, smiles and takes one for herself, returning the others to the suitcase almost as though she were presenting Alice with a gift. She straightens up.

'Turn to face the car. Hands up on the roof. Legs apart.'

'What?'

'You heard.'

So Alice stands spreadeagled while the woman's hands go over her body, under her jacket to feel the sweat of her armpits, then round the front to cradle, for a long moment, her breasts. She can hear the woman's breathing close behind her. The hands move gently, appreciatively against her nipples, then on, down her flanks and over her thighs, then suddenly, with a shocking intrusion, up her skirt so that one of them, the right, cups her between the legs, feeling her through the cotton of her knickers. Alice gasps with outrage. The hand continues, a small exploring rodent, feeling and seeking, up her belly then back down and into the cleft between her buttocks, even touching, through the cotton, her anus. Then both her hands are sweeping down her thighs and the ordeal is suddenly over.

Alice turns. The Alsatian woman is impassive, lighting a cigarette as though nothing has happened, as though her fingers haven't scurried through the most intimate parts of Alice's body, as though all that has taken place is the normal intercourse of search and inquiry, what happens these days in the benighted city. 'You can go,' she says. 'Just go.'

For a moment Alice fumbles with her suitcase, pushing things in order, closing the lid and trying to force the locks closed. Thoughts stumble through her mind, an untidy mix of fear and shock and relief. And gratitude. She can go. She has been violated, but she can go. Her hands are shaking, but she is free to go, the Alsatian woman showing no further interest in her but leaning into the open door of the car and saying something in German to the figure behind the steering wheel.

Don't show relief. Relief is the worst. Anyone can be anxious, fearful even; but relief means that something has happened that merits their attention.

Trying not to show relief, Alice picks up her suitcase and continues her walk across the square towards the far corner, walking calmly and with purpose without looking back. Nothing happened or will happen. Don't hurry, whatever you do, don't hurry.

## IV

She gains the sanctuary of the buildings and turns out of sight. There are few people around, and no one who takes notice of a lone woman carrying a suitcase through the streets of Paris. Half the pedestrians she has seen are carrying suitcases. Suitcases are the motif of the city, redolent of hoarded, trivial treasure and impermanence.

On the wall a plaque announces: RUE DE L'ESTRAPADE.

*L'estrapade* is a torture, she knows that. Something tearing, like the rack. Above the roofs she catches a glimpse of the dome of the Panthéon, where heroes lie buried, the lesser gods of a secular state. But now the God of the Old Testament rules the city, with jealousy and murderous revenge. At the end of

179

the road there's a triangular *place*, a place of convergence with trees and two benches and an old woman sitting talking to sparrows that skip and hop and yearn for breadcrumbs that are no longer found in the starveling city. She stops and considers what to do.

Never hesitate, never appear to be at a loss. If you are undecided you excite interest. People wonder what you are looking for, where you have come from, what your business is. But she *is* at a loss: she has lost all sense of perspective and proportion.

A young woman walks past pushing a pram. She catches Alice's eye and there is a momentary recognition, a faint unvoiced smile of sympathy. For a dreadful moment Alice wants to call out to her, for help, for comfort, for some plain human contact. But the woman has moved on and she is on her own, confronting the door of number two and the board of names and numbers and brass bell pushes. One of them reads *Pelletier, Appartement G.* As she hesitates to ring, the door opens and a man comes out. He nods *bonjour* and holds the door open for her and she slips inside into an archway and the luminous green of an inner courtyard.

To her relief there is no concierge in the *guichet* to ask awkward questions about who she is and what business she has here. Stairs rise into shadows and a lift shaft ascends, one of those open frames within which a platform of steel filigree rises and falls with clocklike precision, a piece of machinery that moves with all the predictability of ordinary mechanics.

*Wave mechanics is not like Newtonian mechanics*, Clément told her. *With wave mechanics you must cast out all idea of certainty.* At the time she had no idea what he was talking about; now it seems perfectly clear. Cast out all ideas of certainty.

She takes the lift to the top floor, where there's an imposing door on the left hand side with the letter G dead in its centre and the name *Pelletier* engraved in brass. When she rings, the door is opened by a maid, a sour and shrivelled creature who must have spent years keeping unwanted visitors at bay. She considers Alice's inquiry as though it might be some kind of affront. 'Mam'selle Pelletier is not at home.'

'Will she be back soon?'

'I have no knowledge of Mam'selle's movements.'

Alice smiles. She needs to win this woman's confidence, at least for a few minutes. 'What a shame. It would have been such fun to surprise her. And Monsieur Clément, is he at home?'

'He is here, yes.'

The answer brings a flood of relief. 'So could you call him?'

The woman sucks on her thoughts. 'Who shall I say ...?'

'Let's keep it a surprise, shall we? Let's see if he remembers me. I haven't seen him for many years. We are old family friends, from Geneva. When I was a young girl I used to worship him.'

Sympathy battles with jealousy across the maid's face. She obviously worships him as well. Eventually sympathy wins and she allows Alice to step forward into her kingdom. 'I will see if he is available.'

Alice waits in the hallway, sitting on an upright chair like a domestic waiting for an interview, her suitcase on the floor beside her. She picks nervously at her nails, thinking of Ned. Ned is here and he is not here, both at the same time, like that bloody cat they told her about, the cat that was both dead and not dead. What was the name? Schrödinger. Schrödinger's Cat.

'It's horrid putting a cat in a box!' she protested, and the two boys laughed at her stupidity.

'It's a thought experiment, you idiot,' Ned exclaimed.

Entanglement was a term they used, entangled particles. And now she feels the entanglement of past and present, of Marian Sutro and Anne-Marie Laroche, of Ned and Madeleine and Clément.

'Can I help you?'

She looks up, startled. He has appeared in the corridor leading off the hall, standing back from the light so that his face is in shadow. But she recognises him just the same, the small, precise agony of recognition that makes her flush as though she has been hit across the cheek.

She gets to her feet, feeling foolish – a child once again, reduced to explaining herself to an adult who probably doesn't care any longer. 'Clément,' she says, 'it's me. Marian.' The name sounds strange in her ears, as though she is talking about another person, someone she, and he, once knew.

'Marian?' His expression changes, from puzzlement to something approaching apprehension. Apprehension in both meanings of the word: recognition, but also fear. 'Good God, what on earth are you doing here?'

'I thought I'd look you and Madeleine up—'

'I thought you were in England—'

'And I need somewhere to stay.'

'To stay? Of course you may stay.' He comes closer and puts his hands on her shoulders. He seems bigger where once he was thin and rather awkward. *Dégingandé*, her mother used to say. His looks seem to have been hardened by the four years since she last saw him, as though a piece of sculpture that was once polished to an unearthly beauty has been roughened up by a chisel. He leans forward and kisses her, on one cheek and then the other. 'My God, how extraordinary,' he says. 'My little Marian is not so little any more.'

'I was exactly the same height then.'

'I wasn't referring to height.' Now he's smiling. Perhaps the apprehension was only an illusion, a trick of the light. His smile is what she remembers, how he found amusement in all things, even the most serious; and the way his mouth articulated the smile, the mouth she so admired and now finds that she admires still – something feminine about it despite the masculine chin in which it is set, something quirky and ironic. 'Come,' he says, with his hand at her back for guidance. 'Come into the *salon*. Leave your suitcase. Marie, who observed that you seemed a little *défraîchie* – how would you say that in English? Unfresh? I see you only as charming and a little wind-blown – anyway,

Marie will see to it. Would you like some coffee? I can offer you some real coffee, believe it or not. Is that what you would like? I seem to remember Squirrel used to loathe coffee, but I suspect things have changed now, haven't they?'

Squirrel. The sound of her nickname, a name that no one ever uses outside her family, ambushes her. Clément's arm is round her shoulders and she finds herself weeping, a fearful sensation of helplessness that she despises at the very moment of feeling it. 'I'm sorry,' she says through a blur of tears; and that small, hard fragment of her personality that calls itself Alice or Anne-Marie Laroche or anything other than Marian or, for God's sake, Squirrel, watches with contempt this lachrymose creature being folded into Clément's arms and comforted by the texture of his pullover against her cheek and the touch of his hand on her head.

'What is there to cry about?'

'Nothing,' she says against his chest. 'Relief, that's all. I've been travelling since yesterday. I'm exhausted.'

He lets her go, slowly as though he fears she might fall. 'Of course,' he says, 'Of course. I'll get Marie to make up a room for you immediately.'

'Actually, I need to use the bathroom, if I may. I ...'

'The bathroom. But certainly. How thoughtless of me. Let me show you ... and meanwhile Marie can make some coffee and even open her secret supply – oh yes, I know she has one – of sugar. Is there sugar in England? I rather imagine there is.'

Once safely inside the bathroom, she locks the door and squats to remove the crystals. It's painful now, a sharp burning, as though something scalding hot were being pulled out of her. She unwraps the package of crystals and slips them into her handbag. Then she pees, and washes her hands and peers into the mirror. A tired, anxious face looks back at her, ravaged by tears, the eyes reddened, the skin flushed. She splashes cold water to try and coax some life back into her appearance and pats her skin dry on a towel that is soft and white, not like the thin grey rags she used at Plasonne.

*Is there sugar in England? I rather imagine there is.*

A small blizzard of questions buffets her mind, matters of logic and logistics, of family and friends and the uneven shifts of loyalty. For a moment she struggles to be Alice once more, trying to calculate her next moves, aware of danger. But she knows that this rationality will only last these few moments of privacy until she confronts Clément once more and all the associations of childhood come crowding in to bury her in a soft, cold snowdrift of memories. She brushes her hair into some semblance of order, pats down her skirt, straightens her jacket and steps out into the hall.

He's waiting in the *salon*. It's a long, ornate and old-fashioned room with three full-height windows overlooking the square outside. There's an air of faded elegance about the furnishings, as though the room has been preserved in memory of an older generation. Clément seems modern against this backdrop, a careless figure in his open-necked shirt and pale blue pullover, with perfectly ironed trousers and brightly polished shoes. So different from Ned. He rises to his feet, looking at her with the faint amusement that he always showed, as though she were about to do or say something delightful and absurd. 'That's better. A metamorphosis. From caterpillar to butterfly.'

She attempts a laugh. 'Where's Madeleine? I expected to find Madeleine.'

'Am I a poor substitute?'

'You're not a substitute at all. You're Clément. But I had hoped to find Madeleine as well.'

He shrugs. 'Paris is no place to be at the moment. She went to Annecy. With my wife.'

She betrays nothing. That much she has learned, to receive any revelation with apparent indifference. There's a pause while coffee is poured before she manages a response. 'You're married, then?'

'Certainly I'm married. With a six-month-old baby.'

'Congratulations.'

'Thank you. It's a shame you couldn't have met Augustine.'

'The baby?'

'The wife.' He offers her a cigarette, lights one himself, watches her through the smoke. She shifts her legs, crossing them and turning herself sideways on the sofa, remembering his look while she did the same thing years ago, in the sitting room in their house in Geneva, his eyes glancing down at her knees. It made her blush. 'The baby's called Rachel.'

'And you let them go without you.'

'They're safe where they are, and this is where my work is.'

'I feared you might have been taken for the STO or something. Been shipped off to some labour camp in Germany.'

Faint laughter. 'Fortunately I'm too old for that kind of thing. But what about you, Marian? What on earth are *you* doing here?'

'I've been in the South-west all this time, living on a farm ...'

'But your parents—'

'Are in London.'

'Didn't you go with them?' His eyes are on her lips, as though reading what she is saying and seeing there the soft tremor of deceit.

'I was in England for a while but then I went back to Switzerland ...' She makes up the story as she goes, extemporising, elaborating, searching ahead for flaws even as she lays down the lies. This is what you were told never to do. Never make up a cover story on the fly. Never try to bluff. Always, always prepare yourself in advance. 'There's nothing flashy about the clandestine life,' one of the instructors said. 'It's dull and methodical and that's what you must be. Dull, quiet, methodical.' And here she is, being silly and capricious and making an exhibition of herself. 'I have dual nationality, you see. From my mother. I went back to Geneva for a while to study, but I always felt drawn to France so I came back last year and' – she shrugs – 'I've been here ever since. It's where my heart is.'

185

Does he believe her? She feels the thrill of panic. She doesn't know this man. She once worshipped him, but she never knew him, then or now. 'That all sounds most patriotic,' he says. 'Although I must admit, I never thought of you as French. English, I thought, with a touch of French élan. A traditional dish served up with an unusual spice.'

'I feel French. I've always felt French, especially in England.'

'And now you've come to Paris ...'

'To find a friend. I've heard she's in trouble. Look, I really must get some sleep. I'm exhausted.'

'Of course, of course.' Suddenly he is solicitous, concerned for her well-being and apologetic for being insensitive. 'I'll have Marie show you your room. You must have a lie-down.' He uses the English expression 'lie-down' with its hints of child-hood, its echoes of family days in Geneva and Annecy. He must have heard it then, on her father's lips, or perhaps her mother's. It is one of those words that her family uses even when speaking French.

'I'll wake you when dinner's ready.'

The bedroom is like the sitting room, redolent of a previous generation. There are heavy velvet curtains and elaborate belle époque furniture and an ormolu clock on the mantelpiece that ticks out the time in magisterial fashion. And evidence of Madeleine's recent presence: her dresses in the wardrobe, her underclothes in one of the drawers and, on the dressing table, a pair of hairbrushes that still have strands of her blond hair among the bristles. A photograph of her and her mother in a silver frame smiles reassuringly at the pre-war world.

Madeleine should be here to bring comfort and security, to defuse the explosive device that lies at the heart of things.

Alice turns off the light and pulls the curtains aside to look out. There is a drop of four storeys down to the courtyard in the middle of the building. No way out. She's trapped and alone, and the trap is one of her own making and she is too tired to care. She draws the curtain, takes off her jacket and skirt and lies down in her slip, pulling the eiderdown over her. In a minute she is asleep.

Then awake. The room is darker now. There is no hint of daylight skulking beyond the curtains. But a figure is standing over her in the shadows and for a moment she has no idea where she is or who this may be. She cries out and grabs the eiderdown, pulling it and herself towards the pillows, cringing from him. And then memory comes crowding in and he's apologising for startling her – 'I should have left you to sleep' – and she's denying it, denying the fright, explaining it away as a bad dream.

'You've slept four hours. Marie has dinner ready.'

'Four hours! My God.'

'Take your time. There's no rush.'

She prepares herself as best she can: a quick wash in the bowl of cold water that the maid has put out, and then some make-up – a dash of crimson lipstick, a hint of eye shadow and mascara, a faint blush. Faced with Clément she cannot be a girl again. She cannot be young and naive. She needs the protection of maturity.

Dinner is laid in the dining room, at one end of a table designed to seat fourteen. Clément sits at the head with Marian beside him, leaving the rest of the table an empty expanse of polished walnut. The maid has an aged mother to look after and has already gone home, leaving the food in the kitchen, so Clément serves, solicitous and attentive, apologetic about the inadequacies of the household, concerned that Marian is quite comfortable. He pours wine ceremoniously, standing at her right-hand side while she tastes. *Château La Mission Haut-Brion* is the name on the label. The wine is excellent, too excellent for her to be able to judge but of a quality out of all proportion to what they have to eat, which is plain and parsimonious – some scrawny chicken legs and a few potatoes.

Barely enough to eat, even if you take advantage of the black market, barely enough fuel to warm two rooms, barely enough of anything. 'This is what we're reduced to,' he observes, poking at the chicken with his fork. 'Great wines and starvation rations. It's ridiculous. Were it peacetime I would take you to the Tour d'Argent and have you eat oysters and *foie gras*.'

She laughs. They ate once in Paris together, that time with her father and Ned. It wasn't at the Tour d'Argent but in a small bistro in the rue des Grands-Augustins where Clément said artists and writers went; but they had seen no one of note. Does he remember?

Of course he does. 'Did you expect me to forget?'

'Things change, don't they?'

'Some things don't.' Outside it is raining hard; inside there is the warmth of this dangerous intimacy that bridges years and memories: a man who was once some kind of deity to her, and is now sitting beside her, his features eloquent and familiar, the blue eyes that seem a brilliant contrast to his black hair, the mobile femininity of his mouth, an expression that used to seem painfully sensitive and alluring and now appears amused and self-deprecating.

What about the family?

His father is in Algiers, playing politics. His mother is at the house in Annecy, with his wife and Madeleine.

And what is he doing?

He shrugs. 'What I have always done. Working at the Collège. Teaching. Trying to keep things as normal as possible. What else can one do?'

'Your research?'

'It continues as far as it's possible these days.' He smiles. 'I used to try and explain it to you, didn't I? Try to turn it into something intelligible to the ordinary person.'

'Is that what I was?'

He looks at her without smiling, as though trying to puzzle out the answer. 'You were much more than that.'

188

Does she blush? Perhaps it's the wine. 'Remember when we went up to Megève that time,' she says. 'To the chalet, just the four of us?'

'When Madeleine skied right over that hut ...'

'And landed in a snowdrift on the other side ...'

'And the door opened and someone came out and asked her what the hell she was doing, that this was private property and how would she like it if someone skied over *her* roof and landed in *her* garden?'

The memories circle round, like predators preparing for a kill. 'And sailing on the lake,' Marian says. 'Remember that? Ned was unwell and Madeleine stayed with him and so it was the two of us alone.'

He does remember that, of course he does. She can see it in his expression. He remembers pushing the boat out into the lake, the two of them wading out thigh-deep and then throwing themselves laughing over the gunwales. He remembers exactly.

'When was it?'

'You know perfectly well when it was. The summer of 1938.'

It was the kind of adventure where familiar places became unreal, pervaded with the strangeness of the whole hot summer's day, dazzled by the glare of sun on water. The two of them lean and brown and laughing. Barefoot and bare-legged. Pushing each other and mock-fighting and he grabbing her hands to stop her hitting him, their difference in age somehow telescoped so that she felt older than her years and he seemed younger. They brought the little boat ashore on a promontory where there were some reeds and a small inlet and a piece of beach. 'Where are we?' she asked, as though they might be lost.

'Who knows?' he said, helping her out of the dinghy, then keeping hold of her hand as they walked up the beach. She'd never held a man's hand before, except her father's and Ned's. Girlfriends', yes, of course. But never a man's. It seemed a gesture imbued with great significance: he likes me, she thought. He wouldn't hold my hand if he didn't like me.

189

*Like.* That equivocal word. More so in French. *Aimer.* The ambiguity of words struck her, their uncertainty and imprecision.

Behind the beach there was a small wood and the roof of a house hidden amid the foliage. They crept up to a garden wall and clambered on rocks to peer over onto lawns and flower beds and a weeping willow. Somewhere a dog barked but the house seemed deserted, its blind windows reflecting the sky and the mountains. Clément's arm was round her waist to steady her. She remembered that more than she remembered the garden. Clément's arm around her. And then his turning her to face him, his face so close that she could feel the warmth of his skin.

She sips her wine and tastes what he suggests she should find there – a hint of cigar, a touch of chocolate, a suggestion of cedar wood – looking at this man beside her whom she knows but doesn't know. 'It almost seems to have happened to other people.'

'Yet it was only a few years ago. Six.'

'Five. You'd come down from Paris and I was back home for the holidays ...' She catches his glance and holds it deliberately. 'I'd never been kissed before.'

'I hardly dared touch you. In case I frightened you.'

'I was only sixteen, Clément. The first time I'd been kissed like that. And embarrassed. God, how I was embarrassed!'

'You seemed older.' Suddenly, disarmingly, he grins. 'You *felt* older.'

She shakes her head, remembering how they climbed down and sat against the wall. He was kissing her and she had closed her eyes because that was what you did, that was what girls said when they discussed it – you close your eyes and let yourself go – and his hand was on her knee and she put her own hand over his. The ambiguity of gesture. Actions as equivocal as words. His hand, her hand, their two hands moved upwards inside her shorts where no one had ever touched her except

190

perhaps a doctor or her mother, where the hair blossomed and, to her intense shame, her flesh protruded like an insolent and vulgar pout. She felt embarrassed and ecstatic at one and the same time, wondering what he might do and what she wanted, neither of which seemed clear. 'I thought ... God knows what I thought,' she says. Unexpectedly she is almost in tears, mourning a distant child whom she vaguely remembers and hardly understands; and a man she loved. 'I thought you'd marry me. I thought I'd get pregnant. I thought you were the most wonderful thing in creation and I was the most despicable. You said – do you remember what you said to me? – one day, you said, one day I will love you properly.'

He watches her now. There is a strange vulnerability to his expression, as though something has been stripped away leaving the younger man exposed beneath. 'I adored you,' he says.

'You went back to Paris—'

'—you disappeared back to school in England—'

'You wrote me those letters. They were the things that kept me alive in that awful place. The bloody nuns used to read them, did you know that? Worse than censorship. Sister Benedict was the French teacher and she hated me because I spoke the language properly and she didn't. She had this dreadful English accent – if you can't hear the language, how on earth can you teach it? Anyway, I'd told them you were my uncle and at first they believed me—'

'You stopped writing.'

She shakes her head. 'That's the point. I didn't stop, but I thought *you* had. You see ...' And suddenly she is that child again, teeming with desire and indignation, her eyes smarting. 'Can you believe it, they confiscated your letters? They became suspicious about *Oncle* Clément and they confiscated your letters without telling me and I thought you'd given me up.' The moment of anguish has become real again, the child trapped in boarding school with no means of contacting the outside world. 'I was desperate, Clément. I wrote asking what had happened, begging you to write, pleading with you. I suppose the nuns simply didn't post them.'

'How very English.'

'How very Catholic. They contacted my parents to find out if you really were my uncle. Maybe it was something I wrote. Did they open my own letters? I've no idea. I begged you to write, and hated myself for doing so. I wrote things I shouldn't have. Maybe they read those too ...' She looks at him, tears battling with laughter. He reaches out and takes her hand and she feels that stirring within her, something undermining, as though the ground beneath her feet has shifted. 'But by then the invasion happened and suddenly you were entirely cut off anyway, with no hope of contact. It's a whole world ago and here I am getting all excited about it.' Carefully, as though it might break, she withdraws her hand from his. 'And now you're married, and a father. What's Augustine like? Tell me about her.'

'You were shocked, weren't you? To discover that I've got married.'

'It was a surprise.'

'You don't think I'm the marrying type?'

'That it could happen without my knowing. Without any of us knowing.'

'Word doesn't get round these days.'

'You haven't answered my question.'

'No, I haven't. Augustine's pretty and wifely and doesn't bother her head with tiresome things like science or scientists. Devoted to her child, like any mother, I suppose.' He smiles. She can't read his expression. Maybe she never was able to. 'Both our families approve. Which is quite surprising, really.'

'Why surprising?'

'Because she's a Jew.'

The word *juive* detonates in the close room, scattering her thoughts like debris. 'Is that why she left Paris?'

He nods. 'She went after the Vél' d'Hiv *rafle*. You know about that, don't you? Augustine wasn't affected by the round-up, of course. She was married to me, and anyway it was the foreign Jews they were after. But we thought it would be best for her and the baby to leave the occupied zone, and the obvious thing was to go to Annecy.'

'And she's safe now?'

He shrugs. 'Now the Italians have gone things have changed, but for the moment she's all right.'

'I'm sorry. It must be terrible to be separated like that.'

He mulls over her question, holding his glass by the stem and swirling the wine so that he can see the colour against the candle flame. When he answers it is carefully, as though he has measured his words. 'Things weren't altogether happy between us. I'm very fond of her, of course. But as with so many matters, the full story is complicated and appears different depending on how you look at it.'

'Like those particles you used to talk about.'

'You remember that, do you? If you know a particle's momentum, you cannot know its position.'

'And what is your position?'

He makes a wry face. 'Or my momentum? Which?'

She looks at him, sensing the danger that lies in shared laughter. Laughter drew them together five years ago, across the gulf of age and education. 'Your momentum was always your research.'

'At the cost of my marriage?'

'You tell me.'

He shrugs. 'The work goes on. With the Germans looking over our shoulders, of course. At the beginning they put Wolfgang Gentner in to supervise what we were doing. He was one of Fred's graduate students before the war, so one of us really. Thanks to him we got the cyclotron going. Did I ever tell you about the cyclotron?'

'I expect so.'

'Fred's pride and joy. The Germans wanted to ship it off to Heidelberg but Gentner insisted that it stay here in Paris.

Gentner was posted back to Germany and now we've got Riezler. He's a good man too.' He shrugs again, that damned Gallic shrug. 'They protect us, Marian. The Germans themselves protect us. They revere Fred and he charms the pants off them and we're all allowed to get on with our work.'

'That sounds like collaboration.'

'It's accommodation. It's what all Frenchmen do, one way or another. Keeping quiet. Turning a blind eye.'

'And that's your contribution to the liberation of France? Obscure research and a bit of Gallic charm? What'll you say when Rachel asks, "What did you do in the war, Daddy?" "Oh, I charmed the enemy and they left me alone."'

'I've not heard you being sarcastic before. It doesn't suit you.'

'There's quite a lot that doesn't suit me these days, but at least I know which side I'm on. You're supping with the devil, Clément – you need a very long spoon. The others in your lab escaped to England, didn't they?'

He frowned. 'You know about that?'

She answered without thinking: 'Ned told me.'

Clément raised his eyebrows. 'Ned told you, did he? Dear old Ned. I'll bet he's feeling smug, tucked up in his nice safe laboratory in England, isn't he? When did he tell you, I wonder? Before you left England for Switzerland?' He considers her, head slightly tilted to one side as though trying to get the measure of her. 'What are you really doing here, Marian?'

'Doing here? I told you, I've come to see this friend.'

'Ah, the mysterious friend. But whose friend is she? Is she Marian Sutro's friend? Or is she Anne-Marie Laroche's?'

There is a sudden stillness in the chilly room. An old portrait, pretending to be some bewigged and waistcoated ancestor, looks down on them with an expression that suggests he would have understood such things as *noms de plume* and *noms de guerre*. Maybe that was how he escaped the Revolution and the Terror.

'You've been going through my handbag.'

He shrugs once more, as though going through someone's handbag is the most natural thing in the world, which perhaps it is in this city of fear and suspicion. 'Marie wondered if you had a ration card, so I went to look. You were asleep and I didn't want to wake you. I told her that you didn't, which is true in a sense, because the only card I found belonged to a certain Anne-Marie Laroche. The same Anne-Marie Laroche who owns the identity card with your picture in it.'

How do you judge your response? How do you balance surprise with mild outrage and make your response convincing? There was no ready formula, nothing the schools could teach you, neither the A School with its assault course and unarmed combat, nor the B School with its clever deceptions and fake interrogations. None of those lessons can help you when you are exposed like this with an old friend who might have been your lover, and you've let your guard down and you have no idea how he feels or where his loyalties lie. She tries to meld indignation with self-righteousness. It's a difficult trick but one that she remembers from school, when caught out breaching one of the arcane rules that governed the convent. 'That's awful! Going through someone's things like a policeman. I was going to mention it when the moment arose. A friend got me the card. I was Marian Sutro when I came from Switzerland but a friend organised another card for me to make it easier. Because the name might seem Jewish, if you want to know. Thousands of people do that kind of thing for one reason or another. Half the country is illegal now, you know that as well as I do.'

Clément considers this idea thoughtfully, and finds it wanting. 'You've come from London, haven't you, Squirrel?' he says. 'How did you get here, I wonder? By plane, I expect. Did you land in a field somewhere, or did my brave Squirrel descend from the air by parachute?' He smiles, an adult humouring a child. 'The daring young girl on the flying trapeze.'

'Don't be ridiculous. And don't call me Squirrel.'

195

'Well, I can't really call you Marian, can I? What about Anne-Marie?'

Carefully – at least her hand is steady – she picks up her wine glass and sips. Can she trust him? Trust no one, they told her at Beaulieu, not even your best friend. But this is Clément, for God's sake – Clément, whom she loved with all the passion of a young girl; Clément, whose letters she waited for with breath held; Clément, the man for whom she first felt that strange emotion that can undermine a whole personality like a river eating away at the foundations of a building, or an earthquake shattering them: sexual desire.

'Yes,' she says as though admitting something shameful. 'I've come from London.'

She's at his mercy now. No cover, no bodyguard of lies. Naked and helpless, with him watching her carefully, like an interrogator who is able at his job, enticing the betrayal of secrets rather than trying to extract them by force. She recalls all the warnings and the play-acting that they did at Beaulieu, how different interrogators might behave, how to stand the glare of lights and the shouting and having your head plunged under water until you were gasping for life. But also the other technique, the quiet, insidious one which, drawing you into a world of compliance and sympathy, makes you share confidences and secrets with the interrogator whom you come, so the story goes, almost to love. But they never taught her how to deal with this.

'So why have you turned up here? Surely not just for old times' sake.'

It's like that game they played, the blind chess. *Kriegspiel.* Only now the barrier between the two players has come down and he can see her board with all its pieces. 'They want you in England, Clément.'

'Who do?'

'People that matter. Ned, of course. But more important than that, Professor Chadwick, Dr Kowarski—'

196

'Lev?'

'He says that the future of the French effort depends on it.'

'Who told you that?'

'Kowarski himself.'

'You've *met* him?'

'In Cambridge. Von Halban has gone to Canada and Kowarski is on his own in Cambridge. And he needs you to keep his group going. Otherwise ...'

'Otherwise what?'

'The Americans will be the only players in the game. That's what he told me.'

He shakes his head in denial or disbelief, it isn't clear which, as though in the course of an experiment he has been faced with some startling observation that goes against all that he has come to expect. The splitting of an atom, maybe. 'And what's your own role in all this, Marian? Are you the bait?'

'What on earth do you mean by that? I'm nothing more than the messenger.'

'A particularly attractive one.'

'Are you suggesting—'

'What do these people, whoever they are, actually *know* about us, Marian? I mean us two.'

She reddens, thinking of Fawley and the avuncular Peters, wondering herself how much they understood. 'They know we were friends.'

'That's a very careful use of the past tense.'

'We haven't seen each other for ages, Clément. Four years. Things have changed. For God's sake, you're married. Isn't that enough?'

'It's something, certainly. But if you'd kept writing, if this bloody war hadn't broken out—'

She shakes her head, as though trying to shake his words out of her ears. 'Clément, you've been drinking, I've been drinking. We mustn't say anything we'll regret in the morning.'

'Are you right? Maybe we *should* say the things now that

we'll regret later. Maybe that's the only way we'll be honest with one another. I'll start. Six years ago I fell in love with my friend's younger sister. She was far too young for me, but that doesn't change the fact. She seemed to feel the same for me, indeed on one occasion we came within a whisper of becoming lovers. And now she suddenly appears in front of me, matured into a rather frightening young woman, and do you know what?'

'I don't want to hear.'

'I find we still laugh at the same things.'

'I told you. We mustn't say anything we'll regret in the morning.'

'But how can we tell we'll regret them until we've said them?' He makes a wry face. 'That sounds like one of the more abstruse aspects of physics. Schrödinger's Cat, neither dead nor alive until—'

'You open the box.'

'You remember.'

'Of course I remember. But that's not why I'm here.' And as though to show how true that is she opens her handbag, takes out the key ring, unclips the Lapreche key and hands it to him.

He examines it curiously. 'The key to your heart?'

'The key to my presence here. There's a letter to you from Professor Chadwick himself. I'm told that makes it important.' She explains the trick, how he can open up a minuscule compartment and take out a microdot. It sounds like a parlour game. 'You'll need a microscope to read it. I presume you can find one easily enough.'

He holds the key exactly as she did, between thumb and forefinger, as though it is something delicate and precious. 'How very ingenious. It goes with the devious Anglo-Saxon mind. I'll read it with interest.' Then he laughs suddenly, and shakes his head in disbelief. 'Do you remember that game we used to play with Ned? Throwing a ball over your head and you trying to catch it?'

'Pig-in-the-middle.'

'We called it "collapsing the wave function".'

'I didn't understand what you were talking about.'

'Neither did we.' Still holding up the key and looking at her with that half amused, half puzzled expression he asks, 'Who's pig in the middle now, I wonder?'

There is no answer to that, really. It's uncertain, like one of his particles.

She lies in bed, awake. She can hear him moving around the flat: the closing of a door, the running of water, a booming in the ancient plumbing.

She remembers. The breathless excitement of returning home for the holidays, hoping that he would be back from Paris as he had promised in his letters. But all they had were a few snatched moments, fragments of time alone when the families were together, mere minutes when she could say things to him that were otherwise unutterable. 'A quantum particle can be in two places at once,' he explained, and she laughed at the stupidity of it all. '*I* can be in two places at once,' she retorted. 'I can be in the dormitory at school lying alone in my bed, and I can be in your arms at the same time.'

'He's only leading you on,' one of her school friends said when she told her about him. She knew that the friend was right but she also knew that she was wrong: it was possible to hold two contradictory ideas at one and the same time just as it was possible, so Clément claimed, for a particle to be in two contradictory states at the same moment. A wave and a particle both at the same time, something like that. She called her own condition Marian's Law of Superposition, and delighted at the idea of sharing it with him.

What collapses the wave function is discovery.

She listens to him walking along the corridor and pausing for a moment outside her door. Then he moves on, and she can hear the door to his own bedroom open and close and there are no further sounds within the apartment other than the shifts and creaking that a building makes as it cools in the night. But there are noises from outside – a car roaring down a nearby street; someone running along the road outside; a door slamming and someone shouting; and late at night she wakes from the fog of sleep to what she thinks must be distant gunfire.

V

Morning seems different. The threats of the day before have receded like a tide. They'll return just as surely but for the moment there is calm and quiet, with the rough sea a long way away. Outside, the grey drab of the previous day has been replaced by a sky of peerless blue, as soft as angora.

She gathers her things and creeps down the corridor to the bathroom to wash. Back in the sanctuary of her room she is half dressed and finishing her hair when there's a knock on the door.

'Come in.'

He wears an expression that she remembers, part contrition, part amusement. 'I've come to apologise,' he says. 'You were right.'

'Right?'

'About conversations that we'll regret in the morning.'

'We'd drunk too much.'

'Or maybe, not enough.'

She shrugs, continuing with the task in hand, conscious of his eyes on her, feeling the thrill of nakedness without the fact of it. 'I'm in a hurry and you're putting me off.'

'I'm only watching.'

'That's the trouble.'

'Where are you going?'

'To see this friend. I told you.'

'But you'll be back this afternoon, won't you? You're not going to run away again?'

'Again?'

'You ran off to school in England.'

'I wasn't running. I was sent.'

'You were sent here as well, weren't you?'

'I could have refused. It was my decision to come.'

'And you won't leave without telling me?'

'No.' The hair is fixed. She turns back to him. 'I'm an adult now, Clément, not your little girl.'

'I never thought of you as a little girl. You always seemed absurdly grown-up to me.' He comes into the room and kisses her chastely on the cheek. 'I'll see you when I get back from the lab. We'll do something. We can't stay cooped up in here. How about the theatre? I can get tickets.'

'The theatre?'

'What could be more Parisian than going to the theatre?'

The theatre seems dangerous, calling attention to oneself. 'Perhaps ...'

But she doesn't finish what she is saying, and he doesn't wait to hear it. 'That's all right then. I've got to go now but I'll try not to be late this afternoon.' He glances back before closing the door. 'Be careful, won't you? Paris is a dangerous place.'

She listens for the front door to slam. In the dining room Marie is in attendance, hovering over the table and the poor apology for breakfast – some grey bread and a yellow slime that isn't butter. But there is coffee, real coffee from the packet Alice has handed over. It isn't clear whether this gift has warmed Marie towards her. The woman watches her carefully, as though she expects her to steal the silver. 'Will Mademoiselle be in for dinner? Monsieur Clément gave me to understand ...'

'I'll be here for dinner, yes. I'll be here for a few days.'

'And you have no ration card?'

Alice looks helpless and makes her apologies, that she left it at home, that it was stupid of her. The woman sniffs. 'That makes my job all the more difficult.'

'I know it does. But I had to leave in a hurry. This girlfriend of mine I've got to see ...' She leaves the rest unsaid but implied: nameless female troubles – a lover, perhaps, or maybe even an errant husband; or pregnancy, unwanted and unexpected. 'I know Monsieur Clément would never accept it, but if some money would help ...'

The maid doesn't flinch. 'That wouldn't be right, would it? You're our guest.'

'But you might be able to get some things on the black market. Some real butter, maybe. Monsieur Clément need never know.'

'I expect you get butter in the country, don't you?'

'Some, yes we do. The farmers keep some back, and if you know the right people ...'

The woman nods. 'My cousin farms in Normandy. We get stuff from him but it's more and more difficult these days.'

The nod seals the matter. The handing over of money takes place with all the discretion of an illegal street-corner transaction, as though even here the police may be watching.

From the moment she steps out of the house she assumes she is being followed. Always assume the worst, one of the instructors warned them: a pessimist makes the best agent. Around the Sorbonne she mingles with students going to lectures, walking into one of the great courts and out by a different exit to see if she can tease a follower out of the crowd. In the rue Saint-Jacques she gazes into shop windows and scans the reflection of the other side of the street, looking for loiterers, looking for anyone who might be looking for her. At the *métro* station on the boulevard Saint-Germain she descends the stairs on one side of the street and emerges on the other, watching for anyone doing the same. No one follows. She is clear and clean, a bright, free woman alone in this anxious city. She makes her way back to the *métro* and pushes among the crowd on the platform to get onto a westbound train. At Odéon she changes to the line that goes under the Seine, going north beneath the city, away from Clément, away from Marian Sutro.

Yvette's address is a block of flats near the cemetery in the twentieth, a grimy, four-storey building with a mansard roof and decaying mouldings on the façade, the kind of place that has come down in the world ever since the plans of Haussmann first put it there. Alice walks straight past the building, looking. There is a *clochard* going through bins; a couple sitting in the window of the café directly across the street; young lovers who stand there debating some issue with typical Parisian intensity; a woman walking her dog; a newspaper seller with copies of *Le Matin* and *Les Nouveaux Temps*. Further down is a street market with a few threadbare stalls selling old clothes and bits of hardware – sewing-machine parts, sections of plumbing, pots and pans, anything that might be of use in a world where everything is reused and nothing is new. People are rummaging through the junk. She turns over a few old sweaters and glances back at the building.

'You'd look lovely in that one, dearie,' the stallholder says.

Alice smiles and considers the possibility of purchase before putting the thing down and walking on up the hill towards the cemetery. People are coming and going through the gates, some with misery etched into their faces. At a stall nearby she stops to buy flowers, a meagre clutch of anemones, to give herself some kind of alibi before going in through the gates. She walks purposefully down one of the lanes between ornate epitaphs and pious weeping angels and finds a bare sepulchre on which to deposit her flowers. The inscription says *Jules Auvergne, poète*. She has never heard of him. Do flowers to the unknown dead from the unknown living have any significance in the afterlife? She returns the way she has come, back past the street market to the opposite side of Yvette's building, watching the people in the street, trying to make an assessment, trying to answer the one question that has to be answered: is Yvette's apartment under surveillance?

At a window seat in the café across the street she sips coffee and reads her book. Time passes. At the next table two girls are discussing a boy in low and urgent voices. He's a bastard, apparently, *un salaud* who is going with two different girls at the same time. Should they tell the victims? The debate goes on without ever reaching a conclusion. Beyond the window the scene shifts in that casual, contingent way of the street: women meeting and talking, complaining; people coming and going at the market stalls. In an *impasse* on the opposite side of the street children are playing tag, three girls and a younger boy, quite oblivious to the world around them. *Chat!* they call and scatter across the *pavé* away from whoever is 'it'. Whenever the door to Yvette's apartment block opens whoever comes out has to manoeuvre through the game. It isn't until half past ten that the figure stepping through the door is Yvette herself. Suddenly she is there, scurrying out into the daylight, wearing a drab brown dress with a fawn gilet thrown over her shoulders. She hurries past the children and disappears up the *impasse*.

Alice calls for the bill. There's no need to rush, she tells herself. The mouse will return to its nest. And sure enough, a few minutes later, clutching a brown paper bag to her chest, Yvette reappears.

Leaving change on the table, Alice grabs her bag and goes out. Across the street Yvette is searching in her bag, then fiddling a key into the lock. Trying not to hurry, Alice reaches the entrance to the building just in time to block the door and push her way inside. Counterweighted by some kind of pulley system, the door slams shut behind her. The hallway is gloomy, illuminated by a dusty fanlight. There are two bicycles propped under the stairs and a battered pram. Yvette is already climbing the stairs, barely glancing at the stranger who has followed her in.

'Hey!' Alice says. 'It's me.'

Yvette grabs the banister and looks round. Even in the shadows Alice can see fear in her wide eyes. 'Who's that?'

'Can we talk?' Alice asks.

Recognition dawns. 'What are you doing here? Go away. I don't want to see you.'

Alice climbs the stairs towards the woman. Outside there are the cries of the children playing, silly, quotidian sounds. Inside, this sudden, unexpected meeting of shadows. 'I've come to see how things are going.'

'You can't come here.'

'Are you on your own?'

'I'm going.'

She turns to climb the stairs. Alice grabs her arm, her fingers locking round the fragile elbow. 'Let's talk. There's no one around. Let's talk here. Like old friends. Who are you these days? I'm Anne-Marie Laroche. Who are you?'

'Yvette,' the woman answers dully. 'Just Yvette.'

'Can we go upstairs? Are you on your own?'

Yvette shrugs. 'Of course I'm on my own. That's it, isn't it? We're all of us on our own.'

'You're not on your own now.'

The woman stands there. It isn't even clear if she is pondering the matter. Then, as though surrendering to the inevitable, she shrugs and goes on up, with Alice following.

Yvette has done well in the choice of flat: it is a typical pianist's apartment right at the top of the building, with sloping ceilings and mansard windows giving out onto a parapet where you can deploy an aerial. Outside the windows, pigeons scratch and scrape on the tiles. The sound of their beating wings is like hands being clapped. In the distance Alice can see the domes of the Sacré-Coeur. Once she loved the building, but Clément had told her it was hideous so now it seems exactly that: hideous, a whited sepulchre.

'I knew they'd come to get me,' Yvette says. 'I just didn't guess it'd be you.' She's making coffee at a paraffin cooker in one corner of the room, the precious coffee that Alice brought.

All the time she looks round, not specifically at Alice but over her shoulder, like an animal on the watch for predators. The scent of coffee mingles with the stench of paraffin.

'I haven't come to get you, Yvette. I've come to help.'

'I don't need help.'

'You went off the air. They thought your set might have a fault. I've brought crystals for you—'

'I don't need fucking crystals. I don't need anything.'

'What's happened, Yvette? What's happened to your circuit? CINÉASTE, isn't it?'

'How do you know that?'

'It was in the signal from London.'

'They sent you specially?'

'I was already in the country. They didn't know what had happened when you went off the air. Tell me what happened, Yvette. To CINÉASTE.'

'They were blown. They were all meeting in a café—'

'We were told not to do that.'

'But that's what happens, isn't it? That's what people actually *do*, whatever they said in training. What the hell do they know? Anyway, I was late. The *métro* broke down or something. So I got there just in time—'

'In time for what?'

'Not to get caught. To see it happen. They knew. The *Frisés*, I mean. They *knew* about the meeting. Someone must have betrayed us. I watched from down the street. There were dozens of them. Soldiers and police. They surrounded the place and grabbed them all and took them away.'

'What did you do?'

Yvette brings the coffee over. 'I laid low. What else could I do?'

'And no one came for you?'

'Nobody. They didn't know this address, see. I'd only just found it. You know, moving around, what you're meant to do.'

'So how did London know?'

She shrugs, as though such matters are of no consequence. 'My final sked, I suppose. I thought they might help me, so I told them about the circuit, and gave this address and then I realised they couldn't do anything for me at all, that I was on my own, that as far as they were concerned I could go and fuck myself. So I cut the transmission. The city is crawling with detector vans. If you're on for more than a minute or two they can get a fix on you and then you're in the shit.'

'Don't you have other places to transmit from?'

'They've all been blown, haven't they? They got Emile, you know that?'

'*Emile?*'

'He'd only arrived a week earlier. A Lysander ...'

'But when I last saw him he was waiting for a drop.'

'He refused to jump. At the last minute, he refused to leave the aircraft—'

'He *refused?*'

'They had to take him all the way back, and the next time they had to get him in by Lysander.'

'He told you this? Surely he wouldn't have admitted it.'

Again she shrugs, looking suddenly embarrassed. 'He told me. He's not like we used to think.' She sips her coffee, holding the cup in both hands for comfort, looking up at Alice with fear and confusion.

'We need to get you out of here,' Alice tells her. 'We need to get you home, back to safety, back to little Violette.'

It's the mention of her daughter that does it. For a moment Yvette's face hesitates, as though it can't make up its mind what expression to adopt. And then suddenly it breaks up like a paper mask dissolving in the rain, the features crumpling, the whole losing its coherence and becoming something else, a mere assembly of ruined features. She sits with her head bowed, convulsed with sobs and apologising for not being up to it. That's what she has always done: apologise for her failures. 'I'm frightened,' she says through the mess of tears. 'I never thought I would be, but I'm frightened. I'm frightened of what they might do to me and frightened of what I might tell them. I'm frightened. And I'm frightened of what might happen to Violette if I don't survive.'

Alice puts her arm round her shoulders. 'Violette's safe, you don't have to worry about that. And we'll sort you out. We'll get a pick-up. How can I get a message to you without coming here?'

'What's wrong with here?'

'You know it's better to have a cut-out. What about the café across the street? Can I leave a message there?'

'I suppose so. I go in occasionally. The owner's a fat guy called Boger. You can leave something with him.'

'Go in regularly to check. Have you still got your wireless?'

Yvette nods. 'It's under my bed. I wanted to get rid of it but I didn't know how.' Her eyes widen. 'You're not going to use it ... for the love of God, I've told you, it's not safe!'

'I'll get rid of it for you. I'll take it.'

'That's dangerous, going out on the street with that thing.'

'It'll be all right. Everyone in Paris is carrying a suitcase these days.'

Yvette attempts a laugh. 'They haven't all got a B2 transceiver in it.' It isn't a bad effort, considering the tears. Alice encourages her. 'You know I brought spare crystals for you? Stuffed up my fanny.'

'Your fanny?'

The idea seems hilarious. They shriek with laughter, a laughter that borders on hysteria. And then the mood veers dangerously, like a vehicle out of control. 'And there's this,' Yvette says, opening a drawer in the table and taking out a bundle of cloth. It's like a conjuring trick: one moment a bundle of grimy cloth, the next moment there is a pistol lying in her narrow hand – a Browning nine millimetre semi-automatic.

'Jesus Christ, Yvette. What are you doing with that?'

'It's standard for a pianist. You can't pretend you're doing anything innocent, can you? So you may as well be armed.'

Alice takes the weapon from her. She is immediately familiar with it, that is the disturbing thing. All those hours spent at Meoble Lodge on weapons training. The different types. More models than a soldier would see in a lifetime. She points the pistol at the floor, flips out the magazine, works the slide back and forth a few times, pulls the trigger and listens for the empty snap of the firing mechanism. 'Ammunition?'

Yvette produces a loaded clip and a box with a dozen rounds in it. 'Take it.' She pushes everything across the table. 'Take the shitty thing away.'


## VI


Alice crosses the city, humping the suitcase. It's a battered, leather-bound thing with a few old hotel labels stuck on it and a handle repaired with tightly whipped twine. She hates it for being dull and ugly and as dangerous as a bomb. It sits on the floor of the *métro* car by her feet where any policeman or soldier might ask her to open it, and that would be enough to detonate the thing.

At Réaumur-Sébastopol she has to change trains, lugging the hateful object through the tunnels where her footsteps echo against the tiled walls. There are others going the same way and she tries not to catch their eyes, tries not to be noticed. 'Let me help you,' a fellow passenger suggests, drawing alongside her and putting his hand down to take the handle. She pulls the case away from him and attempts not to look. But even out of the corner of her eye she can recognise that grey-green uniform, those black and silver flashes plainly enough. A major in the Wehrmacht. 'I'm quite all right, thank you.'

'As you wish.' His French seems good, his manner quiet and courteous. He follows her to the platform and waits beside her as the train draws in. 'Are you going to Montparnasse station?'

'No.'

He glances down. 'The suitcase has become an emblem of our times, hasn't it? So many people have their lives in a suitcase. Regrettably.'

She shrugs, ignoring his question and praying for the train to come. When it draws in the officer follows her into the car and finds a seat opposite. He has a faint smile on his lips, as though he knows her secret. 'Let me guess ...' he says. The train moves away from the platform. Other passengers look away. '... You are not going to the railway station, so you are not travelling. So you are visiting. That's right! You are visiting your aged aunt who lives all by herself in Montparnasse.'

It's about one minute between stations, on average. She has six stops. Allow time for people to get on and off, what does that make it? She tries to do the mathematics in her head while the smiling officer attempts to guess the reason for her journey.

'Or perhaps your boyfriend. You are travelling to see your boyfriend who is one of those left bank intellectuals of whom your family disapproves. A poet, maybe. Or a philosopher.'

'Leave her alone,' a woman says.

'I'm sorry, Madame?'

'I said, leave her alone.' The speaker is a dowdy, middle-aged woman in grey. Her face is grey, her manner is grey but she is the one who is willing to speak out in defence of a young girl. 'Politeness is politeness, whatever uniform you are wearing.'

The major seems nonplussed. 'I'm sorry.' He inclines his head towards the woman and, across the car, towards Alice. 'I apologise if I have offended you. I only wanted to make polite conversation.'

'Politeness is not trying to make conversation with strangers what want to be left alone,' the woman observes, nodding as though to emphasise her point. Alice smiles thankfully in her direction. Embarrassed, the major looks at other things, the passengers crowding on at the stops, the notices posted above the seats, the blackness beyond the windows.

As the train slows for Saint-Michel, Alice gets up and moves to the door. The major follows, standing mere inches from her, waiting for the car to stop and the doors to open. When she steps down, so does he. She walks on, trying to ignore his presence but there is a crowd building up at the foot of the stairs and the officer catches up with her. They edge forwards. Something is blocking the exit above, slowing the crowd. *Rafle*, someone says. The word goes round. *Rafle*. Round-up. At the top of the stairs there is daylight visible, and she can see uniforms, people pushing and shoving, the general disturbance of men and women looking for their papers, opening their bags. A German voice calls out something in French. People mutter and curse. She grips the suitcase. Perhaps she can dump it. Perhaps she can turn back round and wait for the next train. The crowd presses round her. Panic rises, a tide of sweat and heartbeat, a strange ringing in her ears.

'Please,' says the major at her shoulder. 'We cannot wait for this nonsense. Allow me to help you, Mam'selle.' His hand is on hers, easing the suitcase from her grasp.

She lets the thing go, surrenders the bomb that could kill her in an instant. Panic tells her to let him go, to turn round and try to escape through the station. She'd be away before he gets to look inside the case. She'd be free and away. But panic is the worst advisor. Panic can kill. She follows him upwards, pushing up the stairs in his wake. Someone in the crowd calls out, 'Fucking tart.'

She reaches the top. German soldiers and French police are going through papers, going through pockets, going through bags. Maybe they are looking for somebody, or maybe it's no more than one of those random events, the nagging inconvenience of occupation. The major is talking to one of the soldiers. 'I can vouch for the *Fraülein*,' he says. 'She's with me.' The soldier turns and beckons her through. She goes past the *barrage* and onto the sanctuary of the pavement where the fresh air is cool on her face. Corralled to one side is a group of men and women wearing the yellow star. Beyond, two lorries are parked with people being pushed on board. But no one is interested in her. The panic subsides, leaving a debris of racing pulse and weak knees and sweat.

The major hands her the suitcase. 'I'm afraid I have an appointment. Otherwise I would accompany you.'

She takes the thing from him. 'That's all right. It's not very heavy.'

'But you don't look well. Rather pale.'

'It was all those people ...'

'Perhaps ...' Perhaps what? He's a good-looking man, a thoughtful-looking man, a man who would make someone a good lover, a good husband, a good father. 'Perhaps a coffee? I have a few minutes.'

'I'm afraid I can't.'

'Or maybe we could meet up for a drink later?'

'I have a boyfriend, you see.'

'I wasn't suggesting anything—'

'People would misunderstand, wouldn't they?'

He nods, looking crestfallen. 'I suppose they would.'

She attempts a smile and turns and walks away, past the entrance to the *métro*, past the people trickling through the *barrage*. All the time she knows that his eyes are on her.

The suitcase takes on a personality of its own. It lies there in her room, hidden under the bed, waiting. She knows it is there, Marie knows it is there – impossible to disguise the fact of it as she stood at the door of the apartment waiting to be let in. Clément will have to be told it is there. A suitcase. She doesn't know exactly what to do with it, or exactly what to do with Clément. She doesn't know what to do at all. All she knows are the abstract facts – she has to arrange a pick-up; she has to get Yvette back to England; she has to persuade Clément that he should do the same.

## VII

'A Wehrmacht officer tried to chat me up on the *métro*,' she tells him.

'I'm not surprised. I'd try and chat you up on the *métro*.'

'You're married.'

'I expect he was.'

She laughs. She doesn't want to feel at ease like this. She wants to feel anxiety, caution, the wariness that has been drummed into her. But she feels only an absurd and childlike happiness in his presence. And safe – she feels safe. The most dangerous illusion of all.

As promised, he has got tickets for something, a play at the Théâtre de la Cité. It starts early – performances always start early these days, so you can get home before the curfew – and they can easily walk. Does she want to do that?

'I really want to know if you managed to read the letter.'

He shrugs, as though the matter is of little consequence. 'Yes, I did. I went to the workshops in the basement of the Collège and borrowed a file. In order to adjust a key that didn't quite fit, that was my story. The difficulty was persuading the technician that I could manage without his help. And then I had to make up some damn fool excuse to borrow a microscope from the biology lab.'

'And the letter?'

'It's not that easy to keep track of a full stop. I was frightened I'd sneeze or something.' He's teasing her. As he always has. Mockery that is like a secret caress, disturbing and thrilling at the same time.

'But you succeeded?'

'Yes, I did. Very ingenious. Some kind of photographic reduction process ...'

'Never mind all that. What did it *say*?'

'It was most flattering. Flattery from Professor Chadwick is a rare commodity. He was interned in Germany during the last war, did you know that? He knows Germany and German science like the back of his hand. A dangerous enemy. Churchill blusters and calls them the Hun, but Chadwick *knows* them. The question is, do I fall for his flattery?'

'It's not flattery, Clément. For God's sake, they *want* you.'

'But who is it who wants me, and what for?' He laughs and glances at his watch. 'If we don't get a move on we'll be late for the theatre.'

They go out, strolling arm in arm and keeping step with each other as though they are practised at walking together. Her initial fears dissolve in the sunlight of the evening. The city has managed to work some magic at last and deliver a fair imitation of its old self, the Paris before the war. The plane trees in the boulevard Saint-Michel are shedding leaves of gold and red as though nothing has happened out of the ordinary and there has been no war, no invasion, no occupation. Near the Lycée Saint-Louis they pass a café where students congregate, young men with long hair, girls with short skirts and brightly coloured stockings. One of the boys calls out, '*Bonsoir prof!*' and gives him a thumbs-up. Another voice exclaims, '*Quelle bonne gonzesse.*' Laughter follows them down the street.

'*Zazous,*' Clément says. 'The police round them up and cut their hair. Throw them in jail sometimes. The authorities understand how to deal with political dissent. That's easy. But these kids aren't political and that confuses them.'

At the river she pauses and looks. This is where she strolled with him that spring day in 1939 with Ned and her father. The strange contingency of events strikes her: how distant this place is from that sunny afternoon. Within the rigid matrix of three dimensions it appears to be the same: there is the Pont Saint-Michel; there the buttresses and towers of Notre Dame, painted gold in the setting sun; ahead the steep roofs of the Palais de Justice. But it is a different place entirely when the fourth dimension of time is sprung from its shackles. The naive girl in a bright summer frock is there no longer. She no longer walks along the *quai* holding his hand and trying not to skip like a child. She no longer blushes at his compliments. She is a woman now, dressed in grey like the city itself, half a decade and a whole world away. And now she knows that the man beside her was, on that distant summer day, edging his way through the intricacies of nuclear physics towards the possibility of an atomic bomb.

She asks, 'Why didn't you leave France in 1940 when the others did, Clément?'

He doesn't answer immediately, as though surprised by the question. 'I thought I ought to see things through,' he says eventually. 'This is where I belong. Not like Kowarski or von Halban. Not like you. France is all that I have, for better or worse.'

'I love France too.'

'It's nothing to do with love. More mundane than that. More like habit. And something else, a sense of honour, perhaps. Does that sound very pompous?'

'Rather.'

'Obligation. Try that. I'm not proud of what's happened. Almost no one is. But I feel I can't shrug off responsibility.'

'And running away to England would be doing that?'

'Perhaps it would.'

'Or maybe it would be shouldering responsibility.'

He laughs. 'You always were a determined arguer, even when you didn't know what you were talking about.'

They cross the bridge and walk past the Palais de Justice. Swastika banners hang down the front of the building, the colours of sealing wax and boot polish. German soldiers mount guard, apparently indifferent to anyone who passes by; yet still she feels vulnerable, a mouse crossing a field with the hawks hovering overhead. It's a relief to gain the right bank of the river and find Parisians in the place du Châtelet, crowds in the cafés, a scattering of theatregoers around the entrance of the theatre, even though there are some grey-green uniforms among the people shuffling in through the doors to the foyer. Posters announce the play – *Les Mouches*. The playwright is the latest sensation in the literary world of the city, a teacher of philosophy who has one novel and a collection of short stories to his name. 'The novel's called *La Nausée*,' Clément tells her, and she laughs. 'Nausea? Why stop at mere nausea? Why not "vomit"?' But the idea doesn't seem very funny, and neither does the play, which turns out to be a reworking of the myth of Orestes and Electra, an astringent mix of ritual and violence in which the protagonist demonstrates his freedom from the gods by committing murder, and the Furies buzz around the cast like flies around a pile of excrement. The strange dynamic of the piece finds echoes in the half-empty streets of the city, in the sudden raids and the meaningless arrests, in the collusion of the inhabitants and the defiance of a few misfits. '*Pardonnez-nous de vivre alors que vous êtes morts*,' the chorus repeats, and there's an outcry of approval from some people in the half-empty auditorium. Forgive us for being alive when you are dead.

They get back to the flat by nine, having argued about the play on the way back. It was about the occupation and the resistance. It wasn't. It showed how the French people should strive towards the condition of freedom. It showed only how violence could be seen to be heroic. 'And the sets!' she cries, amid laughter. 'And those ridiculous masks!'

Marie has left food for them in the kitchen. They are like students in a shared flat, living on short commons and from hand to mouth. Only the wine remains of high quality. He raises his glass to her, but exactly what he is drinking to isn't clear. A stray hair has come adrift from her chignon and he reaches across to push it behind her ear. She recognises the gesture, feels it in a way she cannot control – more fundamental than a mere

216

emotion, something organic welling up inside her that manifests itself only in trivial things – a quickening of the heart, a flush at the neck, a deepening of her breathing. 'So where do we go from here, Squirrel?' he asks.

'We go nowhere, Clément. I didn't come here to be your mistress. I'm here for one thing only, to get you back to England. All you have to do is make your choice. Can't we at least agree that that is what the damned play was all about? Making a choice?'

He laughs and turns to his food. 'You don't let up, do you? You ought to become a lawyer when this whole mess is over. You'd never let the witness off the hook.'

'I've got a job to do. It's as simple as that. I need to know.'

He pauses, as though trying to construct some kind of answer. 'There's a story going round the lab,' he says eventually. 'A rumour really, but that's all we live on these days – rumour and speculation. It's about Bohr. You know Bohr? I used to talk about him a lot. Niels Bohr, the Danish physicist, the most important man since Einstein.'

Of course she remembers. Bohr was everything that Clément admired – the patient genius who proposed startling ideas while all around were scratching their heads and not knowing what to do, the man who started revolutions and gave a fatherly hand to his followers who struggled in his wake. If I could be any other person than myself, he once confessed, I would be Niels Bohr. The idea seemed absurd. How could one wish to be a person that one was not? And yet here she is, Anne-Marie Laroche; a person whom she is not.

'Ever since the outbreak of war Bohr has been there in Copenhagen like Fred is here in Paris, living quietly and getting on with his own research despite the occupation. But at the end of last month he disappeared from his home and reappeared in Sweden. And now there's a rumour that he's gone to England. Bohr's an outspoken pacifist. He could easily have stayed in Sweden and appealed to the nations of the world to come together in peace and harmony, and yet apparently he has gone to England.'

'What are you trying to say?'

'They seem to be collecting physicists. Consider who they've already got: Chadwick, of course and Cockcroft, and a few lesser types like Oliphant and Feather. But above all there are the Jews who escaped before the war.' He counts them off on his fingers. 'Frisch, Szilárd, Peierls, Franz Simon, a dozen others. And then there's Perrin, von Halban and Kowarski from the Collège. Fermi is already in the US and so is Bruno Pontecorvo, who worked here under Fred a few years ago, and Teller and some others. And now they've got Bohr.' He looks at her. 'If you see most of the grand masters in the world getting together, you've got a pretty good idea there's about to be a game of chess.'

'*Kriegspiel*, perhaps.'

'Perhaps literally.' He toys with his food for a while. 'Do you have any idea what I'm talking about?'

Is this the moment to tell him? She hesitates no more than an instant. 'Yes, I do, Clément. I know exactly what's going on. Ned told me.'

His expression barely falters. 'What did he say?'

'He said it was obvious, that most of the relevant information was published before the war and that anyone could work it out.' She feels the need to defend her brother, as though by telling her he might have been guilty of some heinous crime. 'I blackmailed him into telling me, really. I took advantage of his position, accused him of putting his work before his family, that kind of thing. I even accused him of being a coward, which was unfair considering how hard he's been trying to give up his research and get into the army.'

'And he told you what?'

'He never said it directly. He only explained how it might be possible. To make a bomb.'

There is a great stillness. Only the bare, functional kitchen

218

around them, the tiled range, the sinks, the draining boards and windows now draped with blackout curtains. The voltage of the electricity supply is low and the light bulbs glow like dull anger.

'He told you that?'

'They might be, he said they *might* be. Making an atomic bomb. He told me that all the necessary information had been published shortly before the outbreak of war, that you could work it out from that if you bothered to read the papers.'

He looks around as though searching for a way out. But they are in an *impasse*. 'Is Ned involved? Directly, I mean. Is he working on this?'

'Not directly, no. I don't believe so, at any rate.' For a moment she hesitates, looking at him for some kind of reassurance. 'Is it a possibility, Clément?'

He nods. 'Oh, yes, it's possible. Most certainly, it's possible.' He gets up and walks over to the window, draws the blackout curtain aside and peers into the courtyard of the building, as though perhaps there are people out there looking up at them.

'I heard Ned talk about heavy water. What is it? It sounds ridiculous. Heavy water and light air. Some scientific fantasy.'

He pulls the curtain back and makes sure not a crack of light escapes. 'It's a form of water that can be used to encourage fission. It was Kowarski's pet project. He and von Halban took our entire supply with them when they escaped from Bordeaux, one hundred and eighty-six litres of the stuff, all from Norway. The world's total supply, in fact. We smuggled it into France during the spring of 1940 but we barely had time to start any experiments before we had to get it out.'

'In case the Germans got hold of it?'

'Exactly.'

'The whole thing was started in Germany, wasn't it? Ned talked about Hahn.'

He sits back down at the table. 'Hahn and Strassmann started it, yes – when they did their first work on fission. At the Kaiser

Wilhelm Institute in Berlin. But Irène and Pavel Savitch did the same work here, at the Radium Institute.'

'But if the Germans started it, they could equally well finish it, couldn't they?'

He shrugs. 'I don't know. They've got the men – Hahn, Diebner, Weizsäcker, Heisenberg, above all Heisenberg. They have a group called the *Uranverein*, the Uranium Club. Gentner let it slip in a conversation when he was here. Fred and I assumed ...'

'What did you assume?'

'That they were trying to generate power from the process. Gentner mentioned a *Uranmaschine*, a uranium machine, a kind of nuclear generator that would be able to sustain a controlled chain reaction, giving unlimited energy. It's quite a realistic possibility. Easier than a bomb. That's what the heavy water is for, as a moderator—'

'But they *could* be making a bomb?'

'Possibly. They've got the resources. Czechoslovakia is a good source of uranium, and Norway for heavy water. The difficulty as I see it is getting enough of the right uranium isotope. It's very rare.' He opens his hands helplessly, as though things he has been holding safe have just been scattered all over the floor. 'I shouldn't be telling you this, Marian.'

'But you are.' She casts around for something further to say, anger bubbling up inside her, a lava of hot fury. 'It's Pandora's Box, isn't it? You scientists open it up to see what's inside and all the ills of the world fly out. And once they're out, no one can put them back.'

Clément laughs at her indignation, but it is a laugh without much humour. 'I suppose you're right, more or less.'

'Ned said it would wipe out an entire city. In an instant.'

Clément nods. It's the matter-of-fact gesture that's so frightening. 'My estimate is that the whole of the centre of a city like Paris would be totally destroyed by just one such bomb; as far out as, say, Montmartre in the north and Montparnasse in the south. I mean exactly that – no building left standing. Beyond that it would be the same destruction as an ordinary bombing raid for, what? a further three or four kilometres. Within the inner area everyone would be killed. Outside that a few might survive, only to die days later from the effects of radiation. The question is' – he looks across the table at her – 'how can you expect me to get involved with something like that?'

For a moment his guard is down. Bewilderment makes a child of him. Suddenly she feels older than he, as old as her parents, older than her parents, wiser and sadder than anyone could possibly be. 'A few weeks ago they raided Hamburg,' she tells him. 'Maybe you heard about it. They used ordinary bombs, of course, and they laid waste seven square miles of the city, killing fifty-eight thousand people in the process. Not a few hundred, not even a few thousand. *Fifty-eight thousand*. What particular moral equation do you fit those figures into, Clément? You're good with equations – your wave mechanics, or whatever you call it. How do these figures fit in? The problem with this war, Clément, is that there are no innocents. You can't stand aside and say it wasn't your fault. It's everyone's fault. At this very moment people are being killed on your behalf. You can't say you didn't want it to happen because it *is* happening. Now. And it seems likely a single one of your atomic bombs dropped on Berlin would stop the war in an instant.'

'Would that make it right?'

'When it was all over we'd be free to have an anguished discussion about the morality of it all. Now, if you'll excuse me, I'm going to bed.'

She climbs into her cold bed and waits motionless for her body to bring warmth to the sheets. She thinks of Marian Sutro, a person she has been and, perhaps, will be again; a girl possessed of childlike enthusiasms and the capacity for devotion. Where is Marian now? She thinks of Clément beside the lake at Annecy, and Benoît in London, and Scotland, and here in France. She remembers being in the cinema, with Benoît's arm around her shoulders and that Pathé newsreel – *Hamburg Hammered* – on the screen. Bombers roaring through the night, with a city of glowing embers in the blackness below them. In the Filter Room she plotted raids going out, the RDF operator whispering in her ear: 'New track: Victor Oboe, fife-one, eighter-three, ten plus at five, showing IFF,' while she reached across the table and placed counters on the table where East Anglia bulged into the North Sea, single aircraft growing to dozens, dozens to hundreds, squadrons climbing into a darkening sky and merging into a great stream in their advance towards the Dutch coast, five thousand men setting off into the night. The four o'clock watch used to count them out and the midnight watch would try to count them in as they crept back over the North Sea, battered, shot up, empty of bombs, empty of fuel, empty, finally, of the fear that must have possessed them throughout the hours of the raid. How many dead? And on the ground, how many?

Fifty-five thousand in Hamburg alone.

Or was it fifty-eight? You could lose three thousand people in a mere slip of the memory.

The bear laughs at her out of her dreams. *It means the end of the war; maybe the end of the world.*

## VIII

The café is a short walk from the river in the rue Saint-André des Arts. As she opens the door a bell tinkles somewhere in the back and the man at the bar looks up from wiping glasses. The place is undistinguished inside – brown wooden panelling; some photographs on the wall, scenes of a Paris from before the First War; a poster for *Byrrh*, a chalk board with the word *Menu* but nothing else written on it. She sits at a corner table and orders a coffee. When the barman brings it over she says, 'I'd like to speak to *la patronne*. Is she around?'

He looks her over thoughtfully. 'She may be.'

'Tell her that my aunt in Marseilles sent me.'

The man sniffs, as though there is something implausible about aunts of any kind but especially aunts from Marseilles. Behind the bar he talks on the phone for a few moments. 'You'll have to wait,' he says as he puts the receiver down.

She nurses her coffee. The barman reads a newspaper, the latest edition of *La Gerbe*, running the headline *Le Maréchal Parle à la Nation*. A few people pass by outside; one or two peer in. She stares out into the street and wonders. She wonders about Yvette and she wonders about Clément. In the South-west there was little time to wonder, but here in the city it is different: you have to wait, and waiting brings thoughts and concerns and anxiety. In peacetime the countryside was still and the city a hive of activity; in wartime the circumstances are reversed.

'How long?'

'How long what?'

'Will I have to wait?'

The barman shrugs. 'It all depends.'

*La patronne* arrives half an hour later. She is a middle-aged woman with the relics of beauty in her face and a faint air of concern in her expression, as though she has mislaid something but isn't quite sure what. 'My Aunt Régine in Marseilles sent me,' Alice explains.

The woman purses her lips. 'I haven't heard from her for ages. How's her rheumatism?'

'It only plays up when there's the sirocco. Otherwise she's fine.'

She nods. 'You'd better come round the back.'

Behind the bar is a small room that is part storeroom, part kitchen. There's the ubiquitous picture of Marshal Pétain on the wall and another of Maurice Chevalier. A wall calendar advertises Peugeot bicycles. The woman pulls out a chair and then stands watching as Alice sits, as though this is some kind of interrogation. This isn't how it was meant to go. There was meant to be something more, a sense of welcome, some hint of camaraderie, of shared fear and shared determination. Alice glances back to the doorway. She can see the barman's back blocking any exit.

'I'm Alice,' she says.

'Claire.'

'They told me to come here.'

The woman watches her. It's impossible to work out what she is thinking. Finally she says, 'I heard about you. A week ago. When did you get here?'

A small surge of relief, but relief tempered with caution: they can pull you in, lead you on, drag you so deep in that you'll never get out. 'Two days ago. I've been in the South-west. WORD-SMITH. Do you know WORDSMITH?'

The woman shrugs. 'What do you want with us?'

'I need a pick-up. Can you arrange that?'

'Why from here? If you're in the South-west, Spain's only over the border.'

'It's for people here in Paris.'

'How many passengers?'

'Two.'

'Who are they?'

'I can't say.'

'Are you one of them?'

'No, I'm not.'

The woman chews her lip thoughtfully, then turns to the calendar on the wall. There are a few pencil scribbles – bills to be paid, deliveries made, things like that. But what is most obvious is that it's one of those calendars that has the phases of the moon marked above the date: a black spot for new moon, crescents waxing and waning, a white circle for the full moon. Claire points to the next full. 'Even if we can do it, you'll have to wait at least ten days. Can your passengers manage that?'

'I think so.'

'I've got a flat you could use, but who knows how safe it is these days?'

'They're all right as they are.'

The bell sounds in the bar and some customers come in. Claire pushes the door closed and lowers her voice. 'It's dangerous here in the city, you know that? Not like the countryside. Here everything's in chaos. This place may be under surveillance.'

'I didn't notice anyone—'

The woman laughs. 'You wouldn't. They let you get on with things and then pull you in when they wish. A lot of the time the only reason you are operating is because they allow it. Do you know about PROSPER?'

'I've heard something.'

'Well, it's been blown. Dozens of arrests. Hundreds. And others. INVENTOR, CINÉASTE.' She looks round the tiny room as though in surprise to find the walls still standing. 'At the moment we're lucky.'

'One of my passengers is from CINÉASTE.'

The woman looks incredulous. 'That's impossible. Everyone was taken.'

'Her field name's Marcelle.'

'The pianist? Surely she was picked up with the rest of them.'

Alice shakes her head. 'I've found her. She's been in hiding. Apparently she was late for the rendezvous when the others were arrested ...'

'Do you *know* her? I mean, would you recognise her?'

'Of course. We trained together.'

'Where?'

'Scotland.' But the woman seems to want more. 'Meoble Lodge on Loch Morar,' she adds, and Claire digests this extra piece of information, turning it over in her mind like a dealer turning over a piece of porcelain in his hands. Is it fake or is it genuine? Is it whole or is it damaged?

'How did you find her?'

'Marcelle? She's pretty scared. At least she seems scared—'

'I mean, how did you know where she was?'

'Oh, I see.' Alice smiles at her misunderstanding but searches in vain for a corresponding smile on the woman's face. 'The address came from London. They contacted WORDSMITH, because they knew that I would be able to recognise her. She told me the last thing she gave them was her new address – it's a new place she had just found, so she hadn't told anyone else. Then she went off the air. I've got her wireless now.'

'It's my understanding that she was arrested with the others.'

'It seems not.'

'Can you trust her?'

'Of course I can trust her. She's more than a colleague, she's a friend.'

Claire is silent for a while, as though considering the value of friendship. 'What about the other passenger?'

'Nothing to do with CINÉASTE. Nothing to do with any circuit. London want him out.'

'Safe?'

'I can vouch for him, but I can't tell you who he is.'

Claire shrugs. 'Some shitty politico, I expect.' Then an idea occurs to her. 'If you've got Marcelle's wireless you can ask for a message from London. Do that. Have a message broadcast over the BBC.'

'What message? Why?'

The barman puts his head round the door. 'I've got to go in ten minutes,' he says. 'You'll have to take over.'

'Paul is going in ten minutes,' the woman tells Alice. 'That way I'll know that I can trust you.' For the first time she smiles.

Once more she takes the *métro* across the city, and this time leaves a message with the fat man called Boger at the café, to meet Yvette at the entrance to the cemetery. It's safer like that, out in the open away from eavesdroppers. They walk at random through the city of the dead, past tombs and memorials and epitaphs. Some of them bear sad bunches of decaying flowers. One or two are names one recognises, a poet here, an artist there. Others have lists of letters after their names, as though you ought to recognise them even if you don't.

Alice says, 'I've been speaking to people.'

There's a lurch of anxiety in Yvette's expression. 'What people?'

'People who work for the Organisation.'

'Who are they?'

'It doesn't matter. But they say that every member of CINÉASTE was picked up. Including you.'

'Well, it's not true, is it? I'm here.' There's a snap in her voice, a sharp edge of temper. 'What are you saying? Are you accusing me of something?' Yvette's voice rises up the register. Is it anger or panic? The two emotions feed off each other in a grim symbiosis. 'I'm on my own, Marian. You can see that. I'm alone. Christ, don't you believe me?'

'Calm down. I'm just saying people are suspicious.'

'But who are these people? Who the hell knows anything about me? What have you told them?'

For a moment the whole conversation teeters on the edge of chaos. They seem about to have a shouting match, an inchoate row of recrimination and accusation there among the memorials and the mausoleums. 'It's all right Yvette,' Alice says soothingly. 'I believe you. But you know what it's like. You know how afraid everyone is. Particularly now, particularly with what happened to PROSPER.'

Yvette calms down. PROSPER and the fate of PROSPER bring with them a sudden tide of fear, and fear conquers anger. 'You know what Emile told me? Before they were all arrested, you know what he told me?'

'Emile is a bloody know-all.'

'But you know what he told me? He told me that there was a traitor in PROSPER.'

227

'If he was clever enough to know that, why wasn't he clever enough to avoid being caught?'

Yvette gives a little, apologetic laugh. 'You know what?'

'What?'

'Emile and I ...' She tries a smile but it doesn't really work. 'We were sleeping together.'

'*Sleeping* together?'

Yvette giggles. A hint of her old self. 'Does that sound dreadful?'

Alice smiles. 'He wouldn't be my choice.'

'But he was a comfort. It's a lonely job being a pianist ...'

They reach the tomb of Balzac. There's the writer's head staring imperiously over the city he had once dissected. A single mourner stands in front of it, a long-haired man in a crumpled black suit who stares at the memorial with all the fixation of the mildly deranged. When the man has moved on out of earshot Alice says, 'Anyway it's all organised. The pick-up, I mean. But we'll have to wait. You understand that, don't you? Until the next moon.' It's like talking to a patient, explaining the prognosis, repeating her words to make sure they've been understood. 'Do you understand? We'll have to wait for the next moon period. Meanwhile continue to do what you've been doing up to now – lie low and keep out of harm's way. Have you got money?'

Yvette lights a cigarette, eyeing *Honoré de Balzac, mort à Paris le 18 août 1850* through a pall of smoke. Her fingers – delicate, slender, expert with a knife – are stained yellow. 'I have to buy on the black market. I don't trust my ration cards.'

'I'll give you some cash. All you've got to do is wait for me to contact you again.'

Somewhere in the cemetery a bell begins to toll. People are walking towards the crematorium at the top of the slope. 'There's a funeral,' Yvette says. She pinches off the end of her cigarette. 'Let's go. The last thing I want to see is a funeral.'

228

## IX

She pulls the suitcase out and puts it on the bed. Clément is standing at the door, watching. She opens the case and stands back for him to see.

'There.'

The dull gleam of black metal, of glass dials and Bakelite knobs. He peers at the thing as though it were a new piece of research apparatus. 'You know how it all works?'

She shrugs. 'I hope so. I did the basic course, not the full WT School. My Morse is useless.' She closes the lid and looks up at him. 'So what do I say to them?'

'I've spoken with Fred. I explained about the letter from Chadwick.'

'You've done *what*? What did you tell him?'

'You can trust Fred. He can keep a secret. We all live with our secrets these days, Marian.'

'But I don't want *him* to be living with *mine*. Don't you realise how dangerous this is? For Christ's sake, what else did you say to him?'

'Squirrel, you're becoming heated.'

'Don't call me Squirrel! I'm not a child any more, Clément.'

'Don't worry, I didn't mention you. I told him in the vaguest terms. A letter has come into my possession, that kind of thing.'

'So what did he say?'

'He's been very shaken by Bohr's going over to the Allies. He said that he would go himself if it weren't for Irène and the children. At least he would be able to find out what's going on, that's what he said.'

'Is that all?'

'He thinks I should go in his place. His representative, if you like.'

She can see the conflict in his expression. 'But what do *you* think, Clément? What are *you* going to decide? Because you've got to make a choice. That's the one positive thing that this war has brought: we have to choose. The French more than anyone.' She's angry – at him, at the city, at the whole damn country with its sullen acceptance of its fate, resignation that leaks over into accommodation and becomes, when you look away for a moment, collaboration. When he doesn't answer, she turns away. There is an escritoire in the corner of the room, an elaborate affair with inlaid wood and delicate cabriole legs. Perhaps it is where Madeleine used to sit to write letters. There are paper and pencils in the various little compartments, and a diary with some addresses in it and a photograph of a dark and handsome young woman – Augustine – proudly showing a baby to the camera. She draws up a chair, places a sheet of paper on the desk and sits down to write:

CONTACT MADE WITH MARCELLE, she writes. CINÉASTE BLOWN AND ALL OTHERS ARRESTED MARCELLE NEEDS EVACUATION ALSO MECHANIC CONTACTED HE MAY BE COMPLIANT STOP

Clément stands watching, a cigarette in his hand.

ALSO CONTACT MADE WITH CLAIRE FOR PICK-UP PLEASE BROADCAST FOLLOWING MESSAGE ON BBC START PAUL IS GOING IN TEN MINUTES END REPEAT PAUL IS GOING IN TEN MINUTES AWAIT RESPONSE IN ONE HOUR

'Is all this rather dangerous?' he asks. 'I imagine it is. Transmitting, I mean. I imagine they scan the frequencies …'
'Of course they do.'
'Directional aerials and a little exercise in triangulation to pinpoint the transmitter …'
'You have to get your message through and get off the air as quickly as possible. They say you've got something like thirty minutes for your first transmission. Less for the subsequent ones. The Germans have DF vans out on the streets …'

'DF?'

'Direction Finding. *Radiogoniométrie*. Now be quiet because I've got to encrypt the thing.' On a new sheet of paper she writes out her poem:

> *I wonder whether*
> *Or ever*
> *You'll love me*
> *Forever*
> *Or always*
> *Our pathways*
> *Will keep us apart*
>
> *Perhaps never*
> *But never*
> *We'll share love*
> *Together*
> *Yet always*
> *Through all ways*
> *You're close to my heart*

'Tell me what you are doing.'

'I'm arranging for you to go to England.'

She ignores his laughter and continues with her work, choosing five words from the poem – *whether, or, our, apart, heart* – and numbering their letters to give the key. Then she writes her message out beneath the key and begins to chase the letters through the double transposition to make the plain text appear mere nonsense, a string of random letters with no apparent meaning. When that is done, she adds her personal group to the start of the message, followed by an indicator code to identify the words of the poem, and then her two security checks. Finally she rewrites the whole message in groups of five letters, then checks them through for the slightest error, that single mistake that would shift the whole transposition by one letter and

231

turn apparent nonsense into total gibberish – an *indecipherable*. 'Indecipherables are the bane of our lives,' Marks warned her. 'Make keying errors and we'll sort things out. Get your ciphering wrong and it's a complete SNAFU.'

'What's a SNAFU?'

He grinned. 'It's code. A technical term.'

Clément watches. She tries to block him from her mind. He shouldn't be watching but he is watching. He shouldn't be here alone with her, but he is. She has let her guard down and she knows it. This process – the whole rigmarole of composition and enciphering, the subtle intricacies of transposition keys – is as intimate as washing yourself, or peeing, or any of those bodily functions that you hide from prying eyes. And here she is, her cover abandoned, her defences thrown down, exposed to his gaze. She feels the guilt of transgression.

He asks, mockingly, 'So what have you decided I'm going to do?'

She gathers up her papers, grabs the suitcase and pushes past him into the corridor. 'I've decided what you *ought* to do. The rest is up to you.'

Outside the front door the landing and the stairwell are in darkness, as silent as a church. Access to the roof is through a door on the landing that she discovered just as she found everything else out, checking the place over for escape routes and alternative exits. She even discovered where the key to the roof door was kept, in the kitchen, beneath the eagle eye of Marie. A single bulb casts a pallid light as she lugs the suitcase up the stairs, feigning indifference to his following her.

At the head of the steps is a narrow closet that smells vaguely of soap. There's a cement sink and a washboard and a wooden basket. She puts the suitcase down, opens the door to the roof and steps out. The rooftop is a place of shadows, of slopes and pyramids of slate and a dusty pond of glass through which you can peer down into the hall where they were a few minutes ago.

Above the neighbouring buildings the dome of the Panthéon is touched by the last light of the evening. Clément appears in the doorway watching her.

'Does anyone else come up here?' she asks.

'It's our access. Private. Where Marie hangs the washing.'

She lays the aerial wire out as best she can while he stands there, smoking and watching. Is he considering her proposal? It isn't that she has forgotten how to read him, it is, she realises now, that she never could read him, never could understand whether he was talking seriously or not. His ideas of science always seemed fantastical, and his ideas about life concrete and reliable. But now everything appears in reverse. Now science brooks no doubt, and life seems riddled with contradiction and uncertainty. Only this procedure, the intricacies of encryption and transmission, drummed into her at Meoble and at Beaulieu, appears to have a purpose to it.

She finds a plug in the wall behind a mop and pail, plugs the wireless set into the mains and switches it on. There is the faint, nervous hum of electricity. The voltage dial flicks into life. She lifts the headphones and holds them to her ear, listening to the sound of silence rushing through the airwaves like a stream.

'This is beyond a joke, Marian,' he says.

She looks round. 'It has never been a joke, Clément. Not for me. I'm risking my life to do this, and yours as well. Now if you'll excuse me, I've got to concentrate. I'll be down in half an hour.'

When he has gone, she upends the pail as a seat and props the wireless set on a collapsible picnic table that she found hidden behind some sacking. She glances at her watch, notes the time and puts the headphones on. Then she inserts the crystal, one of those crystals she carried inside her, switches to the five-megacycle band and takes up the position she tried to learn, with scant success, during training, fingers balanced on the knob of the Morse key. Cautiously she starts sending out her call sign, the hesitant dots and dashes vanishing into the wilderness of the evening like faint birdsong.

233

She pauses and listens.

In Brest and Augsburg and Nuremberg receiver stations will have detected that little flutter on the airwaves. Phones will be ringing, one station calling the other while their directional aerials will be shifting round the compass to nose out the bearing of this fragile new intruder. Lines will be drawn on a map of Europe, to intersect in a triangle over the city of Paris … and meanwhile in a country house in southern England, that manor house at Grendon Underwood, a FANY wireless operator may or may not be listening, may or may not be crying out, 'It's Alice!' and calling her supervisor over and putting her hand on her Morse key to tap out a response.

She sends out her call sign again. She can picture the aerials turning, listening, like predatory bats detecting a new call on the night air, the song of a night bird who fears to be captured yet needs to be heard. She counts the seconds, praying to whichever deity might rule the airwaves. And then Grendon's call sign flickers faintly in her ears and brings with it a small thrill of astonishment, as though she has murmured a prayer and God Himself has answered.

She begins her transmission, tapping slowly, knocking on wood, praying for accuracy, the stuttering letters filtered through lessons incompletely learned and inadequately followed. She shifts her backside on the pail and taps on, her words laboriously released into the rush of the ether. There is no such thing as the ether, Ned told her once: it was a figment of the nineteenth-century scientific imagination. And yet she can hear it in her headphones like the roaring of an ocean beating on some distant shoreline, a constant background to the small whisper of her message. She ends the transmission with *Love and kisses*. That is Marks's fault. Don't sign off with 'Message ends', he warned her. Don't do anything that someone might guess. Say 'Cheerio'; say, 'It's been nice talking to you'; say anything except 'Message ends' or 'Over and out', or any of that stuff they tell you at signals school. Because if it's a cliché to you, then it's just as much a cliché to the Germans. And if they guess it right, they'll begin to unpick your knitting. Because your whole bloody enciphered message is no more than a glorious anagram of the original. And that's the trouble with it.

*Love and kisses.*

She puts the headphones aside and turns the power switch to *off*. The voltage dial dies back to zero. Another glance at her watch. Seven minutes thirty-five seconds. The prey's call is no longer on the air and the aerials have stopped straining to hear. If the detector vans have put out from their lairs, they are left with nothing to seek.

She goes downstairs, imagining events in England, her message being hurried to the cipher section, one of the girls getting her poem from the file and starting to unpick the cipher, undoing what she so laboriously did just half an hour ago at Madeleine's desk. Will coherence emerge from the nonsense?

Clément looks up questioningly as she comes in. She shrugs. 'I'll have to wait. I've given them an hour.'

They eat the paltry meal that Marie has prepared. They talk, of nothing, of trivia, of the past, of his father and what he is doing in Algiers, of his sister and mother. And then of Augustine, living a sequestered life in the house in Annecy with her mother-in-law and sister-in-law, knowing that she is a Jew and therefore somehow tainted. Like one of those isotopes he studies. Radioactive.

'I've been on the telephone to them,' he tells her. 'It's not easy talking on the phone these days. Of course you can't say anything openly but I gathered that they're trying to get into Switzerland. It should be possible to arrange a visa. We still have friends there ...'

'So she'll be all right, then.'

'That sounds like an accusation.'

'Well, what about the thousands that won't be all right, who can't cross the Swiss border and be looked after? Tell me about them?'

235

'I don't know about them, Marian.' His tone is weary, as though he has exercised this argument over and over. 'I can't take responsibility for them any more than you can. They have to get by as best they are able.'

'But you can do something about it, can't you? I'm giving you the opportunity. I'm doing that because I believe in what I'm doing. I haven't believed in God for years, but do you know what? I think I've come to believe in Satan. And the only way to combat Satan is to be as ruthless as he is.'

In the cipher room at Grendon her words will be emerging from the blur of nonsense, like a photographic image appearing in the developing tray. The cipher clerk will be signing off the message in clear and dashing with it to the communications room. Teleprinters will chatter between Grendon and London, flimsies will be rushed into offices somewhere in Baker Street. Buckmaster and Atkins will meet up to discuss their response.

And Fawley? The self-effacing Fawley will be informed. *Mechanic may be compliant.* Will he ponder over the meaning of that careful subjunctive?

She gets up from her chair. 'I don't know how long I'll be,' she tells him. 'Don't wait up for me.'

Listening-watch at the top of the stairs, with the receiver on but the transmitter disconnected. The rush of the ether in the headphones, punctuated by muttering and stuttering. Cold seeping into her limbs and her backside growing numb from sitting on the unyielding pail. She blows on her fingers and listens to the empty music of the spheres. Exquisite boredom, inaction underpinned by tension like a bowstring that is never released.

And then comes the small whisper of intimacy like a lover's voice in her ear. Her starved fingers begin to scribble down the twitterings, the dots and dashes, a thin trickle that signifies that someone somewhere is thinking of her.

The message is repeated. She turns on the transmitter and waits for the valves to warm up. A moment's acknowledgement, a few taps of the Morse key and the thing is over, the message received, the fragile moments of contact sundered. She turns the set off and waits for it to cool. There is the housekeeping to do, all those tasks you have to complete: reeling up the aerial, gathering up every scrap of paper, replacing things exactly as they were, removing all the evidence that she has been there. Back downstairs she retreats to her bedroom to decipher Grendon's reply.

Dry acknowledgements, understated praise, all the things one might expect. They want to know more, of course, more about CINÉASTE, more about PROSPER, more about the disaster that has struck the Paris circuits. But she isn't going to tell them. Every minute on air is a minute off your life. She takes a large glass ashtray and carefully burns all the leaves of paper, every scrap of message and code, then goes to the bathroom and flushes the ashes down the lavatory. Feeling exhausted, feeling the damp in her armpits and the sweat on her brow, she goes into the *salon* and finds Clément still up and waiting for her.

'There,' she tells him. 'I've done it.'

Her hand is unsteady as she takes the glass of cognac he offers. He brushes a strand of hair from her forehead. 'You look exhausted.'

'I am.'

'You frighten me,' he says. 'I've never seen you like this. Driven. Obsessed.'

'Don't be ridiculous. I've got a job to do, that's all. I'm not a child any more, Clément.'

'You keep saying that.'

'It's true.'

He puts his arms round her. She feels comforted by the contact. She doesn't want to feel that, but she cannot deny it. She remembers watching the children playing in the *impasse* near Yvette's flat, a little boy falling on his hands and knees, the tears that welled up inside him as he looked for sympathy. But there was no sympathy for him then, and there can be none for her now. Tears are the last thing she needs. Carefully she detaches herself from his embrace.

'It's not safe for me here,' she warns him. 'We can't do anything until the next moon, and I can't just hang around waiting. I'll have to go tomorrow.'

'Go? Where, in God's name? You're safe here, Squirrel.'

This time she laughs at the use of the childhood name. 'Paris is a dangerous place at the moment, you know that. Much as I'd like to, I can't hide in the flat for ten days. My being here is a risk. People notice things. People gossip. It's as simple as that. If you keep moving, you're safer. It's staying in one place that's dangerous. I'll be back in good time, a week from now. And in the meantime you'd better make up your mind about what you are going to do. For my sake, if no one else's.'

# Toulouse

I

The return to Toulouse is like leaving one continent for another, crossing an ocean, making landfall in a different world. The morning is bright and warm, a southern morning ten degrees hotter than Paris with an autumnal sun embedded in enamel blue; and she feels no fear. Apart from the temperature, that is the other noticeable thing – the nagging, incessant fear that she felt in Paris; somehow the rose-red city is immune from that. There is danger here but it is a danger you can see, something you can measure and combat, like the danger of infection. The danger of Paris is a cancer within you, invisible, imponderable and probably incurable.

Feeling elevated, light-headed with lack of sleep, she takes the regional train northwards. The countryside is comforting in its familiarity and when the bus finally dumps her in the main square of Lussac, it is as though she has come home. Gabrielle is overjoyed to see her. How was Paris? Tell me all about Paris! What were the people like, what were the fashions like, how were the crowds and the sights? Oh, and she has heard that Roland is trying to contact her.

Roland?

*Le Patron.* He came round a couple of times. They've been chatting quite a lot. Roland's so hard-working, so *driven.* When she mentions his name, Gabrielle blushes, just faintly, a small flush, not of embarrassment but of heightened awareness.

At Plasonne they greet her like a long-lost daughter, Sophie fussing round her, bringing her food, insisting she sit down and rest, asking how the city was, how people were dressed, how the fashions were. Paris seems a kind of Cockaigne, an earthly paradise beyond their ken, whereas in fact it is nothing more than a grim wartime city with less food and less freedom than here. That evening, they listen to the radio. The set is in the kitchen, a contraption in polished wood with Bakelite knobs and a semicircular tuning dial. Albert tunes it carefully, the volume turned down low, his ear close to the speaker. 'There!' he says with a smile of triumph, standing back to display his prowess. Through the rush of static that comes out of the speaker they hear the familiar call sign that is like the beat of a distant drum:

••• ▬

And then a voice announcing, '*Ici Londres!*' a voice from a world away, a sound that never fails to evoke a sting of emotion. '*Les Français parlent aux Français.*'

Sophie watches her, trying to decipher her expression.

The radio voice says, 'Before we begin, here are some personal messages.' And then the messages come, the absurd and the poetic, lines solemn and comic delivered with the precise phrasing of a man who wants to be heard despite distance and interference and deliberate jamming: *Grandmother has bought the artichokes. The clouds of autumn bring winter rains. All good things come to fruition*. And then:

'*Paul s'en va en dix minutes. Nous le disons deux fois: Paul s'en va en dix minutes.*'

'There,' Alice says with a small stir of happiness, and Sophie smiles at her, knowing that Alice has scored some kind of triumph, that London has spoken, that somehow the end has been brought that little bit nearer.

On the radio the news has started. It's mainly about Russia, a land that Albert espouses but has never seen and can barely envisage. The announcer talks of tens of thousands killed, whole armies captured, so many people thrown on the waste heap that you cannot imagine such a number can be replaced. And yet the war goes on.

'Now you need to sleep,' Sophie says. 'You're exhausted.'


‖


*Le Patron* shouts. White-faced and angry, he's standing in the kitchen of Gabrielle's house, with the old mother in the corner knitting away, not hearing a word. 'What the hell were you doing, gallivanting around in Paris? We've got work to do round here! I need you to be on call!'

She is no longer afraid of him, that is the difference. When she first came he was a terrifying prospect, more terrifying than the Gestapo. But now she sees him for what he is, a small man in a fearful position, trying to balance forces that may crush him in an instant. And finding comfort in Gabrielle's small and devoted attentions.

'I didn't go for my own amusement,' she says when the storm has passed. 'You know that as well as I do.'

He spits something, a shred of tobacco maybe. 'If they want someone in Paris, why the hell don't they drop someone into the city? They can land right on the bloody Eiffel Tower for all I care. Have it stuck up their arse.'

'And I'm afraid I've got to go back.'

'Go *back*? What the hell do you mean, *go back*?'

'I've got to organise a pick-up.'

'I thought it was just those bloody crystals.'

'It wasn't. CINÉASTE has been broken up and Marcelle needs to get out.'

'But there are people in Paris who can arrange that.'

'She's in hiding. The place is a nightmare and she's terrified of being caught. Only I know where she is. Virtually all the Paris circuits have collapsed and there've been dozens of arrests.'

'And you've arranged the pick-up already? How did you make contact?'

Why should he know that she was given instructions about contacting Gilbert? Why should he know anything? 'I used Marcelle's radio.'

He draws on his cigarette and eyes her suspiciously. 'Since when were you a pianist?'

'We all get basic training.'

'Anyway, we're due for a drop the next moon. You can't be away.'

'Gaillard can do it. He knows exactly what to do.'

'He'll bring in Marcel's lot and they'll steal half the stuff.'

She doesn't care. Marcel's men will do useful things with whatever they have. They're communists and are therefore both organised and driven. Too many of the others have mixed motives.

'You've barely been here two months and you're spending most of your time in bloody Paris. I could order you to stay.'

'You'd better ask London about that.'

'What the fuck does London know?' He frowns at her and takes another drag on his cigarette. 'And you've got to go back to Toulouse. Immediately.'

'What for?'

'Another idea of London's. Why don't they keep their bloody noses out of it? This time it's an argument with the RAF. We've got to prove our value by blowing something up, otherwise they'll send Bomber Command to flatten half the bloody town. It's politics. We've got enough politics here among the French. The last thing we need is politics at home. But there you are: our bosses believe that targeted destruction is more effective than area bombing, so they want us to do this as a demo. The idea is simple: we risk the life of a few saboteurs rather than a hundred bomber crews, and at the same time they keep in with the French by not obliterating a few hundred civilians. Simple mathematics. Fine, unless you are one of the terms in the equation.'

She thinks of other equations, with values greater than any imagining. Equations solved by Clément and the big jovial Russian Lev Kowarski. Equations measuring life and death. Fifty-eight thousand. Is that the solution?

'The target is the Ramier factory. César's got to set something up, work out how to attack it and let me have a plan within the week.'

'César?'

'Who else?'

'It sounds risky.'

'Of course it's risky.' He eyes her suspiciously. 'Is there anything going on between you two?'

'César and me? What d'you mean?'

'There'd better not be. We can't have that kind of thing in this circuit. You see to it that he keeps his hands out of your knickers.'

She blushes. 'What on earth are you suggesting?'

'You know perfectly well what I mean, madam. It's a bloody nuisance having a girl like you around. The men here can't keep their eyes off you, and César's practically gagging for it whenever you're around.'

She manages to be angry. It's difficult but she manages it. 'That's outrageous! I barely see him. It's hardly my fault what people think.' She glares at him, seeing him hideous and thwarted, a man who lives with his nerves exposed like something in a butcher's shop, hanging from a hook. He's the first to flinch, to look away from her fury. 'Anyway, you tell him what I said. The Ramier factory. We need a report immediately. I reckon a commando of a dozen men, something like that, but he's to make his own mind up.' He drags on his cigarette and turns pointedly to look out of the window. 'You'd better leave first. I'll wait here until you're well away.'

She opens the door and goes out into the hall. Gabrielle is peering down from the banisters at the top of the stairs. Although it's nine o'clock in the morning, she's still wearing her nightdress. 'Are you going already, Alice?' she calls. 'Is Roland still there?'

Looking up, Alice can see her white legs and awkward knees. 'Don't worry,' she calls up. 'I'm sure he won't leave without saying goodbye.'

III

She emerges from Toulouse station in the early evening and makes her way to an address she has nearby, a safe house she has used before. The owners are a railwayman and his wife who greet her with enthusiasm, eager to do something, anything to contribute. The flat was intended for their son who was planning to get married, but was sent to Germany under the STO. So now the flat lies empty awaiting his return. 'César was asking about you,' the wife says.

Alice finds herself blushing faintly. 'Tell him I'm here.'

The flat is barely furnished – a bed and chest of drawers in one room, a broken-backed sofa and some upright chairs and a table in another, a kitchen with a sink and some cupboards and an ancient gas cooker that doesn't have a cylinder attached and so is entirely useless. As she falls asleep on the bare mattress, the thought of Benoît is a comfort. Benoît is normality, Benoît is comprehensible. Is it easier to love something that you understand?

He comes the next day, letting himself into the house as though it belongs to him. It's not meant to be like this. Meetings are intended to be fleeting, casual, contingent encounters; not the two of them together in an empty apartment with no constraint of time. But this is what she wants. She's smarting from *le Patron*'s words and confused by her three days with Clément. She feels an elevation of mood, as though she has drunk too much, and a depression of spirit, as though she has lost a friend. And Benoît is his usual self – laughing, careless, his clothes awry, his self-confidence complete.

'I've got to go back,' she tells him when he asks about Paris.

'Go *back*, Minou? Why the hell? I'll bet that makes *le Patron* happy. He was calling you all manner of names when I last saw him. That bloody Parisienne, he said, and that was only the mildest. A *garce*, he called you, putting on her airs and graces. Doesn't she know there's a war on?'

They laugh together. She no longer dislikes his calling her Minou. In fact she discovers she enjoys the comfort and the familiarity. He has been part of her life ever since that very first encounter in London when she was a young and fearful girl called Marian Sutro, and now he's a constant when so much is confused and random. And he is not Clément, he doesn't possess that awful potency of childhood memory. When she delivers *le Patron*'s message his expression transforms into one of pure delight – 'The Ramier factory? Wow!' – like a child given a new toy, his face lighting up with excitement. 'Don't you know the Ramier factory? It's explosives. One of the biggest in the country. Do you want to have a look at the place?'

'A look at it?'

'Why not? It's on an island in the river, upstream from the city centre. Come on, it'll be fun.'

Fun seems something alien, something that belongs to other people. 'Why not?' she agrees.

They take bikes, a boy and a girl together, down through the city to the Garonne. The banks of the river are deserted, almost rural. She thinks of the Thames, and the Seine, and now this river, quiet and empty, strewn with islands and brushed with willows, and Benoît cycling beside her, joking

245

with her, bringing sanity to a life that is essentially insane. They cross the bridge to the Ramier island and stroll hand in hand, pushing their bikes past the main gate of the factory while guards watch them incuriously.

'Perhaps we should kiss,' Benoît says. 'Reinforce our cover.'

'You're taking advantage.'

'Of course I am.' He laughs and pulls her towards him while the guards cheer. His smile, that smile of insouciance, is quite unlike Clément's, which is knowing and cynical. 'I miss you so much, Minou. You don't understand.'

But she does. She understands many things, and the things she doesn't understand aren't here in this southern city with the russet brickwork and soft autumn sunlight. They walk on, smiling at each other and at the guards. She even waves, and receives a mock salute in return. When they return to the flat they're still laughing, at the brightness of the day, at their absurd conversations, at the fact that they examined the entire perimeter of the factory and all the while were taken as young lovers out for a stroll together. The flat is bare and indifferent, like Mr Potter's office. Devoid of clues. But there are clues elsewhere, in the way they talk to each other, in the looks she gives and receives. Something new, something shocking and unexpected, is there inside her. It's to do with Clément, with childhood and adolescence, with fear of the past and the future.

'Shall I stay?' Benoît asks. There's a glimmer of uncertainty in his expression, and a hint of understanding.

She shrugs. 'There's nothing to eat.'

'I know somewhere just round the corner.' He always knows somewhere or someone just round the corner. That is how he acquired the bikes. This time it's a small and secretive bistro owned by Basques, where they eat *garbure* and drink rough wine and she evades Benoît's questions about what she was doing in Paris and why she has to return. But there's an easy acceptance of the circumstances. They've learned this – to live for the minute, careless of what might happen. 'Let's get back,' she says, calling for the bill.

They let themselves into the flat stealthily, like thieves. In the hallway there's a moment of awkwardness when he moves to go to the living room with the broken sofa and she stops him, her hand on his arm. For a moment they are like that, as though he is giving her a further chance to reflect. And then they go into the bedroom. 'You know what's wrong with this place as a safe house?' Benoît asks.

'Of course I do. There's no second way out. If anyone comes in through the front door, you're trapped.'

'Do you feel trapped?'

'If I do it's a trap of my own making.'

'That's all right, then.'

She doesn't really know how to do this. The last time was obvious, creeping round her parents' house in the dark. But now, in this tawdry room with the bare mattress and the naked bulb in the ceiling, things are different. She makes a joke – 'They didn't teach us how to do this at Beaulieu' – and then turns her back on him to undress. It ought to be an outrage, against everything and anything she ever imagined, against even that one time in Oxford which seemed then to have a logic to it, a justifiable part of her preparation for life here in France. But it isn't an outrage; it's what she wants to do. The single bulb glows balefully from the ceiling. She'd prefer it if it were dark and there were somewhere she could go to undress. She'd rather creep into the bed in the darkness and pretend that none of this were happening; but then it would be like it was in Oxford, and she's moved on from there, hasn't she? She's moved into different territory, a new world. So she turns and sits on the bed, trying not to cover her breasts, trying not to put one hand in her lap to hide her hair, trying to let him look at her, accepting that the light is on and he's standing shameless in front of the window and there are awkward shadows cast across his body. She has never seen a man naked like this, not blatant in this way. She wants to laugh at the sight and she wants him to laugh with her. She loves his laughter, which seems to her a kind of communion, something almost sacred – it's that which makes her desire him, though the idea of laughter as an aphrodisiac seems absurd. Yet she daren't laugh, in case it would mean something different in this unfamiliar world. The deciphering of what things mean can be so difficult. 'You were afraid of me the last time,' he says.

'I was afraid of everything then.'

'But not now?'

'Only some things.'

'Not me, I hope.'

'Not you,' she agrees.

They lie down together on the mattress, with her entwined in his arms, clinging to him for safety as though if she lets go she'll be swept away. He still has the scent of the day upon him, compounded of sweat and grass, a raw smell that reminds her of the farm at Plasonne: something strange but at the same time comforting. And what happens isn't furtive and silent and bewildering as it was before, but is composed of different elements – shock and delight, the thrill of physical affection and, for a moment or two, a strange annihilation of self in the furnace of this fused existence.

'Was that all right?' he asks when they have finished.

She didn't understand that you could ask such a question, as though what they have done is something you think about and practise and make good or bad, like playing tennis or learning to swim. 'Of course it was all right. It was very all right.'

'And you're not cross with me any longer?'

'I wasn't ever cross with you. It was the circumstances. The wrong place at the wrong time.'

'And now?'

She lies with her head in the crook of his arm looking up at him. 'The right place and the right time, I suppose. For the moment, anyway.'

'What about Paris?' he asks. 'What happened in Paris?'

She laughs, a faint laugh that is no more than an exhalation of breath. 'You know I can't tell you. I can't tell you anything.'

# Paris

|

This time there is no wandering out of the station to look at the river. This time there is purpose and intent, and a sense of confidence. Paris holds no new fears. And she still feels the thrill of transgression, the knowledge of Benoît within her, the startling outrage of it and the comfort. Has he exorcised the ghost of Clément? Is he the man she might love? Perhaps thinking all this is what distracts her, because it is only as she emerges from the *métro* at Maubert-Mutualité that she realises she is being followed.

Anger trips over fear. Why didn't she spot him earlier? Where has he come from? Who is he? Who has sent him? More questions than answers.

From the boulevard she climbs the slope towards the rue des Écoles and the great dome of the Panthéon. At a second-hand bookshop she pauses to pick up a photographic album from one of the bins on the pavement. The book shows Parisian scenes from the early part of the century, the days when the city seemed hopeful and gay, something exquisite created out of silver and platinum rather than the base metal of today. In the reflection of the shop window she can see her follower on the other side of the street standing with his back to her, examining something in another window. He's a slight figure, with his raincoat collar pulled up and his hat pulled down.

She feels the slow churn of nausea. French police? Abwehr? Gestapo? The city is as riddled with spies as a Roquefort cheese with mould.

'Those were the days, eh, Mam'selle?' the bookseller remarks as she puts the book down. 'We won't see their like again.'

She smiles and agrees that he is probably right, and walks on, trying to stroll, trying to be at ease with herself, a woman alone in the city with a man following. Again she pauses to look in a shop window – some ironmongery, a sewing machine, a step ladder that may or may not be part of the window display – and watches him swim towards her in the reflection, then stop to tie his shoelace. He stays down, apparently having difficulty, while she gazes at things she doesn't want. Then she moves on, quickly now so that he has to struggle to keep up.

The street emerges into the great square with the bulk of the Panthéon, that temple to no god whatsoever, standing massive in the centre. She looks round quickly, trying to think, trying to remain calm. On her right is the long façade of the Sainte-Geneviève library with a gaggle of students hanging round the entrance; over to the left the architectural confection of Saint-Étienne-du-Mont. She turns left and crosses the uneven *pavé* towards the church, trying not to hurry, trying to be a young woman who on a whim has decided to say a prayer. Pushing through a leather curtain she finds herself in the shadowy interior, immersed in the smell of incense and obfuscation but free for a moment. Thirty seconds, she reckons, maybe less. The skill is to throw the tail off without giving the impression that you know you are being followed. A delicate art. She looks around at the sanguine glow of stained glass, at flickering candles and shifting shadows of people at their devotions.

Twenty seconds.

The body of the church is divided across by a rood screen, an elaborate amalgam of spirals and arches. She hurries up the side aisle and through a door into the chancel. There are side chapels on the right, one of them holding a gilded sarcophagus where candles flicker and an inscription says *Sainte Geneviève Ora Pro Nobis*. An old woman kneels at prayer before the relic of the saint.

Ten seconds.

The aisle curves round behind the high altar. Ahead is a door to the sacristy and further round the curve, tucked in a shadowy recess, a confessional. The sacristy is too obvious. She walks round to the confessional, pulls aside the curtain, pushes her suitcase inside and crams herself after it. A musty darkness, redolent of anguish and guilt, envelopes her. She holds the curtain so she can peer out like a child playing Hide and Seek.

Beside her the grille slides open. 'Yes, my child?'

Memories come flooding through the open trap – her convent school, the duties of penance and obligation, the odious smear of guilt. On the far side of the lacework of metal is the shadow of the priest's face. 'Oh, I thought ...' What did she think? What could she say? Through the gap in the curtain she watches the old woman get up from her prayers at the tomb of Sainte Geneviève and take her place to wait for the confessional. Immediately behind her the man appears, walking round the curve of the apse, searching.

'Bless me, Father, for I have sinned.'

'When did you make your last confession, my child?'

For a moment the man stands indecisively by the tomb of the saint. He holds his hat against his chest and she can see his face in the candlelight. And she knows him. It is the man who accosted her before, the one who followed her out onto the embankment when she first arrived in the city.

'Years ago, Father. Four, maybe five.'

'That in itself is a sin, my child.'

What should she say? She holds the curtain and watches the man's movements. What is his name? She remembers. Miessen.

Maybe she even has his card somewhere in her bag. Julius Miessen. German? Dutch? French? Who is he?

'So what else do you have to confess, child?'

'Confess?' She hesitates. Impure acts, that's what they used to say at school. I have committed impure acts. And the priest would make careful enquiry as to what these impure acts might have been.

'What nature of acts, my child?'

The man disappears into the sacristy. It's obvious to try there: the open door, a light showing, the possibility of rooms and corridors and another exit. Should she go now while he is out of sight? 'I've touched myself, Father.'

'How many times, my child?'

'How many times have I touched myself? I've no idea. I don't keep a diary. And I've been with a man. Maybe that's a little more important.'

The priest is unfazed by irony. 'How many times have you done that?'

'Twice.'

'With the same man?'

'Of course.'

Miessen reappears at the sacristy door. He's panicking. He's looking this way and that, and there's something repulsive about the sleek look of his face in the light from the clerestory windows. Something shifts in her guts, fear and triumph swimming together.

'And do you love this man?'

Does she love him? She isn't sure. She isn't even sure what love is. She knows fear well enough. Fear she recognises. And hate. But love? 'I'm very fond of him,' she whispers, 'and perhaps he loves me, I don't know. We seem ... suited to each other.' Why is she telling the priest this? Why isn't she making things up, giving Anne-Marie Laroche a whole set of her own sins?

Miessen walks past, mere feet from where she kneels, and

goes down the aisle back towards the body of the church, looking round anxiously, as though what he seeks might be hiding behind one of the pillars. The priest is lecturing her about fornication, its pitfalls and dangers, its effect upon God Himself. 'Remember, you are not your own,' he warns. 'You were bought at a price.'

What will Miessen's next move be? Will he assume that his quarry has left by one of the side doors, or will he guess that she is hidden somewhere inside the building? And why, in God's name, is he following her?

'My child?'

'Yes, Father?'

'If you have finished your confession you must make your act of contrition.'

She gets to her feet. 'Thank you, Father.'

'Your act of contrition, my child. Your penance—'

She picks up her suitcase. 'No penance is needed, Father. You see, my greatest sin is that I no longer believe in God.'

She steps out of the box. The church seems cool and vacant, empty of anyone who matters. She smiles at the old lady who moves to take her place in the confessional, and crosses to the door marked *Sacristie*. There is a corridor, then a room with wardrobes and hanging vestments and a gaunt, polychrome crucifix hanging on the wall. She crouches to open her suitcase, trying to do things as calmly as possible, as surely and exactly as she is able. Don't rush. *Hâte-toi lentement*, her mother always used to tell her when picking her up and tending grazed knees. There are nail scissors in her wash bag. She uses them to cut open the lining of the suitcase exactly between the two hinges. Inside is an identity card and food coupons in the name of one Laurence Aimée Follette. She slips the papers into her shoulder bag, closes the case and straightens up just as someone comes in, a priest in a threadbare soutane looking at her with startled amazement.

'For the refugees,' she says before he can utter a word. 'I

wondered where to leave them.' She takes off her coat, folds it and lays it on the suitcase. 'I only want to help, Father.'

She smiles and slips past him. At the end of the corridor a door opens out onto the street. Daylight brushes her face with drizzle. Students are milling around the entrance of the *lycée* across the street and Laurence Follette hurries through the throng and turns up a side street into the rue de l'Estrapade. No one seems to be following but still she goes directly across the street and then takes two right turns, which bring her round to the familiar square. Marie answers the door to her knock, Marie with her stern face and faint air of disapproval, Marie who cannot be her betrayer because she already knows where she is staying, and surely the whole point of following her from the station is to find out where she has taken refuge in the city.

Who is Julius Miessen? Who is he working for?

She retreats to Madeleine's room. For the first time she is afraid, truly afraid. Not the momentary fear of anticipating a parachute jump, or standing before a *barrage* and waiting to be searched, or finding that a man is tailing you through the streets of Paris. Not fear *of* something. Just fear, like a disease, a growth, thick and putrid, wedged behind her breastbone. Fear in each breath and each heartbeat. Fear rising up her oesophagus and souring the back of her mouth so that she finds herself swallowing a lot. Fear of what might happen, of what might be happening at this very moment while she sits, as helpless as an invalid, on the bed.

'I'm off home, Mademoiselle,' Marie calls through the door. 'Monsieur Clément will be back any minute.'

She listens for the maid's footsteps retreating down the corridor, and the front door opening and closing. What, she wonders, does Marie think about all this? Does she go home and talk about the strange, fraught woman who has appeared at the Pelletier apartment and been welcomed in by Monsieur Clément with open arms? Does she gossip? Does she talk about poor Madame Pelletier and her lovely baby and wonder aloud what the devil is going on, what on earth Monsieur Clément is playing at? Do her words filter through the intricate fabric of the city and reach the ears of the police or the Abwehr or the Gestapo?

She finds some matches in the kitchen and solemnly, in the kitchen sink, performs the cremation of the young student Anne-Marie Laroche.

||

Laurence Follette from Bourg-en-Bresse in the department of Ain is the occupant of this room in the Pelletier apartment now. Laurence. Faintly androgyne, like so many French names, symbolic perhaps of a profound ambiguity at the heart of the French people who once advocated Liberty, Equality, Fraternity but now proclaim Work, Family, Fatherland; a people for whom the same word, *baiser*, does for kiss and fuck.

Laurence waits. She waits for Clément, like a patient nursing her disease and waiting for the doctor who might at least offer a palliative to soothe her pain. The sound of the front door opening brings a great flood of relief, relief that must show in her face when she goes out to greet him for, after embracing her and telling her how wonderful it is to see her again and how much he has missed her, he holds her at arm's length and sees the cold pinch of fear in her face. 'Are you all right, Squirrel? What's the matter?'

'I'm fine. It's just ...' What should she say? Confession or obfuscation? 'Someone followed me. I think from the station. I threw him off but he knows I'm in the city. *They* know.'

'Who knows?'

She shrugs. 'I've no idea. I met him before. He tried to pick me up the last time I came. I thought he was a pimp, or something.'

Pimp. She uses the English word. She doesn't even know the French. *Souteneur?* Perhaps that's it. 'But now I wonder. Maybe he works for the police, maybe the Germans. Who knows? Anyway, now they can guess I'm staying somewhere in this area, in the Latin Quarter.'

They sit in the kitchen, which gives the illusion of being the warmest room in the apartment. The scrubbed deal table replaces the barriers between them that fear has dismantled. He opens a bottle of wine, a Romanée-Conti that, he says, his father would weep to see being drunk like this. 'So what happens now?' His tone is different, as though now he is somehow part of what she does.

She shakes her head. 'Someone knows I'm here. I'm dangerous, Clément, and not only to myself. I'm dangerous to you.'

He smiles. She can see what he is about to say. It's obvious, really. And knowing it makes her want to weep and laugh at the same time. 'You've always been dangerous to me, Squirrel. From the moment I first set eyes on you.'

'You'd be safe from me in England.'

'I wouldn't want that kind of safety. I'd want you with me.'

She looks up. She thinks of *le Patron* and Benoît, of all the people who depend on the circuit – Gaillard and Marcel and the collection of *résistants* who make up the *réseau* WORDSMITH. Gabrielle Mercey, and the family at Plasonne. She can simply step out of their world, without even saying farewell. 'You'd be willing to go if I came with you?'

He makes a small gesture of indifference. 'I got a phone call from Madeleine yesterday. The ducks have flown, she told me. It sounds like one of those messages they transmit on the radio.'

She attempts a smile, as though she has forgotten the trick and is having to relearn it. 'What does it mean?'

'That's my nickname for Augustine. *Mon petit canard*. The ducks are her and Rachel. It means they've got across the border into Switzerland. So I've no reason to stay in France, have I? And if you were to come with me ...'

That evening she goes up to the roof again and sends a wireless message out into the wild autumnal air, a message as quick as she can make it, as sharp and clear as she can be. I have been followed, she wants to write. Someone knows I'm in the city. The city itself is watching, waiting, the detector vans listening for the faintest hint of me. The wolves are circling, sniffing the air, baying for blood. This message – they are listening to this message. But all she transmits is: MECHANIC IS CONFIRMED

She knows what they'll think at Grendon, and in the offices in Baker Street, as it comes off the teleprinters: Alice is winning. But she's not; she's panicking. And when you panic, you drown.

She closes the transmission. The fragile lifeline with England is snapped. She packs the wireless set away and carries it downstairs, struggling to keep afloat, talking to herself, reassuring herself, trying to see the clear light of dawn in the dark of the evening. Fear is like a tide, under the influence of the waxing moon. She can feel gravity's hand, that elemental pull draining the blood from her face and drawing it from her body. The moon period. What was it she told Benoît all that time ago in Oxford? We're minions of the moon. Minions, slaves, worshippers. She takes the pistol from the spares compartment of the wireless case and puts it in her shoulder bag. 'The full moon is next Saturday so we'll go sometime this week,' she tells Clément. 'I'll find out tomorrow.' She feels the weariness in her smile. 'I want to be safe, just for a few minutes I want to be safe. It's so bloody tiring being afraid all the time.'

III

The café in the rue Saint-André des Arts is exactly the same as it was. Small, dull, of no consequence. As far as she can see no one has followed her. She walks in, feeling the weight of the pistol in her pocket, in the pocket of Madeleine's coat that she has borrowed, the hound's-tooth check that says, on the label, Molyneux. The man at the bar, a different man from her last visit, looks up with an equal indifference.

Is *la patronne* around? He shrugs and calls over his shoulder – 'Madame Julienne! Someone for you' – and the door at the back of the bar opens and there she is. Claire. Looking worried, looking suspicious, giving a faint smile of recognition. 'Come,' she says. 'Come round the back.'

Claire's little room has the same pictures, the same calendar with the same messages scrawled against the same dates. How do you recognise a traitor? What are the hints that give betrayal away? What are the lineaments of treachery? Claire is brisk and organised, like a travel agent who has booked an unusual but not entirely unknown itinerary. 'It's all arranged for the day after tomorrow, as long as the weather lifts. You'll have to see Gilbert about the details.'

Gilbert. She recalls that strange, oblique conversation in the office overlooking Portman Square, the tall and awkward Colonel with his even taller superior. *Jill Bear's our air movements man for the Paris area.* The whole thing seemed a kind of fantasy, something that might never happen. And now it is happening – Gilbert is expecting her; she has to meet him in the Tuileries, on the other side of the river. She has to be there at a specific time, at the circular basin in the Grand Carré, beside the statue of Cain. The correct place at the correct time. She must make sure.

'You know the Gardens, don't you?'

'Of course.'

And there is a little rigmarole they'll have to go through, a bit of question-and-answer. She and Claire rehearse it. 'Make sure you get it right. He's a stickler for detail.'

'I'll get it right.' She takes her hand from her pocket and holds it out. 'Thank you,' she says. At the door she pauses, as though the thought has that moment struck her. 'Why do you do it?'

Claire looks puzzled. 'Do what?'

Alice gestures as though to indicate the bar but in reality meaning everything, the planning, the danger, the looking over your shoulder and minding your back, the whole nightmare anxiety of the clandestine life. Fear is a caustic that soaks into everything – your clothes, your possessions, your skin. Perhaps you smell of fear as a heavy smoker smells of tobacco or an alcoholic smells of booze. 'All this,' she says. 'For the Organisation.'

The woman frowns. 'Don't ask fucking questions. You should know better than that. Questions require answers, and you don't always know the answer so you start making things up. I just do it, right? I just do it. So do you.'

There are few people around when she gets to the gardens. She remembers a painting in the Ashmolean museum in Oxford, something by Pissarro – *The Tuileries Gardens in Rainy Weather*. Reality mimics the painting: the autumnal trees, a scattering of rain, gusts of wind blowing women's skirts, puddles gleaming like silver coins, the whole view blended and blurred into cloud and drizzle. She finds the statue of *Cain Coming from Killing His Brother Abel* and strolls towards it, looking for likely watchers. A couple of off-duty German soldiers approach and try to engage her in conversation.

'I'm waiting for a friend,' she tells them.

'*Un Français?*'

'*Bien sûr.*' The gun, now in her shoulder bag, weighs heavily.

'Germans are better men.'

'Not if they haven't got any manners.'

She is saved – it's ridiculous, an absurd risk – by a shout of, 'Goodness, it's been a long time hasn't it?' from a man who comes striding across the gravel towards them. He's good-looking with a mop of wavy hair and eyes that do a lot of smiling. He nods at the Germans and takes her arm to draw her away. 'Didn't we last meet at Aunt Mathilde's?'

'It was ages ago,' she agrees. 'Before she moved to Montpellier.'

He kisses her on both cheeks, then turns to the watching soldiers. If they don't leave his cousin alone they'll find themselves explaining their behaviour to their superior officer. Their expressions fall and they wander off. Gilbert grins. 'The thing about our brave conquerors is that they always obey orders as long as they feel they're coming from someone important.'

'And you are important?'

'I *sound* important. That's what matters. And they have a sneaking suspicion that I have contacts.'

'And do you?'

He laughs. 'You must have contacts in order to survive in this damned city. Let's go somewhere a bit more comfortable.' He folds her arm in his and leads her off towards the rue de Rivoli to a café where he is known, and where you can actually get real coffee if you speak to the right waitress. Over coffee they chat for a while about nothing very much – what he used to do before the war, how he was a pilot, how he wants to get back to flying – and when he has paid, they go round the corner to a flat that he has, a two-roomed place with barely any furniture beyond a couple of chairs and a table and two mattresses on the floor. She feels like a tart, a casual pick-up preparing to negotiate terms. 'You must remember everything I say,' Gilbert tells her. 'Can you do that? Commit nothing to paper.'

'Of course.'

'Claire said two passengers ...'

'It all depends.'

'The pianist from CINÉASTE?'

'I'm not sure about her. I've got a meeting.'

'What's the trouble?'

She shrugs. She isn't going to be quizzed about matters that don't concern him. She should never have mentioned it to Claire, and Claire shouldn't have told Gilbert. This is how things come unravelled. 'I'll have to see. But the other passenger is all right.'

'So we play it by ear, do we?'

'I suppose so.'

'I'll need your help at the landing ground. You've organised drops, I presume? Pick-ups are a bit different.' He grins disarmingly, a little boy planning a prank. 'Of course they're different. The damned kite has to land for a start. But that's the problem – you've got to stand there as it lands, turns and taxies back to the take-off point. It makes the devil of a noise, seems enough to wake the dead, never mind the local police. So you need a bit of nerve to stick to it. Do you have nerve?' He looks her up and down.

'I've got nerve.'

'I'll bet you have. Now listen carefully. We use a three-light L with the long side upwind.' He puts coins on the table. 'A, B and C. A is the touchdown point, and that's where the reception party stands. B is one hundred and fifty metres downwind, but of course you need a greater total length for a landing ground.'

'Six hundred metres—'

'Minimum. And good solid ground underfoot. We had a Lysander bog down last spring and ended up having to torch her. It took a month to get the pilot back home, never mind the passengers. Still, we've not lost anyone yet.' His grin reminds her of Benoît's, the pure insouciance of it, the suggestion that he is sharing something intimate with her. 'The third light, C, is fifty metres to the right. That's the turning marker once the kite is down. He'll turn on that and then come back to A ready for take-off. We stand to the left of A and approach the plane from the port side once it's ready. That's the left.'

'I know it's the left. I know all this. I was briefed in London.'

'Then you'll know it twice. The pilots have instructions to shoot anyone approaching from the other side. It hasn't happened yet.'

'No one's approached from the right, or no one's been shot?'

Again that grin. 'Neither. The pilot keeps the engine running while any passengers get down. There'll be a couple of passengers inbound this time. The last passenger unloads their

262

luggage. Then our passengers climb on board, strap in and they're off. Five, six minutes on the ground if things go well. And Bob's your uncle.' He says it in English. Maybe he wants to show that he knows the language, knows the colloquialisms, knows exactly what he is doing. He produces a Michelin map of northern France and unfolds it on the table. 'Now the travel arrangements. You travel from Austerlitz. I'll be on the same train but I won't recognise you. Whether you travel separately or together is up to you. Whichever you think would be less conspicuous. You get tickets to Libourne. Not Bordeaux because you need a special pass for the coastal area. But you're going to get off at Saint-Pierre-des-Corps anyway. Got that?' He places his finger on the map, near the junction of the two rivers, the Loire and the Cher. 'Saint-Pierre-des-Corps is the through station for Tours—'

'It's miles away from Paris!'

'That's the way we do it. Three, four hours these days. You catch the 13.15 train. If you can't make it for some reason, you can get the next, an hour later. Remember, get your tickets right through to Libourne – not Bordeaux – but get off at Saint-Pierre-des-Corps. When you're there, you purchase a ticket for Vierzon. It's a branch line and you only go two stops to Azay-sur-Cher. But again, buy a ticket for the whole distance. I should be at Azay at the same time, but if not there's a hut behind the station where you'll find bicycles waiting. They'll be locked up.' He roots around in his jacket. 'Here are the keys. Don't lose them. Once you've unlocked the bikes you take the road direct to the village. You cross the railway line and head due south. It's signposted Azay-sur-Cher. After two kilometres, immediately before a woodland, turn left onto a cart track. Follow this track for another two kilometres and park the bikes. The landing ground is the open field on your left. Oh, and bring warm clothes. There'll be a lot of waiting around in the cold.'

It'll go fine, *comme sur des roulettes*, he adds, and she remembers Buckmaster's words: like clockwork. 'There'll be a message on Radio London giving the go-ahead. We're scheduled for tomorrow night, but you never know. "The garage man has greasy hands", that's the message. The whole op is codenamed MECHANIC.' He pauses and looks at her. 'And after the operation, what do you do?'

'I return to my circuit.' She looks at the map. 'Vierzon's on the Toulouse line. I can get the Toulouse train from there.' She pauses. She has said more than she needs, more than she intends. He watches her thoughtfully, his lips pursed.

'You could always return with the Lysander. Return to England, I mean. They can take three passengers at a pinch.'

'I've thought about that.'

'Maybe like that it would be safer for you.'

'I didn't come to France to be safe.'

'Of course you didn't. But these days things are especially difficult. It isn't easy to keep matters under control. Things ...' He waves a hand vaguely, 'fall apart. People do things they shouldn't. It's difficult to keep everyone happy.'

'What people? What are you talking about?'

He ignores her question, but smiles and catches up her hand and shakes it gently. 'You are too beautiful to be here, my dear Alice. I have seen others come here and have ugly things happen to them, others as lovely as yourself.'

Carefully she takes her hand back. 'My looks have nothing to do with it. Look, I must go now. I've got a meeting.'

He shrugs. 'Perhaps you'll think about what I said ...?'

She pushes her chair back and stands up. 'I will.'


IV


At the *métro* station she does the usual things – going in by one entrance and out by another, appearing to lose her way and then doubling back on herself. No one seems to be following. So she takes the train to Yvette's place as she did before and circles warily round the street where Yvette lives, sniffing round like a mammal whose nest has been violated by another. Things seem little different from the last time – people going about their quotidian lives with that listlessness that characterises the occupied city. Customers pick disconsolately through the flea market. A *clochard* with a dog begs for centimes. A busker plays the violin, badly. Women argue, kids shout.

Are there watchers?

She strolls past and turns into the café where the fat guy called Boger stands behind the bar. How do you manage to keep fat these days? 'This is for Yvette,' she says, handing a letter across the zinc. The man sucks his lip as though he hopes it might be nutritious.

'Make sure she gets it,' she says, and walks out.

Balzac's head, the mane of hair, the staring eyes and aggressive nose, the heavy jowls. Alice watches it from afar. She feels detached from everything, as though it's all in a dream, one of those where logic seems iron-bound and yet strange things happen, dreams in which she has a gun in her hand and she's prepared to use it if need be. She's prepared to kill and doesn't care if she gets killed. That's the strange thing. She doesn't care.

Nothing happens. The lanes of the cemetery coil like snakes around the tombs, their scales glistening in the rain.

Two forty-four.

Rules for making a rendezvous: always give a time that's an hour later than the one you intend. Will Yvette understand? Will she understand, and if she does understand, will she come? And if she comes, will she come alone?

In the wind and the drizzle people move among the tombs, placing a flower, standing for a moment in prayer or contemplation. Crows flap their way across the memorials, looking for scraps. There's mistletoe in the trees, clumps of mistletoe like rooks' nests. A quiet, mortifying plant, it seems fit for a cemetery.

What should she do? Figures skulk in the shadows of her imagination. Are they watching her, even now? You'll never know, that's the problem. Not until there is the hand on your shoulder. Like being hit by a rifle bullet – you never hear the shot that gets you. That's what they were told. The bullet travels faster than sound and so it reaches you before the noise of its passage through the air. Just so with an arrest – it'll come when you don't expect it, when you've covered all the options and you think you are safe. The knock on the door at the dead of night. The hand on the shoulder. The sudden stab of a gun barrel in the small of the back. Expect it at any moment and then you won't be surprised.

The third time she looks towards Balzac there is a small figure standing in front of the memorial, a frail figure in a fawn raincoat holding an umbrella against the drizzle, a woman with thin legs and an angular stoop as though she is already an old crone.

Cautiously she walks down the slope and stands beside her. Yvette is looking up at the writer's head on the plinth as though it were some kind of totem. Her face is wet with drizzle.

'I didn't know whether you'd come.'

'Why not?'

'Have you come alone?'

Yvette glances sideways. 'Of course.'

'Someone tailed me from Austerlitz yesterday. They were waiting for me to arrive.'

Silence. Balzac looks solemnly out into the afternoon. The city held no surprises for him; perhaps he wouldn't even have been surprised by this little encounter. Alice adds quietly, 'Did you bring them with you?'

'I don't know what you mean.' Terrified eyes; wide, pleading eyes as she grabs Alice's arm. 'You're going to get me out, aren't you? What's the matter, Marian? What's gone wrong?'

'You've betrayed me, haven't you?'

The wind quickens, stinging like salt in a wound. Yvette's

umbrella shudders and threatens to blow inside out. She struggles to close it. 'What do you mean?'

'I told you, they were waiting for me at the station. I threw them off, but they know I'm here in the city. No one else but you knew when I was due back in Paris and where I was coming from. No one but you.'

Yvette is shivering. She's frail and undernourished and perhaps she is cold. She was like that at Meoble Lodge, always cold. Alice grips the pistol in her pocket, feeling the other thing there as well, the small nut of the L pill against her knuckles. 'I don't trust you, Yvette. Not any more.'

'Of course you can trust me. For the love of God, I'm your friend, Marian. I'm Yvette. You know me.'

Alice looks round at the city of the dead. Living ghosts wander along the paths, peering hopelessly at the memorials. *What you are we were, what we are you will become.* She feels her own life hanging by a thread. 'I'll give you a final chance,' she tells her. 'If you come right now, without going back to your flat, I'll get you to England. You'll be safe. You'll see Violette again. But you've got to come right away. This instant.'

'How *can* I come right now? I can't just walk out.'

'Why the hell not? What's keeping you?'

It's then that she notices the woman. She's about fifty yards away down the slope, bending down to put flowers on a grave. Or maybe she's trying to see the inscription better. There's the same posture, the same manner of holding herself. The same leather jacket with the fur collar. The same blond curls, this time peeping from beneath a cloche hat. It's the Alsatian woman, the one who stopped her in the place de la Contrescarpe.

Alice senses things sliding out of control. Her mind makes calculations – short, desperate additions and subtractions. Where are the others? Who, among the scattered mourners in this city of dead souls, are watching the living? She grabs

Yvette's arm as one might grab hold of a child. She's light, a creature of hollow, sculpted bones. Alice speaks into her face, urgently, hoping that the words will hurt. 'You've lied, Yvette. You've lied the entire bloody time.'

Yvette's voice is the quiet, flaccid sound of despair. 'They've got Emile. They told me they'd let him go.'

'You believe that? They're the enemy, Yvette. They killed your husband, for Christ's sake. They killed Violette's father. Now they'll kill me and in all probability they'll kill you.'

There's a moment of stasis. Crows jeer overhead, like the chorus of some Greek tragedy. Wind rattles the branches. She sees the Alsatian woman turn away for a second and that's the moment she chooses to release her hold on Yvette's arm and run. She runs faster than she has ever run in her life. She runs up the slope, with the rain stinging her face and her feet skidding on the *pavé*. She runs. Whether anyone is pursuing her, she doesn't know. Running is action, running is doing, running isn't standing and waiting for them to get you. Running is freedom, momentary and perhaps illusory but freedom nevertheless. The freedom of the escaped prisoner. She has absurd, tangential thoughts as she runs. How proud her father would be, seeing her running like this. How proud Ned, how proud Benoît and Clément. They'd cheer her on, the men who occupied, in some way or other, her life. Run! They'd cry. Run! And so she runs. Not like the wind but with the wind, past memorial and mausoleum, leaping over tombs and skidding round calvaries, careless of whether they are after her or not. One or two people stare after her. An old man – a gravedigger? – leans on a spade and watches her go. Someone shouts, but the sound is disembodied and might mean anything. Just a young woman running through a cemetery. Curious.

At the gate she stops. There's no one there. She goes out through the gate and crosses the street, walking briskly. A few seconds' lead. Nothing to waste. She takes a side road which cuts the cemetery out of sight. Somewhere nearby there's the roar of a car and the wail of a police siren. Is that for her? She turns and runs to the far end of the street, turns again and runs once more, going by instinct, crossing a wide road at a run, going uphill towards what she remembers from the map as Belleville, a warren of old and decaying buildings perched on a hill at the edge of the city, a hill as high as the butte de Montmartre. They'll be gathering round the north of the cemetery and spreading out from there. You have to second-guess their every move. Cars, vans, they'll be able to muster a fleet if they think her important enough.

She *is* important. A British terrorist trapped in the city – what could be better? As she crosses a street, someone shouts. She looks round. Is it Miessen, that dreadful man who followed her before? Can it be him? But she doesn't wait to find out. She darts across the street and runs down an alleyway, not caring where she's going, desperate to get away from him, from them, from anyone who may be following. She hurries on, now walking, now running, past incurious pedestrians, through streets that become lanes and alleys winding between ancient and dilapidated tenements. A maze. Somewhere in the distance she can hear more sirens, like the dead calling from the cemetery itself. She can feel them at her back, sniffing at the air of the ramshackle quarter, breathing down her neck. Children flock out of a school like starlings in their black smocks, laughing and chattering. She dodges through them and finds herself at an intersection of six streets converging on a small square where housewives queue outside a greengrocer's and a horse-drawn cart stands outside a wine cellar. Where she pauses to get her breath and her bearings.

The horse steams in the damp air. There's dung on the ground and the tang of urine tainting the atmosphere.

Which way to go? It's like a puzzle out of *Alice in Wonderland*. Which exit to choose? One of them might be death, one might be life. Which?

As she hesitates a car drives into the square, another black Citroën, its bonnet like a coffin draped with white chevrons.

Doors open and two men climb out. She ducks away into a side street, hearing a car door slam behind her and footsteps follow. A voice shouts out – German or French, it doesn't matter which because the sense is clear in any language: Halt!

And she has no choice but to obey because the street ahead of her ends in a steep flight of stairs. A cul-de-sac. And at the top of the steps, for a fleeting moment, there's the figure of Julius Miessen.

A tide of panic threatens to overwhelm her. She turns. Behind her two men are silhouetted at the entrance to the *impasse*. She looks back and the stairs are empty. Miessen, if it was Miessen, has vanished.

'You, come here!' one of the men shouts. He's wearing a leather coat, his companion, a fawn mackintosh. Both have trilby hats, as though they have modelled themselves on gangsters seen in American films. They stand in the middle of the street as she walks towards them, one hanging back slightly to the rear of the other. They're nothing more than faces, nondescript, bony. One of them, the nearer one, has a thin moustache. She can hear her father on the subject of such moustaches: travelling salesmen and theatre impresarios. The man at the back has his hand in his pocket. He looks like the fall guy.

Her panic subsides to be replaced by something else, a sense of detachment. 'You frightened me,' she calls out to them. 'What do you expect, charging around like that? What do you want?'

'*Venez.*' The nearer one beckons her forward, and like any innocent civilian she's obeying. She's anxious, but she's obeying. 'I'm coming, I'm coming. Who are you looking for?'

'Take your hand out of your pocket!'

'I'm sorry?' She doesn't understand his accent. She wants to obey but she can't quite understand what he is saying. 'I'm sorry?'

'Your hand!'

'I'm sorry?'

She's closer now. A dozen yards. Too far, but it'll have to do.

She knows the distances and the angles, she knows the timing. Mere fractions of a second. Make the first move and they're always on the back foot, always trying to catch up. It's the only advantage you'll have.

'*Haut les mains!*' the man shouts.

As though trying to obey, she holds her shoulder bag out in front of her and carefully puts it on the ground. Is that what they want? Their eyes follow her movement, watch the bag as if that is what they're after, the bag and all that's in it. Maybe it gives her a second's advantage, maybe as much as that. She pulls the pistol from her pocket and racks the slide all in one movement, like on the range at Meoble Lodge, dropping to a crouch, the pistol extended and gripped with both hands, covering the further of the two. The Fairbairn-Sykes position. Two shots, double tap, the reports sharp and irrevocable in the narrow space of the *impasse*.

Time slows.

The nearer man flinches. His companion folds up as though he's been punched in the stomach. She shifts rightwards, covers the nearer man, squeezes the trigger twice more. Another two shots, quick succession, the slide flashing back and forth, empty cases tinkling out on the ground like something from a Christmas cracker. The man shouts and goes down on one knee, holding up his left hand as though he might ward off further bullets.

Somewhere, someone shouts. Alice runs forward. The man nearer to her is pulling something from his waistband. She fires again, at two yards, into his head. A shot in the abdomen kills, the instructor said. It's the biggest target in the body and it kills because the contents of the gut spill out into the abdominal cavity and infection sets in and there's nothing anyone can do. But it may take a day or two. A head shot's more difficult but it's decisive.

The other man lies there with a vacant expression, staring up at the sky through the one eye that remains intact. She goes to recover her shoulder bag, then runs past the two bodies back into the square. The queue of housewives has dispersed. Two people peer out from a café doorway. Faces watch from windows. The Citroën is still there, the engine running.

Where is Miessen?

She looks round the square at the five other roads that converge on it. Thin slices of buildings like narrow wedges of cheese divide the streets. Beneath the sign for rue des Envierges someone has painted a red hammer and sickle on the wall, by accident or design both dripping blood, and the slogan *Front National*. Is that what attracts her? She runs into the street as fast as she can and down towards the end, oblivious to the pounding of her heart and the straining of her lungs. At the far end of the street there's light and, through a gap in the buildings, the sudden sight of the whole of the city laid out below her. The view brings her to a halt. The cloud has begun to break up and a watery evening sunlight slides across the sea of tiles, catching the odd window, bringing a meretricious shine to the view. The Eiffel Tower stands away in the distance and the dome of Les Invalides, symbols of an ideal Paris; but reality is close by and it's drab and squalid, the ground dropping steeply down what may once have been a country hillside but is now an urban precipice with rotting tenements clinging to the slope.

For a moment she hesitates. Something wells up, bubbling behind her breastbone, something sour and intrusive. She bends over, retching, gasping, spitting out saliva and bitter slime from deep down inside her. And all the while a small fragment of her mind remains cold and objective, watching her from a distance as though detached from all this emotion. They'll encircle the *butte*, it tells her. Once they discover those bodies they'll be deploying troops. They'll come after you and they'll watch all the ways out, guard the *métro* stations, keep you penned up like a rat in a drain. You've got no more than a few minutes in hand.

And where is Miessen? Was he really there, or has he become a creature of her imagination? She draws in air and waits for

272

the nausea to die down. The objective mind is louder now, her thinking clearer. The pistol is more of a liability than an asset. The gutter at her feet runs into a culvert. She swings her arm and throws the weapon into the shadows as far as she can. Then she sets off down the hill, down broken steps and steep, winding alleys, going by instinct, knowing that sooner or later the alleyways will level out into the boulevard that runs across the base of the hill, which is where they'll be waiting. There are few people around. Many of the houses seem abandoned, the windows empty, doors gaping. Washing hangs like bunting celebrating a long-forgotten victory. A woman stands at one door with arms folded across her chest and her mouth turned down in disgust. 'What's the hurry?' she calls. 'It's already too late.'

Her laughter seems to follow Alice down. Already too late? At the bottom of the hill a dog sniffs hopelessly at a pile of rubbish, slinking away as she comes near. Out of a side street a handcart rumbles across her path and brings her to a halt.

An old man peers out from behind a heap of used clothes. He's as wrinkled as a walnut and wears a woollen cap on his head that makes her think of the tumbrels that rolled through the city during the Terror. This is new terror, with new myths and new nightmares.

'One of your coats,' she says. 'I'll swap with mine.'

He looks her up and down, munching on the inside of his lips. 'I dunno about that.'

'It's Molyneux.'

'Why would you want to get rid of that, then? You nick it, or what?'

'And I'll throw in a thousand francs if you'll give me a beret as well.'

A thousand! The deal is done. She scrabbles in her bag, hands the money over, grabs the first coat that seems to be her size and pulls it on. The cloth smells, of damp, of sweat, of age, of decay and despair. Who wore it before? Some Jew, probably. There's a glut of Jewish clothes on the market. She feels in the pocket of Madeleine's coat for the small bullet of the L pill and slips it into the new coat. Then she puts Maddy's on the cart, careful to push it beneath other clothes.

'The beret?'

The old man rummages through the heap of cloth, finds a pancake of black felt and tosses it towards her. What would her mother say? Lice, fleas, scabies, all those creeping parasites that you might catch. She pulls the hat down over her head and tucks her hair up. 'The best deal you'll do today,' she tells him and he shrugs indifferently and rattles off across the cobbles. Cautiously, like a small mammal listening for the sound of predators, she approaches the end of the street and looks out at the boulevard de Belleville.

The street is lined with autumnal trees and wide enough to accommodate two roadways, with a space down the middle that might have once been gardens of a kind but is now just a strip of muddied gravel. Down either side of the street is a line of drab market stalls. There aren't many customers, and those that there are have all stopped to watch an army lorry parked fifty yards away with soldiers piling out of it. Another *rafle*? Whistles blow. More vehicles arrive. Barbed-wire barriers are being dragged into place along the pavement, turning the boulevard into a line of demarcation. A radio babbles from a *Kübelwagen* while an *Unteroffizier* shouts orders. People at the market stalls stare, wondering what is happening, who will be rounded up, who will be searched, whether or not to pack up and go home.

Alice steps back out of sight. Time is racing now, leaving her struggling in its wake. In a few minutes the soldiers will be moving forward into the narrow streets. Can she bluff her way out? They're looking for a woman with long, fair hair and wearing a hound's-tooth check coat. Maybe they know her as Anne-Marie Laroche. Maybe, if Yvette has talked, they know her as Marian Sutro. So maybe they won't think twice about Laurence Aimée Follette from Bourg-en-Bresse, dressed in drab brown and a black beret; maybe she can just walk up to the barricade and show her identity card and be waved through.

But she has only one chance, a single cast of the dice, with her life resting on it. So she hesitates, holding the dice, summoning up the courage to throw.

It's then that she sees the children. They're behind her, coming from a church, shepherded by two nuns with wide, starched headdresses: a gaggle of little boys, maybe three dozen, coming round the corner towards her, their clogs rattling on the *pavé*. They are meant to be walking in pairs but discipline is breaking down – they're jostling and pushing, spilling across the pavement and onto the narrow street. Where, she wonders, are they heading?

'Rue Timbaud,' the nun replies when asked. 'The orphanage of the Daughters of Charity.' She has a pallid face of dough and the smell of sanctity about her, musty and faintly scented, as though she has spent most of her life in an atmosphere of candle smoke and incense. Alice remembers the smell and the look, a world in which cleanliness is equated with godliness, where faces and floors are scrubbed with equal energy.

'There's a *barrage* up ahead.'

'A *barrage*?' Panic opens the nun's eyes. 'We've got to get the children back home. They can't wait.'

'They must be looking for someone. Who knows? Look, if you like, I'll help you.'

The nuns smile. Alice smiles. 'I'm Laurence,' she says, lifting one of the errant children in her arms and moving to the head of the crocodile. 'Come on, let's see if we can march properly,' she calls. 'Can we march like men? Left, right, left right, arms out straight. Can we do that?'

'Ladies don't march,' one of the children complains.

'This one does.'

'Are you a soldier?'

'As a matter of fact, I am.' And as if to demonstrate the fact she strides forward. Giggling and swinging their arms like puppets, the children follow her out into the open space of the boulevard, their clogs clattering. Across the road in front of them, soldiers are now drawn up for a hundred yards or more. Under-officers are calling orders, getting them into line, preparing to advance into the side streets. The children stumble to a halt. Some of the men smile and point. '*Die französische Armee*,' one of them says. The French Army. There's laughter in the ranks.

'*Allons enfants!*' Alice cries. Her squad of infants gathers itself and is about to advance once more when a lieutenant steps forward with hand raised. 'Excuse me, Mademoiselle, I'm afraid you'll have to wait.' He seems no more than eighteen or nineteen, a bright, fresh-faced boy with nervous eyes. His French is solid and accurate, the French of the schoolroom polished perhaps by occasional summer holidays across the border.

'What d'you mean, we can't pass?' she cries. With the toddler still clinging to her neck she turns to display her flock. 'These children need to get home. They need a wash and their supper and then they need to get to bed.'

'We have orders,' the lieutenant insists.

'To stop children? How can that be possible?'

'Not to stop children. To close the area. There's a dangerous terrorist at large.'

'Well, we're leaving, aren't we? So we cannot be in any danger, can we?'

'That's not the point.'

'Surely it is exactly the point. These poor children, victims of the bombing, need to get to their home.'

He looks at the line of children behind her. 'Are they Jews?'

'Of course they're not Jews. They're with the Sisters, aren't they? They're Christians, living with the Sisters on the rue Timbaud. You can check if you like. The Daughters of Charity.'

He sniffs, as though wondering which way the wind's blowing. Then he seems to decide. 'Your papers, please.'

As she rummages in her bag for her identity card, one of the children pulls at her coat. 'Daniel's wet himself, Miss.'

276

She looks round. The child in question stands there with a thread of urine dribbling down his leg. A nun hurries forward. 'This is disgraceful!' she cries as she crouches to deal with the boy. 'Frightening God's creatures.'

Alice turns back to the officer. 'Now look what you've done. May I speak with your superior officer, please? There must be someone in charge round here.'

The young man blushes. 'I'm in charge.'

'Then I demand you stop frightening these children and let us through.'

He's confused, torn between his duty and the palpable stupidity of corralling a bunch of babies. 'Go through,' he says, brushing her identity card aside. 'Get out of here.'

Behind him, the ranks part. One of the soldiers wolf-whistles. '*Die Rattenfänger von Hameln,*' a voice shouts. The Rat-catcher of Hamelin. More laughter. The Pied Piper smiles and makes a gesture that's half a wave, half a salute and the column of children moves forward through the line of soldiers, through the trees and the market stalls of the central reservation, across the roadway on the other side and into the opposite street. Suddenly they are away from the noise of the military and into an illusory calm.

The Sister takes hold of the toddler. 'Thank you for your help,' she says. 'I imagine you'll want to be moving on.'

'I'm afraid I have to.'

'Don't use the *métro*,' the nun warns her. 'They'll shut it down. They always do.' She smiles sympathetically. 'And God bless you,' she adds.

## V

She walks through the gathering dusk of the city, hurrying through the back streets, crossing boulevards like an animal slinking across an open field where predators lie in wait. Military vehicles roar past while she hangs back in doorways.

Crowds issuing up from the *métro* mill around helplessly in the darkness. For some of the way she joins up with two girls who are trying to get home to Issy in the south. They are speculating about what has happened. A power failure was one possibility, but that doesn't explain the military vehicles. 'There's always something going on,' one of the girls complains. 'Maybe it's the Jews again. I mean, there's still hundreds of them around. If not the Jews, then it's communists.'

Once across the river Alice separates from them, apologising for leaving, agreeing that they should meet up again, taking down a phone number. She watches them go with regret. Fear stalks her once she is on her own, fear that is only partly assuaged when the door to the apartment on the place de l'Estrapade finally closes behind her.

'You look a complete mess,' Clément exclaims. 'What have you been up to? And where on earth did you get that coat? Didn't you take one of Maddy's?'

She detaches herself from his embrace and lights a cigarette, her hands shaking. 'I had to give it away.'

'That'll make her happy.'

'They nearly got me, Clément. They had me bottled up in Belleville—'

'What the hell were you doing in Belleville? It's a slum.'

'Meeting Yvette.'

'Who the hell's Yvette?'

'Yvette,' she repeats, as though it's obvious. 'Yvette. I went to meet her and they almost caught me.' She looks round, looks at her watch, looks for distraction. There are things to do, preparations to make, decisions to reach; anything but thinking. 'The radio. *Radio Londres*. We need to know if the pick-up is on.'

He leads her into the salon, pours a glass of wine, tries to sit her down on one of the uncomfortable sofas. 'There's time yet. Tell me what happened.'

But she can't sit down. Sitting down would mean inertia and

she cannot sit still, not at the moment. There are voices in the background, high-pitched, angry voices chattering words that are not quite audible, like an angry conversation taking place in another room. She tries to look at him but somehow she can't do that either, she can't look at anything for any length of time, can't concentrate on anything, can't bring her mind into focus on any single thought, certainly can't sit down. 'Will Madeleine really be cross about the coat?'

He laughs. 'Maddy? I shouldn't think she'll notice.'

Madeleine won't be cross. It's a blessed relief. She pauses to listen to the voices. But the sane part of her mind is still there, struggling for command. You're imagining things, it tells her. It's the stress. Hysteria. She draws on her cigarette, feeling the bite of smoke in her lungs, and looks round for something to do. The cigarette. She concentrates on that, on how to breathe the smoke in and how to expel it. That'll do for now. That, and trying to ignore the voices.

'You haven't told me what happened, Marian.'

'I killed someone.' She says it quietly. Perhaps he won't hear what she said. Would that make the confession invalid, if the priest didn't hear it exactly? But he has heard. He stands there looking at her with confusion in his face. 'You've done *what*?'

She turns her head away. 'Two men. Maybe both. I'm not sure. Yes, I'm sure. Both.'

He bends and puts his hands on her shoulders and tries to look into her eyes, as though he might read the truth there. '*Two men*? What on earth do you mean?'

Isn't it clear enough? She has killed people. That's what the voices seem to be saying. They're murmuring, just below the level of audibility so that she isn't certain they are even there: she has killed two men. Killing is what everyone else seems to be doing at the moment, except that they mostly do it at one remove, dropping a bomb or firing a shell or launching a torpedo, or even sitting at a laboratory bench and designing weapons. But she has done it exactly as they promised at

Meoble Lodge – at close quarters, hand to hand. Double tap. And in cold blood, more or less. A good term that, cold blood. Because blood's never cold. Not until you're dead, anyway.

She makes herself look him in the eye. 'They had me cornered in a cul-de-sac in Belleville. So I shot them. I'm a murderer, Clément. They've turned me into a murderer.'

'Don't be absurd.'

'And that man was there, the man who followed me before. I saw him there. Julius Miessen he's called.'

'Well, he's not following you now.' He reaches out and pulls her against him. She feels the sting of tears. He bends and kisses her cheek and her eyes, and then her mouth. She tries to pull away. 'The radio,' she insists. 'We must listen to the radio.'

'Don't you ever give up?'

'I can't give up,' she replies. 'Don't you understand? If I give up, I'm dead.'

They sit in the *salon* with the wireless on, tuned through the roar of jamming to *Radio Londres*. The drumbeat of the letter V plays out into the room. And then the announcer's voice: '*Ici Londres. Les Français parlent aux Français*. First we have some messages for our friends.'

They wait as the messages are read out, the sentences of nonsense, sometimes poetic, often merely banal. The voice is calm, like a parent reciting a poem to a child, oblivious to the noise all around:

'*Grand-mère a cueilli de belles fleurs ... La pluie tombe sur la plaine ... Jean veut venir chercher ses cadeaux ... Le cadavre exquis boira le vin nouveau ... Le garagiste a les mains pleines de graisse ...*'

'That's it,' she cries. 'The garage man has greasy hands. That's the one.' The mess of emotion that she feels becomes, for a moment, something physical. Nausea, bile bubbling up inside her throat. 'We're going. The pick-up is on. The trouble is ...'

What is the trouble? The trouble is that she feels sick, that the voices are still whispering to her, like a tune going round and round in her head, something that you can't get rid of.

'The trouble is, they'll be watching for me. The whole of bloody Paris will be looking for me now. They know I've organised a pick-up and they've got my description. Yvette will have told them everything. I'm blown wide open, Clément.' *Brûlée* is the word. So much better than the English because that is what she feels – burned, scorched. 'I'm a danger to everyone.' She attempts a smile. 'Radioactive.'

Clément shrugs. 'I'm used to that. All you have to do with something that is radioactive is keep it in a lead-lined container. Where do we have to go tomorrow? You've not told me anything yet.'

'We've got to catch the Bordeaux train.'

'From Austerlitz? That's easy.' He smiles, that infuriating smile that he always uses when he is about to prove you wrong or foolish, the smile she loathed and loved at the same time. 'We catch the train further down the line, at Ivry. We'll use the laboratory van. The Collège has certain privileges and one of them is the van – it runs pretty often between the Collège itself and the lab at Ivry. Tomorrow it'll be going to Ivry. Does it all the time.' He takes her hand and draws her towards him. 'Now you need some rest. More than anything, you need to sleep.'

# Third Moon

|

She dreams. Not the falling dream this time but a running dream, running through alleys, running from people, killing people who won't lie down and die but speak to her in voices she doesn't understand. Sometimes her parents are there, sometimes Ned, once there's Benoît. The alleyways have no end, no way out, all ways blocked. An *impasse*. And then there's another part of the dream that is more dangerous still, a part where she's lying naked, on the borderline between want and need, and Clément's shadow is over her, exploring the inner workings of her body, touching her in places where the machinery seems broken or defective. 'You're beautiful,' he tells her, but she knows otherwise.

She wakes to his presence in the darkness beside her, the corrugations of his spine against her belly and her breasts. The voices, if there were voices, have ceased. She slides away from him, slips out of bed and crosses the cold floor to find Madeleine's dressing gown. The air in the apartment has the dead hand of winter about it. The lavatory seat is cold. Warm vapour rises around her as she pisses.

Memories come slowly, unpicked from her dreams: Yvette at the tomb of Balzac. The running, the shooting, two men dying. And Clément bringing her comfort of a kind. First Benoît, now Clément. Is it fear that has made her like this?

She returns to the bedroom, feeling her way through the darkness. He is sleeping still. She crosses to the window and pulls back the blackout curtains. The moon, a gibbous moon, a hunchbacked moon, is setting. There is the faint flush of dawn to the east but the sky is still dark and if she cranes upwards the stars are visible. She feels the snatch of fear and excitement, a compound emotion like that of sex.

There is movement in the bed behind her. 'What time is it?'

She lets the curtain fall back. 'Time to get up. Marie will be here soon.'

II

'I'm leaving today,' she explains. 'Going back to the South-west.'

The maid nods, tight-lipped, serving them coffee and a few slices of bread with a thin scrape of something that may be margarine. 'I expect it's better that way.' She has to leave before lunch to see to her mother. 'I'll be back this evening to prepare your dinner, Monsieur Clément,' she says, but by the evening all she will find will be a letter from him explaining that he too has left, and where there is money for her, and what to say if anyone asks.

*Monsieur Clément has gone to the country for a while. He left no forwarding address.*

'She'll assume we've gone off together,' Marian says.

'Of course she will.'

'And she'll tell Madeleine, who'll tell Augustine.'

He shrugs, that Gallic shrug.

With Marie gone there are things to do, clothes to pack – borrowed for the duration from Madeleine – food to prepare for the evening meal, a thermos flask of coffee to make. She explains the plan, what train they will take, where they will get off, how the whole operation will go. Clément writes a letter to Madeleine, something anodyne, exhortations to look after *les*

283

*canards* if she can and he'll be in touch as soon as possible. And one for Augustine, to be forwarded if possible. *We'll have to sort things out after the war*, he writes, but after the war seems an impossible concept, something dreamed up by a theoretical physicist, a place and time where anything might be possible, or nothing.

Marian watches him seal the envelope and address it, feeling a curious detachment from what is happening. Nothing around her seems real. The mouldering apartment, Clément, her own presence there, the memories of what happened that night and the day before. She might be enacting a cover story, playing the part with care, getting the lines perfect, but knowing all the time that the whole thing is a careful construct, a lie she is forced to play.

The midday news announces an early curfew. There is talk of security, of terrorists in the city, of the scurrilous and underhand methods of the Anglo-Saxons, of the murder of two officers of the German police in cold blood. They eat a frugal lunch, not saying much, like a married couple who have been so long together that they have exhausted all the possibilities.

'What's the matter, Squirrel?' he asks, but she only shakes her head. Nothing's the matter that can be explained in a few words, and each phrase she wants to utter seems to contradict the one that came before: she loves him and she doesn't love him; she wants to escape with him and she wants to stay here; her loyalty is to no one but herself and her loyalty is to WORD-SMITH. She is a woman who is free and pure; she is a woman polluted. She's a soldier fighting in the front line; she's a murderer. And where does Benoît come into this knot of paradox? She wants Benoît for his normality, for his lack of guile, precisely for his lack of ambiguity.

Afterwards they leave the apartment together, wearing warm coats and hats against the cold and carrying suitcases, like any number of people leaving their homes these days, leaving the city, going into exile, going to the East, vanishing off the face of the earth. She pulls the brim of her hat down to try and hide her face. Are people looking for her? She feels curiously indifferent to whether they are or not, as though it is all happening to someone else, the other person in her life, the girl called Alice who knows what to do and how to do it – the girl who has shot down two pursuers in cold blood, who can summon riches from the sky and communicate with the gods.

III

The service entrance of the Collège de France is only five hundred metres away on rue Saint-Jacques, guarded by wrought-iron gates that open as soon as the gatekeeper recognises Clément. The van is waiting, a brown and lumpish Citroën TUB sitting behind the neoclassical buildings of the Collège like a turd at the backside of an elegant old lady. There are others travelling, a technician who will drive and a woman who is going out to the laboratory to pick up some samples.

'Laurence is an old family friend,' Clément explains as they climb aboard. 'We're going away for the weekend.'

The woman looks askance. 'How's Augustine?' she asks pointedly.

'She's fine, the baby's fine, everyone's fine.'

'They're in the Savoie, aren't they?'

'Annecy, yes.'

'Give them my love when you're next in touch.'

Equipment is loaded into the van after them, instruments for the Ivry lab, some lead-lined containers that hold radioactive isotopes. Clément and the woman talk, of dysprosium and lanthanum, of cross-sections and neutron capture, while Alice sits beside them and feels herself an intruder in a foreign world.

'Did you hear about the shooting in Belleville?' the technician asks over his shoulder as he drives. 'It was on the news.'

They've heard something. Apparently they've arrested someone. The chemist believes they're also looking for a woman. At least, that's the story going round.

'Communists, I expect,' the technician says. 'Don't these bloody people realise that there'll be reprisals? More innocent deaths, and all for what?'

Alice tries to display indifference to the news. From the back of the van she can see little of the journey. There is no traffic beyond the morning rush of bicycles, no roadblocks beyond a moment at the Porte de Choisy when they have to slow as a gendarme flags them down. At the last moment the man appears to recognise the van and waves them on. Within half an hour of leaving the Collège, the van has drawn to a halt outside the station of Ivry-sur-Seine.

It is a morning of brisk breeze and ragged cloud, the southern outskirts of Paris rinsed by the recent rain, littered with leaves and buffed up to a shine by the wind so that one might almost ignore the drab acres of cheap housing and shoddy factories, the wasteland of railway sidings and warehouses.

'Have a good weekend,' the chemist says as they get down. She is not smiling.

'I'll bring you a surprise,' Clément promises her. 'Some *foie gras.*'

'Then it wouldn't be a surprise.'

On the platform a bedraggled collection of people wait for the train. They carry bags and suitcases and have the hungry look of hunter-gatherers in their eyes: Paris is a starveling – the countryside where they are headed is the land of plenty. Alice and Clément stand aloof, huddled against the wind and talking of little, as though none of this really matters. They are just a couple on a suburban station with a plan for the weekend that involves betrayal and deceit.

The Bordeaux train draws in from the Gare d'Austerlitz half an hour late and already packed. Even in the first-class carriages it is only possible to find two seats together by begging people to move. There is grumbling and complaint but eventually they are settled, wrapped up in each other's company, apparently oblivious to their fellow travellers. Clément puts his arm around her. She feels his warmth, a warmth that she has always guessed at but knows now as something intimate, an aura given off to her directly from skin to skin, a fluid like that which courses dangerously inside her. 'If only ...' she says, but she never finishes the sentence and when he asks she only shakes her head. 'Nothing. It doesn't matter.'

*If only we were really going away for the weekend. If only this journey would never end. If only there were no such thing as choice.*

At Étampes, police get on board and walk down the corridors, stepping over people and suitcases, demanding papers and asking questions. An officer stands at the door of the compartment and calls for all identity cards. There is the dutiful pause while people rifle through handbags, search through pockets. Alice takes out the card marked *Laurence Aimée Follette* and hands it over, then reaches up and kisses Clément. Insouciance, carelessness, indifference in the face of daily inconvenience. The policeman glances at her photo, glances at her face, and hands the document back. With great sighs the train traipses on into the flat farmland of La Beauce, where the fields are brushed green with sprouting winter wheat and the sky is a cool autumnal blue.

In the outskirts of Orléans they slow. There was a bombing raid a few nights earlier and the marshalling yards of Fleury-les-Aubrais are wrecked, wagons thrown about, buildings still smoking, rails twisted here and there as though knotted by some bad-tempered child. In silence people stare out of the window at these signs of what is to come, while the carriages stutter and jolt over the single track that has been put back in commission. At the station itself doors slam, people come and go, heavy boots clumping along the corridors, Germans this time, shoving their way down the carriages.

'Why are you travelling to Libourne?' they ask.

Clément glances at Laurence and gives her a kiss. 'We're having a few days away.'

The German looks at her and then at her papers. 'You're a long way from home.' He speaks good French. There is something disturbing about that: no barrier of incomprehension behind which you might hide.

'I've come to see Clément. I've missed him. And in Paris, you know, there's his family around.' She looks the German dead in the eye and gives a little smile. 'It's natural, isn't it, wanting to be on our own?'

'How do you know him?'

She clings to his arm, silly, infatuated, doing dangerous things with an older man. 'From years ago, in Annecy. Our parents knew each other. We used to spend holidays together.'

The man thinks a moment, says, 'Wait,' and goes off with their documents. Alice doesn't move. Time slows, indicated only by the thin trickle of sweat from her armpits. She thinks of Ned. Gravitational time dilation, that is a phrase he used. He tried to explain it to her and only got annoyed when she likened it to how time speeded up when you were enjoying yourself. 'That's subjective!' he cried in exasperation. 'Nothing more than an impression. What I'm talking about is a *real* difference caused by being in a different gravitational field.' Is she now in a different gravitational field? Time seems slowed to the point where this moment in this crowded compartment with her hand gripped in Clément's appears eternal.

'What can they be doing?' she whispers.

'Looking at lists, I expect. Names. Nothing more.' He seems remarkably cool. Maybe he is better suited to the clandestine life than she.

The soldier returns, sliding open the door to the compartment with a crash. 'All right,' he says, passing the documents back. At the same moment, with a peremptory jolt that is like time itself changing gear, the train moves forward, on through the city of Orléans itself, the city of the Maid, la Pucelle, St Joan of Arc. And then they are past the buildings and into the bare fields of the flood plain with the line of the river visible as a distant fringe of willows. She dozes, her head against Clément's shoulder, his arm round her. She recalls the dreams she had as a girl, wanting only this – to be alone with Clément. And now she feels nothing but a strange detachment, a sense of the remoteness of things, as though she were somewhere else, watching their two figures from a distance.

Beaugency, Blois, Amboise. The train rumbles across the river on a stone bridge and edges its way through the drab suburbs of Tours, past factories and marshalling yards, rattling over points, lurching sideways so that passengers, standing to get their cases down, are thrown against one another.

Saint-Pierre-des-Corps, Saint Peter of the Bodies, a name that emerged, presumably, from the charnel house of Catholic guilt and damnation. They stand up to retrieve their suitcases, step over feet, shuffle down the corridor to the end of the carriage. Clément climbs down onto the platform and takes the suitcases from her, then helps her down. The guard blows his whistle and the train draws away, leaving a scattering of passengers on the platform like the debris left behind by an ebbing tide.

And Gilbert.

He has got down from a carriage further up the train. He is carrying a briefcase, looking like a travelling salesman bound for a meeting with a client. Without so much as a glance at them he turns and walks away towards the concourse and the ticket office. They queue behind him, and once they have bought their tickets, follow him to the platform. There is no one around, no one taking the slow train to Vierzon, no one to notice them on this late autumn afternoon with the sun casting long shadows and the wind cold on their faces. When the train appears they climb into the same compartment, talking idly as though they are strangers who have been thrown together by chance. But once the door has closed Gilbert changes. 'I missed you at Austerlitz.' His tone carries a hint of accusation.

'We got on at Ivry. We thought it might be easier.'

'A good thing too. The place was crawling with police. There were posters all over the station, with a description that fits you well enough.'

'Posters!'

He nods. 'And your names. Marian Sutro, is that right? Also known as Alice, also known as Anne-Marie. They call you a Jew. Are you Jewish?'

'Not for generations. Not even for the Nazis.'

'Anyway, there's a price on your head. Five hundred thousand francs. Pretty cheap, I'd say.' He looks at Clément, his eyes flicking down to take in their held hands. 'Where's the second passenger? You said there would be two. Wasn't the other one from CINÉASTE?'

'She's not coming.'

'Why is that?'

'I told you I had my doubts about her.'

'And this is Monsieur Mechanic, I presume. Have you ever flown before?'

'Never.'

'Don't eat too much beforehand.'

'Eat too much? You mean we get dinner?'

'All part of the service.' He turns back to Alice. 'Looks like you got out just in time. Maybe you should leave tonight as well, go back in the other seat.'

'She's going to,' Clément says.

She shrugs and looks out of the window at the fields of France. A price on her head. Five hundred thousand francs. What was that? Two thousand pounds? More. A fortune. Enough to buy a mansion. And a car.

Gilbert asks, 'Is that right?'

She would be back in England tomorrow morning. She could spend Christmas at home, and then maybe return to France in the spring, return to the South-west, to WORDSMITH and to Benoît. 'Yes,' she replies, 'yes, I am.'

'Good,' he says. 'Sensible choice.'

The train draws into a station. Veretz-Montlouis, the sign-board announces. 'We're the next stop,' Gilbert tells them. 'A couple of minutes.'

Clément puts his arm round her. 'Nearly there, Squirrel.'

Gilbert watches them thoughtfully. Outside on the platform a whistle blows. Did anyone get on or off? This quiet corner of rural France seems a universe away from Paris, no one visible on the platform, no crowds, no fear. The train moves on with great asthmatic breaths as though taking in fresh air for the first time in weeks. Away to the right, through their pale reflections in the windows, are the flat fields of the flood plain between the Loire and the Cher, brushed with light from a setting sun. The sky is a luminous blue like the blue of a stained-glass window. Poplars stand like plumes in the drift of sunlight.


IV


At Azay-sur-Cher station the bicycles are waiting, four of them in a shed behind the station house as Gilbert said they would be. He wheels the spare one beside him as they ride – 'We'll need it for the incoming passengers' – and that is the first time Alice thinks of the other side of the operation, that someone will be coming in, maybe people she knows from training, people from a world only a couple of hours away by light air-craft, a world where you don't glance over your shoulder for people following, where you don't have to guard what you say, where fear isn't an endemic disease that eats away at mind and body. Where you don't have five hundred thousand francs on your head and aren't being sought for murder.

They cycle off into the gathering dusk, over a level crossing and through the fields. Some of the land is arable, some has been left for grazing. There are patches of woodland, poplars planted as windbreaks, willows along the rim of a canal. Through the trees to the east the moon is rising, a bone-white globe replacing the dying sunlight with a different kind of illumination, a flat monochrome. *The sun shall not burn thee by day*, she thinks, *neither the moon by night*. It is almost a prayer but not quite a prayer for she doesn't believe in prayer, doesn't believe in God, believes only in the power of evil and the fragile battle of men and women against it.

After a couple of kilometres they turn off onto a farm track and bump over ruts and potholes out into the fields. Gilbert brings them to a halt near a small copse. Beyond the trees a field stretches away to the east, a rough meadow as flat as a billiard table. 'It looks all right,' he says. 'We had to call one op off a few months ago when we found that the farmer had put cows out to graze, but things look OK this evening. The only worry tonight is fog. Fingers crossed.'

On one side of the field is an ancient barn. There's some hay in a corner, a rusted old harrow and some other nameless bits of farm equipment lying around, an ancient leather harness hanging on a hook. Gilbert seems to know his way around, almost as though he is at home. From a bundle of fence posts he selects three stakes about four feet long, each with an end sharpened to a point. 'Let's go and set things up.'

There is still enough light to see by as they walk out into the field. A hundred yards out he stands for a moment with his finger up in the air, like a water diviner detecting things that are outside the range of normal human sensibility. Then solemnly he plants one stake in the ground and sets off into the distance, marching with wide steps as though performing some arcane, hieratic ritual. By the time he comes to a halt and plants the second stake they can only see him as a vague shadow; he paces rightwards, plants the third stake and returns to them with the satisfied air of a job well done. 'Now all we can do is wait.'

Back in the barn they make themselves as comfortable as

possible, unwrapping the food they have brought and sipping ersatz coffee from thermos flasks. There is desultory talk, underpinned with the tension of what might or might not happen. Gilbert briefs them. In the aircraft they'll find parachutes left by the incomers. He explains how to buckle up. There will be two flying helmets already plugged into the intercom. They'll have to put them on to be able to talk to the pilot. The on–off switch is on the front of the oxygen mask.

'Oxygen?'

'You won't need it but that's where the intercom switch is. More likely you'll need the sick bag – the Lizzies fly at eight thousand at the most and it might be a bumpy ride.'

After they've been over and over the procedures two or three times, the men turn to talk of the war, what is happening in Russia, in Italy, in the Far East, how the conflict is progressing and how it might go. Alice clutches Clément's arm and ignores Gilbert's glance of curiosity and answers only in monosyllables when addressed. Orion the hunter drags a whole panoply of constellations across the sky and behind it the moon climbs, flooding milk across the fields. She remembers waiting for the *parachutage*, how boredom merged into a strange state of contemplation in which even the cold became something exterior, something that couldn't hurt you. Clément kisses her in the ear, a startling sound in the silence of the night. 'Soon we'll be in England,' he whispers, and she thinks of England, dull, drab England, and wonders what will happen. She pictures him in an untidy divorce after the war, and then the two of them setting up home together as husband and wife in some other country. Canada, maybe, where the man called von Halban has already gone and where they speak French as well as English.

And Benoît? Two men, both of whom she loves, or thinks she loves, or maybe loves. They occupy different parts of her life, as though she were two people, her personality split by war, the one unknown to the other. But that isn't difficult. She was trained to keep secrets.

'One day we'll look back at this and laugh,' Clément says, but she can't see the joke, or even imagine there is the possibility of one.

At midnight Gilbert gets to his feet and stretches. 'Let's get ready.' He opens his case and takes out four torches, testing each one in turn and issuing instructions like a commander ordering his troops into action. She follows him out into the moonlight. Underfoot the ground is hard with frost. Luminous scarves of mist are wrapped around the trees along the edge of the field and a bank of fog lies over to their right where the river runs. Gilbert is worrying about fog. Fog can ruin a pick-up in the best weather. A completely clear night may become impossible in a matter of minutes – all it takes is for the air temperature to fall below the dew point. 'One minute it's totally clear; the next you're completely invisible.'

But they aren't invisible. They are ghostly shadows moving quietly across the pale countryside, wraiths in the darkness. They walk down to the two furthest stakes and tie the torches in place, then come back to where Clément is waiting with the suitcases. There is something absurd about his appearance, a man in a dark coat standing beside his luggage in the middle of a deserted field, like a passenger translated from a railway platform. He needs a bowler hat, *un melon*, to complete the image.

'And now we wait,' Gilbert says.

V

They wait. Figures in a monochrome landscape, buffeted by a faint breeze, staring at the stars, painted by the moon. Cold seeps into them. Clément puts his arm round Marian and holds her close. There are the sounds of night, the mutterings and scurryings, the distant barking of a dog, the whispering of the breeze as it passes across their ears, and underneath everything a murmur that might be the sound of the nearby river. And then something else comes on the air, a rumour of things to come. She hears it first. Perhaps her younger ears are more sensitive.

'There!'

'What?'

'Shh!'

It dies away. Did she imagine it? The frustration of seeing something that others cannot see, a bird scurrying amid foliage, camouflaged against predators. That day with Yvette on a hillside in Scotland.

'There!'

'Where?'

'Over there. Look!' A grouse or something, slinking through the heather, abjuring flight for being so treacherous – if you flew they shot you down. Safer to walk. The next thing they had seen or heard was the group of students from Swordland, with Benoît ...

'There it is again!' The sound returns with greater certainty, a muttering on the night becoming a grumble, a hint of a roar.

'Yes!' says Gilbert. And now there is no doubt – an aero engine, the sound rising and falling on the breeze and then settling, louder, to a steady drumbeat. They strain to see something as the noise grows. Gilbert points his torch into the night sky, flashing the letter 'M'. And the answer comes back, a small star blinking in the blackness.

'That's it!'

Alice turns the first lamp on and sets off to the other lights, stumbling on the hard, uneven ground, a child again, running through the moonlight. She reaches the second light and snaps the torch on, then crosses to the third. Above her the aero engine drums on the darkness. As she hurries back to where the men are waiting she can see the Lysander moving against the night, a black cloth sweeping away the dust of stars. It turns towards them, hanging from its wings like a raptor stooping to its prey, tilting in the flow of air, the engine note rising and falling as the pilot jazzes the throttle. The shape grows larger and larger. For a moment landing lights come on, eyes staring out of the wheel spats, as brilliant as spotlights in a theatre so that down on the gorund they seem exposed to view like figures on a stage. Then the thing flies past them, the wheels hit, the aircraft bounces, hits again, rumbles down the flarepath, throttling back and going beyond the second lamp but turning as predicted, turning to the right and coming inside the third lamp, coming back to them where they wait, stunned by the din, beside the first.

'What a bloody racket!' she yells against the sound.

The slipstream hits them as the aircraft turns once more and points into wind, its left wing hanging over the first lamp, the pilot waving from the cockpit. Gilbert runs up to talk to him. In the rear of the cockpit two figures are moving. The hatch slides back and someone calls above the engine noise, 'Is this Le Bourget?' He heaves his leg over the edge of the cockpit, finds the first rung of the ladder and in a moment he's on the ground and his colleague is handing suitcases down to him.

'Everything OK?' he yells over his shoulder. 'Had a bloody good flight. Piece of cake, really. I'm David. Goodness, a female!'

'I'm Alice.'

'You flying out?'

'Two of us.'

Clément shakes hands with him. She can see his expression in the half-light – astonishment. Like a child before a Christmas tree.

'Part of the firm?'

'He's not.'

'A bigwig then.'

They pass Clément's case up and then wait while the second passenger climbs down, an older man with a ragged moustache and stubble on his chin. He looks like a bandit. Maybe he *is* a bandit. Gilbert is shouting from beside the nose of the aircraft, his words picked up by the slipstream and thrown back at them in disorder. 'Get ... move ...! No ... time ... waste!'

296

She turns to Clément. 'YOU GO FIRST!' she yells. That song runs through her mind: *Puisque vous partez en voyage/Puisque nous nous quittons ce soir*. Obediently he climbs the ladder up the side of the aircraft and clambers into the cockpit. She follows him up, watches while he settles himself into the seat, helps him buckle the parachute harness.

Then she points down to the ground. 'MY CASE!'

He nods and says something, his words snatched away by the slipstream. She looks round at the field, pallid in the moonlight, like mortified flesh. And the roaring of the engine ahead of her, battering her with a gale. Gilbert is there below the cockpit, looking up. 'Hurry up!' he mouths.

She recalls how time slowed when she shot the men in Belleville. The plasticity of time, the relativity of time, the whole world going slow then, but fast now – the engine roaring, the propeller a blurred disc bisected by a sword of moonlight, the stars rampaging across the sky – and this great stillness inside her. The men on the ground look up at her curiously, their faces white thumbprints of surprise.

She climbs down the ladder and jumps to the ground. From the glasshouse of the cockpit Clément looks down, his face obscured by the oxygen mask, his eyes staring at her. Hard to read the expression in his eyes. Nothing more than globes of jelly and gristle. She shakes her head.

'GO!' she yells into the slipstream from the propeller. And gestures downwind with her hand. 'GO! GO! GO!'

Gilbert runs back from the aircraft. The pilot gives the thumbs-up. The engine gains noise, roaring and raging at the night, straining for a moment against the brakes before lurching forward, bumping, flexing, gathering speed, with Clément staring down from the cockpit, his face no more than a smudge of shadow. Then he has gone and abruptly the Lysander is in the air, climbing up on spread wings, a bat shape against the dark, rising, turning, swinging through the stars and leaving Alice standing in the backwash from the aircraft, her hair blowing in the wind, her coat flapping round her. And she's in tears, fucking bloody silly girlish tears, while Gilbert shouts in her face, his calm insouciance gone for once, dashed away by the aeroplane's slipstream. 'What the hell are you playing at? This isn't a bloody game!'

'I'm not playing a game.'

He grabs her arm. 'Paris is lethal. I told you. You're blown, burned, finished. There's a price on your head.'

'But I'm not going back to Paris.'

'Where then?'

She feels in control again now, decision made, as the sound of the Lysander fades into the minutiae of the night. 'South. I can take the train at Vierzon. My cover is good and I'm safe in the south. I've still got things to do. My mission isn't over yet.' Mission. The word has an almost religious flavour to it. Sent from the sky to work among the people. But Gilbert stands in front of her, almost as though he is going to prevent her from leaving the field, while the other two look on in bewilderment, like children watching adults quarrel.

'It's all right,' she insists. 'I know what I'm doing.'

He shakes his head. 'I don't think you've any idea. You're just another of Buckmaster's amateurs, playing around in a world you don't understand.'

'I've done all right so far.'

'Hey,' one of the men calls. 'Aren't we going to get a move on? We can't stand around here arguing.'

Suddenly it's cold. She needs to move, to get things going again, to be away from here and back in Toulouse, back in Lussac, arguing with le Patron, laughing with Benoît, being where, for the first time for years, she feels at home. She pushes past Gilbert to pull the nearest stake out of the ground and retrieve the torch. 'We need to clear up, don't we? Let's go.'

'Who was he?' Gilbert calls after her as she sets off to fetch the other torches. 'Mechanic, I mean. Who was he?'

She turns. 'An old friend. Maybe I'll tell you when it's all over.'

# Vierzon

She's alone. She's sitting in a corner of a compartment with two other passengers but she's alone. She tries to keep awake by watching the countryside pass by, the alluvial flats of the Cher, the vasty fields of France; but tiredness creeps up on her like a thief and steals away her waking. She sleeps, hearing the roar of an aero engine in her ears, then comes to with a start. Her fellow passengers have turned to reading. She watches the trees and fields pass. There are clusters of mistletoe among the bare branches. There was mistletoe in the cemetery, mistletoe over-head when she met Yvette. The druids' plant. The plant that killed the Norse god Baldur. Kisses at Christmas time, a kiss stolen from Clément. She dozes, dreams, sees herself running in the darkness, feels Clément's body against her.

What will all that mean in the future? How much do such things last? Will they meet again as mere friends, or will there still be this breathless desire? The future seems an uncertain thing, compromised by the present, by the war, by her own strange life here in the dull and battered country that France has become. The future is irrelevant. What is relevant is this train jogging through the French countryside, and the creep of exhaustion.

Clément will be in England by now. How will they deal with him? The man called Fawley with the owl glasses. Kowarski the Russian bear. And Ned, who will presumably be called on to

299

debrief him as he debriefed Kowarski in 1940; Ned whose role in this whole thing is as enigmatic as the physics they all study, a world of uncertainty that yet yields certainty – a bomb that will blow the world to pieces.

Meanwhile the others – Gilbert, and the man called David, and the other agent who looked like a bandit – will be on the train from Tours to Paris, to the Gare d'Austerlitz where there are posters giving her description and a reward for her capture. Five hundred thousand francs.

What would her father say? Or her mother? She can imagine the shriek of horror – their dear little Squirrel, with a price on her head and half the Paris police looking for her! – as though it were a disgrace to be wanted as a criminal, whatever the circumstances. Should she have taken the extra seat and flown back to England? She would have found safety, real safety. Where would have been the disgrace in that? No more glancing over the shoulder, no more living with the flutter of fear trapped in the pit of the stomach. And sleep, she'd have been able to sleep. Instead she's here, somewhere in France. But that is why she came in the first place, after the man called Potter quizzed her in that bare room off Northumberland Avenue: not for Clément, not for Benoît, but for France, that strange abstraction which means so many different things to different people.

The train rattles on, stopping at every station, passengers getting on and off, whistles blowing – the ordinary currency of travel in the heartland of France. Vierzon comes with a clattering of points, the carriage jolting sideways, acres of sidings and rows and rows of goods trains waiting to move and a voice on the public address system announcing 'Vierzon *ville*'. Where Julius Miessen got on the train that time. Julius Miessen who followed her through Paris. Her nemesis. She pulls her suitcase down from the rack and edges along the corridor behind the other passengers. Someone helps her down onto the platform and wishes her '*Bon voyage, Mam'selle*', and she smiles in acknowledgement. The Toulouse train will be arriving at plat-form two.

Toulouse means Benoît. He'll be wondering where she is, what she's doing. She'll appear out of the blue like the last time, perhaps meet with him as they did before in the railwayman's flat. Passion is a crude, physical thing. It makes her feel uncomfortable, walking along the platform with strangers, remembering. Can they smell the passion on her? Does it transmit through the air? Clément and Benoît. How can she have come to this, the convent girl who had kept her virginity until she was twenty years old, whose sexual longings were always clouded with guilt? Two men within days of each other. The kind of thing that once horrified her. Promiscuity, prurience, sin – a whole thesaurus of immorality. Perhaps it's the unnatural life she is leading, her personality split between Alice and Marian, the one doing what the other can ignore. Create yourself a cover for every eventuality. Be real to yourself. Live the person you are pretending to be.

Laurence Follette, a student, returning to the Southwest from Paris where she has been for the last week visiting friends. Laurence Follette, weighed down with tiredness, humping her suitcase over to platform two, thinking of Clément, of a bomb that might blow cities to dust, of Benoît standing before her naked as though nudity is the most natural thing in the world.

She could be in England. Now, at this moment, in England. But she's here in France, which is where she's meant to be, where she wanted to be, where her mission lies. She dozes, awk-wardly, on a bench, trying to stay awake for the train announcements, her head falling towards her chest and then jolting upright.

Yvette. Did Yvette really give her away? Yvette, the mother whom she mothered. Yvette who slept with Emile. Once, that would have been impossible to imagine, yet now everything seems possible, even a voice calling her out of sleep saying, 'Marian? Marian Sutro?'

301

'Yes?'

It's the oldest trick in the book. It's the pitfall of bilingualism, the moment when the wrong switch is thrown, the wrong response given, the wrong word uttered.

*Yes.*

She's not Marian Sutro, she's Laurence Follette, student, living near Toulouse.

*Yes.*

She looks round and they're standing there, two men in dark blue suits and heavy overcoats, and between them, smiling faintly, the Alsatian woman.

It's like the bullet that hits you – you never hear the shot being fired. She moves to rise from the bench but it's too late, far too late. Someone has already grabbed her by the upper arms to hold her down. There's a brief struggle to handcuff her while passengers look on indifferently. A girl being taken into custody. It happens all the time. Who knows why? Who cares?

Simon Mawer was born in England in 1948 and spent his childhood moving backwards and forwards from England to Malta and Cyprus. He has lived in Italy for over thirty years, teaching at an international school in Rome. He is the author of two works of non-fiction and eight other novels, including: *Mendel's Dwarf*, which was longlisted for the Booker Prize; *The Fall*, which won the Boardman Tasker Prize; *A Jealous God*; *The Bitter Cross*; *The Gospel of Judas*; and *The Glass Room*, which was shortlisted for the Man Booker Prize in 2009.